MW01538633

The Uncertainty Principle

A Permeable Press Book
Winner of the 1996 Pocket Rocket Prize

Copyright © 1997 Steven J. Frank

First Edition

All Rights Reserved.
No part of this publication may be reproduced, stored in a re-
trieval system, or transmitted, in any form or by any means, except
for brief passages quoted in reviews, without the express written
permission of the publisher, nor may it be otherwise circulated in
any form of binding or cover other than that in which it is published. Please contact the publisher at the address below for more
information.

This book's story and characters are entirely fictitious. The principle setting is the Massachusetts Institute of Technology, and certain real locations are mentioned, but the story is not intended as a
true account of that institution's faculty, students, educational prac-
tices or policies. The events, action and characters are entirely imaginary.

ISBN 1-882633-26-1

Permeable Press
47 Noe Street #4
San Francisco CA 94114-1017
brian@permeable.com
www.permeable.com

Book design & cover illustration: Brian Clark
The publisher wishes to acknowledge the assistance
of Michael Hemmingson & Ed Heinemann.

These kids today ... the center of percussion
means nothing to them.

                    –lament of Robert Cesari
                    technologist, teacher, mentor, friend
                    (and MIT Class of 1950)

1.0

"TRANSLATION: NO SCREWING AROUND, NO DRUGS, NO BULLSHIT," hissed the fat nurse after the camp director had exited the small outdoor pavilion and was safely out of earshot. Minutes before, the small, wiry-haired and obviously uncomfortable director was stammering through his usual welcome-and-warning speech to this year's counselors, who were assembled around the pavilion. He'd given the speech at least twelve times before, and *still* could not get the damn lump out of his damn throat as he tried, first, to reason with the zombied audience.

"Look, you all know, or at least you should know, how important your job here is, how your kids will look up to you, okay? So the first thing I'm going to remind you about is—and I shouldn't even have to remind you about this at all, since they're illegal—is, well ... enough said, right?"

He looked out over the young blank faces and it suddenly occurred to him that all of them might be drug addicts, what with today's values and their empty stares. Were they even listening or were they high on dope, for crying out loud? Then he felt a breeze kick up from the east, and realized that his comb-over would soon turn to a clump of grizzled steel wool on one side of his face, exposing his bald scalp and probably blinding his entire audience of junkies with the glare of noonday sunlight from his forehead. He tried to remain composed.

And then he tried guilt: "Look, we are actually paying you—I mean, we're not just giving you room and board but actually paying you to have fun all summer and prepare for your own parenthood by rearing these children. So don't let us down, right?" And there was that lump again, since the bulk of the promised payment was only there for those who made it through the entire summer without getting fired—an easy fall from grace, since the camp's budget included full salaries only for about sixty percent of the counselors, and besides, even he was not so stupid as to think that $450 for an entire summer's work was anything but a piece of garbage even for a nineteen-year old.

So he tried bargaining: "And, look, as far as, well, physical contact goes, and you all know what I mean by that," he struggled, forcing himself to scan the eyes of his blank-faced audience as he raised his finger and detected the slightest hint of snickering emanating from somewhere, he wasn't sure where, but he would definitely fire the fucking little creep if he could ever identify him, "what's right and what's wrong. You play fair with us, you don't get into trouble, we play fair with you. Enough said?"

"Now I know we're going to get laid," said Larry, staring at a brown-haired girl in cutoffs toward the front of the crowd. Her name, as it turned out, was Tracy Steakle.

It was just then that a warm, stiff breeze prompted the director's comb-over to rise mightily but then flop over, defeated, into the inevitable grizzled clump. He quickly ended his speech and left, secure in the knowledge that his nurse would say whatever had to be said, filling in anything he might have left out. Which was just about everything, of course, since no one in the audience was there to learn parenting skills or earn much money. We were there for precisely those forbidden activities enumerated by the fat but very savvy and altogether dangerous nurse.

"No way," I assured Larry, trying to be realistic. "It's bimodal."

Larry looked at me, puzzled, but I'm sure he was only pretending not to understand. Romance? With a bimodal population distribution? Might as well hope for massless neutrinos. Just a brief glance at the assembled crowd made it clear that statistics had dealt us a bum hand. We were surrounded by a collection of counselors that included a number of very attractive people, a lot of not-so-attractive people, and not much in between. Not much except us. If you were to graph numbers of people as a function of attractiveness, you would produce a curve with two humps: a bimodal bust. My father, an engineer at IBM, explained this concept to me one day at the beach when he saw me staring at a woman in a G-string. We all know it's virtually impossible to elicit the interest of anyone incrementally more attractive than you are, and also that dipping into the inferior hump is unthinkable, so you're left sitting in the trough—another horny victim of statistical misfortune.

And there was more. The nurse, whether by chance or malevolent design, assigned Larry and me to the most difficult bunk in the most difficult age group, the twelve-year-olds. They were evil and they hated us, in the affectionate sort of way they hated everybody. They also fixated continuously on sex. When they were not asking us questions about sex generally, they were inquiring about our sex lives in particular.

"Get any last night?" one of them would inevitably ask, slyly and just after sunrise, the one of us who had had the previous night off.

"Damn straight," I would answer if I were the unlucky designee, straining to deploy a coherent stream of adjectives and colorful verbs that—believably, I thought—communicated scenes of uninhibited lust, moaning and secretion. I'd developed quite a vivid imagination at college. MIT's motto is *Mens et Manus*—mind and hand.

I would wait for their response.

"Too much detail, you're full of shit," would come the verdict.

Larry's approach was simply to cut a strong, silent figure, hoping to appear discreet and self-confident. This style not only failed to convince but, even worse, failed to entertain, provoking even greater forms of abuse.

As I had predicted, the camp's bimodal population distribution was indeed a problem, amorously speaking. But Larry ultimately turned out to be half right about romantic success. He succeeded; I did not. The end of his misery began the night he managed to cruise within torpedo range of Tracy, who qualified for the higher statistical hump but probably at the lower end. This despite his own failure to so qualify and notwithstanding the fact that Tracy noticed him even less as the summer wore on than she had when he was staring at her that first day, rhapsodizing about imminent sexual conquest, fantasizing as he watched her slam a mosquito biting her knee. But he had her by subterfuge. She thought she had encountered the torpedo of Andre Dupree.

Andre, you see, was a big, blond Canadian who knew his way around a summer camp. His kids loved him and so did the girls. Andre had his pick of the most attractive female counselors, successfully harvesting the top sectors of the better-looking hump. Tracy strove for that hump. And why not? Didn't her trim figure, her fashionably long hair, her toothy smile earn her the dignity? Andre, for his part, noticed none of this. Larry and his own part noticed nothing else. For him, Tracy's frequent but unreturned hormonal stares toward Andre were thermite on his fire.

Nor did Tracy's interest in Andre escape the attention of her co-counselor, Karen Shecter, who more than once upbraided Tracy about it. "All men are pigs," I overheard Shecter announce as Tracy watched Andre play volleyball, clearly thinking, now there's a boy who knows how to hit a volleyball, "and Andre is the worst kind of pig. He uses women. Can't you see that he doesn't respect any of us as an individual? To him, we're just pieces of meat."

Karen's frequent expressions of feminist principle made her an object of some admiration, both on the part of her peers and even the nurse. Karen wore Birkenstocks and headed the Syracuse University chapter of the Feminist Youth Action League.

Digging her eyes into Tracy's, she added, "Don't you have any pride as a woman?"

That hurt. I could tell.

What Karen actually meant by all this was, keep your eyes off Andre, he's mine. Karen was incrementally more attractive than Tracy.

"Sheck, you're so critical of everyone," Tracy replied, clueless.

"And anyway, don't you think you should be paying more attention to our kids?" asked Karen, changing the subject but not her reproachful tone, as the activity whistle prompted the entire bunk of seven-year-old girls to fling their crusty paintbrushes and dried-out magic markers and scramble past the volleyball court down to the pool. Just as Tracy got up to follow them, I saw Karen's and Andre's eyes meet for the first time. Karen, unlike Tracy, had blond hair and fabulous tits.

She was also quite wrong in her public assessment of Andre. In fact, Andre actually held his sexual conquests in rather high esteem. One night, for example, Larry, Andre and I went out to Chet's, the nearby diner that afforded the only worthwhile hangout within light years of the camp, and Andre told us about how, in his most recent tender encounter, he had persuaded his date to bark like a dog.

"*'Oh, Andre, be serious,'*" said Andre in falsetto, raising his hands in mock horror, and then he continued: "So I told her, 'I am serious, now bark,' and then she got down on her knees and went *'aarfy aarf, aarfy aarf.'* I'm not kidding."

Andre gulped down several mouthfuls of beer because he knew that's what Americans expect Canadians to do during male bonding rituals. Larry's lips silently pronounced every word Andre said.

I would soon learn why.

"No way!" cried Larry, encouraging Andre to go on.

Andre leaned forward and lowered his voice. "And do you know why I had her do this?" he asked.

We sat mute, Andre's prisoners. He slammed his beer on the table and raised his voice.

"So I could tell you this story. That's why."

Of course Andre had done no such thing. From what any of us could tell, his sexual tastes were quite ordinary. Andre was merely educating us as to how pathetic we appeared in his eyes. He would treat us to similar untrue sagas as frequently as his other social engagements would permit. We listened because Andre was quite a charismatic fellow, and because he was getting laid and we weren't, and because, essentially, he was correct in his assessment of us. We were in awe.

Larry had no idea what Andre was up to, and I suppose this made me doubly pathetic. On the other hand, Andre was equally ignorant of Larry's intentions.

The plain fact is that Larry had become obsessed. The harder I would try to talk some sense into him, the greater his obsession would grow.

"I'll charm her, you'll see," said Larry after another dateless week. "I see the way she flirts. It's not as if she hates guys."

"Larry," I said, trying to be gentle, "it's got nothing to do with guys generally. It's you in particular. She's obviously placed you outside the class of potential romantic interests. Why don't you just forget it? There's no use chasing after the forbidden transitions."

But no. Larry refused to yield. "Forbidden transitions? What is this, the Twilight Zone? Excuse me," he replied theatrically, extending his arms. "I thought I was in a free country. I thought I was in America. Who are you to tell me what to chase after?"

"Try to be realistic," I implored.

"How long do you plan to hide in that little science world of yours? You know, you used to be fun to hang around with." And stamping his foot, Larry added, "I will *not* go quietly."

He was obviously irrational. Fully aware of his own statistical shortcomings, he nonetheless considered himself worthy in every way of Tracy's heart as well as her other organs and features. And as soon as he understood that Tracy had eyes only for Andre, Larry simply became overwhelmed by the situation's irony. The vagaries of statistics had cast both him and Tracy into perfectly symmetrical roles, each carrying the torch for another. So Larry began to make plans. He started by compiling a systematic inventory of Andre's mannerisms.

For example, Andre usually wore a cap with a glow-in-the-dark Molson logo, so Larry spent his entire day off one week in Binghamton, nearly two hours away, on a successful quest for such a cap. Andre also liked to sneak up behind female counselors and say "Think fast" as he grabbed their waists or ribs, a sport that produced no end of laughter on the part of his kids if the female in question reacted by gasping and dropping something messy or breakable. Andre certainly knew how to charm the ladies, because they always turned and smiled at him, no matter how ridiculous he had made them look; had they done otherwise, the nurse would have canned him like a tuna. He never performed this maneuver on Tracy.

Larry repeated the words "think fast" at every opportunity until he sounded just like Andre. His lips even moved like Andre's. Poor Larry, I thought. Driven nuts by his obsession, he was either humiliating himself trying to become Andre's clone or would suffer an elbow smash to the jaw as soon as Andre caught his imitation. Actually, Larry was preparing for the annual skinny dip.

Camp Cuyahoga, a small patch of scrub pine and asphalt in upstate New York, owed its name to the director's poor sense of geography and its profitability to his shrewd sense of marketing. "Nestled in the cool mountains overlooking Lake Piaget and in continuous operation for over 50 years, Camp Cuyahoga offers unlimited outdoor fun, water sports, a full arts program and a great tradition" was the way the camp's brochure described the place. The great tradition of continuous operation referred to the fact that until four years back, municipal authorities had used the grounds to store and operate front-end loaders, cement mixers and snow plows. The arts program referred to the crusty paintbrushes and dried-out magic markers. And Lake Piaget was a pointless puddle about a mile and a half from the camp and surrounded by as-yet-unsold vacation condos. These had been the real-estate vision of one Hector Piaget, now bankrupt and on the lam. Our man Hector obliterated every public access to the pond except an unused and somewhat dangerous easement path that began near the camp, so overgrown that it could only be travelled on foot. The director had officially placed the lake off-limits to everyone in order to limit insurance premiums. Everyone, that is, except the brochure photographer.

And except us, during the annual skinny dip. Notwithstanding the director's first-day morality harangue, and despite his obvious aversion to thoughts of lust generally, this much-remarked upon yearly spectacle actually enjoyed his grudging approval. Clearly, certain forms of objectionable behavior were out of bounds. That's why he'd hired the nurse. But a celibate atmosphere was unthinkable, intolerable. It was bad for business. No sex, and the curious little campers had nothing to talk about. No chance of sex, and just try recruiting an army of teenagers to punt their summers for 450 bucks.

When the big night arrived, Larry coordinated our departure along the easement so that we trailed Tracy and two of her friends by about 50 yards. There was a new moon and it was pitch dark out, but Larry, expertly wielding our flashlight, managed to keep us on Tracy's trail without letting her see us. We got to the lake and took off our clothes. Larry donned his Molson hat. As we made our way to water's edge, a voice from the lake laughed and said, "Andre, you loon-atick, take yer fucking hat off!"

"Think fast," replied Larry as he followed Tracy into the water, immediately disappearing into the darkness and busily engaging every sensory apparatus he had to keep track of her position. The water was cold and I was alone. Before long I began to ask myself just why it was that I was standing naked in a frigid, malodorous mudhole surrounded by rotting townhouses when I could be back with the eight-weekers in our bunk, luxuriating in their sneers, earning their utter revulsion by sharing with them the humor of calculus. Convincing them, for example, that the integral of e to the x is actually the function of u to the n.

$\int e^x$ is $f(u^n)$

Or treating them to the Math League cheer: Cosine Secant Tangent Sine, Three Point Onc Four One Five Nine, Go Team!

Then I heard some nearby laughter, and then I heard something else.

"Ohhh." That was Andre. Unmistakably Andre.

"Anh Anh Ahhhh!" said a high-pitched voice shortly after. That was Karen. I could picture her open-mouthed gape. Karen and Andre. Andre in Karen. And here I was listening to this gruntfest, this *a capella* serenade to my own empty sex life. The ultimate indignity. Now I was fully disgusted. I waded out, dried off, grabbed the flashlight and left. Larry would have to get back on his own.

Early the next morning Larry was poking me through the wire mesh and thin cloth wafer that served as my mattress. It was day-break. The sun had just begun to filter through the windows, and the Reveille tape wouldn't crackle over the loudspeakers for at least half an hour. I peered over the top of the bunk bed. Larry whispered, "I'm in love, and I'm dying."

"What are you talking about?" I whispered back, annoyed and still half asleep.

"We touched last night. Tracy and me. In the lake."

This woke me up. How could Larry have engineered physical contact from complete indifference, and in a single night at that?

"Tell me more."

"It started out as mischief," said Larry, still whispering. "I was going to make her hate Andre by sneaking up on her, pretending to be Andre and acting like a randy cretin."

"So what happened?"

"She didn't react according to plan. I suppose I shouldn't underestimate my own appeal."

"Wait a minute. She went for your appeal, so now she thinks she's Andre's girlfriend?"

"No, no, no. Eventually she realized I wasn't Andre. She recognized my hankerings for the stupid, cruel joke that they were. But not before she..." Larry was rotating his hands, hoping this would complete the thought.

"You mean she..."

"...soothed the burning embers of my love. Right."

Oh, gag me with a spoon. The sordidness of it all. And now Larry was looking for sympathy from me. Well, he could forget about that. Sympathy was not on the output menu as I slipped into a regression loop of childlike envy, frustration and resentment. Larry had successfully made the leap from pathetic to merely vulgar. Before that night we had been pathetic together.

Larry's soulful expressions of remorse continued all day. They reached a crescendo during "free time," the hour after dinner when everyone was on their own and counselors enjoyed a temporary reprieve from their flocks. "Without her, I want to die," he said, beginning his lamentation as we sat alone in the bunk. "I'm sure she recognized me, and now she hates me."

"Did she say she hates you?" I asked.

"No, but I just know. What the hell was I thinking? Wouldn't you hate me?" the lamentation continued.

"Hey, at least you didn't go quietly," I offered. "And of course your ember—"

"Can't you feel my pain?" Larry interrupted. "I touched her. I touched her and she touched me and it was *perfect*, see? I wish I were dead."

"That's it, I'm done, I'm out of here," I said finally, making my escape from the bunk only to encounter one very angry Tracy just outside, her eyes ablaze.

"You forgot this," she seethed, shoving the Molson cap into my chest.

"Bah buh bah," I babbled, answering her accusation with my usual aplomb in the face of confrontation.

"Bastard," said Tracy, shaking her head as she turned to walk away. What a great ass, I couldn't believe myself thinking. Shecter was right: men really are pigs. I chased after her.

"Wait a minute," I said as I caught up. I hoped Larry would appreciate what I was about to do for him. "I know what you think. You're dead wrong."

"What are you telling me?" she demanded. "That it wasn't you?"

I told her the story Larry had told me. Even embellished it a little. I told her how Larry had so painfully observed her crush on Andre, how he had become Andre to seduce her vicariously like Cyrano de Bergerac in reverse, how he had planned the event for weeks.

Tracy stood motionless for a minute, then looked me straight in the eyes and said, "You ... are ... full of it! That's the sickest thing I ever heard. Larry would never do anything like that. He barely knows I exist!"

"It's true," I persisted. "And do you know why I'm telling you this? To protect Larry. To erase any suspicion of him since you'll never believe me."

She thought about this. Then she laughed and ran her hand through her hair, as if astonished, as if to demonstrate her incredulity with the layers of lies, the depths of my baseness. "You really are a bastard. A pig."

I already knew that.

"Now I get it," said Tracy, slapping her forehead in sudden

realization, "you're obsessed with me, right? Of course you are, that's why you're making up such fantastic lies. All those times I thought you were staring at Karen … it was me, right? God, how I hate being beautiful."

She walked in a circle, kneading her hands against her forehead to help direct her brain, and continued, "You fixate on an attractive woman, fantasize yourself silly…"

Yup, that was Larry.

"…trick her into being, like, intimate, and then you blame it on someone else to avoid responsibility and to hide your feelings of shame. And to pick Larry, of all people. Well," she added, laughing again, "that's about as close as you'll ever get to sex with a woman."

That hurt. I had, over a year ago, been delivered from the ranks of the sexually innocent via the high-energy carnal passages of June Brooke, class valedictorian and sex machine, shortly after her boyfriend announced his intention to pursue a less physically demanding lifestyle with a different girl. I tried to defend my manhood with this fact, but all that came out was: "Bah buh bah."

"Where was Karen when I needed her?" continued Tracy, now talking to herself, starting to walk away.

"You mean you don't know?" I asked.

"Know what?" Tracy demanded, turning around and clenching her fists.

"About Karen and Andre. At the lake." Could she really be that blind?

"What are you talking about? What would Karen be doing with Andre?"

"Fellatio, I think, from the Doppler shift. But I can't be sure. It was dark out last night."

Tracy looked at me, motionless. Her grin was exaggerated and sarcastic. Her eyes were lasers.

"It may be hard to swallow, but it's true," I told her. Tracy turned and stomped off.

When I got back to our bunk, Larry immediately resumed his anguished soliloquy. "You didn't answer me before. Wouldn't you hate me?"

"She doesn't hate you," I said. "She hates me. I just spoke with her, or tried to, anyway."

Larry sat up, excited. "How'd you manage that? Didn't she know who it was? Did you tell her it was you? What a guy!"

"No," I replied. "I actually told her the entire truth."

"You what?" Larry asked, terrified.

"She didn't believe me, of course. And guess what? You, poor soul, are the victim of my perverse and lying nature."

"She's an angel," said Larry, entranced.

"She's a moron," I pointed out.

"How can you say that?" Larry seemed genuinely hurt. "Can't you see the radiant gleam in her eyes?"

Sure, I thought, but only in certain orientations, when one of her ears faces the sun so the incoming light scatters in the empty fog and reflects out her pupils. But I said nothing.

Then Larry pretended to sulk, for days it seemed. He averted his eyes hurtfully whenever he encountered Tracy, which was frequently, since he shadowed her unceasingly. The injured look he wore convinced her she must be persecuting him unconsciously—wrongly blaming him for something she knew was not his fault. Why else would he look at her that way? Soon she could no longer ignore him; it was too awkward, too callous.

They talked for a little while one day, and *voila!* Larry's smile reappeared. And then they had another, longer talk, and another, and soon they were dating—polite teenage locution for humping each other's brains out almost constantly. Not that anyone was allowed to know; Tracy recognized that statistical destiny was being violated, and insisted on strict discretion.

She also revealed herself as supremely compassionate by not turning me in to the nurse, thereby allowing me to fulfill my own statistical destiny, deep in the bimodal trough for the full eight weeks. This compassion had its origin both in deference to Larry and so Tracy could have something to hold over my head.

And she would.

Although I didn't realize it at the time, for Larry all of this was just another tunneling operation. His talent in this area seemed boundless. I am referring, of course, to quantum mechanics, and not to the details of Larry's sexual exploits with Tracy. Tunneling, as you undoubtedly know, is a way of fighting statistical barriers with statistical cunning. My father explained it to me a couple of weeks after the camp season ended, days before the beginning of my second year at MIT, as I lay peacefully absorbing The Doors at high volume.

"Have you ever heard of Heisenberg? The Uncertainty Principle?" he asked me, ending my repose as the voice of Jim Morrison screamed *Break on Through to the Other Side.*

"Yes, Dad," I said, bracing myself for the inevitable explanation, knowing he'd pay no attention to my response. My father was being informative.

"It's like this. Let's say you're a measly one-volt electron and you run head on into a five-volt potential barrier. No go, right?" he asked, and continued without waiting for an answer. "Not necessarily. See, the Uncertainty Principle says that you may be a one-volt weakling, but only most of the time. A little bit of the time you're something more or less than one volt, and a really little bit of the time you're quite a bit more or less than one volt." He wrote "$\Delta E \times \Delta t = constant$" on the window fog next to my bed.

"The trick is to hit the barrier during the incredibly small part of the time that your energy is greater than five volts. It's as if you've stolen energy and gotten away before anyone notices. That's called tunneling. Not easy, but statistics say that if you keep trying you'll do it eventually. On the other hand, if you want to break through within a reasonable amount of time—say, during your lifespan—you've got to be rather clever about coordinating energy and contact. And that," he said proudly, "is what Morrison was talking about." I doubted it.

Then he added: "Larry's much better at tunneling than you are." He said this without sympathy or sentiment. My father preferred solutions. And he was also correct—when Larry won Tracy's heart, he was probably as surprised as some lucky electron after tumbling fortuitously through the potential barrier. My father knew a lot about Larry, and why not? He had helped raise both his children, after all.

But to fully appreciate the significance of this colorful and entirely unrequested digression, you have to know something about my father. Ordinarily he was imperturbable. He didn't get too upset, for example, when my mother toppled the little garden of nitrogen triiodide crystals I had been culturing on my top bookshelf, showering herself and the rest of my room with the tiny explosive particles that detonated with a wild clattering racket and left purple stains all over my bedroom rug, not to mention my mother.

And he smiled indulgently when the police returned me and two of my track teammates of like ethnic extraction to the custody of our parents after we arranged to celebrate Columbus Day by torching our high school's parking lot in the colors of Italy's flag, igniting various pyrotechnic mixtures of gunpowder, magnesium, strontium nitrate and barium nitrate that we'd spread over the pavement. Although the spectacle could not have been more harmless, it did produce a fierce illumination and billows of sulfurous smoke that attracted the attentions of, among others, a hovering police helicopter and later those crusading journalists at the Armonk Gazette. Always eager to lament the idle prankishness of troubled youth, the Gazette's editors went so far as to question the long-term effects of our display on the respiratory well-being of the city's unfortunate populace. I thought of writing to protest this absurd speculation, but who can argue with such good press?

And my father said nothing after those same two hurdlers and I decided for no particular reason to terrorize a group of duffers at the Mill Falls country club, where my father awaited consideration for membership, by bombarding them with homemade mortars constructed from empty tennis-ball cannisters, sending wave after wave of Dunlops onto the crowded putting green, our heads growing giddy contemplating the graceful parabolic trajectories and choking in the stench of lighter fluid as we swung the cannons to aerate them between salvos. We didn't get caught that time, but my poorly hidden weapon suffered mysterious disappearance the next day after the Armonk Gazette reported an unexplained fusillade of tennis balls apparently aimed at disrupting the annual Prestige Putting competition, and launched with blatant disregard for the bodily well-being of the club's unfortunate targets.

Despite all this tolerance, and to my utter amazement, my father almost shot into low orbit the day I suggested that my room would never be tidy as a result of the second law of thermodynamics, which declares the inevitability of disorder and decay. He quaked with anger, too much anger even to formulate a coherent reprimand, sputtered, "Never let me catch you overusing scientific metaphor again!" and then stormed out of the room.

A man of principle, my father. Scientific principle.

"Your father's very upset," my mother deadpanned soon after this brief tirade. "He hates it when people distort science." And then we both burst out laughing at the thought of the most patient, laid-back man either of us knew flipping out over such a scholastic trifle. My mother swaggered across my recently recarpeted bedroom, looking at me with mock sternness. "Your room will get clean if you care to clean it," she said in a phony male voice, jabbing her finger within inches of my nose, "and people will still build Boeing 747s and cars and bicycles and igloos and all sorts of complex things from simple components regardless of the second law." She'd apparently heard this sentiment expressed before.

"Only ignoramuses blithely turn laws of nature, which explain tiny corners of the world, into grandiose metaphors with lives of their own," I said, standing up with my hands on my hips to continue the satire. "Only facile nitwits think general scientific principles dictate the course of everyday human behavior."

"Just remember," she said, mussing my hair as she left the room, "that he's usually right."

My father wasn't exactly original in his objections. Plenty of scientists have decried the eagerness with which advertisers, New Age writers and other assorted bullshit artists have attempted to recruit scientific laws into the pop culture, equating thermodynamic energy with "life force" and blaming the second law for everything from riots to baldness.

And yet for some strange reason, my father drew a single exception to his insistence on definitional rigor. That was the Uncertainty Principle. It was fine with him if this rarefied oddity of quantum mechanics, which by its own terms applies only over unimaginably small distances and time scales, found itself explaining love, business, religion or photosynthesis. And when confronted with this seeming contradiction in his outlook, my father's response was always simple, always the same: "Never argue with Morrison. He's usually right."

2.0

I HATED DRIVING IN THE SAME CAR AS TRACY. WE HAD REACHED THE point of civil accommodation, she and I, but it became awkward when we got near one another. And that always happened when we drove with my parents. It was only natural for her to ride the hump in the back seat since she was shorter than Larry and me. It was only natural for Larry and me to sit on either side of her. So every time my father took a quick turn the wrong way, centripetal acceleration would force Tracy's body against mine and the tense awkwardness would crawl up my spine, cold as ice, as I felt her pulling away.

She hated my guts, basically. And I knew this was not solely a result of ... *the incident.* Now Tracy had an identity. She had been wronged but she stood tall. And she would tolerate me for Larry's sake. In fact, the contrast in her feelings for us seemed to elevate her opinion of Larry. Which, at this point, needed all the elevating it could get. Tracy was presently feeling the relentless pull of statistics.

Tunneling, you see, is usually temporary.

This particular night Dad and the Chrysler drove all of us from Armonk to my aunt and uncle's place in New Jersey for their annual Christmas Eve party. I winced when he turned left, relaxed when he turned right, since that was the way the centripetal acceleration worked that night. But I sure as hell didn't complain. That would be too much like my uncle Tony who, I knew, was presently nattering furiously. The reason I knew this was that we were running ten minutes late, and because that's what he always did anyway. He nattered that his wife's family was never on time. He fretted that the house was messy. He fussed over his children's clothing.

You wouldn't know it to look at him. He was at least six-foot two and muscular, had well-trimmed jet black hair and sported a long, thin mustache that stretched nearly to his chin. With sunglasses he looked like a dangerous mafioso; without them he made a handsome latin lover. But he nattered incessantly.

My aunt Gina dedicated her life to minimizing that nattering. But it was never enough. There was always more to clean, wash, scrub and cook.

Poor Gina. Her life's ambition was so simple. She just wanted Tony to shut up. Longed for the day when Tony would shut up. And according to my mother, who knew about these things, lately her weariness had combined with resentment to produce sheer contempt. Gina felt contempt for Tony because, having sentenced her to a life of nonstop nattering minimization, he had recently begun to proclaim great boredom with his life.

Tony is a dentist, incidentally.

My aunt's labors certainly kept her in shape. She cut a terrific figure with short black hair, intense dark eyes and lines honed sleek by the constant physical demands of her office. My father and my aunt shared a strong family resemblance, obviously siblings. And she kept an immaculate house, thanks both to her exertions and to Tony's bad taste. A small split-level, it had a living room with marble floors, various Baroque statuary, a fountain that didn't work any more and an expensive wrought-iron coffee table that looked weird on the marble. Mirrors and lush purple-and-rose wallpaper covered the walls of the master bedroom. Tony had selected all of this, and Gina went along because everything was relatively easy to keep clean. Today the house also had a big Christmas tree that winked in colors and sagged under the weight of large, bulbous ornaments. In other words, the house was tacky as all hell.

This was New Jersey, after all. Agreeably sanitary but very tacky.

Tony and Gina had three young children, Joey, John and Antonia. As we arrived, these cousins of mine were busily engaging their favorite sport, which was sustained mistreatment of my uncle's father Arturo. Poor Uncle Artie. At seventy-seven years of age he had become a docile robot, completely deterministic, a perfect von Neumann machine: all of his actions were both predictable and selectable. Provide Uncle Artie with the right input and he would issue a known output. To my cousins this made him the ultimate entertainment device, since talking with Artie resembled nothing so much as playing a video game. They would take turns saying something they knew would provoke a characteristic response, then howl with laughter when the response came as they knew it would. And Artie would laugh too, the involuntary laugh of the senile.

"Hey Uncle Artie, that's a pretty *extravagant* vest."

The little man with the egg-shaped head, long bereft of all its hair, dressed in his best brown plaid shirt, brown vest and massively baggy brown pants, appeared to think for a moment with his mouth slightly open, and replied, "In the old country, we'd say, *stravagante.*"

Laughter shook the stucco ceilings as my cousins rolled on the floor, clutching their stomachs and wiping the tears from their eyes. Then Artie's open-mouthed gawk curled into a tranquil, demented smile, signaling his readiness for another round.

I had never known Uncle Artie to act very differently. He'd been in a world of his own since I could remember. It must have been difficult for Tony to watch his father slide downhill like that, I thought, as I watched his children operate their grandfather.

Although he'd been part of the family for over a decade, I knew very little about Artie's active years. I'd heard that he was a welder in the Navy during World War II, and that after the war he worked as a printer, then as a carpenter, and finally as a technician for Fulton Cosmetics. He retired at age 65, just as the company policy statement required.

Larry presented Tracy with an elaborate introduction as we took our coats off. It began with description of their meeting in camp, moved on to how she'd changed his life, and ended, "...and the most fantastic person I've ever met, Tracy Steakle."

No one said much, least of all Tracy, who looked off dreamily. She was thinking of how wonderful it would feel to be there with the man she really loved.

Artie said hello and promptly ambled off to take a nap. He spent most of his life in an "in-law apartment" that my aunt and uncle had added to the house when Artie moved in several years back. His tiny universe consisted of a small living room, a bedroom and a bath.

Then we made the necessary pre-dinner small talk over the nonstop hooting, yelling and scrambling of the little ones. Artie's departure had robbed them of an outlet for their Christmas Eve hyperactivity, and they ricocheted off the walls like fissioning particles in a runaway nuclear reaction. In the midst of discussing what variety of baby this one had had and what species of trouble that one had fallen into, Aunt Gina told us how desperately she needed a week with her friend Rosa at a health spa in Albuquerque. Then she raced off to the kitchen. My parents boasted of their children's success in college. Larry regaled the company with the pleasures and terrors of a freshman's life at SUNY Albany. And Tony tapped his feet impatiently.

"Paul, wake Uncle Artie please," my aunt called out to me from the depths of a mountain of dishes, pots, bowls, cakestands and platters in the kitchen. Why me, I wondered as I obliged my way to his door. Why, just because I'm the only one who doesn't babble his brains out, do I have to venture into Artie's overheated tomb and disturb his geezered prattling? I knocked cautiously. "Just go in," my aunt yelled, unable to see my hesitation but sensing it just the same.

I opened the door, saw a couch, chair, lamp and TV ... but no Artie. Great. Probably in his bedroom. I was grateful for the respite from my little cousins, but I really, *really* didn't want to go into Artie's bedroom. It was an *old man's* bedroom. The bedroom of a crazy geriatric. God only knew what it smelled like or what I'd find. Was Artie dead in there? Would I have to give him CPR? Mouth-to-mouth resuscitation? I peered through the half-open bedroom door, my heart pounding, but saw nothing.

"He's probably playing with his little computer," yelled my aunt from the temple of her toil. "Just go in!" So I took a deep breath and stepped inside. And indeed, Artie was sitting in front of a modest wooden desk that supported a large computer monitor, a keyboard and a mouse. He wore thick black-framed glasses that I had never seen before, and stared intently at his screen. He didn't notice me as I drew closer. All at once I recognized the form displayed on the computer screen as an engineer's drawing. And a fairly elaborate one at that. The legend at the top of the screen said "RAPE-PREVENTION DEVICE". I had learned something during my one and a half years of engineering study (and during my life as my father's son), and understood the illustration of a conical device with inwardly pointing blades.

I couldn't believe my eyes. There was Artie, using the mouse to enlarge the drawing and add a little shading here, a bit of line thickening there. He was a pro, a practiced designer. Obviously not senile.

I just stood there, astonished. Then I thought about what was on the screen.

"It'll never work," I said at last.

Startled, Artie turned to face me. "Why, you little bastard. *Baccala!*" he fumed, raising his hand in the classic Italian gesture of dismissal.

I thought I'd better get out before I provoked him further, but as I turned Artie said, "So what the hell's wrong with it, anyway?"

"Maybe you should explain it to me first."

"What's to explain? You got this little funnel gizmo, which the broad sticks into her nookie before she goes out, right? Your blades here are directed inward, like little spears. If some *porco* shoves his rod into the funnel, it passes through the blade cluster, see, but now the tip of his rod is a flange. *A flange*, see? It's got nowhere to go. Y'know those one-way parking-lot entrances that say, 'Don't back out or severe tire damage will result' or some crap like that? Y'know the ad that says 'roaches check in but they don't check out'?"

"Then what?"

"What do you mean, 'Then what'? Then the broad pushes him off, so his rod gets cut into ribbons, and she calls the cops while he screams and bleeds."

"Uncle Artie, you've designed a hitch-and-trailer setup for unwilling partners. Think about it from the woman's point of view. What's she going to do with a 250-pound gorilla who doesn't want to disengage? He'll just stay on top of her. And being somewhat indignant at the situation, he'll probably beat the hell out of her while he's at it. It's just not practical."

Artie stared at me intently. "Dinner in ten minutes, you two," came my aunt's faraway voice.

"Hey. You like olives? Black olives?" asked Artie, diving into one of his desk drawers to produce a large jar of plump, dark delicacies. "Your auntie would kill me if she saw these. Sodium. Lots of it. What the hell do I care? Life's short," he continued, lifting one of the little orbs out of the jar and gazing at it lovingly before chowing it down. He offered me the jar and I eagerly accepted.

"Good?" asked Artie as I chewed. "Attaboy!" he laughed, slapping my cheek with pride as I gave him the thumbs up. "Y'know, these olives come straight from Positano, in Italy, where your Uncle Arturo comes from." Artie told me that the olive trees that grew sparsely just outside the city of Positano, on the Amalfi coast, were among the best-kept secrets in the country. Commercially grown olives came primarily from Tuscany, much farther to the north, and well beyond the reach of the ocean breezes that Artie declared critical to olivary perfection. He also told me about Positano's steep hills, its winding streets, the fishermen he grew up with and the print shop he'd started with his brother before they both came to America.

"In those days," he told me, "presses weren't automated. Printing was an art. You had to understand color interaction, the way the inks work together. It was a tough, messy job."

"When did you become an engineer?" I asked him.

"Ah, everyone's an engineer in the Navy. Otherwise all the ships'd sink. Besides, this design stuff is only a hobby. I divert myself with it, y'know what I'm saying?" Artie explained.

"Divert yourself from what?"

"From what I do for a living, to keep myself in mail-order olives and pricey computers, and to put something away so those little brats I have for grandchildren can get an education. My genius son is too busy buying marble to put 'em through college." Artie obviously did not think Tony a genius.

But he also seemed to be talking nonsense. He'd retired twelve years ago. Yet he seemed perfectly lucid, so I tried to humor him. "That's very generous of you, Artie," I said.

"Are you humoring me? 'Cause if you are, I'll smack you like Patton slapped that sniveling little private."

"Do Tony and Gina know anything about this?" I asked quickly. "You're always so, uh, quiet around your family."

"The answer to your question is no, Gina's too busy with Tony and Tony's too busy with himself. As for your brilliant observation, I'm 'quiet' because I'm thinking. I turn 'em off, I tune 'em out, see? I go on autopilot so I can think."

Still confused, I asked, "Think about what?"

"What I do for a living, for Chrissakes! I thought your family had all the brains. You're as *sciocco* as my goddamn kid!"

I just wasn't getting it.

"Come *on*, come *on*, everybody's waiting," whined Tony from the entrance to Artie's suite. "You and that computer! Can we *please* get a move on?"

"I'll show you what I'm talking about later," Artie said softly as he got up. "You're a good kid. A little smug, but a good kid." He slapped my cheek again, affectionately. I think.

Artie and I followed my uncle across the house to the dining room. "Hey, that's some computer Uncle Artie's got. A Sun

Microsystems Sparcstation with graphics accelerator, ProCAD and CorelDraw design software ... quite impressive," I said, trying to break the ice. Dad had kindly left an empty seat for me between himself and Tracy. Aunt Gina was passing out salad dishes and serving. The kids had finally quieted down.

Artie sat on the other side of the table. He'd left his glasses in his bedroom.

"Well," replied Tony, "I don't know the model number, but I do know that it cost almost 700 bucks at Radio Shack. And that Coloring Book program was at least another 30. But does he let his grandchildren anywhere near it? Does he use that computer to help balance our checkbooks?"

Tony obviously had no clue that what may once have been a cheap little box with a child's painting program had been transformed into an elaborate system worth well over $25,000. Artie stared blankly ahead, his mouth slightly open.

"Anyway, like I was saying before," Larry interjected, "we may not go to the same school, but we see each other every weekend. She comes out to Albany or I go to Binghamton. Great school, Binghamton."

"*SUNY* Binghamton," Tracy corrected.

She was staring at Tony. It may have occurred to her that if Tony were to shave off his moustache, dye his hair blond and have his facial features completely reconfigured, he would be a dead ringer for Andre Dupree.

"Hey, when are you going to get a girl to bring to Christmas?" Tony asked me. "Don't they have girls at MIT? Huh?"

That hurt.

Then Tony yelled "Ouch!" as my aunt stabbed him with a fork under the table.

"*Girls! Girls! Girls!* Elvis Presley and Stella Stevens, 1962," said Uncle Artie.

"How's your roommate's project coming?" my father asked me. "MIT," he proudly told the table at large, "is the only place where a sophomore can do publishable research. This should interest you, Tony."

"Oh, yeah?" Tony asked me. "So what's he working on?"

"Tissue-compatible glasses," I replied. "He's a biochemist. The glasses he's developing actually bond to your tissue instead of just remaining inert."

"Wouldn't that make them harder to clean?" Tracy asked me.

Tony became interested. "Sure," he said, "glasses like that could be useful for alveolar reconstruction or endoceous ridge maintenance. Of course, most dentists can't even begin to fathom the complexities of implantation. To them, that's oral surgery. It might as well be ancient Greek."

I was confused by Tracy's question. "Why should they be difficult to clean?" I asked. "They'll be highly polished and sterilized as soon as they're manufactured."

"Right, but they won't stay that way forever. What I'm saying is, how are you going to clean them if they stick to the tissue?"

Now I understood. She thought I was talking about eyeglasses. "These are biocompatible glasses that are introduced into the human body," I explained, "to replace bone fragments or to reinforce cartilage. You don't clean them with a tissue. They bond to internal tissue after implantation, which allows them to provide structural support."

"Oh," said Tracy.

"Did I tell you how we met at camp?" Larry asked the table, eager to change the subject. "It was the second day of camp. Two days after I went to church. Remember how I went to church the day before you drove us to camp, Dad? I went to church and I *prayed* to *God*," he said, chopping the air with his hand to emphasize the words. "My prayers were answered."

My father was shaking his head, his eyes closed.

Tony swallowed and said, "That's what a lot of my patients say to me. They say, 'my prayers were answered when I found you for a dentist.' It's because I'm not afraid to extract. I'm not the kind of dentist who says, 'gee, that's just a little crack in the enamel, let's see if we can save it with an expensive crown.' Nope, won't do it. Just extract the damn tooth. Makes us both feel good."

My mother turned to Tracy and said, "Larry says you're thinking of majoring in psychology."

Tony said, "I remember when I was in college, God, it was wonderful. I was *appreciated*, you know? Smokers, coeds, boozy times at Sigma Delta Omega ... now I just drill 'em, fill 'em and bill 'em." Just as Tony finished this short plaint he snatched the bottle of red wine that Artie had just picked up and said, "Da-a-a-d, you know what the doctor told you about alcohol. No wine, okay?"

"You're the only one at this table who whines," replied Artie.

"Hey, you think it's easy putting a big spread like this together?" Tony snapped.

"Oh, how would you know?" asked Aunt Gina as she cleared the salad dishes. "You don't do the cooking."

"Not in the kitchen, anyway," Tony leered, slapping her behind as she made her way into the kitchen.

Then he looked over at Tracy, catching her glance. You've got to be quick to be a dentist of Tony's caliber.

The next course was pasta with some kind of seafood sauce, at least five pounds of it, which arrived by the armload in great porcelain bowls. Before I had even finished chewing my first mouthful, my aunt was back in the kitchen, working on the main fish course.

"OWWWWW!" bellowed Joey all of a sudden. "Hey Mom, Dad, Antonia bit me! She bit me for no reason!"

"Maybe you should stop giving her wedgies," yelled Aunt Gina from the kitchen. How could she have seen?

Tony said, "That's exactly why I like to extract. Hey, Toni, come here, let Daddy see your teeth."

Antonia turned white and clasped her hands over her mouth. At eight years old, she'd absorbed quite a bit of dental jargon.

"Dentistry is a metaphor for life," Tony proclaimed to everyone at the table. He looked directly at Tracy, interested but slightly rueful. Not bad ... could use a little more up top, eh Tony? "With my drill I am artist and scientist," he continued. "The drill is my tool—"

"But life is your substrate, right Tony?" my father interrupted. "Lighten up and chew. It's good for your teeth."

Everyone laughed. Tony's eyeballs seemed to sink into their white surroundings as his gaze widened into a glare. He eyed my father brutally. My father ate pasta, oblivious.

I, meanwhile, observed Artie throughout dinner. It seemed as if he had somehow partitioned his brain so that one little segment always remained available for autonomous processing. That little segment executed a response algorithm which conveyed the illusion of awareness by allowing Artie to contribute to a conversation. But it was entirely unconscious. The rest of Artie's brain was free to wander elsewhere, loft into formless flights of fancy if he wished. More probably, however, to concentrate on whatever it was he did 'for a living.'

The algorithm was triggered, and the autonomous control segment activated, by certain conversational cues. It spotted and announced double entendres. It identified areas of conversation where a reference to an old movie or show tune would be relevant. And it picked up on unusual words and translated them into Italian, appending, "In the old country, we used to say..." to the translation.

I decided to test the hypothesis. "Hey Artie," I said, "better eat your food while it's still hot. Don't you like it hot?"

The part of Artie's brain that spoke without thinking said, "*Some Like It Hot*. Marilyn Monroe, Jack Lemmon, Tony Curtis, 1959."

"What year was that?" I asked him.

"What year was what?"

Proof positive. Everyone else at the table fidgeted uncomfortably, forced to swallow yet another token of Artie's senility.

Artie caught my eye as Aunt Gina cleared the last of the dinner dishes. He nodded toward his apartment. "Artie and I have some unfinished business," I announced as we withdrew from the table.

Artie closed the door to his bedroom as we entered, and once again produced the jar of olives. "Want another before dessert? They're great after dinner."

"Why not," I said, taking one as Artie continued rummaging through his drawer. After what appeared to be great effort he finally produced a small silver flask and a champagne glass.

"They're especially good," he said, dropping an olive into the glass, "in martinis." He poured the contents of the flask over the olive as he sat down at his desk. "Your uncle would kill me. He'd have a goddamn conniption," Artie added, laughing.

"Do you do design work for a living?" I asked cautiously.

"In a sense I do," said Artie, leaning back in contemplation. "But not like you think. Your Uncle Artie is an artist. An artiste, really, a *maestro*. You know what I'm saying?"

"What kind of art do you make," I asked, still not quite sure whether I was hearing fact, senile fiction or a strange combination of both.

Artie leaned forward and looked at me with great seriousness, drawing his eyebrows together and gathering his breath slowly. "Album-cover art," he said finally.

"Album-cover art," I repeated, not believing him for a second, amazed at the altitude of this fanciful flight, not knowing whether to ride it out or eject.

"Album-cover art," he said again, this time solemnly. Then he got up and hauled a portfolio case out of his closet. Opening it on his desk he said, in one of the world's great understatements, "Now

I know you may find this a little tough to believe, but these here are all mine. I do at least two covers a month for Zeta Records. Maybe you got some of these at home."

His portfolio case was like a tour through the last ten years of my life. Zeta had produced at least a third of my record collection. Top forty, underground, jazz, you name it. Each of Artie's works was a painting on Bristol board, itself barely bigger than an album cover.

"They let me keep the originals. I insist on it. If they want the hand of Arturo Sebastiani," said Artie as he raised his finger, "they gotta do what he says."

The first entry in the box was sort of a pen-and-ink drawing of a chain-link fence. Behind the fence a mass of dark, impersonal heads receded into the background. Each head was actually a fingerprint. I recognized it immediately as the *Let Me Out!!* album by The Scavengers. Great rock-and-roll.

"Do you listen to this stuff?" I asked, not knowing what else to ask.

"Your uncle thought I'd lost control of my bowels when he saw the stains on my fingers from this cover," Artie remarked, shaking his head. Then my question registered. "Listen? To this crap? You kidding me? Zeta's art director of the month tells me about the group, tells me who we're marketing to, and then I send him something. I'm supposedly freelance but they never turn down anything I submit. Then they send me a big fat check."

Artie had also done a number of heavy-metal covers. He showed me the design from PowerTool's first album, called *Hardware Department*. The painting was colorful and detailed, showing a buxom woman with flowing dark hair against a red storm-drenched background. She stood on a rock at the edge of a choppy sea, holding an electric drill above her head. Her breasts practically poured out of her Viking tunic.

I'd seen the album before but PowerTool was strictly for the lowlifes. Their latest album, *Rip Cut*, featured the hit *Meat-Seeking Missile*—a brain-deadening brew of distorted guitar power chords, animal noises, and nonstop screaming. They set a hotel on fire once.

"I met that Nickerson fellow a couple years back—you know, their lead singer." When Toby Nickerson wasn't screaming he liked to moon his audience and show off his right ass cheek, which featured a tattoo of half a snake. The other half appeared to have departed into sunless regions.

"I liked him," Artie continued. "You know he went to Yale? Now those guys are way out, crazy. The marketers got hold of 'em ... let's see, what else do I have here?"

"How on earth did you get started in this trade? I mean..."

"It's not a TRADE, see, it's ART! When I was a printer, now, that was a trade. My brother and I used to print covers for two or three big record companies, since they used to job all the work out in those days. And their covers were CRAP, you hear me? Lousy photographs, stupid illustrations. But you gotta run what they give you, see? At first I liked being a printer—getting the colors just right, making the press listen to you. But bad art is like a fungus, it rots your brain. So I got out. Got out of the whole business. Became a carpenter, a technician, anything just so I wouldn't poison my eyes with that garbage. Y'know," Artie said, poking me on the chest with each important syllable, "*al*bum *cov*ers are the *only true form* of com*mer*cial art. You want to know why?"

I didn't. He told me anyway.

"Because they stand on their own. Because they have to sell the product but they're also *part* of the product they sell, see? Advertisements sell, but no one *buys* the *ad*, right? When you think of your favorite album, you picture the cover as you hear the music in your head. You can't separate the music from the art. You think you're dishing out for songs, but you're also buying what I put in front of your eyes. Album covers are the biggest-selling form of art in the world. Only people are too stupid to realize it."

"All right, so when did you begin life as an *artiste*?"

"I started the day after I retired," said Artie. "I'd been saving up ideas for years. I made two boards, put copyright notices on them, and shipped them off to Zeta Records with a note telling them that their album covers stunk like crap. Within two weeks I was working. That's it, the whole story."

"So where do you paint, where do you do all your work?"

"Ahhh," replied Artie, waving off the question. "I don't paint anymore, my hands aren't steady enough. I use the box." He pointed to the computer. "That little jewel under the desk is the best color printer you can buy."

I tried to make sense of all of this. "Artie," I asked, "You've got a life. What you do is important. How can you stand to play the senile simp every time you interact with someone?"

"What do I care? Everyone I like is dead. Besides, I need every minute to think about my work."

I pressed on. "Then why don't you just clam up, say nothing?"

"Because then my son would send me to a nursing home. Right now I'm an entertaining, pathetic *vecchio*, you know what that means?"

"Old man," I said, a little ashamed at my earlier opinion of him.

"You got it. Your auntie takes care of me, but not so much that she wants to ship me off. My idiot son forgets that I exist, thank God. And no one's a critic."

"Who buys your engineering design efforts?" I asked.

"No one, yet, but the Patent Office agrees they're new and different. Here, look at this."

Artie pulled a document from his drawer. It said "United States Patent", and underneath, "Sebastiani", and underneath that, "Childbirth Assistance Device." On the bottom half of the first page, a professionally drafted diagram showed a round platform to which a woman was strapped with her legs spread. Although lacking in detail, the woman was anatomically correct. I couldn't help but notice a striking resemblance to the Italian film star Laura Antonelli, actually, but with a bulbous belly. An arrow indicated that the platform rotated clockwise.

"The OB-GYN sits here," Artie explained, pointing to a location on the platform between the woman's knees. "The platform turns and centrifugal force pops the kid out. Just pushes it right out! The doctor hardly has to do anything. He just catches."

"You don't like women, do you?" I asked.

"Why, you little son of a bitch," said Uncle Artie. "Shut up and eat your goddamn olive!"

Just then a loud series of thumps and crashes from outside the room startled us. I rushed to Artie's door and saw Tracy crumpled on the floor at the bottom of the marble steps across the living room. Aunt Gina, who had been nearby in the kitchen, was there in a flash. And then Larry was also there.

"Oh my God, oh my God, are you all right?" panted Larry.

Apparently, Tracy had lost her footing at the top of the stairs after visiting the bathroom. Maybe she was still swooning from the sight of the flame-cut red marble vanity or the green marble shower with three heads, or perhaps she was allergic to the onyx fixtures, but in any case the potential energy she had accumulated on her way up the stairs rapidly turned into kinetic energy as she tumbled down, and she sank her front teeth into the inside of her lower lip when she hit the floor.

The children giggled. Tony, seeing the blood dripping from Tracy's mouth onto the white marble, jumped from his seat. As he stumbled around the table, tripping over chairs and toys left on the floor, Tony uttered the line he had waited to utter since the day he graduated dental school. Tony said, "Let me through, for God's sake, I'm a dentist!"

He lifted Tracy's head and examined her mouth. Tracy's eyes rolled. "Hold her head back, like this," Tony commanded Larry, "while I get my emergency kit." Tracy clearly fell within the class of females Tony found interesting, a generous class that included every human female other than his wife. He disappeared, up the marble stairs and into his bedroom.

Tracy said, "Ummagum…"

Returning with a small black shaving pouch, Tony dug through its contents. He tossed aside tooth brushes, dental floss and "No Cavities" smiley-face buttons until he found what he was looking for: a needle and suture, which he held aloft in triumph, looking just like his father with a Positano olive. Tony got to work immediately on the bleeding gash inside Tracy's mouth, sewing methodically as he stretched her lip down to her jaw. Tracy's eyes stopped rolling and began to focus on Tony. "Now there's a man who knows how to handle a suture," her eyes said. I'd seen that gaze before.

The dessert, the gifts, Tony and Gina playing a duet of Silent Night on the piano, retina-searing camera flashes, more yelling and foot-thumping madness courtesy of the children, assorted expressions of bonhomie and concern for Tracy, and then it was time to take off. Tracy was in lust again. Sewn lip notwithstanding, she looked like she felt great.

3.0

THE DRIVE FROM ARMONK TO CAMBRIDGE, MASSACHUSETTS, HOME to MIT and other, lesser institutions of higher learning, is long and tedious. Up Interstate 684 into Connecticut, through dreary Waterbury and Hartford on Interstate 84 and then mile after mile of monotony on Interstate 90, the Massachusetts Turnpike. It is an uncommonly unpleasant drive when the roads are filthy with snow and the diffuse winter sun nearly clenches your eyes shut and your brother is sullying the family's reputation by his supine worship of a dipshit bimbo and you know that, as soon as you've hauled the last of your luggage up the three long and musty flights of stairs and into your dormroom, your roommate will regale you with tales of exciting research developments when you haven't got the foggiest notion what direction your own investigations should take and it's becoming rather embarrassing.

I was mad. Very mad. And also rather grateful, actually, for the waves of blissful anger lapping over my thought centers, clearing them like a mental laxative, sharpening my senses. Thank God for Tracy. Thank God for my aimless academic wanderings. And special thanks for the ancient vehicle I was driving—my tiny mean machine, which I'd worked two summers cutting green grass at Big Blue to buy—whose inoperative radio left me to enjoy the whooshes of passing cars, irregular and unpredictable, at full volume. Not to mention the random rumbles and thumps under the car's wheels. Worst of all, the dashboard had acquired a rattle whose frequency varied with the car's speed, and of course the absence of musical diversion led me into an obsessive search for its pattern— a techie's substitute for counting the cracks in a sidewalk.

For the longest time it was twice a second, one-two, every fourth second, which wasn't so bad—one-two *shim*my *shim*my *shim*my, one-two *shim*my *shim*my *shim*my. But when I accelerated to pass a slow-moving pickup, the pattern bifurcated so the one-two rattle occurred every second and fifth seconds, and as I went faster still the pattern become very complex but not quite random, and the not-quite-randomness absolutely drove me nuts because I knew it should be predictable and why the hell wasn't I able to figure it out, dammit? I'd always been pretty good with patterns.

Oh, I was really irritated now. Bifurcations leading into pure chaos. It was nonlinearity all over again.

My only relief from this persistent rattle addle was a cure worse than the disease itself—unwanted nostalgia, my memories of June Brooke, class valedictorian and sex machine, forever invading my thoughts whenever time grew idle. June, wearing ripped jeans and a cowl-neck sweater, smiling and waving, catching up with me on my way to track practice back when I had a life. June sitting beside me in chemistry class, hunching her shoulders and giggling at my latest imitation of Mr. Misrach, our teacher. June answering the phone while she undressed, repeating my imitation of Misrach to another chemistry classmate who could not possibly have imagined the low-frequency, oh-so-large-amplitude bounce of her breasts, breaking free as she undid her bra, bobbing as she laughed and laughed.

Chemistry class was where we met.

And there she was again, in the piercing reflection from the chrome fender of a passing car—whoosh!—as the haze of clouds momentarily brightened, still at least three hours from Cambridge. June sitting next to me with her hand on my knee as I drove. The strong May sun low to the west, glinting perfect red fire off the hood of my car. June getting too friendly and distracting me from the road so I nearly tanked us into a telephone pole. Loud music gushing from the radio, chunky guitar riffs and thumping percussion pounding in our heads and pumping hot through our veins, Here comes Johnny with the power and the glory...

But not today, I reminded myself. Not with the radio broken, the shimmy shimmy one-two rattle and the sky becoming ominously dark. About ten miles past Danbury it began to snow, one of those unanticipated squalls that bedevil weather forecasters and their helpless congregations. Within minutes a white frosting covered the highway shoulder and the grassy island. The atmosphere, MIT meteorologist Edward N. Lorenz informed the world in 1963, is a secretive beast even as it circulates all around us, and will forever defy our efforts to understand and predict its habits. Reliable long-term weather forecasts are nothing but a fantasy. Lorenz recognized that all parts of the air we breathe are so thoroughly interconnected, from the smallest to the largest scales, that tiny disturbances in one place will spread out and kick around and finally produce big weather changes in many other places. The atmosphere is just too complex an organism for us to fully perceive. And you can't predict what you can't see.

Now the traffic slowed down and my car crawled through a loud construction zone. Whatever they were doing must have been pretty important to carry on in the snow. I nodded politely to the stuporous but undoubtedly well-paid flagman who pointed me to the safety of the left two lanes, as if the regiment of bright orange cones and the chest-thumping *rap rap rap* din of pneumatic jackhammers were insufficient to alert me to the beehive of activity to our right. I tapped the wheel to a Scavengers song, "Most of Life is Waiting," trying to overcome the noise and fill the car with imagined music and my imagination with ideas for research.

"Most of life is waiting," my father told me once, unwittingly quoting the Scavengers, "and the rest is statistics."

The snow began to intensify. More chaos. And more nonlinearity. The weather owes its hypersensitivity to nonlinearity, a mathematical oddity with big consequences for the real world. Nonlinearity is nature's ultimate taunt, defying us, standing in the way of our efforts to understand, predict, model. Nonlinear quantities intertwine with themselves in unsolvably complex ways. Systems built on such quantities effectively write their own rules as they evolve.

Nonlinearity sends planets and satellites and billiard balls jittering off the even, linear trajectories Newton promised into elaborate tangles of self-dependent migration. Nonlinearity underlies the infinite variety of snowflakes and the skies that create them, it's in our imperfectly beating hearts and the crazy swirls of rising smoke, it's in the sounds we hear, in the breaths we take and probably in the emotions we feel and the impressions we sense. Nonlinearity is the lawless rule; predictability the chance exception.

Usually we're too oblivious even to notice or to care. Usually the nonlinear terms remain pleasantly small. Real things may wobble and waddle slightly instead of following neat orbits, but no one pays any attention. Most of the time life stays simple and easy to understand. Newton isn't gospel truth but he's close enough.

How easily all that can change! Stress happens. Stir a system up and the nonlinear terms awaken. Wobbles begin to overpower linear smoothness, and orderly progressions dissolve into shapeless pandemonium. It's not random, this chaos—just so impossibly complex that things seem random, and they may as well be. Even an infinitely powerful computer couldn't predict chaotic behavior any faster than the behavior actually happens. And nonlinear chaos is where small disturbances make big differences.

It can happen anywhere, really. A pendulum swings freely, a stream of water flows gently. But just add some energy, a tiny bit more viscosity, and boom, disorder is everywhere and the once-tidy swing or flow becomes turbulent, as hopelessly mysterious as the tumult of the largest thunderstorm and much like, I observed, the powerful eddies and impressive vorticity vectors being generated by the huge, no—absolutely *colossal* two-trailer truck now bearing down from my left, driving too fast for these narrow temporary lanes, heaving clouds of wet grit and pebbles against the side of my car and then into the windshield to completely obscure my vision and buffeting me toward the closed-off lane so my tiny tires left the road and of course I panicked, I hit the brakes and glided, as though in slow motion, past the orange cones and then into the construction area. When it was finally over I was sinking into the fresh, steaming asphalt.

Thank you, truck-driving jerk. Just what the day lacked.

Now the flagman was running toward me. I opened the window and the freezing cold and the roar of heavy equipment poured into the car and I could hear June, bursting into loud and unwelcome laughter at a clever comment I whispered to her during a serious movie in a crowded theater. And there she was reading Walt Whitman as the Ferris wheel at Great Adventures amusement park reached its apogee, the broad world dropping all around us and as I looked in her eyes I saw, for the first time, so many other worlds she held in secret and I wondered whether I was part of them, and I hoped desperately she would decide to go Princeton, where we had visited that day, a hefty but not inconceivable ride from MIT.

"I think I'll need some help pushing the car back up onto the shoulder," I yelled toward Mr. Flag as I leaned out the window, hoping he could hear me over the deafening growls of those jackhammers. I thought about Walt Whitman again.

O Flagman! my flagman! rise up and hear my yells!

But he wasn't listening. He positioned himself just behind the car and waved his mighty fluorescent baton at the traffic, just in case any of the drivers felt tempted to drive across the line of cones, over the shoulder and into this sweltering, gluey cauldron that held my car prisoner and filled my head with the stench of petroleum and rubber. As if there were anything he could do about cars spinning out of control. And as if everyone else weren't behaving themselves anyway.

"Can you get us some help? Some help? I need some he-e-e-lp!" I hollered and hollered. I really didn't want to get out of the car.

My flagman does not answer, his lips are pale and still,
My flagman does not give a damn, he's got some time to kill.

And finally three of the road crew made their way over to my window, slogging through the muck in their tall shiny boots. The biggest one smiled, not unkindly, and said with a thick Slavic accent, "You fuck up, boy." Then he said, "We move you." The three of them leaned into the rear fender, lifting and bouncing and grunting in a futile attempt to drag my poor suffering car through the viscous goo. We went nowhere. Finally, just when I thought I'd surely lose my breakfast to the jolting bounces and sickening fumes, I noticed a row of fat wooden boards leaning against one of the official orange detail trucks. With frantic gestures I convinced my ineffective benefactors to jam those boards under my rear wheels and lay a path of them back up to the shoulder. My poor suffering car moaned and spat as it slowly hauled itself from captivity, riding over the boards but leaving them undamaged. The flagman marched several feet ahead, dutifully wagging his baton at oncoming traffic.

O Flagman! my flagman! Our fearful trip is done,
The car has weather'd every whack, I can't say it's been fun.

As I reached the shoulder I waved at my saviors, who smiled and clapped; I was off again. And angry again. Friction with the road loosened the asphalt that had encrusted on the tires and wheel rims. Tiny gravel particles scattered and echoed in the wheel wells, adding to the general cacophony of rumbles and thumps and chaotic rattles. Thanks, serendipity.

A car trailing a bright orange ribbon from its antenna flew past me on the left. The fluttering ribbon looked so much like June's hair the day she took me for a spin in her father's sputtering old convertible, that flaming red hair streaming behind us like the bright plume of a rocket, propelling the car ahead. I hoped my mean red machine hadn't suffered any expensive damage from its gooey encounter with stress. I wished my head would stop pounding. Stress happens. I wished my heart would stop racing so furiously, return to equilibrium.

Equilibrium, yes.

Drive a nail through my heart.

"Equilibrium," lectured Misrach just about two years before, "is a canonical problem. Today we'll go over some of the mathematical elements." I looked over at my beautiful lab partner with smooth, shapely legs and a tiny nose with just enough freckles, and whose touch had just stood my hair on end like a the crackling dome of a van de Graaf generator. June Brooke was rolling her eyes. She wanted to let me know she was bored to death with Misrach's mechanical explanations. I smirked in agreement. I'd had a crush on her for months.

Misrach was attempting to explain Le Chatelier's Principle, which has to do with the way systems react to stress. Explaining might be too strong a term; actually, he was reading from a mental script. June leaned over and whispered to me that she could do with some Le Chatelier magic herself, since her latest boyfriend had broken up with her the previous night and thereby introduced significant stress into her life.

"If a chemical system at equilibrium is subjected to a disturbance that changes any of the factors that determine the state of equilibrium," Misrach intoned, "then the magnitudes of such factors will adjust so as to minimize the effect of the disturbance on the system ... everybody get that?"

"There's no place like homeostasis," June said to me, a little too loudly, as she tapped her pencil against her desk.

"What was that?" Misrach asked sharply.

"What you mean, I think," explained June, "is that systems always try to re-establish equilibrium. They want to be at peace."

He looked at her quizzically. "Isn't that what I just said?" he asked, annoyed that she had interrupted the efficient transfer of data from his notes to his students' notes. Shaking his head, he began drawing equations on the board that described the principle mathematically. But neither he nor his chalk was as elegant as June, and he knew it, and he didn't like it, and there wasn't a damn thing he could do about it. June and her perfect grade-point average were beyond reproach, and besides, her observation was entirely correct.

June's eyes caught mine again as Misrach's chalk squeaked out variable after variable. Only this time her eyes didn't let go. Then we were eating lunch together, then she was cheering me on as I cleared all ten intermediate hurdles to win the 400 meters in that day's track meet. I'd never had an audience before. And the next day I returned the favor, attending the awards ceremony at the Armonk Gazette's offices where June received their annual prize for literary criticism. I hoped none of the editors would recognize me. And then there we were after our second real date, late at night, in her house, we'd known each other long enough and she said she could trust me.

Trust me? Give me a break. Oh, I may have looked suave in chinos with my hair slicked back, but that was just image. In fact, my experience in matters romantic was actually rather narrow.

The house was silent, dark. June led me by the hand through a foyer and up some stairs and there was her bedroom on the right—uncharted territory to me. I don't think I'd ever been in a girl's bedroom before.

And then there was a noise. *What was that?!* Her father with a shotgun? The onset of a terrorist assault? Or was it the house settling? Did someone just open the refrigerator door? A dog started barking outside—no one could possibly sleep through that, the dog would certainly wake her parents. I searched frantically for a place to hide.

Sensing my discomfort, June laughed conspiratorially as she turned on her bedroom light and closed the door. So *that's* what a girl's bedroom looks like! Not all that different from my bedroom, actually, except frillier. But the smell! So feminine! An ineffable bouquet of hygiene and soft fragrance, of wildflowers, talcum and a hint of jasmine.

The first detail I noticed was the picture of June and her mother on top of a desk-like structure. Both of them had those many-worlded eyes that seemed to drop behind the rest of the flat image like holograms. Apparently June's night table was the proud owner of the same cheapo clock radio that sat next to my bed, but it was impossible to be sure, because June's was covered with a thick crust of scratches and dents.

Another noise! And this one definitely sounded like successive footsteps. Her mother and father! Should I make a dash for the closet?

Easy now, I told myself, squelching the startle. Nothing to worry about, just a burp in the heating pipes. June's parents were safely asleep. Catatonic, in fact.

"Come closer," she whispered, stretching twin cones from my shirt as she drew my stiff carcass toward her very unstiff self. "You know, I'm really attracted to you." And I thought of pointing out that this was untrue as a matter of strict Newtonian mechanics since she was the one exerting the force on me as she tugged on my shirt, and besides, what did gravitational fields have to do with romance anyway, and perhaps I should warn her that I tend to intellectualize just about everything when I get uptight, so maybe we should just call it a night, okay? Then I looked down at the pointy little stretch marks on my chest and realized they made a perfect complement to the two marbles pressing through June's clingy blouse.

There was no turning back.

Marbles and stretch marks flattened each other as we entwined. The time for nervous humor and hesitance had passed. June was serious now. And soon she was naked, like me. I kissed her and touched her on the bed, striving to appear relaxed and experienced, running my hands over her topography the way I thought you were supposed to run your hands over such topography.

But she was not convinced. Sitting up, June looked into my eyes and delivered her opinion: "You're not too familiar with ... what goes on down there. Right?"

I wasn't. I mean, I'd seen pictures, but never had one to call my own.

She smiled and shook her head, not unkindly, and her long red hair shimmered gloriously in the light of the high-intensity lamp she had trained on her bed. Here she was—in the buff, in the every living detail of my daydream transformed into flesh, in the web of florid blood vessels beneath that flesh transporting the desire in her eyes throughout her overwhelmingly real body. No longer a daydream but a *woman*, just eighteen, like me, but fully self-aware in her every want and need. And here she was stuck with me—all I could offer were my unskillfully scalar caresses, all magnitude and no direction.

"All right," she continued patiently, "time for Anatomy 1."

She opened her legs and pulled my head down, delivering herself of tender instruction, of prim euphemism, of little men in slender boats.

Heady down here, I noted.

"Think you've got it?"

I heard what she said and my finger began to dance elaborate flowing patterns through her warm creases. Supporting herself on her elbows, June watched my actions intently at first. Then she felt comfortable enough to close her eyes, then she was smiling a twisted smile, then she was throwing her head back in pleasure as her folds swelled into glistening, veiny little sausages.

I'm serious.

Her glance returned to me to communicate her enjoyment, but the limp hose she saw told her my own fire was out. She turned onto her side to face me, gently raised my head, held my cheeks and looked into my eyes. "Don't get paranoid on me, I wasn't criticizing you before," she reassured me. "You're turning me on incredibly, and you'll be a wonderful lover. I promise. You just need a little orientation, okay?"

She had me paralyzed and mesmerized in her grace, in the boundless sensual generosity of her forgiveness.

"Come next to me," she said, running her hand down my side. Immediately the fire was back. "We're going to start off slowly, very slowly." She dragged her hand through my hair so I could feel her nails and gave me a deep, gyrating kiss. Wow.

"Don't even think about technique. The Kama Sutra teaches sixty-four separate paths to fulfillment, each its own journey without destination or direction. There are no wrong turns. You can't get lost."

She slithered underneath me and showed me how to climb on top of her without crushing her ribs. She cupped Max Planck in her hands. Then she deftly slid it inside her and arched her back, kissing me, grabbing clumps of my hair with each hand, and suddenly we were moving in synchrony with one another. I almost screamed with ecstasy at the sensation—the silky longitudinal friction on the way in, the grippy hydraulic drag on the way out. A magnificent reciprocation!

But then June started to talk. She talked a lot, in fact.

"Ease in, now ease out, like that, now again, now again ... yes, you're marvelous, marvelous! Now slide your body up, use long, deep strokes, push in slowly like a snake entering his lair, remember what I showed you about my anatomy ... that's right ... Now pause, pause and strike hard, strike like a hawk swooping down at his prey ... oh, you're wonderful ... now try shallow, teasing strokes before you push all the way in, like a stealthy otter testing the water before he dives ... strike out to the left, strike out to the right, you're a brave warrior fighting two enemies at once! ... Move your body up and down, up and down, like a wild horse refusing to be broken ... that's it! ... Now make your strokes progressively deeper, like a spelunker exploring a cave ... deeper, struggle deeper into the darkness ... you're marvelous, oh, you're wonderful, a little to the left ... Thrust swiftly now, chase the frightened rabbit into his hole!"

Then a crash: her night table took a nosedive. That explained the bruised clock radio.

Could her parents possibly be asleep? Or had she killed them?

And then June was fighting me, opposing my movements, wrestling away from me, making me work harder. That explained why her old boyfriend always looked so tired.

"...Oh, baby, I want you, I *want you!*"

"You got me, you got me!" I managed.

"SHUT UP, SHUT UP!" cried June. "I was being figurative! You've got enough to concentrate on, let me do the talking ... oh, God, I'm sorry, I'm so sorry, I didn't mean to insult you ... I'm such a bad girl ... Push harder, push *harder*, I don't deserve you, I'm so bad ... A little to the left, if you don't mind."

Then she sensed something. "Don't come yet!" she warned, "don't give up on me. Think about Misrach's kinetics lecture. Think about quadratic equations. Think about anything but don't give up on me! Don't give up! Don't give ... I'm so close, I'm ALMOST THERE! I'm..."

Now her voice trailed off as she strained and arched until the tendons in her neck billowed out. June's face was bright red and her skin slick as her head shook from side to side, her breath short, gasping in rhythmic staccato, again gripping my hair in clumps. Then, at last, her shaking began to subside and her eyes opened. "How are you doing?" she asked with concern, slowly regaining consciousness.

My little tremor had passed what seemed like ages ago, a wispy transient lost amidst seismic convulsions and aftershocks. I melted into her arms and fell asleep—barely able to comprehend her distant reminders about the time as they dissolved into space, fully absorbed and triumphantly adrift in the gaze and the sounds and the sex of the redoubtable June Brooke.

There's no place like homeostasis.

o   o   o

"Can someone give me the pH of a 0.1 molar solution of ammonia at the equivalence point?" Misrach asked, turning from the blackboard and the little white cloud his chalk had kicked up to face the class. "What about you, Paul? You're looking a little drowsy today."

Misrach, you inert byproduct, I screamed silently in response, don't try to conceal yourself in some drippy titration exercise. You know, I know you know, and I can only imagine the stretching frequencies your lone pair must be suffering at this moment.

How I pity you, encased in this acetone-drenched dungeon of periodic charts, rusty clamps and glassware supports, permanently stained lab benches. Don't you know I can see you marveling at her frontier orbital lobes (*dream on!*) and agonizing over her catalytic reaction crevice (*oh, baby!*) and dying to know whether she goes down like a hungry ligand (*does she ever!*)?

Look at this smug expression on my face and tell me you don't rue the day you ever decided to teach chemistry to an endless parade of tight-bodied high-school seniors sparging hormones who think you're ridiculous and pathetic and would eat you for lunch if it weren't for that miserable little grade book of yours.

"5.1," I responded.

Quick thinking like that got me into MIT.

o   o   o

We talked endlessly.

I swam in the sweetness of the soap she wore.

And we dated. We dated constantly.

"You're a magnificent partner," June said one late-spring day as she lay on top of me. She was looking off to my right with her ear pressed against my naked chest. And then out of nowhere the words "I love you" convected up from somewhere deep in her diaphragm, humid and throaty, as if somehow rising under their own power, free from so clumsy a bearer as conscious thought.

Respond, you idiot! I knew I should say something, tell her how entirely and urgently I felt the same, ask her how many kids she wants and where we should get married and if she minds Royal Oak china, since that's my mother's pattern, and whether we should hyphenate our last names together and how she figures we'll ever be able to afford a house, what with prices these days ...

But I didn't have the words. I said nothing. And June was not

45

one to repeat herself.

o   o   o

And I should, of course, have been able to predict that June would accept the offer from Stanford. And I ought to have realized that she would want to go her own way. It should have been perfectly obvious that she would not return a single one of my letters or phone calls.

And I should have known from the outset that when it finally ended I would dread normalizing every woman I would ever love to June, gauging them against her, and how desperately I would wonder when the worlds in her eyes would finally leave my eyes and how long it would take to forget the scent of her blood and her heat.

I should have been able to predict all this. But I didn't.

And that hurt.

o   o   o

Then there was an intruder, come to remind me what a pitiful mess my life had become.

"Are you treating?" I remembered joking to Andre as we got ready to pay the check and leave Chet's.

He smiled. "I have been. All night."

What a guy.

o   o   o

Soon I passed Waterbury, Connecticut, at one time the brass capital of the free world but now mostly forgotten except for a stern, tacky cross atop a prominent hill just outside the downtown district. You can't miss it from the main highway. The cross serves as the centerpiece of Holy Land U.S.A., one man's vision of biblical Jerusalem, now an empty, fenced-off wasteland. The cross still lights up red at night. Once a landmark, today a pitiful distraction.

Things change. Stress happens.

And then I was slowly winding my way through the ceaseless construction in Hartford that seems to draw the road into new meanders every time I pass through. How I hated construction. I detested the snow. I cursed all flagmen.

The rattles returned as the traffic sped up, one-two shimmy shimmy shimmy, and you can believe I was now monumentally pissed off as I drove through the Connecticut hinterlands, one-two shimmy shimmy shimmy in my mind and out my ears the pattern of this goddamn rattle through my brain like herds of cattle, catch the rhythm feel the meter prisoner of this two-seater, speak to me you teasing slattern let me understand your pattern, even intricate equations are no match for my persuasions, spill me all your secrets now before I have a fucking cow! ... and then I accelerated and the chaos was back and the rhythm was gone. I stopped pounding the steering wheel with my fist.

And that's when it suddenly occurred to me: the snow had begun as a dusting on the gray pavement, now it covered like a carpet. Suppose you could imagine dust into down—connect points into completeness. Snow is nonlinear. It falls chaotically.

Suppose you could just compute away the uncertainty. Suppose you could find harmony within the chaos, meld driving swirls and mad darting flakes into a quiet blanket of order. Suppose life and snow were as tractable, as well-behaved as Newton's apple falling from a tree. Imagine: an end to the unexpected, a roadmap to the future...

A light dawned. Why not? Why couldn't you just get rid of the chaos? Pretend it doesn't matter. Ignore it. Filter it out. Start with scattered snowflakes and use mathematics to sew up the gaps, fill in the missing pieces with approximate solutions.

Yes, of course, missing pieces—that's when you use an obscure branch of statistics that lets you draw conclusions without complete information. Missing-data statistics. My father had mentioned it once in an almost occult way, some mystical black magic strange to all but the hardest core number jockeys.

My skin was prickling. Isolate the turbulence, corral the chaos, and a patchwork picture just might begin to resemble reality. Like stipples coalescing into a clear image. Like a curtain rising, the future revealing itself!

But wait. How do you ride an elusive thread of reason through galloping seas of confusion? In the eternal brawl between harmony and disorder, how could you keep score? What you would need is ... yes, now that was interesting.

O flagman! my flagman!

4.0

"P<small>ATIL'S FINISHED,</small>" <small>SAID MY ROOMMATE,</small> D<small>EXTER</small> D. D<small>RAIN,</small> III—Dexter to his mother, 3-D or D-cube to his friends—after I'd hauled the last of my luggage up the three long and musty flights of stairs and into our dormroom. "Gone. Blew his qualifiers."

He was talking about Ramesh Patil, the graduate student with whom he worked on the bioactive glass project. A nice guy, actually. Probably too nice for their adviser, Charles Pappadallas, one of the darlings of Course 7—the biology degree program. Curricula, like everything else at MIT, get numbers, and it's more consistent with the overall atmosphere to tell someone you're in Course 7 than to say you're a bio major.

Lounging on Dex's desk was another biodarling and Dex's good friend, Don Boyer. "Ramesh never really fit in here," he said. "An organism eliminates what it can't process. Ramesh just wasn't right for MIT."

"And now the machine has ejected him," I said, trying to emphasize my sarcasm.

"Precisely," said Don, not noticing or not caring.

I couldn't stand him. Dex had met Don Boyer at one of those awful parties the Biology Department liked to throw, where most of the people were insufferably pretentious to disguise their premed terror and the rest had learned to cultivate that terror into a state of comatose indifference. Nervous whispers about last week's cell biology exam. White, blank stares (from the comatose ones) and vicious bravado—"you thought it was *hard?* You're not premed, are you?" (from the pretentious ones).

Don was of the latter stripe. He and Dex encountered each other within five minutes of our arrival at the party—my first and last—and they hit it off almost instantly. "Don Boyer. Calcium transport," announced the big, tall owner of a hand extended in greeting to Dex and also, incidentally, blocking our progress toward the cheese whiz and warm soda. A delighted grin spread across Dex's face as he gripped the hand. "Aha, a heart man, eh?" he said, and they went off together, biobuddies.

"What about the company you're putting together?" I now asked Dex. "Does that mean Ramesh will get his masters and start working full-time for, uh ... what's the name of your outfit?"

"BioVitrics," said Dex. "And it doesn't look that way. He's pretty broken up, thinking of going back to Bangalore."

"I don't imagine Pap did much for his chances on the qualifiers," I said. Certainly the august Pappadallas engaged more pressing matters than Ramesh's interest in the Ph.D. program. Fully spelled out, that's M-I-T, P-H-D, M-O-N-E-Y.

"Well, that's not really fair," said Dex. "Pap was the only judge who passed him on the Physiology orals. And as soon as he got the bad news, he talked the VCs into creating a permanent position for Ramesh at BioVitrics." Dex was referring to the venture capitalists who had just seed funded the company to the tune of $500 K. "I just don't think he's interested."

As I stuffed my coat into my half of the closet it occurred to me that now it was just Pap and Dex in this bioventure. That meant fewer gruntwork hands to stir the vitreous mixtures in their platinum crucibles until they domed up and hardened over, like little glass eggs, after hours of painstaking care. But also fewer hungry hands grabbing for stock options and founder shares. I now shared a room—and a rather small one at that, just big enough for two standard-issue MIT beds, desks and bureaus, provided they were creatively arranged—with a 19-year-old whose net present value was about to skyrocket.

Christ, everyone but me was tunneling.

"How was break?" he asked me.

"All right, the usual," I said. Actually I was dying to tell him about my idea, but not with Don Boyer, calcium transport, in the room. Not only was Don personally insufferable, but he had the effect of making Dex insufferable as well. Dex thought the world of him. So much so that in his presence Dex became protective of everyone in the vicinity, shielding them lest they be crushed like a bug in the titanic vice of Don's intellect. To Dex, Don Boyer was a towering, fearsome genius. And no one could have agreed more with that assessment than Don Boyer himself.

"Have you been here all through break?" I asked Dex, suddenly realizing I hadn't seen him leave in December and here he was three days before the beginning of the January Independent Activities Period. IAP is when you're supposed to take one of these ooh-ahh 3.5-week intro courses on topics at the cutting edge of technology or hook up with a faculty member to do research.

"Well, not *all* through break," Dex smiled. That meant he just might have taken part of Christmas Day off to visit his family in Dedham, about eight miles south. Dex was local. "We had some annealing to do."

"You mean *you* had some annealing to do," I smiled. Pap wouldn't be caught dead doing spade work, particularly on either side of a holiday. Dex nodded absently.

"So, Paul. What have you got planned for IAP?" Don asked me in his slow Midwestern monotone. He spoke without affect or accent, as if each word exiting his mouth were a pearl that could be properly admired only when unadorned. And I was sure he posed the question not out of curiosity or concern, but to afford himself yet another opportunity to talk about his own research.

In fact, I hadn't yet decided. I hadn't decided about a lot of things. Like what I should major in. A year and a half into my MIT tenure and still I was bopping around among computer science (Course 6) and mechanical engineering (Course 2) and physics (Course 8) classes. But now my wanderings seemed divinely inspired, about to end on the shores of the promised land, since they all related in one way or another to my Idea.

And it was time to announce that idea to neutralize the incipient biogloatings of the odious Don Boyer. "I'm glad you asked," I told him. "I've got a research idea I'd like to pitch to you guys."

"Something you hatched over Christmas break?" Dex asked.

"Still mostly in the ovum, really," I replied, and began telling them about my approach to the beastly math of chaos that defies solution. How I would plumb the secrets of the unknown with fancy statistical tools.

I'd just finished this engaging little intro when Rita Dorfman, who lived down the hall, poked her head in the door. Rita was a year ahead of us and the senior teaching assistant in the basic computer programming class, Electrical Engineering and Computer Science ("EECS", pronounced Eeeeks!) 6.001, Structure and Interpretation of Computer Programs. That made her my boss. And her presence usually meant that her shadow, Wiseman Hsu (Course 2) wasn't far behind.

"You mean you've finally got a research project?" came her uninvited question.

That made me defensive. Rita frequently made me defensive. "That's what we've been talking about," I sniffed.

Now she was fully inside our room, looking ever so Rita, the way she looked every day of her life—facial features stretched tight by the torque she exerted on her dark hair, extruding each and every strand back into a tight helix she coiled around a plastic stick pin, and wearing her usual ensemble of sneakers, blue sweatpants and a loose gray sweatshirt. Rita was studying psycholinguistics (Course 9, Brain and Cognitive Sciences). The practical side of her research focused on speech recognition—teaching computers to understand and directly process the spoken word. But Rita was more interested in her work's philosophical pedigree: the merciless slicing and dicing of all forms of communication they call information theory. Strip away meaning, strip away emotional impact, strip away redundancy and rhetorical flourish and communication becomes data transfer, pure and simple.

If you're a communication engineer, redundancy drives you crazy. You listen in shorthand, talk in monosyllables and never repeat yourself. If you're Rita, you're no fan of excess either but you accept it, use it to your advantage. You know computers are stupid. You know they can't think. And you know that, as a result, they have trouble understanding human speech.

So you collect every bit of redundancy in sentences, words and letters, and use it to help sharpen uncertain computer ears. You even teach yourself several languages—to gather more clues, find more kinds of redundancy, make computers better listeners.

And then you let yourself loose on the world. Rita's hunt for the meaning in the message had become her personal ideology, her sense of mission. Watch out for Rita. She'll spot the information contained in your everyday behavior and deduce your motives. Those designer clothes you're wearing? Rita knows you're doing more than trying to look good. You're displaying an emblem, sending a message, engaging in communication: "I can afford these duds."

Which, incidentally, is why Rita only wore sweats. She had long ago decided that if people want to know her they would have to look beyond her clothes, and if they refused, who the hell cares what they thought?

Wiseman arrived, as expected, just moments after Rita's entrance. He also maintained strong personal views on the subject of communication. He hated it entirely. An information theorist's pride, he discharged his words in impatient bursts, eager to rid himself of their inefficient spoken nuisance. He could time-shift an entire conversation so it was mostly over before you could say anything. A telephone greeting might begin, *Hello this is Wiseman Hsu how are you fine thank you very much in case you forgot I am calling to remind you that our design-and-build project for 2.70 class is due shortly and I continue to encounter vibrations in your reciprocating swing arm I wonder if you have made any progress in your efforts to ameliorate the same since as you know it interferes noticeably with the operation of my clutch....*

Whenever anyone managed to shoehorn a thought into Wiseman's continuous transmission he would immediately begin to fidget, rubbing his fingers together, nodding furiously, hissing through his nose and saying *yes, yes, yes* to indicate you could clam up already, your ideas have been fully absorbed and you're becoming an unbearable irritation. It was fun to watch him interact with Don Boyer and his slow, persistent drawl, like dueling phonographs set at different speeds.

Wiseman's narrow frame always seemed to chase after the large silver-rimmed glasses that preceded his face. Both he and his glasses now pressed through the doorway. "Oh, Rita, I'm sorry, I did not realize that you were engaged. Oh, hi Paul, hi Dex, hi Don," said Wiseman as he barged past Rita into our room. Terrific. Now we were a conclave. Now discussing my idea would be like defending a thesis I hadn't even started yet. Five people crammed into our tiny room, Don reclining across Dex's desktop and leaning back on his hands, Dex in his creaky wooden desk chair with his knee over the arm, me sitting tensely in my own creaky wooden desk chair, Wiseman leaning against the only patch of empty space on the walls and Rita wandering around the pitifully small amount of unoccupied floor space. The room quickly grew stuffy and the snow-stained windows fogged over.

It was group therapy, MIT style.

Wiseman's tee shirt caught my attention. It said:

... and GOD said:
$$\nabla \cdot D = \rho$$
$$\nabla \times E = -\partial B/\partial t$$
$$\nabla \times H = J + \partial D/\partial t$$

$$\nabla \cdot \mathbf{B} = 0$$
$$\nabla \cdot \mathbf{J} = -\partial\rho/\partial t$$

... and there was light.

Bravo to you, Wiseman, always finding new propellers to wear on your head so people will think you're smart. Maybe Maxwell's equations will diffuse through your shirt and up into your brain by osmosis.

No one was exactly sure why Wiseman followed Rita so assiduously. He already possessed that rarest of assets at MIT, an acquaintance of the opposite sex who was crazy about him. And that was because Donna something-or-other, a cornsilk princess from Illinois, where Wiseman grew up, possessed that bizarrest of quirks, an appreciation for the sex appeal of MIT students. Engineers turned her on. Go figure. She was in school at Wellesley and Wiseman "saw," perhaps even "dated" her nearly every weekend.

"Welcome to our show," Rita said to Wiseman. "Paul here has an idea. He's sharing it with us so we can trash it. Find yourself a comfortable spot with a clear line of sight."

So once again I began my introduction. And once again I never got to finish. About two-thirds of the way through my discourse Rita brusquely announced her verdict. "Sounds like Bayesian black magic to me," she said, gleeful titters erupting all around her. "It's also the nerdiest, most boring thing I've ever heard."

The reference to Bayesian statistics was truly unkind. Such unvarnished cruelty, accusing me of soft-numbered subjectivity. Rita was a whiz at hard, pure statistics. She was showing off.

"It's not Bayesian," I assured her.

"Who will you get as a faculty sponsor?" asked Dex.

"That Bayesian sorcerer Watt, perhaps?" Rita followed.

"It's *not* Bayesian," I protested. It really isn't.

"Why don't you just use covariance, or better yet, derive a sample correlation coefficient?" Dex asked.

"Because things are constantly changing so there's nothing to correlate. It would be like averaging the temperature over a year and then trying to predict how cold it will be tomorrow based on the average."

"Oh, so it's a form of regression."

"No," I told him, trying not to sigh impatiently. Jesus, the guy takes one lousy course in population statistics and now he's Louis Harris. "Regression is just a guess. My method is exact."

"You mean the method you don't have yet?" asked Rita, turning the knife. "But I think I see what you're up to. You use mathematical equations, which you can't solve, to guide your statistics, which would otherwise be useless."

"Right."

"And you use the souped-up statistics to filter out the crap while solving the equations you thought you couldn't solve. Hopefully without sacrificing too much accuracy. Correct?"

"Exactly." There was hope. "It becomes a missing-data exercise."

"Sounds Bayesian to me."

"It's not Bayesian, godfuckingdammit!"

Then the great pistons of Don Boyer's cerebral engines began to groan into action as he at last turned his attentions to my proposal. "I don't understand it," he said. But with contempt, as if to suggest it wasn't worthy of being understood.

"If you're interested in chaos, though," he continued, "you should see what we're doing in the cardio lab. It's truly cutting edge. You know about heart fibrillation, right? Where the heart turns into a useless bag of squirming worms instead of beating normally? That's a chaotic phenomenon, and you die from it. Fritz Sauer's found a way of identifying heart-attack victims at high risk for fibrillation. He takes an EKG signal and plays it *backwards!* Pretty wild, huh? And as you know, I'm looking into the role of..."

"Calcium transport." We said it together. I knew he'd find a way to talk about his own research. I smiled icily.

Wiseman could no longer hold himself back. "This whole deal strikes me as kind of dumb, yes, dumb, precisely," he offered, racing through the words. "There are of course already plenty of ways of solving differential equations. You can approximate them with a power series, you can use the recursion formula, parameter variation..."

"Dumb? You think my idea is dumb?" They certainly were piling on.

"I did not say your idea is dumb, or even that I think it is dumb. I said it strikes me as dumb."

"Great, thanks for clarifying. Wiseman, can you—right now—name the two basic types of differential equations?" I asked.

"Certainly, of course," he said. "Homogeneous and non-homogeneous."

"Wrong!" I announced triumphantly. "The correct answer is 'hard' and 'easy.' The techniques you're talking about work for easy equations with a few variables. And you need to set boundary conditions. I'm talking about hard equations in environments without effective boundaries, like the atmosphere." Running this quadrophonic gauntlet was getting on my nerves. I had to clear the decks. "Let me ask you another question. Do you have any naked pictures of Donna?"

"Why … no," said Wiseman, in an unusually slow cadence.

"Wanna buy some?"

Dex laughed through his nose.

"Where, may I ask, did you obtain these photographs?" asked Wiseman, astonished.

Rita stood up. "This is getting disgusting. I'll see you later when you're through with this masculine protest ritual." She walked out the door.

"And I suppose I've got to make a call, yes, that's just what I'll do," said Wiseman, following Rita.

"I'll catch you at ten," said Don Boyer as he too left the room, glancing at Dex.

Dex was smiling. "Like, totally awesome concept, dude!" he said, swooning and creasing his eyes to more effectively imitate the California contingent of the late-night crowd at the computer lab.

Then he got serious. "But you've got it backwards. To do research in this place, you need faculty sponsorship and a source of funding. Professors have their own ideas. If they're lucky they can get funding, and then if you're lucky you can go to work for them. It doesn't work the other way. You won't get funded on your own, and don't expect anyone here to drop their own research agenda to be your champion."

"Unless they've got nothing better to do," said Rita, once again poking her head in the door. "Really, Paul, talk to Watt. His expertise goes beyond Bayes, and more importantly, he genuinely has nothing better to do."

"Wait a minute, even I've heard of Watt," said Dex. "That guy's reputation has spread all the way to Course 7. Jeff Watt hasn't gotten a grant in, what, eight years? Nine years?"

"Talk to Watt," Rita repeated, ignoring Dex. "It sounds like the only resource you'll need up front is computer time. If that ridiculous nerdalert idea of yours pans out, you can get funding with Watt or in spite of him." She slammed the door.

"She is your boss," smiled Dex. "Maybe you should do what

she says."

It was true. I owed my job to her. Last year I'd done well enough in EECS 6.001 that Rita, the head TA, asked me to join the corps under her charge. That offer came just in time. IBM had just announced a summer hiring freeze. The $10K I thought I'd earn from three months' toil there—gone. And Big Blue wouldn't be renewing my small scholarship.

The previous summer, just after I'd graduated high school, IBM had seemed ready to unleash a perpetual bitstream of bucks in my direction. A guaranteed summer engineering position, a $2K annual scholarship award, vague promises of a job after graduation—the works. All because I'd picked up some computer-programming techniques from my father over the years, the way other kids pick up fade-away jump shots and bigoted ideas from their fathers, and one day made a helpful suggestion to his group director about a data pipelining problem they were working on. It wasn't a particularly brilliant suggestion, but no one else had thought of it, and it got me off the John Deere for the rest of August and into the cavernous, air-conditioned warren of partitioned pigpens where the engineers worked.

But you know the rest. The recession, the layoffs, the staff reductions across the computer industry. IBM wouldn't even let me cut their lawns as I began to accumulate a mountain of student loans, and my Camp Cuyahoga pittance trimmed my growing debt burden no more than the shaves I gave the grassy hillocks at IBM reduced their height.

So it was Rita to the rescue. Although she'd doubtless forgotten, I met Rita much earlier, on my second day at MIT in fact. I was lost. It isn't hard. Much of the campus is a seemingly endless progression of identical rectangular courtyards surrounded by undifferentiated institutional buildings. And so, clearly confused, wandering through a sunny courtyard where dozens of greased bodies busily manufactured melanin, I attracted Rita's attentions as I meandered and twirled and gawked. She walked up to me and said, "If you're hunting nerds, they're the ones sunbathing with all their clothes on. You have no idea where you are, right?"

"I'm looking for Hayden."

"Come on, get with the program, huh?" she said as she rolled her eyes. "They don't *name* buildings around here. They *count* them. What you want is Building 62. Go through that doorway and keep walking straight. The end of the hall is Building 10. Make a left and walk through the infinite corridor, through Building 4 and into Building 8, and then make a right into Building 6 ... oh, shit, delete that last instruction, you'll probably get yourself lost again. Just walk all the way through the infinite corridor and out. You'll be facing Building 18. Walk around that building to the right, and Building 62 will be straight ahead to the left. Got it?"

"What's the infinite corridor?" I asked, feeling increasingly worthless.

"It's the techie tool term for the ugly hallway that runs all the way from Building 7 to Building 8 and never seems to end. It's nearly a quarter of a mile long. The sun shines clear through its hideous depths on November 12 and January 31. There. Now you have something to tell your grandoffspring about MIT."

And she walked off.

One of the less stressful aspects of my first days at MIT was meeting Dex. Like the Reverend Thomas Bayes, who invented Bayesian statistics in an effort to prove the existence of God with scientific rigor, and like Albert Einstein, who already believed passionately in God and vainly pursued a unified theory of everything to show God left nothing to chance, Dex had a sense of mission when he arrived at MIT. That mission was sweat, or more precisely, its control. Dex had a nightmarish perspiration problem and he fixated on it.

When he left home his parents doted over him and told him how proud and delighted they were and said it was the happiest day of their lives, and no, really, it wasn't necessary to live at home and commute, your mother and I have been working two jobs each for the last three years to raise enough money for room and board so you can devote your full attentions to your studies and live with the other MIT students and lord knows we—that is, you—deserve it. Bye bye! We'll visit you, honey! Maybe take in a football game, watch the Head of the Charles together ... something outdoors in the fresh, breezy autumn air.

And wouldn't you know that no sooner had Dex shown up at MIT—literally right in the middle of orientation week!—Dr. George Preti of the Monell Chemical Senses Center in Philadelphia announced that he had isolated the most noisome component of the chemical signal we recognize as B.O. And there was more. Dr. Preti's discovery of *essence de l'armpit*—3-methyl-2-hexenoic acid—gave a few smart MIT researchers a good idea, and in no time Dex was guinea pigging an experimental enzyme that chewed the offending molecules into inoffensiveness.

Odoriferously cured and stunned at the sudden irrelevance of perspiration-related projects, Dex somehow followed his nose for the strong research topics and ultimately bioattached himself to Pappadallas. This prickly prof held a keen gift for obtaining private and government funding. His research assistants were always gainfully employed.

Pappadallas introduced him to grantmakers and proposal takers, to financiers and peer-review panels. Dex learned to gladhand. He acquired confidence. He learned to make pie charts and bar graphs and to wield a mean spreadsheet. Soon my roommate, olfactorily challenged high-school recluse, embarrassed scourge of locker room and schoolbus, who had earned his high-school valedictorianship in the crucible of a lonely upstairs bedroom with only his own crowd-clearing, sinus-spearing emanations for company, began to cut a formidable presence.

Yet there remained a certain detachment, a remnant of reserve about him. The kind of emotional distance that allows bio majors to whack unsuspecting frogs against benchtops and remove their live innards while discussing what's for lunch. We were best friends, Dex and I, yet so often he seemed a step away and a world apart.

There was no arguing his savvy, however, and when he concurred with Rita's suggestion that I contact Jeff Watt, I found myself hard-pressed to disagree. It was a simple matter. I just logged onto EDGAR, the third sentient entity that occupied our room. EDGAR was the name of our computer. Actually, EDGAR was the name of everyone's computer. It stood for EDucational Guidance And Resources. A massive project that took MIT over a decade to implement, EDGAR provided its users with access to numerous databases, library catalogs, calendars, event schedules, bulletin boards, central printers and even some application programs—design software (not as good as Artie's, but occasionally useful), word processing and spreadsheets. It also offered some programming capability, although for the really big jobs you still needed to go to the computer lab.

EDGAR's central mainframe was linked to what appeared a limitless number of remote terminals. Every MIT dormroom had one. EDGAR was definitely a hit, an unqualified success. The smudges and wear marks on terminals just recently installed proved it. Ours was a lived-in future.

To contact Jeff Watt, all I needed to do after logging on was select MITnet, the computer network that served all of MIT, find Watt's electronic-mail address, and send him a message like this:

MITnet To:jwatt@csl.mit.edu From:busta@mit.62.410 6:15p

Professor Watt:
I wonder if I could arrange a time to talk to you about a research project.

Perfect. I didn't tell him I was trying to jockey my idea. At least I'll get the appointment if he thinks I'm just looking for an RA spot.

People usually read their e-mail once, maybe twice a day, so I didn't expect a response any time soon.

And yet not five minutes later there was a message in my mailbox:

MITnet To:busta@mit.62.410 From:jwatt@csl.mit.edu 6:18p

How about tomorrow at 10 AM?

Interesting. Maybe this guy really didn't have anything else to do.

5.0

As I headed out of the dormroom for my meeting with Watt, I noticed a blinking smiley face on EDGAR's screen:

First-semester grades to be distributed today
Check your private electronic mailbox after 3 P.M.

I'd totally forgotten. The first year at MIT is all pass/fail (pass/pass, really, if your mental circuits carry more than a milliwatt), and now I faced my first set of real grades. I hoped I hadn't screwed up big-time on any of my finals. They all seemed pretty straightforward, although one pathetic soul of limited intestinal fortitude decided to collapse about halfway through the Physics III exam. The proctors had to carry him out. He began screaming wildly as the classroom door clicked closed behind him, the echoes of his howls diminishing with the square of his progress down the corridor—a sad example of the very law of field intensity that had stumped him into fitful retreat. The rest of us pressed dutifully onward, of course, calculators at full throttle, trying not to notice.

Choking victim, Physics III, Problem 4. Wheel in the gurney. An organism eliminates what it can't process....

I'd gotten the lowdown on Professor Jeffrey S. Watt when Rita called the previous night, a couple of hours after her visit. It wasn't as if I'd never heard of him. He taught 6.001 that year so I saw his lectures every so often, but the plain-vanilla syllabus gave no clue to his own interests. All I really knew was that Jeff Watt dealt in simulation. He modeled reality. He could put an oil refinery or an airplane wing or an integrated circuit on the screen and let you play with it, search for the process bottlenecks and try different pipe arrangements, determine whether the wing will fly or if the circuit will work.

The problem with simulation is that sometimes you get lost between the model and the reality.

Jeff Watt's particular problem, Rita told me, lurked in his past. Watt had been *persona non grata* not merely in his department but throughout all of MIT for a decade now. Since he spread the first computer virus MIT had ever seen. Not out of malice or mischievous intent, Rita insisted. The reason was obsession. It was a metaphysical issue, really. Very Zen. In a way.

Jeff Watt, you see, had become a prisoner of thinkable things.

It had begun with a ferocious mental assault on some ancient conundrum of truth. Something to do with thinkable things. Soon Jeff Watt became lost as he thought his way through labyrinthine layers of logic. So lost, in fact, that at last he reached a dead end, exhausted, unable to think further. Yet somehow his thoughts persisted. They began to think on their own. Or so he thought, because he was no longer thinking, yet here were all these thinkable thoughts still flying around in his head. But can a thought really think? Or was this mere thinking about thought? After all, is a thought thinkable without a thinker? If a thought forms in the forest and there's no one there to think it, can it still confound?

Without even thinking he had thought up all these new conundrums and forgot the original one. On the other hand, if he only *thought* he hadn't been thinking, he might well have been all along! The point was this: Can a thinkable thing think? Or must it be thought?

Jeff Watt was a simulationist, an intrepid cognitive explorer, an avid reader of Jack Kerouac and, according to rumor, had once smoked marijuana. And inhaled.

He was also, of course, an MIT computer science professor. He had the massive data-processing resources of the world's greatest technical university at his disposal. Jeff Watt decided to plumb the mysteries of thinkable thoughts. He would create a model, develop the ultimate simulation to answer their cosmic riddle. He would conduct his experiments on MIT's main computer system and the world would soon gasp in astonished gratitude.

Jeff Watt's experimental technique went something like this. He would write a little program, a clever burrowing gremlin that knew how to slip itself into the master control program of the MIT computer. If the gremlin survived, it would retain its own existence and yet fit seamlessly within the program logic, becoming part of its basic identity and behavior while remaining completely undetectable in the vast ocean of ones and zeroes. Independent, yet part of a larger cognitive process. Like a thinkable thought that can think on its own yet is also the thought of a thinking thing.

Far out!

And so Jeff Watt, recently tenured Professor of Computer Science (Course 6) and sometime Zen mystic, showed up late one night at the main computer center at MIT and slipped his gremlin into the master compiler. Not a malevolent gremlin, certainly. Just one that would fill a terminal's screen with a message and make a little noise. And then he recompiled the compiler and left. And lo and behold! his program survived.

Now every time someone logged into the main computer system and executed a program, that program would retrieve the gremlin the first time it fetched data from memory. And at some random point, you could never tell when, the gremlin would suddenly make the terminal go blank and then display the words JACK IS GONE BUT THE BEAT GOES ON, repeated over and over again until they filled the entire screen, after which it would list every one of Jack Kerouac's books beginning with *The Town and the City* and ending with *Vanity of Duluoz*, repeated over and over again until they now filled the screen, all the while engaging the terminal's internal speaker to play some obscure be-bop jazz number that surely would have brought tears to Kerouac's eyes if by some grace he could have been returned to life to enjoy the tribute. Then the sequence would repeat. Over and over again.

The problem was that the entire computer system had to be brought down and re-initialized just to restore a single disrupted terminal. To Jeff Watt, this seemed a pittance to pay for the great truth confirmed by his program's survival. But then again, it did happen quite a bit. And a lot of people were growing very, very unhappy. Jeff Watt decided to sacrifice the glory and recognition that were his due and maintain his philosophical triumph as a private matter.

So no one could pin the blame on Jeff Watt. The *cognoscenti* harbored their suspicions, however, and they let him know it. Jeff Watt wasn't exactly received like a hero when he volunteered, after two days of electronic mayhem, to do his level best, darn it, to get this baby running in the groove again. And no one attributed his quick success to Zen enlightenment.

Now these many years later, the bitterness had faded. Jeff Watt's Faculty Club pass had been restored. His office had a penthouse view and a central location. Jeff Watt hacked away in Building E42, situated just off Main Street, offering easy vehicular access as well as ample vehicular parking. At work or deep in thought, Jeff Watt was never far from his set of wheels. Or a lot of other sets of wheels.

The non-numerical name for Building E42 is the Hayward Garage. MIT had recently built a single floor of offices above six stories of grimy parking lot to help absorb the ever-metastasizing Computer Science Department. Now Course 6 real estate, those offices received the full Course 6 treatment. Construction crews added high-capacity electrical wiring to feed all the computers, network cabling so they could talk to one another and, to tickle their static-sensitive toes, covered the concrete floors and the new elevators with blue rubber sheeting—the really smelly stuff pimpled with raised half-dollar-sized disks.

I was beginning to feel truly out of my element as I made my way to Jeff Watt's office. Peeling my crepe-soled shoes off the sticky, tacky disks each time I took a step, totally engulfed by their anti-septic stench and watching the constant parade of computer equipment rolling by on little carts, I felt as if I'd just entered a nursing home for silicon seniors.

Watt's office was nowhere near the elevators, all the way on the other side of the building, right next to the old garage stair-case—worn concrete steps and bent metal railings—that now extended up to the new office floor. The unventilated shaft allowed exhaust fumes to seep into Jeff Watt's side of the building, and they combined with the gamey rubbery smell to produce an absolutely nauseating odor that made my eyes tear. I could also hear the faint sound of screeching tires and an occasional car horn. Watt's appeared to be the only faculty office in these quarters.

His door opened by itself just as I raised my knuckles to knock.

How clever. Try to look impressed, I thought, as I walked inside. I need this guy.

Outside the sun's reflection off the snow made the day blindingly bright, but Jeff Watt's office was subdued, almost dark. He had the blinds drawn and sat intently at his desk, his face bathed in the blue glow of the computer screen in front of him. With his beard and longish, wavy brown hair, he looked like a bhikku in the midst of a religious experience.

"I'm Jeff, you're Paul," he said, looking up. "Ever read any Jack Kerouac?"

"No," I answered truthfully.

"Me neither. So, Rita told me all about you and your hot idea last night. You really impressed her."

What happened to nerdalert?

Then Jeff looked straight into my eyes and said, "You know, I've already sim'd this entire meeting, and my simulation says we're going to work together. You can go now."

His gaze returned to his screen. There was something unreachable, something profoundly melancholy, in his eyes. My jaw dropped.

"Just kidding. It's a *joke*, okay? A *joke*," he said as he looked back at me with not-quite-a-smile.

I hauled my jaw back into place.

"That's the problem with this place," he growled. "No senses of humor. Refined senses of the political, however. Oh, yes, expertise in backstabbing, intrigue, retribution—all you want, right here." Clicking his computer's mouse, he said, "But—" and then the amplified digitized voice of Robert Plant, thundering a Led Zeppelin concert memory out of the computer's speaker, completed his question: *"Does anybody remember laughtuh?"*

"Not at MIT," answered Jeff Watt.

If I didn't get this screwball's signature on my IAP form within 48 hours, I'd be slogging through the mathematical fever swamps of group theory for almost a month. My nausea graduated into a full-fledged headache.

"All right, sit down, take a load off. Tell me how you go about taming those gnarly diffy q's." So I shook off the throbbing in my head and gave him the short version of my pitch, feeling intensely grateful toward Rita for paving the way for me. Now he knew I had an idea of my own I wanted to pursue.

"I think I'd like to work with you on this," he said to my utter relief after I had finished. "I'm intrigued. And it's not like I have anything else … I'd rather do than work with you on this. Okay, so what about funding?" It was obviously too much to hope that Jeff

Watt would not only take me seriously, but also pull out his wallet.

An uncomfortable moment of silence made it clear I'd come with no visible means of support. "This is MIT!" Jeff declared finally, slapping his hands on his desk and heaving himself out of his chair. "Sponsorship grants are what it's all about here. Begging for bucks. Hustling for handouts. Pimping for pesos. There's no MIT money for projects like this!"

"I understand that," I said, "and I was thinking about all those private grants..."

"Hah!" said Jeff, now leaning over his desk. "Forget about it. Corporations don't fund basic research. They'd rather have us fix things. They want to know why a big eight-cylinder can't get 45 miles to the gallon, or why their anti-ICBM missiles prefer to prowl for Canadian geese. See? Get it? We're kindred spirits, Paul, my friend. Hunters of the unseen, chasing after the big secrets. But lost in the night of MIT politics and corporate financial priorities. I guess I've pretty much discouraged you by now, right?"

"What about federal funds?" I asked. Jeff was beginning to scare me.

He sank back into his chair, leaned his head back and scratched the bottom of his beard. Then he began to squint, almost painfully it seemed, as he answered, "Ah, yes, Uncle Sam ... funding by and for fascists ... Are you a registered blackshirt?"

I blinked. "I could be..." I began.

"Let's see," he continued, "National Oceanic and Atmospheric Administration ... I don't think they give direct grants anyway. And of course most of NSF's money now goes to medical research, especially AIDS. ARPA? Well, Congress has cut their R&D budget to shreds and this doesn't seem to have any direct battlefield application. Unless I'm missing something ... can you kill people with it?"

"Who's ARPA?" I asked.

"Advanced Research Projects Agency. It's the research arm of DoD—the Defense Department. NSF is the National Science Foundation. The National Oceanic and Atmospheric people call themselves Noah."

He began to scratch the bottom of his beard again. "I think I read something about NRC—I mean, the National Research Council and weather recently, something about a committee trying to modernize the National Weather Service with new radar and computers. That'll probably soak up any remaining federal funds for weather-related projects. The point is, I'm not confident your idea is fundable at all. At least not until it's proven."

"I just know that..." I began.

"Good heavens!" cried Jeff. "How you persist! Very well, I obviously cannot discourage your strength. You bend without breaking, like the bamboo. Go home, then, and forage for funding. Oh, and write me, say, a one or two-page research proposal. Then we shall journey together."

"But..."

"Now, now, I know what you're thinking. I have read the *Chuang-tzu*; I recognize that language can never do justice to pure ideas. But all I want is a little summary. And funding, of course."

He rose from his chair and clasped my hand in both of his. "Lonesome travellers on the road, in the town and the city, desolation angels of the subterranean in search of *satori*."

Give me a break already, I wanted to tell him, but instead I smiled and said, "I'll get back to you right away."

I became more and more discouraged as the hours dragged by after my meeting with Jeff. My one chance to be taken seriously and I'm already blowing it. I wandered through the melting slush, across the rectilinear courtyards, down the Infinite Corridor. For the first time I noticed the endless-loop slide show projected from an invisible source onto the wall above one of the door jambs, its title echoing Jeff's cry: *This is MIT!* Color-enhanced slides featuring aerial views of the MIT campus, happy professors at their blackboards, inquisitive students and gleaming new lab space. Like a huckster trying to convince you that no, these decaying walls with peeling paint and cracking floors and exposed pipes and squeaky, warped doors, no, these aren't MIT—look up here, *this* is the real MIT! Such sales tactics may have ruined lakefront condo builder Hector Piaget, but MIT had a $1.5 billion endowment. Go figure.

And then I noticed, also for the first time, the bulletin board that said Peace, Justice, Freedom & Liberation Issues Only, filled with yellowed newspaper clips and handwritten notes. Liberation from what, the laws of physics? I doubted that those little inscriptions could possibly have been placed there by MIT students, since no one I knew at MIT talked about politics. Why bother? The problems are intractable. Political forces don't resolve like vector forces, crime and poverty statistics don't converge to a solution. You improve one situation, you make another worse, and the best we can do is elect the people who put on the best slide shows and know how to disguise the peeling paint and cracking floors. It's all the same.

Finally I made my way to Morss Hall in Building 50 for lunch. Most people ate alone, occasional heads in a sea of empty chairs, and that was fine with me today. I studied my macaroniandcheez, inspected the limp green beans and began to calculate the odds against my ever finding somebody or something to rescue my idea from fundlessness. Dex could get funded because he was in Course 7 and everyone loves a Course 7 idea since they *help* people and the health-care system possesses an infinite capacity to welcome new products with open arms and wallets and then *wham!*—a crash of silverware and glasses and plates startled the hell out of me. I looked up and there was Rita, standing over me and drilling her eyes into mine, clearly unconcerned with the puddle of cola slowly oozing its way toward the pile of mashed potatoes that had jumped from her dish to her tray when she slammed it on my table.

"Your potatoes will undergo irreversible interfacial dissolution if you don't act quickly," I said, trying to break the tension. I was mystified at the hostility.

"I thought you'd have the courtesy to call and tell me how it went." She didn't care that the once-edible potatoblob was now melting into a brown muck.

"How what went?"

"Exactly."

"What?"

"Right, Watt. Don't play Abbott and Costello with me."

"I'm confused," I confessed, "but if you're talking about my discussion with Jeff, I didn't realize I was supposed to give you an immediate report. I just got out of the meeting."

"You got out of the meeting hours ago," said Rita as she sat down. Just pull up a chair, make yourself at home.

"Jeff really has both feet firmly planted in Shangri-La, doesn't he?" I observed, once again trying to break the tension.

"So?" asked Rita, reinvigorating the tension.

"So he's a flake, a character. I mean, what's this guy going to be like to work with?"

"Like you have any other options?" replied Rita. "Count your blessings. Here you are, hooked up with a senior faculty member—"

"Playing with half a deck and speaking from a Lotus position," I interrupted.

"—and you're in phase with each other. In tune. In sync, like two electrical waveforms exactly superposed." She swallowed a forkful of meat loaf.

"All very Zen," I said, touching the fingertips of both hands together and bowing slightly.

"And it's like you don't even care. First he takes the time to listen to you. God, I would have killed to impress an MIT prof with some whimsical idea when I was a soph. And you know, if he becomes your adviser, he's taking a big chance. He'll look like a schmuck if you putter around for two and a half years and come up with zilch. They'll blame him. They'll say he dispatched you on a snipe hunt to satisfy his own curiosities. As if he doesn't have enough trouble already."

I thought of the sadness in Jeff's eyes and grew embarrassed. Insensitivity comes with surprising ease in MIT's obstinately rational environment. "Sorry, Rita, you're right. I guess I didn't realize you were such a fan."

She shook her head and started to laugh. "Incredible," she sighed. "I try to give you the reality of the situation, and that makes me Jeff Watt's fan?"

"Well no, but you must like him to be so concerned. Right?"

"Wrong. I can't stand him. Any other questions?"

"Yeah, I'll bite. Why? Can't you stand Jeff, I mean."

"Because he's a flake," said Rita. "Now will you please tell me what that has to do with anything?" Then she looked sourly at my plate. "No wonder you're so confused. How can you survive on those nanoportions?" she demanded as she scooped up the brown muck from her tray and gulped it down.

That was too much. "You're not my mother," I reminded her sharply.

"Obviously not, because no son of mine would forget to call the woman who not only saved his academic career but also hands him his paycheck every month."

A pause.

"So when are you supposed to get back to him?" Rita asked.

"He wants me to write a proposal. Didn't give me a deadline, but IAP registration closes in two days. Jeff is worried about funding. I think he wants some ideas before we go forward."

"Funding? Why do you need money for mental masturbation?"

Now there was a good question. I had no idea. I thought everybody needed funding.

"Just tell him you want computer time, tell him you want to hook into one of the supercomputers and onanize your gray matter till it's pink. Tell him that," she insisted. Then she got up with her depleted tray and stalked off.

This was a typical Rita repast, helpful advice served up surly. Too bad she couldn't decouple the helpfulness from the surliness, since she would then have enjoyed a passable social life. Rita would have been able to pick and choose among the swarms of bewildered MIT stragglers, their brain cells too fragile to withstand the ceaseless onslaught of equations, reactions and command sequences, all perfectly eager to heap friendship on any source of cerebral support. Except an honest one, that is.

And no one was more honest than Rita. For a disciple of information theory, tact is even worse than inefficient communication. Tact conveys misinformation. Hurt feelings can't justify faulty data transmission. So if you were confused, Rita would be more than happy to explain what had eluded you, and happier still to tell you to find a different major, transfer to another school, get a new life if your confusion appeared terminal. Any other questions?

Rita reserved her most scathing expressions of tact-free honesty for Dex—D-cube, as I said, to his friends; to Rita he was Drano. Sometimes she referred to him as the descented Sultan of Sweat. Dex, who makes a point of being unflappable, didn't particularly care; and of course that drove Rita, who makes a point of never failing to elicit a response, crazy.

So when Dex expressed trepidation at the prospect of final exams that would spawn real letter-type grades, Rita told him not to worry, even normal men can experience castration anxiety once in a while, although most don't, and besides, professional therapists sometimes have great success effecting a cure, although not often. And Dex's suggestion that perhaps an unusually crowded cafeteria did not provide the ideal venue for such observations only led Rita to thunder that none of the four people now staring at Dex had any desire to hear him pay such pathetic tribute to his mother.

Nor did she make any secret of her disdain for Don Boyer, calcium transport, whom she call DonBoy. And one Saturday morning when Wiseman finally and mercifully excused himself from our room to visit Donna what's-her-name at Wellesley, Rita, walking by our door without stopping said, "She's a lucky girl," and two beats later bellowed the word "NOT!" which resounded through the hall and confused the hell out of Wiseman, imposing on us several additional, painful minutes of his presence as he tried to interpret Rita's use of the logical inverse. "What was she negating?" Wiseman wanted to know. "Was she insulting Donna?"

Me she always left wondering. Just a couple of months before, I'd been playing the model TA, helping an EECS 6.001 neophyte struggle through a nested loop problem on his Olivetti laptop. And then along came Rita, leaning over both of us, looking admiringly at the little twit right across my line of sight and telling him, "Nice equipment. And *very* Italian."

What the devil did that mean? What was wrong with my equipment? Was I insufficiently Italian?

But all this, I told myself, was Rita's problem. Not mine. Right now I was desperate to know more about funding.

"Watt? Jeffrey S. Watt?" my father asked me. I had decided to call him at work for a few thoughts.

As I said, I was desperate.

"You know him?" I replied, somewhat incredulous. But then it occurred to me that they were both computer engineers, and my father had no more than five years on Jeff. They might easily have run across each other, somewhere.

"Oh, your mom will love this. Wait, I'll conference her in."

A moment later my mother was on the line. "I've only got a minute," she said, "I'm expecting the head of the Horticultural Society."

My mother worked for a fundraising agency in Westchester, and she had been trying to land the Horticultural Society as a client for months now.

"Hey, hon," my father said, "remember that guy Jeff Watt from the IBM picnic, oh, I don't know, a dozen summers ago or so?"

A pause. "A *dozen* years ago? Not really, dear."

"Sure you do, sure you do," my father insisted. "He was the one who made those off-color jokes about multinode pin testing for microchannel-architecture components. Remember now?"

Another pause. At this point I knew my mother had given up trying to remember. She was trying to think of a graceful way to get off the phone without embarrassing her husband in front of his son. "I guess I just don't..."

"Oh yes, you know, the only male not dressed in a shirt and tie. He was wearing that orange-and-blue nehru jacket, just the thing to drive starched-shirt supervisors to distraction, eh? I knew you'd remember. Anyway, Paul's thought of a really interesting research project, and so he's shopping for a supervisor, and so who do you think is now a tenured professor at MIT?"

"Jeff Watt?" asked my mother. I could hear her tapping a pencil on her desk.

"Did I tell you she'd get a kick out of this?" asked my father. "Did I tell you? Frankly, I'm a little worried. Jeff Watt didn't exactly distinguish himself as a consultant for IBM."

"So you worked with him?" I asked.

"No, he was over in heat sinks. I don't know exactly why, but he made everyone berserk. And the heat-sink boys, of all people. Such a mild bunch. Not an obsessive in the lot."

"No personality, either," said my mother.

"Well, there's my point," my father replied. "If he can disrupt heat sinks, what will he do to our son? I don't think Paul should work with him. What do you think?"

"It's craziness," my mother gushed.

"It's nuts," I echoed.

"It's insanity," added my mother.

"All right, all right. I can see where this is going. I wasn't born yesterday, you know. I'll lay off. Jeez, wait till they hear about this over in heat sinks."

"Gotta go now," said my mother.

"Bye, Mom. Hey Dad, got any ideas for funding?"

"Funding? You mean for your project? Ha ha! I can't even get a wretched NAND gate around here without filling out two requisition forms and saying a prayer to Tom Watson."

"Come on, Dad. THINK."

Now Eric, our dorm tutor, inserted his head through the door. I wasn't getting anywhere with my father anyway. "Hey, Dad, gotta run. Talk to you later, okay?"

"Certainly. Always happy to help."

A tutor is MIT's version of a resident counselor or adviser. At other schools the duties of such individuals include academic support, spiritual uplift, and relentless pursuit of datable young freshmen. At MIT it boils down to suicide patrol.

"Get your grades?" Eric asked me as I hung up the phone.

"Yup."

"Gonna kill yourself?"

"Nope." Who'd kill himself over four As?

"Mmm-hmm," said Eric with mechanical satisfaction as he made a check mark on his clipboard. "Is Dex gonna off himself?"

"Don't think so."

"Could you have him check in with me later?"

"Absolutely."

Eric was gone before I'd even finished the one-word response. He was the soul of efficiency, as if either efficiency or Eric could possibly possess anything as human as a soul. I don't think he ever told us his last name.

I heard Eric repeat his little inquiry with each of our neighbors, the exchanges growing quieter as Eric progressed down the hall. Until he hit Rita's room.

"Yes!" I heard her yell. "But I'm not going alone, you little worm! I'm taking every scab-face bureaucrat in this whole place with me, you hear what I'm saying?" And then her voice and Eric's plaintive, half-uttered protests disappeared in a shuffle of footsteps down the main stairway. Rita wanted Eric to earn his stipend.

Soon Dex was back from whatever he had been doing that day to secure the fortunes of BioVitrics and earn himself great wealth and fame. I asked him about funding, whether you really needed it, if there was some way I could do without it.

"Everyone needs money," said Dex, amazed at the stupidity of the question.

"Why?" I asked.

He turned his head askew and stared at me with one eye. "Because," he said slowly, "that's how ideas turn into profit. That's what turns privates into captains of industry."

"Then I'm in a bind. Jeff seems to think funding is a disallowed state until we can show the idea's got merit, but I'm not sure he wants anything to do with me if I can't lay my hands on some cash."

"Sounds like Watt knows nothing about the private sector. Venture capitalists care more about marketing than merit. You need a story line, an angle that will pique the interest of corporate America. What need will this hot new advance fulfill? What weakness in current technology will it exploit? Why will people buy it?"

"Oh, come on, Dex," I said. "It's a technique, a method. People don't buy methods like cameras or diet books."

"You've got to think *story*," Dex admonished. "*Someone* will buy it, or else it's nothing but an academic curiosity. What if you could enhance the accuracy of National Weather Service forecasts?

Wouldn't the government mint you a fortune? Wouldn't television stations pay you to help keep their meteorologists from slipping up? Hey, there you go!" Dex was heating up. "Yes, an auction! A bidding war! Every national TV station would kill for the ability to outdo everyone else's forecast accuracy. You'll sell this idea to the highest bidder!"

His enthusiasm was becoming infectious. "You know," I said, "the last Geostationary Operational Environment Satellite will run out of fuel and drift out of geosynchronous orbit in less than two years. At that point the National Weather Service loses its eye in the sky, and they won't get another GOES into orbit any time soon. The government will be desperate for this invention. They'll be sorry they didn't fund me when I came cheap."

"There you go," said Dex. "Let the auction winner license it to the National Weather Service for a big fee."

"What about MIT?" I asked. "They own whatever we produce while we're here."

"Oh, they'll be happy to give you an exclusive license. They do it all the time. So what if they take a small cut?"

"And just how do you find these generous venture impresarios?" I asked.

"Because I'm a nice guy, and because you're turning pitiable on me, let me check with our VC. Star Ventures may not be interested in weather, but maybe they can point you somewhere. Just give me a couple of days so I can work it into a conversation about other things. I don't want to look like a promoter."

Hawking ideas, selling your soul.

Now this is science, I thought.

This is MIT!

I finished my proposal and e-mailed it to Jeff just after 7 AM. It was a beauty. I discussed my approach. I elaborated on the potential federal interest. I mentioned Star Ventures.

Soon I found a response in my mailbox:

MITnet To:busta@mit.62.410 From:jwatt@csl.mit.edu 7:19a

Get your gluteus over here. Now now now!

What what what? I thought as I hurried to comply with the wishes of my surreal savant, my resonant circuit, my superposed waveform. Why do you haul my butt through these many snow-sloshed steps from my dormroom in W70, all the way on the west side of campus, to your stinky little hovel in the easternmost reaches? Trouble not, I come at your beckon. Your wallet is empty but our souls are simpatico.

This time I didn't even have to raise my hand before Jeff's door opened by itself. How clever. The door must be hooked up to a recognition system that improves its performance each time it sees someone.

I looked inside and there was Jeff in the dark again, but this time he kept his eyes on the screen and his fingers tapping the keyboard as I walked in.

"You're an undergraduate," he said in an accusing voice.

"Well..." I struggled as my heart sank, thinking I had somehow misled him and once again picturing my stillborn idea hurtling into oblivion.

"Don't deny it!" he roared. "I have your transcript! You're an *undergraduate*! Shoot him, Philly!"

Jeff's fingers mashed the keys as the sound of two gunshots *pow! pow!* rang out from one corner of the office and then someone yelled *oooof!* from another corner and the thud of a limp body and rumpled clothing hitting the floor came from I know not where as the whole sequence sent me diving for cover beneath the overhang of Jeff's desk.

Jeff's entire office was wired for sound.

I peered over the desk just as a loud, husky voice from somewhere else suddenly said, "He was a rat bastard!" and the fluorescent ceiling lamps buzzed on, flooding the office with harsh light and startling me into the duck-and-cover all over again. Once more, finally, I peered over the desk.

Jeff smiled weakly. "Get up, boy, tell me the story," he sighed.

I could see no loudspeakers anywhere in the room. "What story?" I asked.

"Go ahead, go on, just tell me the story." Jeff was nodding his head, gesturing with his hand for me to come closer or come clean, I wasn't sure which. "Really," he continued. "You'll feel better. Tell me how you thought of this idea of yours. Was it a vision in the shower? Was it a kismet-charged revelation as you peered off a mountain in western Peru? Something Moses gave you on some rocks? Were you bungee jumping?"

I climbed back onto the standard-issue MIT metal-and-vinyl side chair and came clean, told him about the incident on the highway, my nonlinear insights.

"So the discriminator function, the filter, is your flagman. Is that it?"

"I guess ... well, yes."

"And your flagman will allow the good data in and keep the turbulent data out."

"Right. Exactly, see—"

"You know, I thought you were a grad student," Jeff interrupted. "You seemed to really know what you were talking about yesterday. But now you send me this dungweed, this seedbag. Of all things, to think you can model the atmosphere weather station by weather station."

"But you've got to start somewhere," I replied, "and it'll be a lot easier than trying to—"

"Trying to do it right," he interrupted. "Trying to shoulder the burdens of the true seeker. Do it your way and your statistics will instantly fall apart."

And he proceeded to tell me just why they would fall apart. He spoke of time derivatives and space derivatives. He lost me totally. His words floated through my ears like melodious yammerings in Bhojpuri. I said: "Of course."

"You're not *hearing* me," he growled, now mashing the keys again, raising his palm as I took a breath to tell him I was totally clueless and that maybe group theory wasn't looking so bad after all, I'm going to leave now, it's been real. Peace. "You come along, you've actually got a fresh idea or two. You make a little sense. You whet my eagerness for adventure. *But you have no idea what you're talking about!* The atmosphere, chemistry, your brain— anything nonlinear is one, not many. There's no such thing as a local solution. That is the ignorance of *avidya*!"

Jeff wheeled himself back in his chair, as if recoiling.

"Don't you see what you're onto?" he exclaimed. "You're eliminating the guesses with your statistics. But you need all the data you can get your hands on, from all over, hear their voices combined like a single choir instead of a crowd of babblers. You can't just look at a piece of the whole. Get it? Brahman. Dharma. Tao. Gestalt. Understand? Oneness. Wholeness. Space first, then time. Am I *penetrating*? Am I doing any *penetrating* here?"

"I'm lost in space," I finally confessed, and there was Jeff Watt, Course 6 pariah and philosopher of fluid dynamics, getting that pained expression on his face. He began typing again.

"What courses have you taken that you feel prepare you for the journey you now propose to drag me along on?"

"I know about fluids, I know about the Navier Stokes equations—"

"Big deal," Jeff said, and continued typing. When he'd finished he said, "There, I've just selected your class schedule. Say bye-bye to three of your four course choices. You can keep the Analysis, but make sure you sign up for Option B—for mathematically mature adults. You know, you've got pretty good instincts, but you basically don't know squat."

All that would all change, obviously, since now I had an all-weather course load. So much for the multimedia class I was looking forward to.

"And I'm putting together a list of books I want you to get from the Lindgren Library ... there, that's done too. You can pick it up at the main printer on your way out, through the door next to the elevator. But first I want to talk at you. I'm going to talk at you now, okay?"

"All right," I said, reflecting on how much I enjoy being beaten about the head and shoulders.

"You propose a weather project, yet you know nothing about the atmosphere. Are you really interested in forecasting? Or are you chasing something bigger?"

"Bigger like what?" I asked uncomfortably.

"Bigger like universal truth, karma. Understanding life and eliminating its guesswork. Stuff like that."

"Absolutely not," I assured him.

"Too bad," sighed Jeff. "All right, does it bother you that you'll have millions of data points to contend with?"

"I suppose it's—"

"Doesn't bother me," Jeff interrupted. "Does it bother you that no one has so much as thought of using statistics to reach into the chaotic void?"

"No," I said firmly.

"Now you're getting the idea."

"So how on earth do I do it?" I asked.

Jeff leaned back and scratched the bottom of his stubble. "Let us understand each other. This is your journey. You lead, I follow.

I am your spiritual mentor; nothing more. If I were to place you on a path, I would betray your trust and wind up as an unwelcome co-inventor on your patent application. Just take my word. It's doable. I think."

"Just thought I'd try," I said, attempting a smile.

"And don't worry about the IAP form. I've taken care of it electronically. So," Jeff said, "our voyage begins."

"I just have one question. Did you study meteorology? I mean, I thought you were a simulationist from day one."

"I learned about weather when I learned about fluids, and I learned about fluids when I did consulting work for IBM. I modeled the way the airflows from their miserable computer cooling fans interacted with the heat sinks on their miserable electronic components."

"When did you stop working for IBM?" I asked, fishing for a little more info.

"A long time ago," said Jeff, wrapping his hands around his face. Then he added, "Heat sinks are really political."

I didn't ask. Suddenly I just didn't want to know.

6.0

LADIES AND GENTLEMEN OF THE ROYAL SWEDISH ACADEMY, IT IS OF course my utmost privilege to address you this evening. As a scientist, I can imagine no greater honor than the one you have bestowed upon me tonight. To be chosen as a recipient of the Nobel Prize represents the researcher's loftiest aspiration, the culmination of a lifetime of work. And to receive the award on the soil of this nation, which has produced so many luminaries in the study of weather systems, elevates the privilege still further. Without the contributions of professor Carl-Gustaf Rossby, who identified the fundamental variable in day-to-day weather changes, or professor Tor Bergeron, who explained the mechanics of rainfall, I sincerely doubt I would be standing before you this evening.

I began my study of weather as an MIT undergraduate, oh, more decades ago than I can presently count, and no, none of you need assist me with the arithmetic. *(Hushed laughter.)* Back then we were prisoners of nonlinearity, and meteorology was as dry a subject as you can imagine. I'll never forget my first weather course at MIT. Our instructor, a young Hungarian fellow whose name escapes me now, told us he was almost embarrassed to teach a subject whose entire soul reduces to a mere seven variables: pressure, temperature, density, moisture, and the three directional components of wind speed. And that if we could just grasp these variables, learn their values at every point on the face of the earth at one single instant, we would know everything. Know why hurricanes form. Know when tornadoes will strike. Forecast the next cool breeze, the next frost, the next ice age.

In fact, weather prediction wouldn't involve prediction at all; it would be routine calculation. Then our instructor told us that despite the seemingly trivial simplicity of it all, half the ten or eleven of us in the room would come close to failing his embarrassing little course and the rest of us would come close to hating the subject matter. And that the ones who merely came close, who managed to avoid developing unqualified hatred for the reams of numbers and complex models and endless sequences of computation, would go on to win Nobel Prizes in meteorology. And so I find myself here today, just a happy result of his supremely accurate forecast. *(More hushed laughter.)*

A very rare bit of accuracy, I might add, for the late twentieth century. Most of you are probably too old to remember how unreliable weather forecasts used to be in those days. It wasn't for lack of trying. Our weather models were unimaginably elaborate. They shook the innards of the very biggest computers. After all, five million billion tons of air swirl, blow, meander, and stagnate over the earth, lifting trillions of tons of water skyward and dragging it thousands of feet up and thousands of miles away, absorbing and releasing heat, generating electricity, all the while nudged by pressure differences, variations in surface temperature, gravity, Coriolis forces, and tidal effects. It takes a lot of math to tease even mediocre forecasts from all that.

You might say I was tired of worshiping at the great wall of numbers. You might say I was tired of limitations, of predictability ceilings, of restrictions on what we can know. And I suppose it had to do with more than the weather. My first faculty adviser certainly suspected as much. "I thought you were after bigger game," he told me once....

o   o   o

"There's a word for people who sleep with their eyes open," said Dex, jarring me back into reality. "I need to run some numbers on EDGAR. Are you done with it?"

"You don't seem the least bit curious," I said. The first traces of spring had arrived at MIT. We were well into our classes, and I'd learned enough meteorology to hack some basic weather routines on the computer. And there it was, the beginnings of my research, right there in front of him and he could care less.

"All right," Dex indulged. "What is it?"

"It's a general circulation model. It gives a very rough picture of the way the atmosphere moves."

Dex didn't seem impressed. And why should he have been? All the screen showed were numbers. They were important numbers, varying and jumping engagingly, but numbers nonetheless.

"You want to describe this to me, am I right?" asked Dex. He knew me so well. "Go ahead."

I took a breath but immediately realized that an explanation of any rigor would be wholly wasted on a Course 7 softie. "It's actually a very general model," I told him. "You can represent any kind of circulation by changing the parameterization. So let's say D-cube wants to get a date. He wants to know how long it will take. It depends on his own attractiveness, the attractiveness of the population, how well and how quickly the population mixes, and whether D-cube is a sociable guy. Make sense?"

"Sure, I guess. I'm not sure I like the direction this is taking."

"So we recognize that population, like atmospheric temperature, reflects a statistical distribution. Santa Monica in summer absolutely brims with gorgeous people. It has a high attractiveness temperature, a bell curve shifted to the beautiful side. MIT? Just the opposite, as you well know. A fearfully low-temperature place, its bell curve way over in the bleachers. So we'll enter an appropriate equation..." I said as I stroked away on the keyboard.

"That's only if I stick around MIT. Suppose I take the Red Line over to Harvard?" Dex asked.

"They'd laugh you out of Harvard," I told him.

"What, then, do you plan to enter for your roommie's attractiveness level, recognizing that he's twenty pounds heavier than you and reacts poorly to insult?"

Twenty pounds heavier? On the left side of your ass, maybe, you enormous warthog. And don't think you scare me. Overweight, acne-scarred skin, a premature bald spot beginning to spread like a pink desert across your oversized scalp ... Five out of ten, at best. "What do you suggest?"

"Well, where did you rate yourself?" Dex asked.

"Eight point two. On a logarithmic ten scale," I told him. It seemed fair. After all, every point represented a factor of ten. I hadn't exactly put myself in the stratosphere.

"Same for me, then."

"Fine."

Fine, really. Throw the results off. Go ahead.

"Okay, then," I said. "We've replaced temperature with population. I figure attractiveness is like air pressure, since it determines how big a crowd you can draw and how hard they'll push to get near you. So we replace air pressure with attractiveness level." I typed 8.2, jabbing the keys loudly to emphasize my displeasure.

"What's mixing rate?" asked Dex. At least he was getting interested.

"It reflects how often people put themselves in social situations, accessible to you, so you can meet them. That's a simple variable, analogous to wind speed. MIT's got frat parties and intramurals. There are plenty of social opportunities here, even though people always seem to stay in their rooms since EDGAR came on line."

"And that leaves, what, non-shyness or something?"

"That's one way to put it. Friendliness reflects the way you carry yourself, the way others see you as carrying yourself. It's like angular momentum, which transports heat and fluid."

"Six out of ten," said Dex. "I know I'm no Arsenio."

The numbers on the screen began to blink more slowly, and finally stopped.

"So how long till I meet a woman I'm not afraid to exchange genetic material with?" Dex asked.

"A year for someone at your own attractiveness level." I almost choked on the words. "Much longer if you want to wait for someone slightly better looking. February 17, 3037 if you're looking for someone a lot better looking. Of course, it's never too early to embark on a program of cardiovascular fitness."

"How can you reduce attractiveness to a unitary number?" asked Dex, shaking his head. "People have different tastes."

"Oh, come on. There are certain assumptions we can all agree on."

"Like the importance of big tits?" he asked.

I had to think about this. "Well, not big tits *per se*. That would send Rosanne Barr off the scale. I'd say the ratio of breast volume to waist circumference is what's important."

"Not to me," dismissed Dex. "I don't care if she lactates. I want a woman who mentates."

"Suit yourself. Besides, the model can account for that too, whatever characteristics you consider important. Just takes a different state vector and more number crunching."

Dex started to laugh. "God, how long have you spent reformulating your circulation model into a dating oracle? Those analogies of yours—they're far from perfect. You must have tortured your weather equations inside out. It must have taken ages."

"It took one night. It's just statistics."

"Bullshit it took one night," he persisted. Then he looked at me slyly. "So how long until you meet the redoubtable June Brooke's double?"

Oh, cut my heart out, you dermabrasive, depilating endomorph! Stand tall, Bustamante! Do not fold!

"Eighteen years," I responded as blandly as I could. "But if I tunnel two of the variables, twenty-six months."

"How convenient," said Dex. "Just in time for graduation. Invite me to the wedding, please." He looked at me sternly. "Now can I log onto EDGAR?"

I yielded the terminal.

"I'm doing this for you, you know," he continued as he turned on the stereo and began typing. "I got a slight rise out of our VC when I described your project."

And sure enough, there on the screen were scattered remnants of my little research proposal, which Dex had turned into something titled "Marketing Statement." He had even thrown some important-sounding numbers: revenue projections, year-to-year expenses, return-on-investment estimates.

"I don't know what to say," I told the balding warthog with a heart of gold. "You must have spent ages on this."

"Not at all," he assured me. "I'm starting to get used to these kinds of documents. They're just cookie-cutter. You define the market, pick plausible starting numbers, and let the financial-analysis software do the rest."

I was going to ask more but it was too late. Dex had caught the riff of the tune on the radio, hitting the keys on the downbeat, his forehead creased in concentration. Both lobes of his brain were fully occupied.

I walked out of the room, out of the dorm and into an unusually warm day in late March. Time for my first hard run of the season, I decided, and jogged across Memorial Drive onto the Charles River embankment. I could smell just a whiff of airborne chlorophyll, the balmy, fertile odor reminding me of the faraway day my dad first taught me to swing a baseball bat just right, so it strikes at the center of percussion, driving its energy into the ball instead of stinging your own hands. And the time he showed me how to snap spin onto a football as I tossed it so gyroscopic rotation would prevent the oblate spheroid from tumbling in flight. And how he spent half a weekend modeling my hurdling stride on a biomechanical analysis program developed at IBM, concluding that I was going too vertical, dragging me down to the track at 5:30 in the Monday morning so we could work on it. He poured some water in front of each hurdle, where my left foot pushed off the ground, and damn if his stop watch didn't give me a full two seconds off my best time.

It was definitely getting to be spring because some of the civil engineers were already hanging off the ever-decaying Longfellow Bridge, measuring and cataloging and scraping test samples. A gang of Course 6 long-hairs, wearing jeans and tee-shirts but keying away on hyperexpensive laptops, laughed at the dangling civvies from the safety of the river bank, blissfully unaware they were being stalked by two experimental planetary-explorer vehicles advancing on them from behind some tall grass. Those crazy guys in Course 16, Aeronautics and Astronautics; they just loved to scare the shit out of people with their mechanized minions, and for this reason were much beloved and frequently followed by the Media Lab crew, camera equipment in perpetual tow, ever alert for entertaining footage. I passed four of them operating a digital videocam tethered to a wireless modem, stealthily sampling the unhappy but highly mediagenic misfortunes of the latest Course 16 victims.

More than chlorophyll sweetened the air. The romance of engineering had emerged.

And soon spring would be percolating through all the computer labs, hundreds and hundreds of mouse-rolling, keyboard-striking fingers sublimating renewed hormonal energy into virtual pointers and virtual objects, their display screens full of virtual life. Everyone would be chasing the paradigm.

When I first ventured into the EECS 6.001 computer lab my freshman year, I expected to find row after row of determined research initiates racking their brains to drive the frontiers of computer science forward. Just like in the MIT slide show. This, I soon found out, was mere propaganda. The paradigm is what it was all about. No one, it seemed, talked of anything else.

The paradigm is whatever sells. It usually starts out small, just a twinkle in the eye of some cola-swigging, bleary-eyed infomaniac who's worked 100 hours straight and desperately needs to appease his unforgiving computer terminal. He tries something new, something drastic. The computer purrs and now he can go home to catch some sleep. His professor is impressed. His fellow hackers are impressed. They adopt the approach in their own programs, and it catches on. Soon the public falls in love with it. No one will buy anything that fails to carry it. No investor will fund any project that fails to incorporate it. A new paradigm is born.

Maybe it's a dazzling new programming fillip. Maybe it's a spiffy new screen display. It doesn't matter as long as it catches on. And the originator's reward? Being there first. Even if he can't collect a dime, he was still there first. Now he's back in the lab, spreading his sore eyelids with his fingers, chasing new paradigms as the old ones go out of fashion like trendy hairstyles and swell the landfills of paradigms lost.

Selling, the central paradigm of science, I thought as I turned left at the Longfellow Bridge. I jogged down Broadway past One Kendall Square, a sprawling thud of red brick and glass strips that provided research and office space to a number of MIT start-up companies, including BioVitrics. Dex and Pap would be moving their electric stirrers and gas burners and crucibles of every shape and size over there during the summer.

I, for one, hadn't had any luck advancing the central paradigm in support of my own project, although it wasn't for lack of trying. I'd visited the MIT Project Development Office, the official grapevine for funding leads. It was horrible. The efficient, spectacled woman in charge flipped pamphlet after pamphlet describing various federal grants into my hands, then shook her head with grim finality and told me just to forget about it. There was a look of disgust in her eyes—the kind of disgust such a woman feels only for one not a small business within the criteria and size standards of 13 C.F.R. 121, and not a woman-owned, minority-run, disadvantaged, disabled, Viet Nam-veteran affirmative-action employer within the meaning of 41 C.F.R. 60-1 and 60-2, and not even a qualified labor surplus area, one who might not try to influence federal officials but who knows, since I had no performance record to prove otherwise ... And yes, yes, it's true the National Science Foundation does have that Atmospheric Sciences Section, and they've got a Climate Dynamics Program going, but ... who's your faculty adviser? Jeff Watt? You don't say! He still around? He hasn't gotten a grant in what, eight years, nine years?

Jeff's office was just to the left now, I could see the light that perpetually illuminated his window; I think he lived in E42. Following Rita's advice, I'd convinced him to let me start on my project without financial support. But my lack of progress on that front was starting to make him nervous. He was convinced of the need for cash.

Jeff had arranged a pass-through from EDGAR to one of the Artificial Intelligence Laboratory's parallel-processing timeshare machines, so now I could access high-speed computer power whenever I wanted. This wouldn't have been an easy feat even if Jeff had been a popular faculty member, since pass-through slots were jealously guarded commodities: the groups that owned the machines didn't want the rest of the world horning in on their computer time. Jeff must have called in a favor or two. But that was the most he could do.

Except send me e-mail messages, of course, and my spiritual mentor was careful always to temper each of his exhortations with a kernel of inspiration.

MITnet To:busta@mit.62.410 From:jwatt@csl.mit.edu 3:16p

The time is now and now is the time.
Yogi Bhajan

I hope you're working on getting funding.

MITnet To:busta@mit.62.410 From:jwatt@csl.mit.edu 11:18p

Sitting quietly, doing nothing,
Spring comes, and the grass grows by itself.
Zenrin kushu

Money ain't grass. Did you get my last message?

I stayed to the left and jogged down Main Street, down to Technology Square, a small cluster of bland, blocklike buildings that housed all the AI equipment, including the state-of-the-art parallel processor Jeff had sunk his talons into for me. I never saw the thing, but could imagine its thousands of individual microprocessors processing away, splitting calculations up into little bits and pieces and distributing the pieces among themselves in the most efficient possible way.

Although probably not as well Jeff's own personal machine.

He'd designed the bizarrest bitbox imaginable. Thousands of little processor chips lined the inside surface of a spherical housing like quartz crystals in the hollow of a geode. They talked to one another by flashes of light. The whole business looked and sounded like a little too much Hollywood, but upturned Course 6 noses became raised eyebrows when people saw what it could do. The little demon chips attacked every complex calculation, every package of screwy logic operations and broke them open like so many piñatas, scraping up and devouring the exploded contents even while vying to conquer the next one.

Not that Jeff held his tireless creation in particularly high esteem. The silvery globe-like structure, about the size of a decent beach ball, was stuffed like an afterthought onto a standard-issue metal-and-formica table in the corner behind Jeff's desk. Often it supported a floppy green fishing hat or a casually tossed jacket—an incidental accessory about as relevant to the outside world as any of the simulations Jeff carried out on it. Which wasn't much.

As I turned onto Albany Street, ready to head back, my legs started to ache—the pleasant soreness of snoozing limbs beginning to reawaken. *Amore, amore! gaudio tormento ....* love, love! what joyous agony, I remembered hearing my mother sing one evening. She was accompanying Larry's rendition of a duet from *Aida* on the massive piano my grandfather had left us—an oversized monument to himself that occupied not only most of the space in the living room but most of the sound as well. On the other side of the room my father was hollering over the din, determined to teach me about homologous pairing, meiotic division, recombination, and, of course, missing data. He hollered not only for my benefit, since I was sitting right next to him, but also in the hope that some of his words would unconsciously sink into Larry's skull as he pounded the ivories. My father, you see, was explaining the birds and the bees. Years later Larry pointed out that my mother had been attempting the same thing.

I heard Don's voice as I reached the top of the stairwell. There goes the neighborhood, I thought.

"You should have seen these mice," he was saying, "cardiac tissue shriveled almost beyond recognition, nearly every one of them."

I wanted to strangle those slow, interminable sentences of his. I knew exactly how they would end before he even got started.

"And I'll bet the ones in the control group looked pretty bad, too," I joked as I entered the room.

Don looked at me blandly. "I've noted quite an improvement in your humor lately," he said, sloughing a precious nugget from those mountainous deposits of cognitive bullion. "You've left puns and improbable verbal juxtaposition behind for the sophistication of irony. Very impressive."

"Don's always admired your wit," said Dex, jumping in protectively.

"At least the half I've been able to meter," Don snorted.

"Meter, you say," I nodded, as if impressed. "You almost sound like the engineer you wish you were."

"You think you're an engineer?" he replied tartly. "There are exactly two engineers in this room right now, and one of them's about to leave. As for the other," Don said, turning to Dex, "I'll see you later. You won't be sorry."

I had to laugh at that little display. Course 7ers sometimes called themselves "bioengineers" to show they really belonged at MIT. But deep down they all knew words provide no more than empty reassurance, sanitation engineers are still garbage men, and Course 7 is still liberal arts even if its followers know how to wheedle research funds.

"Why won't you be sorry?" I asked Dex after Don Boyer finally disappeared.

"This summer he'll be BioVitrics's first outside employee. We're going to need help moving, and then we start a limited production run for our clinical trials. If they ever happen, that is. We haven't even identified any participants yet."

"You know, my uncle was pretty intrigued with the concept of biocompatible glass when I told him about it last Christmas. He's a dentist, in addition to being a pain in the ass."

"That's terrific! You know how hard it is drumming up interest for something this new? When can I meet him?" Dex was breathless.

"I'm sure he'll be visiting us for Easter dinner. Consider yourself invited."

Maybe we'd have some venture funding to celebrate. And maybe Dex could get me a summer job, too.

o   o   o

Converge, goddamn it!

Now it's just EDGAR and me, no one here but the hacker and the hacked. I'm sitting at the desk playing technogames in the middle of the night with a million blinking numbers jumping off the screen and stinging my eyes like dust motes, flickering soft light throughout the room—over my left shoulder along the bed I'd love to jump into, to my right across Dex's slumbering silhouette as it rhythmically rises and falls. Mounting frustration and graveyard silence. EDGAR's souped-up parallel-processing *mens* and my very weary *manus*.

And I am quietly going crazy, this I know. No longer can I differentiate among the crazy, stupid and brilliant, and you must be going crazy if you think you are, since a sane person knows he's not turning loony and only a crazy person lost in the misty illusion of sanity can never be sure.

Iteration after iteration brings me no closer to success. I've planted my hopes on something called the E-M Algorithm, the Ferrari of missing-data statistics, a number-guzzling bullet built for speed. You can tell it's caught the road when the numbers it spits out start getting closer and closer together, approaching a single unchanging value: the elusive convergence. Otherwise you've got a fancy jalopy. Like the wreck on my screen.

It shouldn't be this hard. What I'm doing is trivial.

I'm just trying to see if the E-M Algorithm can keep pace with my circulation model. I want to feed it a few data points and have it digest them into an entire weather pattern. "E" stands for expectation; we try to connect the dots with guesses, sketch out a picture of how we think the air circulates. In the "M" step we see how well we did, comparing our rough sketch with the nicest weather picture my circulation model can paint. Then we repeat the process, again and again, each time using the results of the comparison to help fine-tune the guesses until there's no difference between the E-M sketch and the model's circulation picture. Convergence.

My computer screen is a colorful patchwork of windows, scattered rectangular boxes that overlap one another, each containing something independently useful. I've got my circulation model in a red window at the top left corner. My E-M equations appear in green at the right. And the growing column of values they discharge stands tall in the center, bright white to pry my eyes open.

It's the Italian flag.

And working about as well as the Italian government. Definitely not brilliant, not even a first step, so: crazy or stupid?

Now I'm slogging through the garbage, looking for patterns. Maybe I'll figure out where I'm going wrong if I can find some kind of structure in the field of useless numbers.

Or conclude that the whole enterprise is a snipe hunt, as Rita put it, a mathematical impossibility, a waste of my time and Jeff's hope and confidence. A crazy idea. Stupid to persist.

Soon the numbers are just formless white noise, empty symbols climbing up the screen like effervescent bubbles. I'm starting to see them as hieroglyphics. I'm eyeing them like little pictograms instead of absorbing their information. It's nighttime. It's gawking time. It's show time. It's amok time.

... amok time!

I'm dreaming. It's time to quit.

And just then I get e-mail:

MITnet To:busta@mit.62.410 From:jwatt@csl.mit.edu 4:01a

Try increasing your sampling density, and assume censored data.

And get some sleep.

Thank you, guardian guru. Don't mind if I do.

7.0

MIDTERMS WERE NO PROBLEM. MY HUNGARIAN METEOROLOGY instructor had obviously exaggerated. Analysis was just more math. And Dynamics was just more computer programming.

But my nerves were fraying anyway, for different reasons. For one thing, I'd heard nothing else about Star Ventures. Not even a hint! Not a single mention! It got to the point where I felt an icy shot of adrenaline at every hint of enthusiasm in Dex's voice, at every chirp of his new pocket cellular phone, every time a transmission came in on the plain-paper fax/copier he'd just installed. I shuddered like an expectant father waiting for the slap-and-wail.

And I was equally terrified he would succeed. The E-M Algorithm wasn't cooperating. I'd yet to achieve anything close to convergence.

To top it off, Easter plans had taken a strange turn. Since when did we have Easter dinner at Tony and Gina's instead of my parents'? Why wasn't Larry going to Tracy's folks for a change? And where was Dex, dammit, we were way behind schedule and now I'd have to drive all the way down to New Jersey without a break.

When he finally returned to our dorm, Dex was panting, full of apologies, and two hours late. Animal surgery, he explained. Couldn't get away. The operation took over three hours instead of one. And guess what, the block and tackle almost fell apart, which not only would have killed the pitiful cow but set the research schedule back two months and at least three grand, and would I mind if he took a quick shower to get rid of the blood stains and scrape the hardened fatty grime off his fingertips and out from under his fingernails?

No problem, I told him. As if it made a difference. Stains were as much a part of Dex's everyday wardrobe as extra-large jockey briefs. To the bio crowd every indelible splotch was a badge of honor, each shirtsleeve encrustation an epaulet. Pappadallas cultivated this battle-scar aesthetic in all his research assistants—the better to suggest productive utilization of funds to flint-hearted investors when they visited the lab, and also to sharpen the line between cufflinked commander and trudging troops.

Scheduling surgery on an Easter Sunday struck me as another Pap strategy for attitude reinforcement. So on the long journey south I did a little probing for signs of disaffection, invited a bit of resentment at the needless subordinations, but Dexter D. Drain, III, my high-powered finance angel and blithe tormenter of cattle, was a company man through and through.

Artie ambled in the front door with his characteristic shuffling gait just moments after we arrived. In stark contrast to Dex, dressed to impress in threadbare jeans and a once-monotone pullover that now resembled a map, Artie looked unusually spiffy. Why were the old guy's shoes so shiny? What gives with the bow tie and braces? "Arturo Sebastiani," he said slowly as he extended his hand to Dex. "Maybe later we'll talk." Then he slapped my cheek affectionately and disappeared into that little two-room refuge of his.

Tony, dressed in a pink shirt and a tie full of Easter Bunnies one of his kids had obviously given to him as a gift, took our coats and handed them to Gina. He was upset; we were late. And he wanted to make sure we appreciated the causal connection between these two phenomena. "After you ... *Dex*," said Tony, gesturing toward the end of the foyer, pausing just a little too long before the name and overpronouncing it. "And after you," said Tony to me, bending over slightly and extending his hand in a flourish.

"Thanks, Tony," I said as he nodded his head let's-get-on-with-it rapidly, his eyes closed. Then he repeated the hand flourish, still nodding, flicking his fingers to emphasize the monumental effort he had to make to contain his exasperation.

Tony was anxious to get into the living room so he could tap his feet impatiently. The small talk was well under way.

"How was your trip, guys?" asked my father, a bit overenthusiastically from the living room couch—small talk central.

Something was wrong. The kids were too quiet.

"Thomas Eakins," said Larry to Tracy as he pointed over the pink travertine coffee table to the television, a crisscross pattern of shadows from the new chandelier covering their faces, "had an extraordinary sense of perspective. Look at the way the river recedes behind the boat..."

"Not bad," I said to my father. "No land speed records, though."

"It's good to have you here," said my mother, "and nice to see you, too, Dex."

Dex, who was at least half a head taller than I, had to duck to avoid capture by the chandelier as he made his way across the marble floor to an empty wrought-iron chair. The house had now passed beyond the event horizon and was hurtling toward a black hole of perfect, infinite vulgarity.

"Look at the arms on that rower. Every muscle precisely rendered. Did you know Eakins studied medicine in Philadelphia?" continued Larry, clearly intent on narrating the PBS special over the small talk. He lowered the television volume with the remote control, dropping an obvious hint, and now the inoffensive PBS organ melody fell completely out of audible range.

"Did you know I rowed crew in college?" echoed Tony as he plopped down into the velour easy chair next to Tracy's side of the couch. "Didn't look much like that picture, though, one guy in the middle of a river wrestling with his soul or something. I'm talking eight big, burly guys rowing like Volga warriors against a stiff wind, mile after mile."

"Really," said Dex, looking for an opening, leaning in Tony's direction. Tony glanced sourly at his coarsely attired guest.

"I was referring to the aesthetics," Larry replied.

"So was I," laughed Tony. "The kind the girls just adore." Then he corrected himself: "I mean, adored. That was three kids ago."

"How can you sit there and advertise your ignorance by laughing at art?" asked Aunt Gina, obviously annoyed, as she dropped a plate of stuffed clams onto the coffee table.

"I've been clearing the gutters all morning. It's tough work."

"So you're laughing at art because you're tired?" Gina demanded.

"No, I'm sitting here because I'm tired."

"Oh yeah? Try being *sick* and tired!" she raged. "Nice to see you boys," she said, her voice temporarily gentle as she turned to Dex and me before disappearing back into the kitchen.

"I *am* sick and tired," Tony yelled after her, the implied message clear.

And the small talk continued. Dex inquired of Tony's dentistry exploits. Tony warmed to the question and recounted bicuspids newly capped, gums newly scraped and fresh hope for gingivitis sufferers. I felt tension rise again the next time Gina emerged from the kitchen with a bowl of cocktail shrimp in her hands and disappointment heavy in her heart. Thanks to Tony's boundless concern for the oral afflictions of others, Gina told us, she couldn't accompany Rosa to Albuquerque. She couldn't because that was the week big-hearted Tony gave his big-shot talk at the periodontal convention in Binghamton, you see, and little Johnny had croupe, and...

Mention of Binghamton sent my eyes reflexively to Tracy, whose own eyes had found Tony. "Small planet," I said to Tracy. "So did you—"

"No, I didn't hear Tony's talk," she replied quickly, "because I was away from college that weekend, visiting a friend in upstate New York. She's got a place on Lake Surprise, you know where that is? *Lake Surprise?*"

Gina's eyes landed on Tony. "If we could do something about *your* oral affliction," he told her, "you wouldn't need to spend a week in an overpriced cult eating grass and searching for the thin within."

"Don't you get me started, you," Gina warned.

So what the hell was Tracy talking about, anyway? Where was Lake Surprise? Then I studied her face, the look of desperate anger I'd seen before, and all at once it became clear: to keep me from prying further, she was threatening to reveal the "truth" about *the incident* to Larry—unaware just how familiar he was with those particulars. What a joke! And no wonder there was so much tension in the air. I thought I owed it to Larry to press the issue, but the livid expression on his face nearly knocked me over. He and Tracy glared at me with the same fiery rage, roasting my flesh with their eyes. Fine, I decided, I'll shut up. I've already made my point. What are *you* so worried about, Larry? Afraid I'll crack, convince her of the *real* truth this time? You should be red with anger!

"Rancho Albuquerque?" asked Dex, eager, it seemed, for a hook into the conversation. "My second cousin just came back from another one of those vacation spas, the one in Duluth, Montana. Duluth Springs, I think it's called."

"Yes, that's right," said Gina, distracted from her husband's guilty expression. "It's run by the same people. And they're open year round, too. How much did it cost? Do they have natural mineral springs? Do they rolf?"

"You guys really should appreciate this," said Larry, again attempting artistic commentary. "Eakins was very scientific in his painting. Maybe they'll show *The Gross Clinic*, his fully realistic rendition of a gory surgical operation."

Pathetic cuckolded sap, I thought.

"Eeeyuuuw," said Tracy. "Sure sounds gross!" She searched the room for appreciative laughter, but there was none. By the time Tony caught the pun it was too late.

"I'm going to show you some of my regatta photographs," said Tony, the kids promptly making their escape downstairs to the den. And soon he was passing around color glossies of the smiling Tony and seven smiling others posing in their shell, and then straining to the coxswain's demands, and then standing on dry land around a trophy.

Rowing. Manual propulsion of a slender boat in polluted water using a shaft of wood with a shaped blade as a lever, and with the ultimate aim of producing photographs for subsequent presentation to unfaithful tramps. Some sport.

Larry kept quiet, his discourse overwhelmed, and Tracy also offered no comment as the pictures made the rounds. Very discreet, that Tracy.

My mother, on the other hand, didn't even glance at the pictures, staring impassively ahead. At least someone's brain cells were sufficiently active to appreciate what was going on. She said, "I liked the Eakinses better. Larry, why don't you turn up the volume?"

But it was too late. Gina was summoning us to the dining room table.

"I'm please to report that both occupants of W70-503 are now productively occupied with compelling research projects. Tell everyone about your work, Paul," said my father as he sat down.

My "work." I liked the official sound of that. My work. My opus. My oeuvre. Eat your heart out, Larry, you artiste of a doormat.

"Well, it may sound technical, but I'm playing with the equations that govern damped, driven systems. They're very hard, if not impossible to solve. But I've got a new approach. I use a funny kind of statistics."

"Tell us all about it," my father pushed. "Tell us about the E-M Algorithm. You know, people have known about it for decades, but the military tried to suppress its versatility. No one knows why."

"I'll try to keep it simple," I said. "Basically, it's a trick, a way to draw conclusions even though some important pieces of information are missing. It's as if you've only got one good eye, and my procedure fills in what your other eye would see, so you get a complete picture."

"So you're working on eyes?" asked Tony the lecherous dentist as he gnawed on a bread stick.

"Actually, my son's going to revolutionize weather forecasting," beamed my father.

"Oooh, maybe we'll hear your name every night on the news when they give us the five-day computer-enhanced guaranteed-accurate forecast," said Gina. "The Bustamante Barometer says…"

"Tomorrow it shall rain," said Tracy, completing the sentence in a bogus baritone. "Just like the DJ on the radio who pretends he's God giving the weather forecast."

Again nobody laughed. Again Tony caught the humor too late.

"What do eyes have to do with the weather?" asked Tony, sounding annoyed.

"You need to see if you want to predict. The more you can see at any one time, the farther ahead you can forecast. Damped, driven systems like the weather are impossible to see completely all at one time. My approach enhances your vision."

Now Tony was really indignant, looking at me like I was from Mars. "So I've got a half-blind weather man with a damp eye who's being driven through some weather system by a top-secret procedure, and his other eye opens, and now he's a prophet squinting into the future. Is that it?"

The coveter of my brother's girlfriend was unable or unwilling to unravel my metaphor. I tried to remain civil. "The vision thing is just a figure of speech," I told him. "You're not really seeing—"

"You're right, I'm not," he interrupted.

"— you're just better able to understand what's going on."

"Tell him what you mean by 'damped' and 'driven,'" my father suggested.

"Suppose Joey here is on a swing. You're pushing him from behind, that's the driving part. Air resistance slows him down, siphoning off some of the energy you introduced. That's the dampening part."

Now Gina was passing out the pasta course. She served Tony last, dropping the bowl on his serving plate with just a little extra noise.

"Okay, this I can understand," said Tony. "In fact some people think the economy works like that. You know," he added as he twirled his fork, "economics is what's killing dentistry. Just last week I'm treating an indigent patient, right? The guy's on Medicaid, okay, fine. He needs three teeth extracted and one filling. But Medicaid only covers oral surgery, see? And the brilliant economist who wrote the regs decided extractions are merely dentistry, unless you do seven of them, in which case it becomes oral surgery. So what could I do?"

"Falsify the record keeping?" I asked.

He looked at me, nodding his head slowly, as if impressed with a terrific new idea. "Didn't think of that," he said.

"So what did you do?" I wanted to know.

"Just yanked seven, clean out. He won't miss 'em. This guy's only got one oar in the water, hardly knows his own name. I treat waste products like that out of charitable instincts. Keeps me in touch with humanity, you know?"

"Dentist to the downtrodden, eh, Tony?" my father asked good naturedly, if somewhat absentmindedly.

Instantly Tony turned a deep shade of crimson. His head lunged forward and his eyes bugged out as he sucked in the last few centimeters of a linguini strand with a loud snap. A piece of crabmeat glanced off his chin and landed on his tie, creating a spreading pool of red grease that coated several of the little Easter bunny faces. Tony glared at my father, who was too busy eating to notice, but caught himself as he turned toward me. Cocking his head and forcing his lips into a tight smile, Tony asked, "Hey, how come only your brother brings girls home to meet his family? Are you ashamed of us, or you having trouble with the girls?"

Artie said: "*Girl Trouble*, Don Ameche and Joan Bennett, 1942. What a year."

But Artie's verbal belch was ineffective as a distraction, and Aunt Gina wasn't around to stab Tony with a fork. "Actually, I've dated a whole number of women since I've been at MIT," I told Tony. That was no lie. Zero is a number, and a whole number at that.

"Do tell," he said, still leaning forward, feigning interest. "So I guess you're ashamed of us, then. Is that it? Larry doesn't seem ashamed. He's brought a lovely, *lovely* young woman to meet us not once, but twice now, right Larry?" Tony turned to Tracy.

I was incensed but wordless. Fortunately, the equally dateless

Dex came to the rescue just as my mother slammed her knife against her plate. She'd had enough of Tony, and was ready for action.

"Speaking of oral surgery," said Dex, even though we weren't, "I think you'd be interested in some products I'm working on. You could get in on the ground floor, since we haven't introduced them to the dental community yet. I've got some literature with me..."

"Forget about it, he doesn't have time," said Aunt Gina to Tony as she marched in from the kitchen with a huge roast lamb. "After dinner Dex is going to tell me all about Duluth Springs."

"Here, let me take the laboring oar," said Tony, standing up and drawing the lamb away from Gina. He looked at Tracy. "You know, I'm not the first Sebastiani to distinguish himself at sea. Generations of us have fished off the Amalfi Coast, hauling in those endless water-laden nets" (setting down the lamb and beginning a strenuous hand-over-hand action) "and wrestling with giant sword-fish" (now leaning back, struggling to pacify an imaginary monster). "That's why we're so vigorous." Then Tony turned to Gina. "Speaking of which, did we get an Easter card from my fisherman cousin Rodolfo this year?"

"Of course not," Gina said as she walked back into the kitchen with the empty pasta bowls. "The Italian mail is awful. You know that."

"The Italian male is not awful," Artie observed, "but you cannot trust him." He looked directly at Tony.

And Dex looked over at me, smirking at Tony's previous suggestion that you could pass acquired characteristics, like nautical prowess or developed physical strength, on to your children. That ridiculous Lamarckian idea had gone out of scientific fashion with patent leather. Something to chortle about on the way back to MIT.

"I am happy to report that our other son appears to have selected a major for himself at college," my mother said, attempting to give Larry equal billing. She always did love him more.

"Larry is Art Man," said Tracy, her voice tinged with pride.

"I hate art!" Antonia bellowed.

"Yeah!" followed Joey and Johnny.

That prompted Artie to disengage autopilot. "What do you little pip-squeaks know about art?" he demanded, the contents of his mouth spilling onto his plate. "Art is what separates us from apes. Let me teach you a thing or two before you go hating what you know nothing about."

"Don't try to flash your oars in unfamiliar waters, Dad," Tony advised.

"Ahhh, what do you know either?" growled Artie with a swipe of his hand. "I'm surrounded by ignoramuses."

"Art isn't very different from engineering, really," I said to Artie, hoping this would gratify that secret renaissance man. "Both are about optimizing parameters. Engineers work with stresses and tolerances, artists with color, form, and texture."

Artie drew his eyebrows together as he looked at me, then he began to stare at the wall as his mouth opened. He'd receded; left the cockpit.

"Ridiculous," said Larry. "You don't assemble beauty. You can't quantify aesthetics."

Tony said: "Sure you can, 36-24-36 ... now that's aesthetic. A beautiful assembly. Heh heh."

"More parameters define a greater challenge, higher art," I told Larry, ignoring Tony. "The best art forms are the ones with the most parameters that can be varied, and the best artists are the ones who can assign optimum values to the most free parameters."

"So sculpture is 'better' than painting since it extends over three dimensions instead of two, is that what you're saying?" Larry asked. This was great.

"Sure," I said. "And so is music, with its ordered progressions of tones, harmonies, intervals and pulses of rhythm, its timbre and varying volume levels. The Puccini records our grandfather used to listen to—now that's great art."

My mother was shaking her head. "Art is a gift, a talent," she said.

"Talent is velocity, nothing more," I said. "It's just the rate at which you can increase your ability level. I could be as fast and accurate a hurdler as Edwin Corley Moses, given enough time and devotion. But so what? I'm constantly aging; we all are, and we've only a limited time window within which to excel. Theoretical physicists and gymnastics competitors burn out before age 30, so talent is paramount. Artists can be more leisurely, and overcome lack of talent with dedication. Picasso and O'Keeffe painted into their eighties, right?"

"And Seurat was dead at 31," said Larry.

"Meaning what?" I wanted to know.

"Meaning, get yourself a life before it's over."

"Get yourself a diaper," I replied. "You know I'm right, you just won't admit it."

"Did you teach him this?" my mother demanded, turning to my father.

"Just a minute here," said my father, playing peacemaker. "Let's talk about something less divisive. All right?"

"Like politics," Gina recommended, finally relaxing in her chair. "So Tony can give you his speech about how dumb and insincere all the politicians are."

"Sincerity's got nothing to do with it," I said, intrepidly seeking new ears to enlighten. "At MIT we believe in the Turing Test, right D-cube?"

Dex shot me an evil glance. I'd forgotten that D-cube was a designation reserved solely for techies.

"Yeah? And what the hell's that, smart guy?" asked Tony, prompting Gina to slap his head with her free hand as she balanced a bowl of mushrooms with the other. Gina pointed at the children as Tony looked over at her—no swearing!

"Not on the head!" said Tony, stroking his hair back into place.

"Someone asked the mathematician Alan Turing whether a computer could ever 'think.' He said, well, if an isolated interrogator can't tell whether he's talking to a person or a machine, the computer is thinking or might as well be. It passes the test. Same for politics. So what if the candidate is just pretending? Anyone who can fake sincerity so convincingly that you absolutely can't tell is as good as the real thing, as far as I'm concerned."

"Turing..." repeated Tony. "Wasn't he a homo?"

"Hey, I get it!" Tracy exclaimed, several sentences too late. "D-cube, like D D D, three Ds, right?"

Tony produced an elaborate laugh to make up for his earlier lapses. "Oh, Tracy," he said. "You slay me."

"No, I'm serious," she chided. "It's Dex's nickname."

"Oh, right, of course. That's what I meant, it's so clever, and clever of you to see it," said Tony, attempting recovery. And then, tasting a mushroom, he scooped up the bowl of them and made his getaway. "Cold cold cold," he nattered as he stomped into the kitchen to fire up the microwave.

"Cold rolled steel," said Artie.

"Time for pictures," Gina announced.

"Jesus, Gina, we're still eating," Tony complained from the kitchen as the microwave whirred.

"Three generations of Sebastianis," she said, rising as Tony returned with the steaming mushrooms that by now had been irradiated into tastelessness. "And who knows," she added in a whisper, eyeing Artie portentously. "This could be the last time we'll all be together."

"Yeah, right," muttered Tony as Gina scampered off.

"Keep eating, pay no attention," said Gina when she returned with her auto-everything camera. She began snapping away. Dex launched into his pitch. "The cellular response is extraordinary," he told Tony, shirt stains testifying to his credibility. Soon they slipped away downstairs as the flashing and munching began to wind down. Dex, you salesman, you.

Then Artie winked at me. I followed his shuffle into his bedroom.

"You're a weird kid," he confided.

I noticed a strange sort of weapon in the corner. It was a rifle, probably a .22, standing vertically on its heel. But it had been modified. A rectangular metal box flanked by a series of little knobs rested on the barrel where the eyepiece should have been.

"What's that?" I asked him.

"Oh, nothing. The latest thing I'm playing with. You use it to get rid of rodents."

"*Rodents?* Seems like mighty heavy artillery for mice. What happened to rape and childbirth?" I asked.

"My lady friend says I should stay out from under women's skirts. People will start to talk, you know?"

His lady friend. That explained the cuff links and other fashion accoutrements. Artie, you old dog!

"As I was saying before..." he began.

"Is that a laser on the barrel?" I asked him. "Show me how it works. I've never seen anything like it."

He stared at me for a second, a trace of disappointment playing in the expressive wrinkles around his eyes. Then he picked up the rifle and said, "Yeah, that's right. I had this double micrometer mount sitting around for ages doing nothing. So one day I decided to slap one of these lasers on it, see, and throw the whole shebang on a twenty-two. It's fully adjustable, you know."

"What does the laser do?"

"First you find a comfortable blind for yourself, a place where you can see and hear the little bastards late at night. You set the laser—did I mention it's fully adjustable?—so whatever it lights up, the bullet rips through. Then you wait. When you see the beady little eyes, you paint them with the laser the way the Air Force targets its smart bombs. The rodent doesn't notice since he can't see red light too great. Then you whack him." Artie closed his finger around the trigger without pulling it, and jumped back as if the rifle had actually recoiled.

"Have you tested it yet?" I asked him.

"Of course! I use a silencer. Not that anyone would notice around here anyway. Come."

He led me outside to a spot next to the garage, and pointed to some off-square wood trim near the overhanging gutter. "That's where I site 'em," he said.

"And then the bullets lodge in that tree over there?" I asked, pointing to the ancient oak about fifty feet ahead.

"Only when they miss."

"What does your lady friend say about all this?" I asked.

"I guess she thinks I've got better ways to spend my time than torching mice. So what? I've whacked at least a dozen. There isn't even much cleanup—all that's left are the tails."

Then Artie spun around and poked his finger in my chest. "But listen!" he said. "The issue isn't rodents. The issue is you, see? What's all this business with engineering being like art ... ah, never mind, you don't wanna hear this, I know. Everything okay at school?"

"Couldn't be better," I told him.

Artie looked at me intensely. "They got, like, marketers at MIT? They get to you?" he asked.

"I don't ... huh?"

"It's the way you talk, it's *reducing*, you know'd I mean? Everything's *reduced* to something until you forget what you started with. It's like some high-tech marketing gimmick. I'm sitting there waiting for the encore. I'm sitting there worried you're gonna show everyone a tattoo on your rear end. Or something. See?"

It was a cold Easter and neither of us had bothered to put on a coat. I saw the concern on his face and I tried to listen as I watched him raise his finger, then hunch his shoulders against the stinging wind. But it was as if I couldn't hear him.

"Artie, you're freezing. Let's go back in."

He nodded. We walked in and soon Dex and I walked back out, back on the road.

I called Larry at school the next day. Let's just say I expressed incredulity at his girlfriend's all-too-obvious interests. Let's just say

I didn't mince words at my opinion of Tony. And as for Larry, let's just say he wasn't buying a word of it.

"You're jumping to conclusions," he told me.

"And Tracy's jumping your uncle's bones!" I shouted. "You've got eyes, ears—how else do you explain what went on?"

"You know," he said, "you just don't understand women one bit. I think you spent too much time with Dad growing up. You're clueless! Completely and totally and fatally clueless."

Is this how you talk when you decide to major in art history?

"Dammit, Larry!" I yelled. "Wake up and smell the gravity! He's drawn her out of your orbit, it's simple physics."

"You know, when it comes to matters physical, I believe I'm enjoying somewhat greater success of late than you. Right?"

I ignored the taunt. "Look," I implored, "if you don't care about yourself, at least think about Gina and your three cousins. At least confront Tracy for their sakes!"

"Gina's marriage is her business," Larry said coldly, "and may I suggest you mind yours."

Sometimes there was just no talking to the guy.

8.0

MITnet To:jwatt@csl.mit.edu From:busta@mit.62.410 9:14a

PROGRESS REPORT

My finals start in just over a week, and I wanted to update you before I go into hiding. First, I've got a funding lead—my well-financed roommate, Dex Drain, passed the concept by his venture group and got us a nibble. They want to meet with you and me ASAP, tomorrow or Thursday if you can make it. Dex is very positive and thinks we have a real chance.

As to the project itself, your advice was right on target. I got the E-M to converge—talk about progress! Looks like we can use missing data to forecast weather after all! To accurately model a hunk of the atmosphere, we just need a sufficient number of observation points. Big relief given the imminent venture-capital prospects. But of course, it's only the beginning.

Next step: tackle turbulence. Use the algorithm to improve the performance of a standard weather forecasting model under windy, stormy conditions. I'll use the approach you told me about back in January, now that I understand it. Data from just a few points lets us represent an entire region of the atmosphere—sort of like imagining a detailed landscape from a few minimalist flecks. From our snapshot of how things are changing through space, we can calculate how they're changing over time, and make predictions. Space first, then time. Just like you said.

You were also right about the money. We'll need it. Lots of it, if we ever want to perform field operations in the real world. Satellites, weather stations, balloons spread far and wide—all pouring data down our insatiable gullets, all just so we can test ourselves against today's forecasting models. But if we can't do better than the local weather report, why should anyone care about our arcane approach? Why buy a Ferrari to chase mules?

So our initial meeting with the venture people may turn out to be critical if we want to get this project off the screen. I've been assured, however, that it's altogether preliminary. They just want to sniff us over, see whether further investigation would be worth their time. We won't need to demonstrate technical feasibility for weeks, maybe months. I assume everything will be put on hold for the summer while I toil away at some menial job somewhere; I'll probably repeat my experience as a counselor at Camp Cuyahoga if nothing else comes up.

Over and out.

MITnet To:busta@mit.62.410 From:jwatt@csl.mit.edu 9:20a

Glad to hear about the progress on funding. As for your summer employment, I assume you were joking about Camp Cucamonga. Rita put your name in for a summer-session TAship weeks ago. Better call the Residence Office right away if you want to keep your room.

Regarding your proposed approach, let me kick the tires by doing a little modeling of my own. Then we can talk.

Good luck studying for finals, by the way. When they're over, heed the words of the sage:

Levitate your consciousness to total nothingness.
Yogi Bhajan

I need not know how you accomplish this.

"Blair E. Stille," said Dex, flipping through the pages of a glossy annual report. "She's the head honcho, the maximum leader of Star Ventures, and she personally interviews every prospect they seriously consider. Let's see ... where's her picture in here, anyway?" His voice began to trail off.

"Aha!" he said suddenly, planting the booklet on my desk and pointing at a large color reproduction. "Blair E. Stille." He looked up and smiled. "She'll scare you silly."

Great. My roommate was frightening the crap out of me in verse.

Her picture didn't ease the dread. Blair E. Stille looked young, blond and hard. I wondered how she'd react to Jeff.

"She's got the marketing statement," said Dex, "but you and Jeff had better be familiar with every line, every number. Star Ventures isn't that big. They've only got around 11 mil to throw around, so they can't go out on a limb with projects that look too speculative."

"On the other hand," I said, my eyes still fixated on the glossy page, "we're not asking for the moon. Twenty-five kilodollars won't exhaust the treasury."

"True. Now after you finish memorizing your marketing statement, start soaking up the details of this annual report. Be ready to tell Blair why your project fits into the Star portfolio. Make me proud."

Yes, daddy, I thought for a second, but then suppressed the reflexive resentment with feelings of gratitude for this, my sole opportunity for financial support. It wasn't *my* marketing statement at all, and Dex knew it. He'd entered every figure. I called Blair E. Stille's secretary and made an appointment for Thursday. I assumed Jeff would be available, since, well, he just always seemed available.

But I was wrong. A couple of hours later I returned from a particularly invigorating Analysis class, blithely wondering whether a thirteenth-century math whiz named Fibonacci could possibly have imagined the little numerical sequence he devised explaining the breeding of rabbits, the number of ancestors of a male honeybee in different generations and, until the '87 crash anyway, the behavior of the stock market. 1, 1, 2, 3, 5 ... the pattern is easy, it's rhythmic, it's got a beat—8, 13, 21 ... It seemed I'd had a visitor during class: an envelope was taped to the door 34, 55, 89. The envelope was wrapped in a note 144, 233. From Jeff. Can't make it to the VC meeting, it said. But not to worry. Just give them the attached letter, it should answer any questions. And stay cool.

377, 610, 987.

My mother always told me to count to ten before going ballistic. But I'm up to 1597, 2584, 4181 and I'm not staying cool—I'm going into shock instead!

The questions raced through my mind like clouds leading a

cold front. Was Jeff afraid he'd make a fatally bad impression? Did he think someone at Star would remember his adventures with IBM heat sinks? Or was he queasy about selling an idea not yet half-baked? Maybe he'd sim'd it already, found that my approach could never work, but didn't have the heart to tell me; now he was trying to dissociate himself from a boondoggle and preserve whatever was left of his reputation. There were too many possibilities, too little data to draw a reliable conclusion. I plunged into the room, reeling in confusion and frustration, ready to hurl the letter against a wall, but fortunately there was Dex, calmly sitting at his desk, smiling beatifically. Thank heaven for Dex. I began to relax, certain he'd know just what to say, how best to proceed.

"HE *WHAT?*" Dex screamed when I told him. "This is a *disaster!* I'll look like a fool! You'll look like twice the fool! What the hell are we going to do?"

"Such huffing and puffing," said Rita, poking her head through the door. "Someone forget to feed his id this morning?"

Rita grew quiet when she read the note. "He's sim'd it, I just know," I said. "He's decided the whole thing's ridiculous and now he wants out. He's embarrassed."

"How do you know he's sim'd anything?" Dex asked. "Maybe..."

"He doesn't eat lunch without simming his colon first," said Rita. "He's sim'd the thing all right, but I doubt it flunked. Don't you get it? Jeff models for a living. Your direct solution poses a threat to his simulationist fakery. He was *hoping* you'd fail. And now that he sees that you haven't, he's out to sabotage you."

"Well, we've got to find out," I said. "I've got to know where I stand before I sink any deeper or turn into a laughingstock."

"What do you mean, turn *into?*" Rita snapped. "I'm sure he's already having a good laugh. Guess we'll just have to do a little breaking and entering to see what he's found out." She dug her hand into her backpack and produced a single gold key hanging from a multicolored keyring that said 'Peter Max.' I'd heard of him. "Good thing he gave his head TA a key to his office."

"Why don't you just walk up to Jeff and ask him?" Dex wanted to know. His mood had shifted from panic to mere gloom.

Rita looked at him and drove her fists into her hips. "Are we inaudible? What we're saying is that his motives are selfish and destructive. You think he'd stand up and admit that?"

"But he's always in his office," I complained. "How are we..."

"Not when he lectures," she interrupted. "He's got a class tomorrow morning. Remember? 6.001? The one you're supposed to be a TA in?"

"And what if his system is locked?" I asked.

"I can off-load the memory directly from the CPU. No problem," said Rita.

"And store it on what?" I asked.

"Oh, don't worry about that, I've got at least a dozen spare floppies," said Dex, noisily extracting a box of 3-1/2" diskettes from his desk drawer.

Rita and I looked at each other and burst into laughter, a welcome relief from the bitter apprehension gripping my stomach. Rita spoke first. "You'd need thirty of those to store one of his simplest sims."

"Thanks anyway," I said, trying to back off the meanness of my laughter.

But he persisted. "Well, if the keyboard is locked, why can't you just exchange it with another one, or use a laptop instead?"

"Oh!" grunted Rita, expressing great pain. "It's the whole interface that's locked, not just a particular keyboard. And anyway, you think Jeff is considerate enough to leave us a menu of his sims? You think this is pick and choose, like an EDGAR screen?"

"That's it!" I cried. "EDGAR! We'll transmit the entire memory contents through EDGAR to the parallel machine I'm working on. Then we can take as much time as we want to sift through the sims."

"Brilliant deduction, Sherlock," Rita sneered. "That part is obvious. Did it occur to you that we'd have to reprocess all his instructions so your parallel box can understand them? Don't worry, it occurred to me, and I know how to access Jeff's conversion program. Have you thought of a way to connect to EDGAR from a locked terminal?"

"He's got cables taped to the floor between his terminal and that round monster of his," I said. "So—"

"So forget about it," Rita replied. "I know what you're thinking, pick up signals from the cables. It'll never work, they're too weak. Besides, we'd have to hang around his office for most of his lecture since we can't just leave the setup hanging around. That's too risky."

She began to pace back and forth, to the extent the two-step shuffle our room accommodated could be called a pace, and touched her fingertips to her lips as she walked. "I know," she said finally.

"Ever watch the cooling ports on Jeff's computer, the way light flashes out of them? The whole computer thinks in flashes. Read the flash pattern and you know what it's thinking. So we make a light sensor, a remote pickup that can send every flicker our way—transmit them wirelessly like a walkie-talkie. We aim our pickup at those cooling ports. We get past the locked keyboard by using the panel switches. We flip some switches, tell the computer to dump its memory, and whatever's in the memory turns into light flashes. So Jeff's computer spills its guts; our pickup reads its flashing lips through the cooling ports, and passes every last detail along to us." She thought for another moment and continued, "Sure. And we store everything on tape. We plant a radio connected to a tape drive in one of the nearby storage rooms, where no one will even notice amidst all the technocrap. Then Mr. Pickup's a radio personality. He talks right to the tape drive. We can make sense of it later."

"In fact," I said, "we can stick the pickup behind the ventilation grate in Jeff's ceiling so he'll never even notice. We'll retrieve it some other time. That grate is conveniently huge, I guess because of all the car fumes. One of us can climb up in there and aim the pickup."

"Yeah, but then how does said person get back out? The aim has to be precise. It would have to be done with the grate in place. The pickup can't be moved after it's aimed, see?"

"Fine," I rejoined. "The other one of us enters the ventilation system through an access grate or an air intake. It's still too early for air conditioning, and probably too late for heat. The crawler listens for the aimer's whistle or tap or some other signal, wends through the tunnels, finds the aimer, and leads the way back out."

"An air intake? That's fine if crawler doesn't mind putting on a show for everyone in the hall and then getting puréed in the compressor unit. I've got a better idea. There's probably a manifold where all the outflow ducts come together. Crawler sets up the tape drive in a storage room, climbs through that room's ventilation grate, slithers into the manifold and waits for aimer. When aimer arrives, crawler leads the way back out. That's how we do it."

Dex was shifting his eyes back and forth as Rita and I spoke; he watched our exchange like a tennis spectator. I figured we'd dazzled him.

"So you're not even going to try the computer before you dissect it?" Dex asked, shaking his head. "Maybe you could avoid all this James Bond stuff."

Those guys in Course 7 just don't get it.

"We need to lay our hands on a cheap kid's telescope," said Rita. "That's your mission, nothing a trip to Central Square won't take care of. I'll borrow transducer and transmitter chips and an optical reader from one of the electronics labs, and scout out a tape drive. Maybe there's already one in E42."

Dex said, "You realize that all of this is beside the point, don't you? None of this brings Jeff to the meeting. What are you going to tell Blair? What's she going to think when you show up without Jeff?"

"Hey, hey, one crisis at a time," I said.

"That *is* the crisis, goddamn it!" cried Dex, heating up again. "The rest is just idle curiosity!"

Rita slapped her thighs and twisted her head toward the door, as if ready to walk out in anger.

"D-cube," I said patiently, "look. Jeff said his letter would explain everything, so..."

"Let me see it," barked Dex as he grabbed at the envelope I still held in my hand.

I jerked my hand upward to avoid his grasp. "You can't open it!" I told him, bringing the envelope behind my back. "That's Jeff's personal stationery. The letter would look pretty stupid sitting in a blank envelope after you've ripped this one apart. We'll just have to trust him."

"That was your first mistake," said Rita.

"Trust him to a first-order approximation, then. Listen. I'm going through with the meeting, okay? I'm not ready to toss the opportunity."

"And you're going to hand her that crackpot twaddle?" Dex asked, still upset but resigned again. "Watt probably wrote it in Sanskrit."

"That's exactly what I'm going to do," I said, and then looking over at Rita, asked, "meet you at his office tomorrow?"

"10:45 AM. We'll set up the drive and then do the deed."

Outside my window I could see the tip of a thunderhead inching over the horizon, advancing over the dilapidated low buildings across Briggs Field and promising an end to our three-day sunshine streak. I figured I had an hour to get to Central Square and back before the sky opened up.

Our dose of good weather had used itself up. Unfiltered sun

finally began to stir the low-lying air during the morning. Soon bunches of fluffy clouds were forming as the rising air cooled to its dew point, and without a renewed blast of Canadian frost to sweep the system clean, continued heating just sent more and more columns of warm air racing to horn in on the crowded adiabatic cooling party now going on upstairs, where things were beginning to get out of hand and some of the moisture was starting to tumble back down like swarms of kicked-out crashers who butted heads with the oncoming party seekers until updrafts and downpours drove each other into a turbulent frenzy to create the humongous anvil thunderhead in the distance that would spit lightning and roll thunder as soon as its lunatic nonlinear chase brought it within earshot.

What a compulsive meteorology freak I'd become. And a good thing, too, I realized, since an early start on studying for finals was beginning to look less and less likely. Not that MIT encourages excessive preparation. They scheduled my Analysis exam just four days after the last class. Maybe they figure that if the problem sets and lab assignments haven't gotten under your skin by the end of the semester, it just won't happen no matter how hard you study. I sure hoped they were right. Whoever they were.

Conspicuous. No two ways about it. No way to avoid it. Absurdly, garishly, and noisily conspicuous—that was yours truly as I made my way to Jeff's office the next day, toting a bright telescope with colorful pictures of Bart Simpson spying on his dowdy school-teacher as she undressed behind a window. Even worse, my shoes made loud squishing noises and left wet imprints as I traipsed along the smelly rubber pimples in E42. I had incorrectly estimated the thunderstorm's progress the day before; I got drenched walking to, from, and around Central Square. So much for conventional forecasts.

"Give me that!" hissed a hand extending past a corner I was about to round. The hand was quick and I was startled; suddenly the telescope was gone.

"Are you sapient?" Rita whispered scornfully as she emerged from around the corner. "You trying to advertise this caper?"

She stashed the telescope in her backpack and scanned the corridor up and down. I started to imitate her side-to-side glances in unconscious paranoid resonance, but she caught me by the collar from behind and yanked me into the room we'd been standing in front of. It was a storeroom, littered with monitors, loose keyboards, an oscilloscope, and piles of circuit boards bristling with electronic components and skaggy wire ends. Incredible. The whole floor couldn't have been more than a couple of years old and already it had its ancient burial ground.

"Look!" she exclaimed in a whisper, pointing at a cable connector mounted on the wall.

"What?"

"This room is wired for EDGAR! We don't need a tape drive, just a terminal that works. You can log on and send the data right through to your parallel machine." But then she slapped her forehead. "Forget it, forget it. We have no way to demodulate the radio signal. We'll just use the tape drive."

"No, you're right, that was good," I told her. "We'll feed EDGAR the signal and store it as a waveform. I can demodulate and digitize it later. I've written a hundred filter programs."

"Then let's find a terminal that works and get cracking."

And after about fifteen minutes of try this one's and bring me that one—no that one's, we finally had an operating screen that flashed the familiar EDGAR logo at us.

"You can log on later," Rita said, standing up suddenly. "I want to be the hell out of Jeff's office as fast as possible."

She flung the door open and marched out, but instantly stopped as she turned the next corner. I nearly plowed into her. She was really making me nervous.

"What?" I said, but quickly recognized the problem. A fresh-faced, tender nerd sat in front of Jeff's office door. He awaited Jeff's wisdom and guidance.

"Do you have an appointment?" Rita growled at the callow petitioner.

"Uh, no. I didn't know..."

"Then clock yourself into the input buffer like everyone else," she interrupted. "His office hours don't begin until one."

But the guy didn't move, he just gaped. Rita's bearing had immobilized him. I knew the feeling.

"Scram!" she said, stomping her foot just in front of his crossed legs. He untangled himself and scampered off like a skittish puppy.

"Why do they always come to Jeff?" Rita sighed as she slipped her key into the deadbolt lock. The tumblers fell with a loud *clack*. "I mean, I've got office hours too. I'm the head TA, right? But they always show up here instead. I just don't understand it." (I did.)

Jeff's office was dark. He had drawn the blinds, which admitted only slivers of light.

"Excellent," said Rita. Satisfied with our isolation from the outside world, she removed a towel from her backpack and jammed it into the crack at the base of the door, perfecting our privacy. Then she flipped the light on and got right to work. The transmitter she'd assembled was extraordinarily simple: a perforated breadboard no bigger than an index card held two integrated circuits that looked like centipedes with metallic legs, a five-volt lithium battery, an antenna coil, and a set of tiny dipswitches that you need a sharp pencil and great eyesight to set. Underneath the board, an ordered tangle of wires made the whole thing work.

The top of one of the centipedes contained a little round window. Rita taped the telescope to the board with duct tape so the eyepiece lay flush against the window. Then she popped the telescope out of the tape, leaving a sticky sleeve projecting from the board. I get it, I thought. Aim the telescope, secure it, and now you can slip the tape sleeve back over the eyepiece. The window will see what the telescope sees. Squeeze the tape and the board will stay put.

Rita made her way across the room, stepping lightly between piles of journal articles, half-read technical manuals, and a pair of sandals neither of us wanted to approach too closely. She powered up the computer and wordlessly began playing the panel switches on the base. Through the vents I could see the central lamp begin to glow. But it shined continuously—not what I'd expected.

"Don't worry," Rita reassured me as she continued to operate the panel. "It's flashing. Human eyes are just too sluggish to tell."

She stood up and walked to the file cabinet that stood underneath the black metal ceiling grate. "I don't suppose you brought tools," she said.

I sensed the derision and cheerily proclaimed, "Got my screwdrivers right here." I patted my back pocket.

"Too bad the grates have hex bolts," she replied. "Don't worry. I've got a ratchet set." She drew a red metal box from the bountiful backpack. When she'd finished assembling the ratchet she looked at me and said, "Listen. I'm the aimer. After I'm in, replace the grate and turn the light off. Then go back and program your computer. Connect the radio to the terminal's analog input. But if it takes you more than ten minutes, fuck it. Just come get me and we'll finish it after."

She climbed up onto Jeff's file cabinet and removed the bolts, then the grate like a seasoned mechanic. In fact, she looked kind of like a mechanic in those sweats, a rangy proletarian working under a raised chassis. Soon she disappeared into the duct. Seeing her squirm and kick her legs as she hoisted herself up made me realize that the passage really wasn't all that wide after all, and I grew terrified at the bulging groans and crunches the ceiling made under her weight. I was about to raise the grate when she slid back out.

"No room to turn around," she panted. "You'll have to lift me in."

There wasn't time for discussion. As I climbed onto the file cabinet I raised her feet and then her legs until she was upside-down vertical against me. I could picture Jeff's reaction if he were to walk in: "Gnarly sex position, guys. Think you could do that somewhere else?"

Then I began to lift and she pushed up on my knees, I threaded her legs into the vent and struggled to catch her shoulders to raise them up like a curling bar when her sweatshirt sagged down, revealing, to my amazement, a bodybuilder's waistline: razor-sharp lines and well-defined abdominal muscles that emerged in squares and strips as Rita's torso undulated from side to side. I had always assumed the body buried underneath all those sweats would exhibit far more drag than lift, as they say in Aerodynamics. But it wasn't so.

"You having a problem?" asked Rita, her voice garbled with her face pressed into my shirt. She'd caught my hesitation.

I sank into my knees and then hefted her with a mighty effort of legs, arms and shoulders. A smooth clean and jerk, just like the weightlifters. Now she was high enough to grab the edges of the vent and she pushed herself back. I handed her the telescope and her transducer circuit. I resealed the grate. I wondered what she'd look like without her clothes on.

Back to the storeroom I raced. I'd forgotten to close the door but everything was as I'd left it. I accessed my pass-through and jumped through menu after menu to find the waveform-capture routine. Good thing for those Media Lab folks, who had been kind enough to create the specialized software I'd need. They used it to analyze musical performances; I needed it to see into Jeff's head.

I had to go through list after list to find it, my ten minutes disappeared in an instant, but there it finally was—the program called CATCH_A_WAVE. I'd activate it when I got back. I dragged one of those rolling carts under the grate, locked the wheels, and clambered on top, hoping it wouldn't give, petrified it would start to roll. My whole body swayed as I turned the ratchet, rocking its rotation axis so it took forever to remove the bolts. Again I thought of Jeff walking in. "Gnarly hula, for sure. But where's your audience?"

I tied the end of a twine ball onto the grate and lowered it down to the floor, then stuffed the ball into my back pocket. I figured I might need a trail back if the tunnels turned labyrinthine. Then I looked up. The vent was brushed stainless steel. I could see nothing to grab onto except a fat plastic seam where the flared vent section met the rectangular shaft. Hope it doesn't give, I thought as I clenched my eyes shut and jumped, giving myself the old heave-ho into the darkness. The tunnel provided just enough clearance for me to reach back and withdraw the twine ball and a compact flashlight from my pocket, then wriggle forward. The walls banked to the left about fifteen feet ahead, and I was relieved to see that the plastic seams repeated every six feet or so. That would give me something to grab onto other than the barely textured metal sides, which squealed like a chalkboard under my nails, sending that icy shiver down my spine. On the other hand, my genitalia didn't particularly appreciate the intrusive bumps of those seams as I writhed ahead slowly, without sufficient room to get a good crawl going, around the bend and sure enough the vent opened into a boxlike volume with outflow ports on every side: the manifold.

I stuck my head into each of the ports until I heard scratching noises. Had to be Rita. Good thing for the twine, I realized, because I'd completely lost my orientation in the perfectly symmetrical manifold. Without the stringy trail I'd have no idea which port led back to the storeroom. I found I could sit up in a crouch, and listened to my heart race until Rita finally snaked her way in, feet-first. Two was definitely a crowd in the little cubicle and Rita ordered, "Let's go. We're set."

That's when I made a big mistake. I spun around to follow the twine without leaving the crouch, pivoting on the ball of my left foot, and the sudden enormous force density caused the floor of the manifold to buckle under my concentrated weight and bring part of the ceiling down with it in a thunderous metallic reverberation.

"Shit. I hope no one heard that!" cried Rita in a whisper.

And then when things had fully quieted down, and no suspicious voices came through any of the ports, Rita jabbed me and whispered, "Move it! Move it! Move it!"

But I couldn't. I was absolutely, totally, and firmly stuck. My foot was wedged into the crater I'd sunk into the floor, the ceiling had draped over my head like a sloped roof, and with Rita behind me I was unable to rock backward. It soon occurred to me that she was now stuck, too.

"I believe I'm entrained," I said with as little emotion as possible. "What about you?"

"You *idiot!*" she hissed.

Yes, she was stuck, too, all right.

The recriminations were immediate and forceful. "I can't believe it," she complained. "All that planning, all that effort lost in an instant to your bonehead clodhopping. We'll be expelled, you know. But don't worry. I'll find work. My arms are strong, they can bus dishes or push a mop. If the Jaws of Life don't pry all my limbs off first, that is."

"We're not going to be expelled, because they won't catch us," I assured her.

"What's the alternative? To rot here like vermin?"

"We're getting out the same way I got in. I just have to free myself up."

"And just how do you plan to do that?"

"Pipe down, dammit, I'm thinking."

"I thought I heard something rattling," Rita muttered.

"If you can't..." I began.

"To think, after all this time, it turns out like this. I just can't believe it. I should have known better."

"What are you talking about now?" I demanded.

"I'm talking about what a dope I am. Do you have even the slightest idea why I'm doing this? Why I'd volunteer to waste half a day building a stupid data transmitter and half of another twisting through filthy disgusting pipes and putting my entire future earning capacity at risk? And all of this just before finals?"

I knew what was coming.

"Because I had a crush on you, you insensitive double-digit-IQ numbskull archetype."

Now, I wasn't so blind that I couldn't see her interest all this time, but I'd simply never considered Rita a serious candidate for romantic involvement with that extruded hair of hers and those ridiculous sweats. And then of course there was her attitude.

"It was when I first saw you wearing that tennis shirt," she whispered. Now her voice was thin, almost like a child's. "In 6.001. You were chewing out that big goon tormenting the others, the one hitting everyone else's keys and ruining their programs..."

The big goon was a female sophomore, she was just overeager, and I had merely admonished her. But I said nothing. I rather liked this.

"I could see your physique through your shirt and hear the keenness of your intellect in the words you chose. I'm just teasing when I call you stupid, you know. And I work out, too. Sometimes I would envision you next to me in the Nautilus room, straining on the chest machine, browbeating some DonBoy lookalike Course 7 clown with your unassailable logic..."

"Rita, this really isn't the time or the place," I said. "The humidity in this god-awful cell is already making me sweat." I was becoming more and more aware of the details of our confinement, how tight the manifold was, the acrid air-conditioner odor, the cramping stiffness I was beginning to feel in my calves and ankles.

"I know," she replied. "Drano would be proud. And to think how I'd picture you when I became lonely. You know, I could practically feel your heartbeat sometimes, I'd see you next to me, feel you holding me, touching me ..."

"Rita, cut it out already!"

"I'd think of you taking off that tennis shirt, I'd imagine the sinew of your body, the firmness of your cogitation..."

"Enough!"

"Filling my desperate, aching emptiness, gorging me with your manly strength and cerebral potency, driving my fears and desires into endless waves of wet, glorious passion..."

"Goddamn it, Rita, I can't take this right now, I can barely breathe and you're turning me into a miserable aqueous mess!"

And that's when she somehow wedged her feet onto the small of my back and drove her legs forward with all her might, suddenly freeing my body from contortion and launching me headlong into the tunnel ahead of me like a torpedo into its tube. I'd been facing the correct vent, I realized: the twine was right there. And so I writhed and wriggled and hauled myself ahead until I popped out the storeroom vent. Rita was right behind me. She looked sourly at the grease stains on her sweatshirt as she climbed off the cart, and began to remove her sweatpants in disgust.

The legs. They were the only key anatomical item I hadn't assessed as I lifted her into the vent. I watched with great interest as she unsheathed one, then the other long, tapered extremity and balled the sweatpants up with a guttural *ucchh*. Her hair glob had come undone, and she shook what remained of it into a long, shaggy mess. Then the sweatshirt came off. You know, in gym pants and with a tee shirt tacked to her body by wetness and her hair in complete disarray, she looked, well, really not half bad at all.

"What are you waiting for?" she snapped. "Get EDGAR ready to accept transmission and tune the radio to my signal. I'll start the dump going."

She took off for Jeff's office. Soon the waveforms began to show up on the screen, safely absorbed, processed and stored by CATCH_A_WAVE.

And then Rita was back. "You won't believe this," she said. "Jeff doesn't lock his keyboard."

"Let me ask you something. Did you mean all those things you said up there, or were you just trying to make me perspire to loosen me up?"

She smiled wryly and tossed her hair in apparent disbelief. "You really are *so* stupid!" was her reply. "Your obtuseness knows no limits."

It didn't matter. I was so happy to be through with this adventure I could feel nothing but playful relief. "Stupid, you say? Obtuse? We're sleuths, stealthy detectives. You think just anyone could have executed this piece of high-tech burglary? I just may embark on a whole new career!"

"Yeah, well *don't* quit your day job," she said, shoving me with both hands on the word 'don't.'

Then she walked off, her head high, dragging her backpack like a hunter's kill. I watched her legs quiver into firmness each time she took a step. She really looked, well, pretty damn good! How could I have failed all this time to appreciate her handsome, angular features and the grace of her stride? Clearly within, at most, half a standard deviation of me on the attractiveness scale.

And so there I was, admiring a stranger I'd known for over a year, feeling like a character in one of those ridiculous sci-fi genre movies—the mad scientist who suddenly realizes his devoted lab assistant is actually one heck of a looker, and now finds himself ready to cast aside the lonely world of solo science for the greater rewards of domestic pursuit.

My life imitates kitsch. How utterly revolting.

9.0

IT TOOK ALL NIGHT, OR AT LEAST MOST OF IT, BUT I DID IT: I FOUND A serviceable analysis option on CATCH_A_WAVE and hacked it into a digitizer. Soon all of the messy, scribbly waveforms were transformed into an orderly array of ones and zeroes, packed into the parallel computer's optical memory like a sea of eggs neatly distributed among the wells of a vast carton. Rita loaded the conversion program the next morning.

"It'll take a long time—hours, maybe—for EDGAR to unscramble Jeff's instructions and put them in a dataflow format your parallel machine can understand," Rita said. "I've got a class. I'll stop by later."

By lunchtime the conversion was complete. The next chore would be to slog through the endless chain of instructions to determine where one sim stopped and the next one began. Unless, of course, Jeff had organized the sims as ordinary data files and ... no, impossible, I decided. They were much too complicated. It couldn't be done.

But then again, if he *had*, that would mean the files would have names, and we could just order up a directory to see those names, and then we could make selections and play sims as if we were operating a juke box and the sims were top-forty hits.

Just like Dex suggested.

"I'm not bothering you with all this keyboard activity, am I?" I asked Dex, hoping he'd say yes and get up and leave and then I could see whether he'd been right all along, that our ventilation-shaft burrowing maneuvers had been an absurd waste of effort. He knew what a directory looked like. Laying across his bed with his nose in a molecular biology textbook, the slightest sideward glance would tell him just how foolish we'd been to ignore his sensible suggestion to try Jeff's computer out first.

"Hardly," he replied.

"You don't need to use EDGAR, do you?" I asked, hoping he'd say yes and get up and leave to find a free terminal somewhere else.

"Nope."

I dithered. I studied my fingernails. I scribbled out some thoughts on my final Dynamics problem set. I looked over at Dex and tried to count the number of amino acids in the oligopeptide he was poring over—seventeen, it looked like, an utterly trivial molecule, yet illustrated in multiple colors like a third grader's picture book. Anything to simplify the already easy for technologically challenged biobrats. It was an insult to the sturdy black-and-white words and vector diagrams of my Dynamics text.

By now the curiosity had grown so strong I could feel it pounding in the front of my head and tingling the tips of my fingers. The hell with it, I decided at last. I typed the directory command and turned my head as I hit the <ENTER> key, unable to witness the truth on the screen, feeling like a condemned man refusing to face the firing squad about to do him in.

I peeked. And there it was! Yes indeed, a directory all right, and a full-fledged one at that: file titles, the date each was last fiddled with, even the amount of memory each sim occupied in Jeff's machine. There were dozens of files, but only one with a date more recent than January. That had to be the sim I was looking for.

Dex didn't notice. I was about to clear the screen when Rita's voice startled the life out of me: "Holy shit!" she bellowed from behind me.

The door to our room had been open and I didn't hear her come in. I gestured for her to shut up shut up shut up but she just kept going. "He had a goddamn directory! And his keyboard wasn't even locked!"

Dex's eyes didn't move from his book, but he shook his head in private disapproval. Just like my father.

"Oh, well," Rita continued. "So let's see what we've got."

We ran the sim we'd risked our lives to retrieve, the one that contained the key to my fate, the one that would explain whether Jeff was friend or foe. We watched the screen intently.

"This is garbage," I said finally. "There's nothing here but financial analysis. It's an econometric model."

We played the next three most recent sims. Pipes, a propeller in cavitation, and something that involved a matrix of vertical and horizontal lines connected at various points by little spaced-apart triangles. Dex immediately recognized this as a neurological schematic: the lines represented nerve filaments, and the triangles were their little heads that signal one another by spitting chemical messengers across the spaces—synapses—between them.

"Well, apparently Jeff isn't the traitorous wretch I pegged him for after all," said Rita. "Maybe he's just being Jeff. Anyway, good luck tomorrow. You'll probably need it, but who knows."

After she left I wondered vaguely why she'd been so absolutely sure the keyboard *would be* locked and Jeff's computer *wouldn't have* a menu. And for that matter, why was she so quick to suspect Jeff in the first place? Something smelled.

"Oh, and by the way, I know what it is you're wondering," she said, reentering the room. "Don't worry, I'll save you the trouble of asking. Yes. I'm free for dinner Saturday night."

Or else I was being seduced.

The prim and dreaded Blair E. Stille sat behind a long glass desk with her legs crossed, stroking one of the glass-block supports with her toe. Her desk was completely empty except for a flat black phone, a computer screen, and a black halogen desk lamp with a long, stringy neck that arched over the screen and cast an eye-piercing reflection in the transparent desktop. As I looked around it occurred to me that the entire office, big and anonymously, generically lush like the cavernous lobby downstairs, declared: you're in the citadel of power now, so watch your step. Look out the windows on two sides, gaze at Logan Airport and Boston Harbor, but remember who owns that picturesque view. And draw no comfort from the lush hanging plants. They may add a splash of life to the cold black lines and steel details, but they're just expensive touches.

The secretary who had shown me into the office quickly left. Surrounded on all sides by empty space, I stood alone—a conspicuous alien, a stray cipher. Blair E. Stille spoke into the air, her wire-rimmed glasses pointed at the ceiling, her voice as creaseless as the dark blue suit and white blouse she wore. A small pale man with a bloom of wet black hair huddled at a table to her left.

"Can we start with our term sheet, please? Redemption at investor discretion. Automatic conversion of the preferred at public offering. Full-ratchet antidilution. Full pre-emption. Two demand registrations at company expense. That's our term sheet. Can we start with our term sheet?"

A tinny voice grew out of the phone on the desk. "You know, we've got other sources of financing we can look to. This is a company with depth."

Blair E. Stille laughed tightly. "As much depth as piss on a flat rock."

A pause, as she gestured for me to sit down in a dark leather chair that looked sleek but swallowed me.

The tinny voice grew hesitant.

"Blair, look, I'm just one little guy on the board, all right? We've already got a hunk of change in this venture."

"And that hunk will be sunk when your dog takes a dunk because no one would throw it a bone. Not to mention the bad press your fund will get when the papers find out that two hundred jobs could have been saved if the money men had been just a little more reasonable with their prospective partners. Let's see, how shall I word our press release..."

"Blair, I'll get back to you by four, okay?" said the phone.

"Jerry. Make it two. Okay?" She stabbed a little button on the phone with her finger, cutting the line with a brief burst of static. It sounded as if Jerry had been sucked into oblivion.

"Go!" she said, turning to me. But then she started flipping her fingers back and forth, as if calling me closer. Not sure whether I was coming or going, I said, "Ah—" and then the back of my throat locked up. I sat there helpless. Blair E. Stille saw my confusion.

"Your pitch. Go. Let's hear your story."

"It's about weather forecasting," I managed. "Enhancing it. Making it better, uh, more accurate."

"Why I am talking to you?"

This took me by surprise. "We have an appointment," I stammered, "don't we? I spoke to your secretary early in the week..."

"I had an appointment with Professor Watt and his research assistant. You're not Watt, and we don't finance undergraduates. This isn't the student loan office. Where's your project adviser?"

Probably immersed in thinkable things, I thought, but I said, "Professor Watt asked me to give you this." I handed her the sealed envelope.

Without taking her eyes off me she handed it off to the small pale man, who opened it and passed the contents back to his liege. Then her phone erupted again, this time in a female voice.

"Sorry to interrupt, Ms. Stille," said the phone. "Mr. Trump is on the line."

Blair E. Stille turned quickly to the small pale man. "Archibald, take Mr. Bustamante for some coffee." Looking up at the ceiling again she said, "I'll take it."

Archibald ushered me out of the office, back through the reception area where the receptionist appeared to stifle a giggle, and out to the elevator bank. "Mr. Trump is an investor in one of our funds," he said as the gilt-edged elevator doors opened, and then he muttered, "a very minor investor."

Downstairs at the Au Bon Pain, Archibald treated me to coffee, which I really needed, and a glutinous corn muffin secreting butter, which I definitely didn't. Then he proceeded to tell me about his life, about how he'd studied classics in college and won an award for his thesis on the hellenization of Carthage. And how he had just begun graduate studies at the University of Pennsylvania when he developed an acute terror at the thought of spending his life as an itinerant academic, chasing a dwindling number of permanent tenure positions, wandering for years like Odysseus in search of Ithaca. Had no less a moral authority than Phaedrus exhorted against the futile pursuit of unreachable dreams—"Out of breath to no purpose, in doing much doing nothing"?

At about this time Archibald also discovered—much to his own surprise, mind you!—a hitherto unknown weakness for Porsches, in particular the red 911 with a 3.3 liter turbo and full leather interior and a Blaupunkt slide-out CD sound system. He had to have one. And why not? Archibald was not ashamed, knowing as he did that such cravings reflect naught but the purest altruism. Had Aeschylus not observed that it is easier when we are in prosperity to give advice to the afflicted? So Archibald switched to Wharton. Star Ventures L.P. was his first real job after business school.

Archibald was animated as he related his life's story. He looked taller than he had in Blair E. Stille's office, and his face had color. I also learned that he preferred the name Ronald.

Then a small beeper somewhere on his side went off. "Time to go back," he announced abruptly, scraping his chair against the floor as he rose. I wondered whether the beeper was surgically affixed.

And so we returned to the citadel of power. Archibald marched by the receptionist, waiting just long enough before barking "Hi,

Nancy" to make his contempt for her clear. In the office, Blair E. Stille looked spent. We had been gone perhaps fifteen minutes but now she looked as if she had run a marathon. Her face was shiny with perspiration. The top button of her blouse was open. And the earthy fragrance of the hanging plants seemed stronger, but I may have only imagined this.

Blair E. Stille stared at me, slouching in her chair. She blew a lock of hair out of her left eye and back over her forehead.

"There's really no one like the Don," she said at last, shifting her gaze off to somewhere.

Then she leaned forward and tapped all ten of her fingernails against the desk and said, "Let me explain a few things to you about venture capital. We're not a bank. We don't lend money. We invest in promising new companies, hoping for a big—no, I mean gigantic return. And we're hands-on players. *We'll* structure the company, *we'll* take charge of its board, *we'll* select the officers."

"Then ... what's left for the founders to do?" I asked, genuinely mystified.

Blair E. Stille smiled indulgently through her weariness. "We are to emerging business what the recording industry is to musical talent. Record companies take chances on ridiculous new performers, and we back a portfolio of farfetched entrepreneurial visionaries. Music houses are also hands-on players. They manage the artists, book their concerts, sell their personalities. They can't afford to leave their investments in unguided hands, and neither can we. In fact, we've got about the same win percentage as your average record company, maybe fifteen percent of our portfolio companies earn us a net return. But just one Springsteen, one Scavengers and we're in fat city. We take a hot company public or sell it to a generous conglomerate. What do the founders do? They get rich, and we keep our investors happy."

She got up and walked over to the window behind her desk. "You see that brick building just in front of the Hancock Tower? That's one of our gems. The three top floors of that building are the executive offices of Big-As-Life, Inc. Net income of $11 million on $300 million worldwide gross. Not a great ratio, but we're working on the expense side. We'll have them on NASDAQ by year end."

"What do they make?" I asked.

"Celebrity cut-outs. You know, those stand-up photographs of Roger Clemens and Clinton and Queen Elizabeth that tourists pose in front of. Big-As-Life offers street vendors a very attractive financing package." Perhaps I did not seem sufficiently impressed because she hastily added, "Not that this is a one-product company. They have depth. They're diversifying. Now they sell a line of small-scale stand-ups for the home. 'No-Care Companions,' they're called. Babies in diapers, dogs, cats, that sort of thing. Quite lifelike. And of course they're a lot easier to store than the real thing." She turned around and looked directly at me again. "You know, it took us a long time to locate this little start-up and grow it into a viable business. We had to assess the market very carefully. We had to determine just how many childless, petless consumers would shell out for a hassle-free alternative."

I wondered whether Big-As-Life might further diversify into childbirth-assistance and rape-prevention devices.

"I know you're a researcher," Blair E. Stille continued, returning to her desk, "but try to indulge us. Can your system detect microbursts?"

"No. The scale is too small. But it could probably locate high-risk regions where..."

She shook her head and turned to Archibald/Ronald, who was taking notes. "Scratch the aviation market. What about premature frosts? Can it predict unexpected freezes?"

"Sure! I would certainly hope so. Maybe. I don't know."

"Scratch agriculture, citrus. How about ozone depletion?"

"No."

"So much for the tree huggers. All right, let's try bottom up instead of top down. Exactly what, if any, commercial possibility does your system have?"

She obviously hadn't read our marketing statement. I told her about the value of enhancing long-range weather predictions, how reliable monthly forecasts of temperature range, rainfall levels, wind speeds, and sunshine durations could save mankind untold billions of dollars annually. I stressed the licensing prospects, the government, and the hungry television stations.

Blair E. Stille was staring at me again. Then the female voice in her phone announced, "Ms. Stille, it's Jerry Taylor."

"I'll take it," she replied. "Welcome back, Jerry."

She looked at me and mouthed "ciao" silently, her raised fingertips falling in arpeggio to emphasize the point. We're done, see you later.

Go.

"You call this a date?" Rita complained during our culinary excursion to an Indian restaurant in Central Square. It was Saturday night. "All we've done is harp on the details of your deep freeze by chilly Stille. Can't we talk about something else?"

My limited experience waging romantic protocol had not prevented me from internalizing some important lessons, like the criticality of keeping your dignity and reserve. I knew to a mathematical certainty that eagerness or fluster promised nothing but catastrophic failure. I would not betray discomfort.

"Like what?" I asked casually.

"What about my research? Has it occurred to you that you have never, once, asked me how my work is progressing?"

"You're right," I admitted. "How's your project going, by the way?"

"Don't ask."

Did I need this?

Then she continued, "I just don't know what to do. Every time I identify another linguistic cue, my workload seems to increase exponentially. I feel like I'm farther away from a UROP thesis than when I started."

She was referring to the Undergraduate Research Opportunities Program. Although UROP is open to everyone at MIT, only the brightest and luckiest find a research spot that can lead to a thesis. Dex had one also. My research project wasn't official UROP since Jeff never filled out the paperwork.

What now? *Look into her eyes, caress her with yours!* Yes, that's it. Radiate sensuality. Exude confidence and charm. Formulate a coherent response.

"Hello?" Rita said, dipping her head and staring at my eyes. "You still with me?"

"Don't they all fit into a single speech-recognition model?" I asked hastily.

"Only in the broadest sense. Each new entry causes a disruption at the lowest level, see? So I have to patch things up to accommodate. Too much patching and the whole model starts to unravel. Then I have to start again."

"Maybe you should close the gate on new entries," I suggested. "Develop one approach and stick with it."

"Even though it may be the *wrong* one?" Rita was incredulous. "I'd never get to sleep at night, my blood pressure would shoot out of sight. Why would I waste my time fine-tuning a kluge?"

"To finish a thesis within your lifespan, maybe."

"That's a bullshit approach," said Rita, shaking her head in horror. "You ever hear of that translation program someone developed back in the fifties? The thing was supposed to understand Russian and English, and the day it was unveiled someone told it to translate an English sentence into Russian and then back into English. The sentence was, 'The spirit is willing but the flesh is weak.' The computer came back with, 'The vodka is fine but the meat is rotten.' That's what happens if all you're concerned with is scraping out a thesis. You wind up with a *bête noire* instead of a breakthrough."

Wind up with a what? God, I love it when you're abrasive in another language! But I felt myself losing ground. What started out as a conversation was turning into an embarrassment. My first non-trivial statements of the evening were being received like faulty input data, and I could feel the system about to crash. My dignity was sliding away. I knew this.

"How's the vindaloo?" I asked.

"*Meharbani hai, sab thik hai,*" Rita nodded with what might have been a smile. "Yours?"

"Fine," I answered. I hoped whatever she said didn't mean loathesome. "Say, where'd you grow up?"

"Baltimore. You?"

"Armonk."

"Your father an IBMer?"

"Yup. Taught me everything I know about missing data."

"So again we're back to your project."

I changed the subject. "How often do you work out?"

"Every day," she replied. "You?"

"Close to that." I was on the hairy edge of a fib but not over it, since it all depends on relative proportions. Once a week is close to seven times a week, logarithmically speaking. "You play on any intramural teams?"

"No. You?"

"No."

A few gulps later Rita asked me, "Are you an older child?"

"Yeah. How'd you know?"

"No reason."

So now I tried to analyze this tantalizing little clue from every possible angle as the last of the little curried lumps slid down my throat. Was she offering an explanation for my lackluster conversation or hopelessly naïve research observations? Was she providing me with an excuse or recommending professional help? Either way, I realized, I'd obviously blown it. I just couldn't do anything right.

"Ready to go?" Rita asked. I nodded and paid the check.

A thick fog had settled over the area. Streetlights sprayed bright grainy cones into the mist. Before they visit Cambridge, most people picture a quiet collegiate town laced with narrow Gothic lanes and quaint gabled houses. Actually the place is mostly rather a dump. We walked back toward MIT, down Mass. Ave.—a busy, dirty, noisy city street where oily air rising from the underground subway mixes with grubby urban decay and an occasional, inexplicable smell of stale fish to produce a unique olfactory experience. And yet somehow, despite the stench and gloom, all around us the world seemed colorful and vibrant. Street musicians practiced their raucous refrains. Groups of partyers out on the town, some duded up sharp and others dressed down funky, laughed as they strutted along the sidewalk, not even noticing when they pushed past us. Rita seemed sullen. We were outside the magic, orthogonal to all the activity, our footsteps out of phase with the rhythm of the street. For us there was nothing but the empty strangeness of being separate and apart.

"Sorry for the lack of sparkling dinner conversation," Rita said as we ducked out of the intensifying drizzle for a quick dessert. "I'm not very good at contrived social situations or chitchat."

Come to think of it, neither was I.

Going down in flames I thought as we reached W70 and started up the stairs. *Initiate escape sequence.*

Wiseman, who had apparently been hanging around Rita's door, loped off when he saw us coming. My door was just ahead. "I guess…" I began.

"I'm soaked," said Rita. "You?"

"Pretty much," I agreed.

"Well, I've got a clothesline. Maybe we should stop by my room first."

Reverse fields, neutralize escape sequence! Now this was unexpected. *I suppose I shouldn't underestimate my own appeal*, I thought. Hadn't Larry said that?

It was a warm, still night, and the small window in Rita's single dormroom couldn't even manage basic ventilation, much less meaningful circulation. Rita didn't own a fan. She did, however, own a shelf-top stereo unit. She pressed the SCAN button and the obedient digital circuitry stepped through Aerosmith's erudite analysis of libidinous juvenile appetites and then Madonna's examination of egocentric post-consumerist piety.

Stop it! I admonished myself. No intellectualizing!

Rita stopped the scanning when it came to rest on a syrupy Barry Manilow number. Now I briefly considered leaving.

She switched off the ceiling light and turned on the dime-store lamp with a stained conical shade next to her bed. Without gesture, without words, we began to kiss.

The temperature rose as our clothing fell, and I tried to prepare myself for my first sexual scrimmage since my days and nights with June, all muscle and twitch, her sure hands and prying tongue—distant fires that still burned bright. But now Rita, her naked body a landscape of sinewy spline curves and earthy bramble, was surging over those exothermic memories like a rising sea, consuming them in the irresistible promise of renewed combustion, of steam heat, of simmering reaction enthalpies, all that good stuff.

I promised myself I wouldn't get uptight. I vowed to modulate the cerebral activity.

But it didn't matter, in the end. I would have been right at home. This was no primeval carnal wilderness. This was sex in nerdland.

"How's your nitric acid level?" asked Rita from behind a terrycloth robe on the other side of the room, making sly inquiry as to the current dimensions and rigidity modulus of Max Planck as she fussed with birth control.

And what birth control.

Before I could answer she emerged from the robe in a snugly fitting elastic garment that encircled her hips and extended down to the middle of her thighs. An impregnable chastity corset. Gray bike pants from hell.

I stared at her.

"*Non avere paura, piccolino,*" she reassured me in Italian. "*Riscalderà il tuo spirito come le foreste virgine di Toscano sulla mattina d'ora nell'estate.*"

Whatever she said was of little comfort to me. My knowledge of Italian is confined mostly to the expletives, although I did recognize something about golden summer mornings.

"Surely you don't propose ... a condom just won't do it, huh?"

I asked.

"Not until you've had your AIDS test. The entire perineum is highly vulnerable to viral infiltration, and condoms offer incomplete protection. Particularly when both participants are supine as I plan to suggest."

Incredibly, she looked, well, pretty good, actually, in spite of herself and the absurdity of the appliance she wore. Hands bracing trim hips and fingers curling over her flat, muscular belly, Rita walked like a fashion model showing off a designer girdle she obviously didn't need, bringing tears of envy to the eyes of her girdle-buying audience. Or maybe this was a raunchy ad for topless scuba gear. Fear began to subside into expectation.

We continued to stare at each other.

"Yum!" I said finally, challenging the mounting awkwardness with an attempt at lustful humor.

"What does that mean?" she asked, escalating the awkwardness and then, reconstructing my line of sight, she pointed with her thumbs and reproached, "Watch it, mister. These are the life-giving orbs of nurture, not some adolescent fetish objects."

"Hey, don't get so bent," I said. "I thought we're supposed to enjoy ourselves."

"Oh God, please, let me out of this pre-Oedipal fantasy. I am not your sex toy. Consensual intimacy between two adults is no occasion to celebrate arrested oral development."

"You're not doing much for my nitric acid levels, you know."

"That's just a counterphobic response," Rita retorted. "I'm obviously threatening you, am I not?"

"Do you think all men are pigs?" I suddenly had to know.

"Only when they rut like amorous boars," she replied. "Any other precoital questions?"

"No, I'd say it's time we got started."

And get started we did. It began with diagrams. Rita drew figures and arrows on the standard-issue MIT whiteboard above her bed with a green marking pen that smelled like goocy children's candy, mapping out a proposed series of engagements and looking like nothing so much as John Madden delivering the NFL play-by-play with a grease pencil.

"What do you think?" she asked.

"Seems well thought out," I answered. We stared at each other again.

"What's your problem?" she demanded finally. "Don't you

know that pursuit and seduction are the essence of sexuality?"

Please don't be scared, crooned the stereo. It was Barry Manilow again. There was nothing left to do but assume whiteboard position (A).

I found that the appliance was topologically complete, seamlessly covering the surface, a trap section fully lining the interior. And somehow it was ventilated so the inside portion didn't burst on entry—ingenious!

Not terribly fun, however. The static and dynamic coefficients of friction were mismatched. Worse, interior shifts occurred frequently, sometimes painfully. A kinematic purgatory if ever there was one.

"You're doing a lot better than my old boyfriend," Rita remarked casually as I labored and struggled. "He experienced serious mechanical difficulties the first time. Collapsed like a concertina, then he buckled like an Euler column in failure mode f_2, you know, like in Mechanics of Solids. You took MechE 2.01, right?"

That's when something snapped. I lurched forward, toppling Rita out of Position (A), clamping my lips over the fleshy part of her neck and tickling her mercilessly with my tongue. She yelped, temporarily deafening me as she wriggled out of my grip and caught me in a half nelson, flipping us over in a cascade of flailing arms and tangled legs. We rolled. We tumbled. We disengaged and recoupled. We deviated seriously from the whiteboard game plan.

"Pretty good," Rita said when it was over. She began to erase the whiteboard. "We strayed from my position sequence, but meaningfully."

She may well have been right.

"175 kcal, minimum," she added with approval, shaking her head and billowing her hair with her fingertips. "So much for that Mrs. Field's cookie."

She was referring to the number of calories (kilocalories, technically, as calorimetrists always point out) we had expended. Rita never failed to announce her estimate after a bout, I would soon learn. Average was 150. Somebody was dozing if we didn't make it past 120. We hit 200 and sent out for pizza once.

Once.

"So who was this old boyfriend of limited bending moment?" I asked her.

"Who? Oh, that was rubbish. You were having trouble getting off the dime so I manipulated you. You don't mind, do you?"

"Of course not. I don't expect you to validate the male need to hunt and conquer," I told her. It seemed like the right thing to say.

"Now you're getting it." The birth control came off and Rita slid under the sheets. She began to draw fingernail patterns on my chest, where the hair is a bit sparse, and I thought she was making fun of me until she said, "Time for some intimate exchange, don't you think?"

"What did you have in mind?" I asked.

"Ask me a question. About anything."

"All right. So why are you always copping this attitude of yours, giving people such a hard time?" I knew I had just planted my foot on dangerous ground.

"Good, honest interrogatory, straight to the point," she said. "You don't waste time with diplomacy. I like that."

Was she going to rate my questions or answer them?

"I challenge people I'm fond of," she continued. "I don't mean it as sarcasm. It's my way of expressing affection."

"Then I'm jealous of my roommie. You must adore Dex to pieces."

"No, it really is sarcasm with Drano. I genuinely can't stand him."

"And Boyer?" I asked.

"Nothing but indifference for that presexual narcissist. I tend not to be very interested in people who are only interested in themselves."

"For crying out loud, what does it take to win your approval? I mean, Dex is the nicest guy I know."

Now Rita was getting all serious. The chest designs stopped. "First of all," she said, "nice people make me uncomfortable. They hurt without meaning to. When my father remarried after my parents' divorce, he was so nice to his new wife that he began to confuse his stepdaughter with his real daughter, and now we see each other three, maybe four times a year. If he hadn't been so nice to me when I was growing up, maybe it wouldn't have cut so deep, you know what I'm saying?"

"Rita, I..." I began as my face flushed with regret at initiating this whole discussion.

But without missing a beat she continued, "Second of all, Drano isn't so nice."

"How can you say that?" I countered. "You know, he's the one who introduced me to Star."

"Sure I know that. Did you ask him whether he got a finder's fee?"

I must have looked stricken. How could she say such a thing about Dex? What did she have against him? And what if it were true?

"He's a mechanic," she continued. "A robot. You like him because he seems easygoing, and he is, in a detached sense. But one day he'll just be another faceless bureaucrat building his empire, pampering his budget. Like the one that turned my too-nice father into an unemployed neurotic."

"I thought your father was a physicist," I said.

"He is. That doesn't mean he gets paid."

"So why isn't anyone paying him?"

"He was working on Star Wars over at Stinson, in their Shreveport facility of all places—ninety-four locations worldwide and they send this quiet little Jew with his pregnant new wife to David Duke land. Anyway, what's left of Star Wars is really two separate programs—a laser program, which is supposed to knock incoming missiles down with directed-energy beams, and a ballistic program, which is supposed to knock them down with precisely aimed little cannon balls. Stinson has engineers and scientists working in each group. As you can imagine, they compete fiercely with each other for dwindling federal money. But the unwritten rule is you never, ever question the feasibility of the other group's research, since that could jeopardize funding for the entire program. My father broke the rule. He was trying to be helpful. He made a suggestion to a manager in lasers, told him why their current approach wasn't working. The manager smelled criticism and got pissed off, and my father's ballistics buddies turned on him as if he were a traitor."

"And he's been out of work ever since?" I asked.

"Can I finish, please? Stinson fired him, told him he'd never work for another defense contractor again. But the Pentagon procurement team had him reinstated. If he was so sure the Stinson lasers wouldn't work, they figured, maybe he could come up with a way to make them work. But six months later he proved mathematically that they *couldn't* work, ever, period. So this time the government had him fired. He was an irritant..."

"And the machine just ejected him," I said.

"You got it. Engineers play by the rules. Scientists discover them. My father would rather be an out-of-work scientist than a bureaucrat who toasts every miserable little efficiency increase."

She reached over me and switched off the lamp on the desk. "Just don't turn into Dex, okay?" she said as she curled her arm around my chest. What an exquisite feeling to have another body next to mine, pressed up against me from head to toe.

We fell asleep. After what seemed like only minutes, the sun spread a brilliant parallelogram of morning light onto the far wall of the room, and I awoke, hot and still tired, turning over to smile at Rita and stroke her hair gently but there she was already, hovering over me like a rubberized mermaid from the Frederick's of Hollywood catalog. She was up, sitting on her knees next to me, waiting. This time the protective girdle was a fashionable lime green.

"You're inexhaustible," I marveled. "A true serial port."

Rita rolled her eyes. "And so now I'm supposed to tell you what a big dynamic RAM you have? Pay homage to your refresh rate?"

I wondered if I could get used to this for the next twenty-six months or so.

Definitely, I concluded.

10

IN JULY I HIT MY FIRST CRISIS POINT. THANKS TO THE MUSHROOM.

At the very center of the MIT campus a slim, twenty-story concrete block called Building 54, sometimes known as the Cecil and Ida Green Building, suddenly juts out of the ground and towers over everything else like a brooding monolith. It houses the Department of Earth, Atmospheric, and Planetary Sciences, their chemistry laboratories, and a networked array of VAX minicomputers. Perched on its roof is a great white mushroom. The mushroom belongs to the Center for Meteorology and Physical Oceanography. It contains a Doppler weather radar array.

Finals come and go without incident, the technology I've learned firmly encrusted under my skin. My summer TAship is a breeze. The mushroom is an unnoticed detail, a curiosity that greets every MIT visitor between thoughts and glances before disappearing from attention.

The summer advances. And in the quiet that suffuses the campus between spring and fall semesters, I begin to draw connections. The damn thing looks like Jeff's computer up there with its round body, its fan-bladed underside, its slender support stem. I haven't heard from Jeff in weeks. Maybe it's been months. I wonder if I've still got a faculty adviser. I wonder if I'm even getting course credit for my project. I wonder why I keep noticing that stupid mushroom.

It seems fitting for MIT to own a Doppler radar system. The mushroom's belly carries the youngest lineal descendant of the very first weather radar system, invented right here, and provides its progenitor with the most advanced meteorology electronics available. Only a world-class institution churning out leading-edge work could possibly acquire so costly an apparatus, not to warn aircraft of high wind shear or impending storms, not to steer ships clear of waterspouts, but strictly as a research prop—a gigantic test instrument for speculation and fancy. An extravagant gamble on the ingenuity of its keepers.

The mushroom is a monument to MIT's legacy. It rests proudly and awkwardly atop Cecil and Ida, a ludicrous crown, usurping the building's dignity and casting it into the servile role of pedestal—as inconsequential as the little formica table underneath Jeff's computer whose only purpose is to support the weight of overlying spherical eminence.

And now the mushroom is everywhere.

Approach the building from the south, walk beneath or to the side of the ugly Calder sculpture that stands in your way and the globular beast is there already, eyeing you and the Calder like an alien come to view abstract art. Stroll down Memorial Drive past Building 50, the Walker Memorial, with its somber Ionic columns and bronze doors and there it is again, suspiciously peering at you over the friezes and their inscribed paeans to the Great Men of Science. And now it's right outside my window, every day, off in the distance over the indoor-tennis bubble, proclaiming the greatness of MIT, impersonating Jeff's electronic masterpiece, chastising my scant research progress, roaring the silence of its implacable other-worldly symmetry until I can't keep a thought in my head.

And so I finally begin spending most of my free time in the Lindgren Library, located in Building 54 and boasting the best view on campus—namely, the only one from which you can't see the hated mushroom since it's directly overhead on the roof. And occasionally I wander away from the laptop I've plugged into EDGAR at one of the study carrels and roam the silent, secluded stacks of meteorology treatises and periodicals. And I flip through *Tellus* and the *Journal of the Atmospheric Sciences* until I become lost in the sea of Greek squiggles and hessian matrices and isobar diagrams and finally it strikes me like a lightning shock wave: I'm barely a college junior trying not only to understand the excruciatingly complex work of distinguished professors and graduate students, but also to build on that work. It's an absurd, quixotic conceit!

That's what I tell my parents. I explain that I understand my statistics but feel hopelessly lost and inadequate, like a woodworking neophyte who only knows how to use the band saw trying to make a better coffee table than anyone else in the shop even though they all know how to rip and sand and drill and rout. I tell them I'm lost. That I'm drowning in self-doubt and despair. That I'm in way over my head.

My mother says, "For this they charge $25,000 a year?"

My father listens. He thinks it over. Finally he points out, with some disapproval, that woodshops do not provide a useful metaphor for scientific investigation. "And remember: a power tool is not a toy. Ha ha! Ever hear that one? Come on, cheer up."

Rita is also helpful. She says, "How come we never go out?"

It occurs to me: we've made substantial progress, Rita and I. Now I draw the whiteboard diagrams as often as she does. And who needs to go out? I'm fully wired into all of life's essentials right here. A keystroke delivers limitless computing power. EDGAR tells me the time, keeps my calendar, clocks my laundry, reminds me when it's time to eat, sorts my electronic mail, plays bingo, calculates in real and imaginary numbers of any dimension, checks my grammar, balances my checkbook, could probably devise innovative new whiteboard diagrams. And I teach it nothing. EDGAR has recently been outfitted with an assimilation feature that monitors my habits and activity patterns.

It knows, for instance, that I'm working on weather and missing data; it can tell because I log on at Lindgren so often and from the statistical techniques I use. So EDGAR constantly searches through the MIT library database for new journal entries to tell me about without my even asking. It's discovered I tend to check the clock every twenty minutes or so, and now the clock window appears automatically just before I'm tempted to click it on. Last month it asked me where I go every Tuesday morning from ten to twelve-thirty since it has my TA schedule and knows there are no classes, and now it inquires if I've had a good workout when I log on Tuesday after lunch. They're talking about adding a newspaper-access feature. If they do and if I had the time to read newspapers, EDGAR would learn my news-reading proclivities and assemble a custom on-screen journal heavy on technology features with a sprinkling of sports and no metro. They're talking about electronic problem sets. They're talking about electronic interviews and career advice.

EDGAR cares. It understands me thoroughly. EDGAR is my biggest fan.

So what if my girlfriend drags herself around in baggy, frumpy sweats? So what if she gets on my nerves sometimes and fails to fulfill my every dream? We satisfy for each other the needs EDGAR can't reach. We laugh sometimes. We share the security of knowing what to expect. Besides, it would just be another, what, twenty months?

So I answer Rita's question by pointing out that although it's summer and most of the students have dispersed from the area, we'd still probably have to wait at least an hour to get into any worthwhile restaurant since many of them close for the season due to lack of foot traffic, keeping the diner-to-seating ratio not only constant but well in excess of one. And as for movies, sure you can get in, but it's axiomatic that the film selection will be limited to the most juvenile tripe imaginable since studios aim their summer sights squarely at the bored out-of-school crowd, assuring not only inferior cinema but high-decibel audience participation as well.

That dose of statistical reality is enough to end the matter. Before she leaves Rita warns me that objects in motion tend to remain in motion, but an object sitting at his desk is in danger of remaining forever at his desk. I knew she'd say that.

And now the crisis eases, the despair lifts. Because I realize I can think of no greater joy than to live the pure harmony of scientific precision and consistency, to acquire knowledge of the universe's operational details denied to those not equipped to pass through these MIT halls, to master the unending mysteries presented in impossible problem sets, obscure textbooks and fast-paced lectures filled with arcane equations and symbols—the exclusive language of a closed priesthood.

How fortunate I am just to be sitting in the air-conditioned stillness of the Lindgren Library, interacting with EDGAR, fighting with the parallel computer to get my numbers to work, tormenting myself as I pore over obscure journal entries, understanding just a hair more than I did before, and basking in the beneficent grace of the stern but endlessly patient mushroom. The journey has become as important as the destination. At last I belong.

o   o   o

"Have you heard anything from Star yet?" Dex asked me.

"Not a thing," I replied. It had been almost three months.

"Don't worry. They take their time unless they sense blood in the water—when you're being chased by other VCs, that is. They'll call soon."

I wasn't worried, actually. I'd formulated a plan. During my last meteorology class before finals, our instructor had launched into a sudden tirade against the corruption of scientific research and its appalling neglect of the environment. How do these fools expect to diagnose the effects of pollution and population, he lamented, without understanding the atmosphere's fundamental physiology and metabolic quirks? Not since 1978, when the World Meteorological Organization's Global Atmospheric Research Program (GARP) got into action, had the air and oceans gotten a real physical. A yearlong, $500 million megaproject involving 149 countries, five geosynchronous satellites, four polar-orbiting satellites, 50 research ships, 110 aircraft, 300 weather balloons, 300 instrument-drifting buoys and dozens of compound acronyms, GARP sampled, probed, poked, prodded, and listened to the atmosphere's vital signs around the world and at different vertical levels.

The world according to GARP, that gargantuan mountain of data, was the answer to my financing frustrations. So what if I couldn't afford field tests? I could grab a hunk of data, pretend they were current observations, use them to make predictions, and then consult the historical records to check my accuracy. It smacked of spectatorship rather than participation, but what the heck. Maybe some promising results would earn the price of admission to a GARP of my own. Then Star could keep its money.

A knock at the door.

It was Boyer. So few undergraduates around MIT during the summer, and he had to be one of them.

He and Dex began to talk as I tapped away at the keyboard and clicked my mouse, struggling with EDGAR as usual. I was vaguely aware they were discussing the upcoming BioVitrics move, the crating schedule, locations for new research equipment not yet arrived. Finally I stored my data, getting ready to head over to Lindgren, when I realized I had become the topic of their conversation.

"Hey Paul," said Dex oh so eagerly, "show him your dating-game circulation model." And turning to Don he said, "You'll love this. Paul here has a multidimensional model, you see, and it's got him slated to meet his permanent zygote counterpart come graduation. What about you? Ready to face the truth?"

"It's just some common-sense statistical footwork," I said in my best self-effacing reserve after Dex's introduction, which might have been glowing or mocking, I couldn't tell which. "Nothing all that elaborate, really."

Don said: "Uh-duh."

I detested this puerile habit of his, the way he proclaimed the obviousness of a proposition with a sarcastic suggestion of imbecility.

"Go ahead," Dex gestured to Don, and to my growing annoyance. "One to ten. Tell him how attractive you want your future gamete partner to be."

"Six point five," said Don without hesitation.

I was shocked. How could someone with as high an opinion of himself as Don Boyer request such a modest ranking?

Don recognized my surprise. "Orgasm intensity is not a function of beauty, you know," he said. "Besides. The high-end models are unreliable and cost too much in upkeep. I'm looking for a source, not a sink." We faced each other in silence. "I suppose this realistic notion offends you?" Don asked derisively.

"Not particularly," I told him. "I'm a realist myself, in case you hadn't noticed."

"Well, then maybe there's hope for you yet." Don turned to Dex. "Anyhow," he said, "I thought we were going to start the inventory."

Thank God.

"Sure, we can begin with the pen. Paul, why don't you come along? You've never even seen what it is I do for a living. It'll be a lot harder to get access once we've moved." Then he looked at me reproachfully, as if to forestall any excuses. "I know all about *your* research pursuits, do I not?"

You don't know a damn thing if you think I'm still screwing around with a circulation model that crude, but what can I say?

We all walked up to the northern reaches of the MIT campus, toward Central Square, where sterile university buildings begin to share space with abandoned brick warehouses and forlorn housing projects. Not your ideal research neighborhood, but probably safe enough in daylight.

Dex led us into an unmarked, unnamed brick building, indistinguishable from its surroundings except for the concrete handicap-access ramp, new windows, and stylish signs warning of the building's security system—the emblems of university ownership. We took a small freight elevator, its hoists and metal fittings recently masked with a thick coat of light blue paint, downstairs. It was a basement, sort of: high ceilings, painted cinder-block walls, and modern fluorescent lights presiding over unimproved dirt floors. There were no solid partitions; I could see from one end of the large space to the other.

A number of research groups had staked out patches of territory. Their little plots were demarcated by cordons of electronic equipment on metal racks, fencing struts, and chicken wire. Animals were everywhere—lumbering across the floor, slithering up the walls, pawing at the walls of their prisons. The low-frequency drones of massive dehumidifiers and air-exchange units blended with bleats and squeals and gobbles into a confused, buzzing chorus. At least the place didn't smell all that bad despite the abundance of fauna. Car fumes in E42, animal odors here—MIT must have been pioneering the techniques of mass-scale ventilation.

It certainly made sense for MIT to keep this *in vivo* research building as anonymous as possible. Just a little notoriety would have all the curious pranksters and animal-rights activists descending on the place, causing all kinds of havoc.

We dodged the scattered research parcels until we reached the far end of the space, where a cow stood in a small pen formed by wooden struts set against two corner walls. Hay was scattered about the floor within the pen. The cow munched away. This little arrangement was ridiculous, it looked manufactured, like someone was shooting a low-budget sagebrush movie and this was the ersatz ranch set. Even the cow was overdone—black-and-white markings, patient chewing and a near constant whipping of its tail: an absurd bovine quintessence.

The only piece of equipment anywhere near the pen was an old hydraulic winch on wheels, positioned off to one side now but which could easily be brought to the fencing so its boom would reach over the cow's little virtual pasture.

Dex gestured to Don, who promptly opened the gate to the pen. Well, well: what a difference employment makes. Once admired, now you're hired, eh Don? Maybe six point five shouldn't have come as such a surprise.

"We implanted four bone replacement segments, one in each leg," Dex explained as he entered the pen. "The replacements are sturdy as hell, thick metal rods coated with our glass. The rods fit into the marrow of the natural bone and the glass bonds with surrounding muscle and cartilage. That's what I was doing on Easter, helping implant them."

"Why did the cow need bone replacements?" I asked.

Dex looked at me quizzically, the way I looked at him when my talk of math or computers left him clueless. "An old skiing injury," he said, rolling his eyes. "What do you think? We removed fifteen-centimeter sections from each of its legs so we could test our replacements. That's the whole point."

Dex scratched the cow's head. "Look at her forelegs," he said, bending down. "Good as new, no scars even."

"Mooo-o-o-o," said the cow, shaking its head. Its eyes shined like mammoth black pearls.

"What's her name?" I asked.

"Oscar," said Dex.

"Why did you name a cow Oscar?"

"Because if it hadn't stood up after we unhooked the winch, it'd be Oscar Mayer cold cuts by now. Right Oscar?" said Dex as he scratched the cow's head again.

Don snickered. Those Course 7 types were so clever.

"Mooo-o-o-o," said the cow.

"But it's a female," I protested, earning a pair of irritated looks.

"Uh-duh," said Don.

God, I hated it when he did that.

"It's a subject, is what it is," Dex responded.

"So who's the grunt responsible for cleaning up the mess when Oscar does what cows do?" I asked, glancing briefly at Don, hoping he'd turn out to be the designated grunt.

"All contracted out. Our original NIH grant took care of that. Paul, watch your sleeve, unless you're into cow snot," Dex warned as Oscar nudged me with her wet nose.

"Have you figured out how your glass stuff works yet?" I asked.

"We have a few chemical theories, an ion-exchange mechanism or two. It's not that important. We're more concerned with results. And these," said Dex, looking approvingly at Oscar's gams as he paced around her, "are terrific results."

"Does that mean you can start selling the stuff?" I asked.

Dex laughed. "All it means for now is we'll get more money. VCs like milestones. They give you a little money first, set progressive goals, and make additional money contingent on reaching those goals. Oscar was our first. Star's scientific advisory board wanted us to prove that our implants could support twice the weight of an average human. Oscar weighs 1,200 pounds, so that's 300 pounds per leg—a perfect test creature."

"Who's on the board setting these milestones?" I asked.

"Oh, let's see, a couple of other MIT profs, a Harvard emeritus, two or three docs from Mass. General Hospital. The usual suspects."

"And what will you do with the new money?"

"Begin our clinicals. Get enough results to convince a pharmaceutical company to buy us out, or just go public. Maybe spend a couple of weeks on St. Tropez." They laughed. "Your uncle Tony's on board, you know. He'll be our premier evaluator for dentistry applications."

Grant money from the National Institutes of Health to dispatch dung, venture money to fund commercialization, and a group of Pap's fellow scientists to set achievable money-liberating milestones so everyone could dance south to ogle topless Europeans. What a racket!

And was I jealous.

It wasn't long before the good news arrived in a triplet burst.

Rita's adviser had gotten his federal matching grant renewed. That meant she and the rest of her research team would be able to travel to Scottsdale, Arizona, the site of this year's International Conference on Speech Recognition. Who knows, maybe Rita would have a paper of her own to present—that is, read verbatim in front of a collection of name tags that read, "HELLO my name is—" pinned to a motley mob of mandarins, some of whom would applaud politely, others who would vie for the opportunity to skewer your research in the hope of advancing their own.

And then I got a call. "This is Archibald," said the voice on the phone. "You remember, Ronald."

How could I forget? Make an appointment with Maurice Herman, Star's patent attorney, right away, he told me. Jeff and I should be prepared to provide Mr. Herman with a full written description of our concept to enable him to evaluate the prospects for patent protection. That would be the next step in the review process.

Yeah, baby!

And then the third momentous piece of news: in two weeks Dex and Pap would appear on the *Today Show*. BioVitrics had attracted the attentions of media giants.

"They want you to talk to the patent lawyer?" Dex exclaimed when I told him. "Then you're in! Star never hires expensive outside consultants unless they're really serious. I'll bet Blair's already preparing her presentation to the board."

Even Jeff, it seemed, became caught up in the mounting excitement. The big chief was back on the reservation. Said he'd be happy to connect, meet with the patent lawyers, smoke peace-pipe, whatever. Whenever and wherever.

Good thing I'd trusted him. That mystery letter of his to Blair E. Stille clearly hadn't hurt us, Ronald's call proved that. Maybe Jeff had even made the difference.

Maurice Herman's law firm was in one of those tall, ungainly granite-panel buildings in downtown Boston. They were all over the place now. Sterile, nondescript, efficient and completely out of place in this strongly traditional city, they seemed to signal the onset of sober, pragmatic times. Realism was everywhere now.

Maurice Herman emerged from the corridor on the left of the receptionist's station in a march of heavy footsteps and an intense vapor zone of Old Spice. Maurice Herman, Esquire. A man to be reckoned with. Tall with an important lantern jaw, an important bald head and a big important gut, he wore a silk bow tie, red braces, and sensible shoes. Elite but pragmatic, urbane yet rational.

The whole office was set up that way. Lots of chrome, no gold or marble. We followed Maurice Herman—"Call me Mo, please"—as he strode purposefully down a hall chock full of computer equipment but only an occasional staff person.

"No word-processing center," he announced proudly, "no billing department, no operations retinue. We're lean and mean."

So was his office. The spare surroundings doubled as a trophy room: laminated degrees from Cal Tech and Harvard Law School, Tau Beta Pi engineering honors, admission certificates from three states and the Patent and Trademark Office, and a halfway decent view of the city to boot. But his desk, while large, was scratched-up teak.

"Is everyone here an engineer?" I asked.

Mo Herman scowled. "We're more than technologists. We're lawyers," he explained in a deep, resonant voice.

"You know, you look just like George Forman," said Jeff, which was probably exactly what everyone thought when they met Mo Herman, and probably exactly what he didn't want to hear. "Did you play, like ... ball once?"

The scowl intensified. At least Jeff was relatively presentable in a tweed sportjacket and faded jeans. But those sandals.

A junior-looking lawyer came into the room carrying a yellow pad. "My associate, Suzanne Harris," said Mo Herman.

She gripped our hands firmly as she said, "Call me Sue. I've been looking forward to meeting you both." Her manner was confident but her eyes gentle. She looked like someone who could have a jury eating out of her hand.

"Let me explain who Frederick & Williams are and what we do," Mo Herman began as Sue dragged a chair next to him. "This is an intellectual property law firm. Anything worthwhile that seeps out of your brain, we can protect. Inventions, books, art—we'll make sure the law covers it, and if someone tries to steal it"—he slammed his huge palm against the desk, sending a pen flying overhead—"we'll land all over them." No one made a move to pick up the pen, which was leaking bright blue ink onto the well-worn institutional carpet.

He continued, "For our venture capital clients, we assess just how much protection a potential investment is likely to get for its inventions. Protection is money. An investment isn't worth much if everyone can steal its technology, can we all agree on this?"

We could.

"Now, I have reviewed the details of your disclosure. Elegant approach. Deft mathematics, I'm sure. But I'm not convinced what you have is an invention."

"So I guess we're done, then?" asked Jeff. He seemed anxious to leave.

Mo Herman's scowl returned. "Not so fast. I didn't say we couldn't patent it. I said I don't think it's an invention. But that's just my opinion. I'm difficult to impress, and we're very skillful about dealing with the Patent Office."

"So we're in!" I exclaimed. "I'm going to get a patent!"

"I didn't say that either," the scowl replied. "What I said was, you won't be denied a patent because your idea is not an invention. There are other grounds on which your application may be rejected."

"What concerns us," said Sue, "is that your whole approach seems to boil down to the math. But you can't patent the latest way to crunch numbers unless you do something with the solution besides displaying it. That's how the Patent Office stops people from getting monopolies over mother nature."

I looked over at Jeff. He stared silently ahead.

"Well, of course we do more than parade numbers. We create

forecasts," I said.

Mo Herman held up the huge palm, now stained blue with ink from the injured pen. "Not enough," he announced. "The forecast is still just reportage. It's what the Patent Office calls insignificant post-solution activity. The cases cited in 1106 O.G. 5, September 5, 1989 explain all this."

"Is that correct?" Sue asked us. "Or do you do something more with the output?"

Jeff said: "I always remember Kiangsu in March—the cry of the partridge, the mass of fragrant flowers."

The lawyers looked at each other. I wanted to die.

"Let's try something different. How do you acquire your data?" Sue asked.

"From satellites, land stations, ship reports..." I said.

"So it's transmitted from observation points?" she continued.

"Exactly."

"Well," said Mo Herman, "that's mere data-gathering. And not enough to satisfy the patent laws, I'm afraid. *See, e.g., In re Richman,* 195 USPQ 340 (1977), *In re Gelnovatch...*" His head rocked left and right.

"Wait a minute," interjected Sue. "Sounds like something we could characterize as signal processing." For our benefit she explained, "If your input is an electrical signal, and you monkey around with it, the courts have ruled you're not guilty of mere data-gathering. Even though that's just what you're doing. Thank heaven for *In re Johnson* and progeny."

"But you heard him," Mo Herman protested. "It's not a signal, it's just a stream of numbers. Well within the principles announced in *In re Sarkar,* 200 USPQ 132, and, I might add, some of the more recent cases I trust you've perused."

"If it's a continuous stream, it's no different from a signal," she insisted. "And remember, if you've got a signal, it doesn't matter whether it's represented mathematically or electrically. *In re Taner* started that ball rolling."

"Taner, eh?" asked Mo Herman as he stroked his chin. "That a CAFC case?"

"CCPA, actually, 214 USPQ 678, 681 F.2d 787 (1982). It's still good law, believe me."

"In spite of *In re Grams?*"

"It was cited in *Grams.*"

Now Mo Herman pursed his lips into an embarrassed, pointy

smile and taptaptapped his fingertips together. "Well," he exhaled, "perhaps there is room for optimism after all. Perhaps so. We shall get back to Ms. Stille, and she will get back to you if she so chooses."

"Multithanks," said Jeff to Sue as he rose from his chair. As he shook Mo Herman's hand he said, "And to you, too. I enjoyed the half-cycle phase shift."

Mo Herman smiled indulgently. "My secretary will call you a taxi. Opal!"

"We'll take the T," said Jeff.

"No intercoms," muttered Mo Herman, not hearing Jeff. "Opal! Opal!"

We finally extracted ourselves from the office, politely and with some shred of dignity, but I could hardly contain my rage. Why did Jeff have to compound his Zen non sequitur with that obnoxious, gratuitous parting comment? Why did he have to tell Mo Herman what a kick he got out of the guy's 180° change of heart? Why had he agreed to come along at all? Just so he could blow this whole goddamn deal?

"Don't worry," said Jeff, sensing my discomfort as the elevator doors closed. "He didn't understand me. Mr. Herman is no electrical engineer; probably mechanical, or worse yet, chemical. I just wanted to be sure. From this point forward we deal with Sue."

"Where's the Kiangsu, anyway?" I asked.

"Ah ... the Kiangsu," he said wistfully. "Actually, I threw that in to break Herman's stranglehold on the meeting. I wanted to give Sue an opportunity to express her own ideas. And I was pretty impressed, what about you?"

There was just no figuring Jeff.

11

"YOU'RE JUST NOT GETTING THIS, ARE YOU?" RITA ASKED ME. DEX
had already pretty much given up. "It's an argot, just another language to learn. And not a terribly hard one, either. The buzzwords
are so superficial."

I fingered the fax transmission nervously. A presentation to
potential investors! Term sheet to follow. Appearance at 10:00 AM
in the John Philips Salon at the Boston Harbor Hotel. Star also
faxed a copy of the investor invitation, engraved in flowing script.
The invitation doubled as a return postcard. In addition to the
scheduling particulars it said: *Yes! I want to know more about this
exciting investment opportunity!** And at the bottom, in plain fine
print: **Nothing in this invitation shall be construed as an offer to
buy or sell securities. Purchases and/or sales of securities are made
solely by way of a prospectus, which when furnished is hereby
incorporated herein and made a part hereof.*

At no point did they ask me whether I would be free to attend.
I'd just better be.

Gone, I realized, were my early days at MIT, lazy Sunday after-
noons drinking illicit beers with Dex and his friends, marvelling at
the latest research news out of the different Institute laboratories
or lost in hopelessly earnest debate over the great science questions—what's the fundamental building block of matter? what's
the reach of the universe and how will it end?—blissfully unconcerned about our hermetic isolation from the lazy Sunday after-
noons of college freshmen everywhere else, the overwhelming *importance* of what was being discussed obscuring the comic mysti-
cism of the discussion itself.

But now the real world had intruded. That place outside where
the sincerest form of flattery is the sound of money changing hands.

"You've read newspapers, right?" Rita continued. "Cracked

the business section every now and then? All the vocabulary you need is right there. Just look at your audience and see who they are, so you can custom-tailor the jargon. If they look athletic, say you're recruiting an unbeatable management team. If someone's wearing a sailor's cap, tell him your hand is firmly on the tiller. Praise the fundamentals for the fundamentalists. Get it?"

Dex decided to try again. "And when it comes to the technology, story rules. Talk people instead of science. Lament the ill-timed vacations on the Riviera scuttled by unexpected storms, the 70-foot yachts sunk by hurricanes." Dex was standing now, lecturing with his thumb and index finger pinched together, bouncing his hand up and down with the cadence of his voice. "Don't get too detailed. Stick to metaphor. Talk about the nonlinearity of everyday existence. Compare violent weather to life's struggles and the mysteries of life to, oh I don't know, the caprice of the zephyr."

Scientific metaphor! My father would collapse with rage. That made it fun. But I still wasn't getting it, the words weren't coming. Dex somehow knew zephyrs but my brain went blank on business. And with just one week to prepare. Blair had done her part by Fed Exing me a copy of Donald Trump's book, *The Art of the Deal*. Useless. I'd even tried to read it.

I reminded myself that the same day I would be trying to avoid looking stupid in front of twenty or so prospective investors, Dex would be risking full frontal humiliation before millions at the hands of the evil Bryant Gumbel.

Star had pointedly failed to invite Jeff to their dog-and-pony show. The only emissary besides me would be Ronald, whose job would be to keep the presentation honest and thereby save Star from promoter liability. They were taking no chances.

So to complete the fullness of my suffering, or maybe to express resentment, Jeff had managed to replace the EDGAR logo on our screen with the Eastern symbol of yin and yang—you know, the circle with black and white halves separated by a wiggly S-shaped line, each half containing, at its fat end, a small dot of the opposite shade. That symbol spooked me from the very first time I saw it—on a sign inside the window of a new-age bookstore in Armonk, where June bought me the paperback edition of the Kama Sutra. I thought it depicted two one-eyed fish endlessly swimming around one another with perfect rotational symmetry.

Maybe Jeff thought it would calm me down. That in itself was enough to make me nervous. When you think too much, others' good intentions usually produce opposite effects. As a kid I would grow terrified at the sight of the aquarium in my pediatrician's office. I figured if this guy went to the trouble and expense of ripping up his walls to install an elaborate backlit tank with fancy fish just to distract his frightened subject from the silvery arc of fluid streaming out the business end of a syringe, it was a sure bet the needle would hurt like hell and there was every reason to be scared.

"Well, I think that completes tonight's tutorial," Rita said. "You know epsilon more than when we started, and I've got to put in some time at the lab. You coming by later?" I wondered if Dex was at all intrigued with our relationship. He hadn't had a single date since we'd begun MIT together nearly two years before. Did he get jealous when I wouldn't return until morning? Did he whisper about us with Don? Surely he boiled with curiosity. He just held himself back with that New England discretion and reticence, that was all.

Epsilon, incidentally, is a very small number.

"I'll be there," I told her.

I turned to Dex as the door closed behind her. "This really means a lot to me. I can't thank you enough."

"Please. You're making me moist."

"No, really. I wish there were something in it for you."

I was taking a sounding. Dex said nothing.

"You deserve a finder's fee," I said finally.

"Oh, I'll probably land a couple of K or something equally trifling if this thing flies." Then Dex looked up at me, as if surprised. "Perhaps we should split it. Yes, that seems fair, doesn't it? I mean, why should I profit from your work and good fortune without sharing it with you?"

Now I didn't know what to think. His willingness to divvy what to him were obviously negligible spoils made me feel petty. He was entitled to reward for his efforts, and who was I, the beneficiary, to deny it to him? But maybe he also sensed the subterranean sleaziness of marketing your roommate for financial gain and was trying to wriggle out of shame by trivializing his motives.

"I'm not worried about it," I punted.

As if to emphasize his virtue, Dex added, "I've designed some presentation-graphics transparencies for you to display from an overhead, if you want. They show the year-to-year projections as bar graphs in three colors. Investors eat this stuff up."

I thanked him profusely and again the yin-yang thing on the

screen caught my eye. It occurred to me that this might be a good time to visit Jeff and ask him to get rid of it.

The frats along Memorial Drive were getting ready for fall. As I walked past them I could hear a stereo booming from Kappa Sig and someone drumming a trap set in Theta Delta Xi. Frat parties at MIT can be pretty loud and grungy affairs. That's why women rarely show up, which, of course, largely defeats the whole purpose. The weather was also hinting at autumn as the isotherms began their southward retreat, dragging away the summer haze. Clear sunlight turned all the brick buildings a vivid deep red and a steady wind ruffled the sails of small boats in the Charles River. Across the water all of Boston wore an aqua sheen, washed in the intense blue-light scatter of a cloudless sky.

These days a brief stare was enough to persuade Jeff's door to open itself. The office was unlit, as usual, and filled with the odor of something that smelled a little like tea, but more like straw or raw wood.

"Ho!" said Jeff in the dim light of his screen.

"...Right. I just came to ask—"

"And I have answered you."

"But—"

"Ho!" said Jeff. "End of discussion." His gaze returned to his screen.

I left feeling strangely satisfied. I knew stopping by Jeff's would be a good idea.

o   o   o

"Who or what are you thinking about?" Rita demanded with acutely unfortunate timing later that night, truncating a perfectly serviceable rising sexual peak.

"What?" I panted as the excitement dissipated.

"Cindy Crawford? Claudia Schiffer?"

"What ... are you talking about?"

"You think my eyesight shuts down when I'm on my back?" she persisted, raising herself on her elbows. "I look up and see you swooning off into space with your eyes closed. What am I supposed to think?"

"That I'm enjoying what we're doing!"

"Do I disappoint you?"

"No!"

"Do you wish I were someone else?"

"I wouldn't be here if I wanted someone else!"

"Well, I suppose that's plausible," said Rita, sinking back onto her pillow. "Then I'm sorry. I really am. Please continue."

"It's not that easy, goddammit!" I said, now fully flexile and completely useless.

"You have every right to be upset. Feel free to access your rage."

Now I really was upset. I glared at Rita brutally.

"Oh, I'm just kidding," she said. "Here, I have a surprise for you."

I was in pain at this point.

She pulled a box out from under her bed, put on her robe and left the room. When she returned a few minutes later the box was gone. "Close your eyes," she told me.

When they were permitted to reopen Rita was standing at the foot of her bed, wearing a seductive floral bustier with ruffled edges and strapped to a set of garters. She raised her arms as if unveiling herself. Astonished, I looked her up and I looked her down: it was a sharp refraction of identity, she had reinvented herself, and the theatrical contrast between appearance and personality was intensely exciting—like a peek at a secret life. Like a performance. The weak glow of her lamp lit her bewitchingly, heightening the drama.

"How did you know of my weakness for black lace?" I asked.

"Because all men are—look, can we get back to business now?" she asked.

"Pleasure before business," I replied, moving in tight.

Rather suave, I thought.

o   o   o

A week later, early in the morning, the EDGAR terminal in Rita's room screeched *I feel good* ... in the voice of James Brown. Jeff had taught me how to program EDGAR's alarm feature for rock-and-roll. It was nearly time for Dex's television debut.

Rita was already up. Dressed too. She lay on her side next to me, bracing her head against her hand, staring at me.

"Are you counting kcals again?" I asked.

"No, I know that bothers you." She kept looking at my eyes. She said, "You're having an effect on me."

What type of effect did she mean? Where was the cause? Another mystery. Rita frequently spoke mysteries.

Moments later we were back in my room, and Dex's new twenty-seven inch color remote TV crackled into action. There he was, seated, looking scared stiff on the *Today Show* family couch, Bryant Gumbel and Katie Couric all smiles. Dex's adviser sat beside him. I'd never even seen Charlie Pappadallas but there he was too, in full color, with thick black glasses and a long rectangular face that extended into an even longer rectangular black beard. He looked like Cat Stevens after his conversion to Islam but with slicked-down hair and a tweedy jacket. Of course.

And now Bryant Gumbel, former industrial paper salesman cum video icon, was getting comfortable, wearing a perfectly tailored dark-blue Joseph Abboud suit, pursing his eyebrows, doing his best to appear scientific and serious.

"As part of our continuing series on health-care financing, today we look at biotechnology start-ups. A few years ago the idea of tinkering with life processes on a microscopic level was just a twinkle in the eye of a handful of obscure academics. But that twinkle has blossomed into a remarkable multibillion-dollar industry responsible for innovations ranging from disease-resistant crops to promising new drugs to renewed hope for a cure for cancer.

"Yet there is another side to this success story, one involving the success of the practitioners themselves. Academics who once spent their lives cloistered in ivory towers now pocket huge sums of cash if their ideas can be sold to investors. Today we welcome two of the founders of BioVitrics Corporation, a company recently formed to commercialize their discovery that certain kinds of glass materials bond directly to human tissue. Dr. Charles Pappadallas is professor of biochemistry at the Massachusetts Institute of Technology and Dexter Drain the third is one of his students good morning gentlemen."

"Good morning," said Papadallas and Dex in unison.

"Guys, tell me. Who can your product help?"

"Well," said Papadallas, a little too breathless, "we're talking about improved bone prostheses..."

"By which you mean artificial bones," interjected Bryant Gumbel for the little people in listener land.

"... that the body will not only accept, but which will also withstand greater stress. And we're also talking about a whole range of dental implants." His beard kept stroking the lavaliere microphone clipped to his tie, producing loud swishing and rubbing noises, muffling his speech.

"Let me ask you this. Many people feel that a lot of today's science is pure hype. So-called breakthroughs like cold fusion and artificial intelligence haven't lived up to their advertisements, and now just about any well-publicized discovery raises suspicion. How big is the science-to-salestalk ratio in your own work?" Bryant Gumbel creased his forehead.

Dex and his adviser looked at each other. "First of all," said Pappadallas, swishing away, "BioVitrics is not really a biotech company in the sense you described before. And we're not the ones writing those exaggerated news stories."

"Well, that's just my point," glibbed the impeccably attired egomaniac. Bryant Gumbel's hands were forming the letter A, fingertips on his lips as he looked thoughtfully into the camera. He spoke slowly. "Cer-tain-ly the venture-capital and investment-banking communities are responsible for a lot of the commotion, since their business is to stimulate investment interest." Now he looked over at Dex. "Isn't it fair to say that a lot of promising scientific ideas have been oversold or sold prematurely?"

"That's undeniable," Dex replied.

You fuck up, boy, I said to myself. Right into the bitumen and pitch.

"Now, I understand that you've received over $15 million in what venture capitalists call a 'private placement', is that right?"

"Yes, but I thought you wanted to talk about our technology, our products. And another thing anugamugwumpwump" *swishrub*, said Pappadallas and his beard.

Bryant Gumbel smiled. "You guys are one step ahead of me, I was about to bring that up. Do you folks have a product to sell? I mean, is what you have real?"

"Absolutely," Dex effused. "We've got an investigational device exemption from the FDA, and we're about to start our first clinical trials."

"You sound so enthusiastic," Bryant Gumbel interrupted. "That seems to be one of the big stumbling blocks in the biotechnology business, isn't it? Sort of an ... *excess* of enthusiasm?"

"You can't achieve success if you don't believe in what you're doing," said Dex.

"Sure, but some would say that for every success you can also point to a boondoggle like tPA, the designer drug that cost umpteen million dollars to develop yet in most cases is riskier and more expensive than conventional treatment. Have you determined that your product is free of side effects?"

"That's just what the clinical trials are all about. Over the next two years…"

"Years?" Bryant Gumbel interrupted again. "You mean you won't know whether you've got another tPA on your hands for years? Do your investors know this?" Why, Bryant, you look positively aghast. Someone had clearly done his background research.

"Of course," swished Pappadallas. "We couldn't afford human testing without that funding. Have you any idea how much it costs to set up a double blind study?"

"But do your *investors* know how long it will be before you've tested for side effects?"

"We don't give our investors daily progress reports," said Pappadallas, pointing with his finger. "But—well, of course they know the status of our clinical trials. It's in our offering literature." Pappadallas leaned over to confer with Dex.

Swish.

"Gentlemen … gentlemen? We've got one of your investors on the line. Mrs. Mendoza? Can you hear us?"

A still photograph of a middle-aged Spanish woman now filled the screen. The little white caption said:

MARIA MENDOZA
Investor, BIOVITRICS CORP.

And now the voice-over said, "Mrs. Mendoza, this is Bryant Gumbel. How are you today?"

"Fine, sir," a Spanish female voice responded.

"Mrs. Mendoza, you've invested quite a bit of money in BioVitrics, haven't you?"

"Oh, yes, sir. I have indeed."

"And is investing in biotechnology companies something you do often?"

"What is this 'biotechnology'?"

"Mrs. Mendoza, how much do you really know about the company? Have you ever met Dr. Pappadallas or Mr. Drain, BioVitrics' principal scientists?"

Something that sounded like garbled Spanish laughter.

"I'm sorry," continued the voice of Bryant Gumbel, "I couldn't hear that. Were you aware that BioVitrics had not even started clinical trials on its biotechnology glass product?"

"Oh, well." Giggling, definitely. "My people say I have nothing to worry about. We are in the hands of very smart men, you know."

"Mrs. Mendoza, do you want to ask either of these two scientists anything about their company? Such as what kinds of side effects their product may have?"

"No, that is all right. But I believe I will say good luck, we are counting on you. All right?"

Bryant was back on the screen. "Thank you Mrs. Mendoza." He turned to Dex and his adviser. "Looks like our time is up. Interesting, gentlemen, a pleasure to have you this morning. And take care of yourselves, okay?" Close-up of Bryant Gumbel's face. "Coming next, questions and answers with astrologer Lucien Demain. After this."

Bum bum bum-bum ... bum-bum ... bum ... bummmmmmmmm, went the *Today* theme.

A couple of hours later it was my turn. I stared out over the faces beginning to assemble in the small function room. It was New England plush. Soft velvet cushions bulged from white carved-wood chairs neatly arranged into three rows. The carpeting was a quiet green, trimmed with gold appointments around the edges. Brocaded wallpaper, tasseled drapery, glass ship's lanterns, and neatly rendered lithographs of fox hunting scenes decorated the walls. From my lectern the entire right side of the room was a lofty, spacious bay window that looked out over Boston Harbor and the airport, like magnified detail from Blair Stille's view. It was still morning and fiery shimmers off the harbor surface made it impossible to glance toward the window for more than an instant.

There was something very sturdy, very responsible about the room. Why had Star reserved *this* particular room? To clothe the presentation in respectability? To convey a sense of refined elegance suggesting business success? To calm me down like some goddamn dentist's aquarium?

A woman with light brown hair and blond temples flitted efficiently into the room on low-heeled black pumps. She had a thin face and lips, a pale complexion and a pointy nose and chin. Her short hair was parted on the right and swept over in a shock to her left. As she inspected the contents of her small briefcase the spotlights illuminating the room occasionally flashed off her gold wire eyeglass frames.

A guy with thinning, wavy hair sat in a corner, bent over his folded Wall Street Journal. He had a puffy face with a gray beard trimmed tight against his cheeks. His sleeves were rolled up. His hump of a body rose and fell as he breathed; I could practically hear it.

Then Ronald came in, carrying an armload of Velobound booklets that he set down onto the speaker's table next to the lectern. He nodded at me warmly. The booklets said, PROSPECTUS AND BUSINESS PLAN, and underneath they said, ATMOSPHERIC RESEARCH GROUP, INC. What the hell was that?

A short woman, well-packed into a boxy black dress bisected by a shiny black belt spouted a hearty, "Hiya Ronald" as she claimed a front row center seat. A rolled-up scarf—colorful blues, reds, yellows and chips of black—surrounded her neck. Her eyes were distorted through thick glasses, but the speckled black frames matched her graying hair perfectly.

I silently rehearsed my little speech as more of them began to show up: A forty-something woman with short feathered blond hair that matched her turtleneck, heavy ribbed hoops stretching her earlobes; her chin creased when she looked down; cashmere jacket; leather riding boots; no wedding ring. Some people just shouldn't wear stretch pants. A tawny guy in a black leather jacket, his full head of wetted hair shorn into little porcupine spikes, carefully checking out the room as if it were a singles bar; he picked a chair in back and chewed gum. An older fellow in a blue oxford-cloth shirt and expensive jeans leaned back and stared at the ceiling.

And as the words I had prepared travelled through my mind I began to feel them slipping away, as if through some hidden orifice in my head. I scanned the little pile of index cards I'd prepared. The words were there but they weren't in my head. They had leaked out. It occurred to me that I had nothing to say to these people.

A nondescript bald fellow lumbered in, his shoulders seeming to sag under the weight of two Neiman Marcus shopping bags. He was followed by a rather striking woman in a bright crimson business suit with a short skirt and gold buttons, sheer red stockings, and matching heels, who marched with confidence into the room. She looked almost like ... *it was Rita!*

First there was the astonishment, then the rush of reassuring warmth that greets fire rescue squads and computer-repair technicians. Rita's lips were painted juicy red, her face buffed with makeup powder and rouge, her eyes defined into prominence by mascara and eyeliner. She looked like a perfect match for this crowd.

But then there was the terror. She'd be discovered instantly. They would banish her and blame me. I'd never get funding again, I'd spend my life in a forgotten E42 office right near Jeff and hack programs no one cared about until someone decided MIT needed more parking spaces and without warning paved and lined my miserable life right out of existence.

I began to say "Bah—" but Rita tightened her lips and drew her pencil-enhanced eyebrows together. The message was: can it! Then she caught the eye of porcupine man. I heard her say *buon giorno* before she sat down next to him and struck up a conversation whose signal disappeared into the general murmuring noise level. Ronald didn't notice her; maybe he had no idea who was coming, there were no guest lists or name badges. I seated myself behind an overhead someone had been thoughtful enough to set out.

As if responding to some unseen cue Ronald suddenly rose and began passing out booklets, nodding and smiling as he progressed. I leafed through the stack of transparencies. Were they in the correct order? I couldn't remember for the life of me. It wasn't clear from the index cards.

"On behalf of Star Ventures I'd like to welcome you all this morning," Ronald began as he reached the podium. "Atmospheric Research Group is a seed-stage company formed to develop and commercialize a promising new approach to weather forecasting. The brainchild of an eminent MIT professor and his gifted research assistant..."

In my mind his words trailed off into a colorful, silent world of leather boots and hoop earrings. The guy next to Rita wore a pink-and-white striped shirt with a white collar. I hated those shirts, they're so tastelessly asymmetric. Almost vulgar, really. He was reading the booklet. Who formed this company, anyway? Was I even part of it? The prospects for new MIT graduates continued to recede with the economic downturn and reductions in defense funding. Was Atmospheric Research Group my future? Would it pay off my student loans?

"... and without further ado, allow me to introduce Paul Bustamante." Now Ronald was finished. It was my curtain call. I turned on the overhead, slowly, savoring my remaining moments of peace before baring my chest to the firing squad of thin-lipped matrons and plump stockbrokers. I cleared my throat. I tapped my index cards against the lectern. Were they in the correct order? It wasn't clear from the transparencies.

"Thank you," I said. "Maybe we should begin with some graphics to put all this into context." I turned the overhead on and placed the first transparency on the glass. It looked great on the screen but I couldn't connect with its meaning or significance. I said, "Now here's a nice chart..."

Immediately there was a comment. It was the well-packed woman front and center. She said, "Excuse me, I see you predict a linear increase in operating revenues over five years. Can you tell me what assumptions you're making in terms of market penetration and economic losses due to weather-forecasting errors?"

As she spoke she held her thumb against her index finger and bounced her hand up and down, using the rhythm to pace her speech—just like Dex. It was mesmerizing, hypnotic. I said: "What?"

"*Signor BOO-sta-montay*," said Rita in a perfect Italian accent, "you must forgive me. I had a similar question, but my command of English is so meager. Might I ask you to turn to page 14 of this *libretto*?" She held up the prospectus.

I grabbed an undistributed copy and flipped through the pages and there it all was, neatly typeset, right in front of me: a complete narrative, financial conjectures woven around enthusiastic descriptions like an authoritative business suit. All the underlying assumptions were there, presented objectively but leading ineluctably to modest, conservative conclusions. It was a brilliant job of advocacy. I wished I had enough time to replenish my leaky memory from this fountain of frothy tribute.

"Perhaps the question is answered in the first full paragraph? In the discussion of the pro for-r-rma statements?" Silence as I scanned the paragraph. "And perhaps your next, *come si dice*, graphic..." she growled with a smile.

I fumbled to replace the transparency but Ms. Blond Temples had a question. It was an elaborate, rambling oration about share conversion and liquidation preferences that ended, at last, with a question mark. I recalled the discussion Blair E. Stille was having with that Jerry guy when I first entered her office. She had been talking about a term sheet. Star still hadn't sent me a term sheet— they probably didn't want to go to the trouble until they scratched some investor interest.

Ronald rose and answered the inquiry with two words: "Standard terms."

"Thank you."

It had turned cloudy outside. A plane glided softly, gracefully onto the runway at Logan Airport, fully visible through the window behind the blond temples. Airplanes fly for a simple and straightforward reason, yet the sight of such behemoth contraptions floating so slowly above the runway, hanging there in apparent defiance of gravity, never ceased to entrance me. Wouldn't it be fun to fly to Cancùn with Rita and sun ourselves on Mayan ruins and snorkel in the emerald waters and pump like tan, wet sex fiends on the soft white sand?

"Young feller," said the geezer staring at the ceiling, "I been in weather forty years. My comp'ny sends forecasts by computer to aviation contractors nationwide. Now, I seen you staring out that window at Logan, and I see them planes landing and taking off, and I begin to wonder: what do these guys bring to the party with their fancy techniques? We use statistical forecasting already. We correlate weather elements, we use these regression formulas and what not, all the data we need we get from the National Weather Service. It ain't exactly elegant, what we do, but it gets the job done pretty good I guess. Otherwise we'd have a lot more disasters, right?"

I explained that ordinary statistical methods are no more than guesses at the future based on the recent past, not on any understanding of how weather actually works. I described the way our approach actually represents the atmosphere's inner workings, how our forecasts are grounded in deeper understanding of its behavior and processes. I'd given this little speech before. But he wasn't convinced.

"I think yer missing my point. You got the same data we got. They don't make any more of it, right? Now I could see maybe using some complicated new technique if the gov'ment decided to expand the observational system, double or triple the number of weather stations or satellites. But that won't happen anytime soon, and it's the small-scale stuff, the data we can't see, that get blown up and *destroy* our large-scale forecasts. Yer telling me y'can achieve fundamentally improved results with the same old synoptic data? That yer gonna predict local conditions using spotty information from all over?" He shook his head, smiling, still staring at the ceiling with his hands in his pockets.

"That's what missing data is all about," I told him. "Filling in what we can't measure with accurate guesses, then making forecasts based on the enhanced picture."

"What I'm asking you is, how much real measurements do you need to make them accurate guesses? How do you know you'll ever have enough?"

His skepticism was dead on target, of course. He'd lanced at the heart of our speculations. We—I—had no clue where the threshold lay, how much actual data you'd need to guide the statistics and improve a local forecast. All I had right now was a concept, yet here we were merchandising it as hard science. Maybe it would be totally useless without vast swarms of numbers to operate on. Maybe it would be totally useless altogether; no one had tested it on anything real yet. That's why we wanted their money, after all— if we were sure it would work we could probably get government funds. But asking investors to buy something you don't have in the hope that their money will help you get it isn't a very effective sales pitch.

I was terrified, I was even a little angry, but I had an idea. "We're confident," I told him.

"Why?" he wanted to know. "How?"

It was a recurrent theme I kept running across in the pages of *Tellus*—the idea that the atmosphere, or portions of it, is fractal, meaning everything looks pretty much the same whether you're close up or far away. The same math that delivers chaos and tumult can also limn delicate, repeating designs, self-similar designs, patterns repeated within patterns. An enchanting concept, really, the stuff of many daydreams in the Lindgren carrels: my eyes closed, my mind lost in vast jet stream winds bending down from Canada over the plains and surging back up the East Coast, my imagination taking the massive ribbon apart only to find an endlessly layered cascade of smaller and smaller ribbons, all of a piece, all following the same twisting trajectory. Other times I could picture the great lumbering cyclonic regions that span entire oceans decomposing into vortices and then into smaller and smaller whorls all the way down to the texture of the air itself.

So I explained fractal geometries, how these dwindling repetitive patterns create topologies that defy familiar Euclidean descriptions—wavier than a line but not fully spread into a two-dimensional plane, bushier and bumpier than a flat plane but not solid like a three-dimensional volume. I mentioned a recent study demonstrating that the perimeters of clouds tend toward a fractal dimension of 1.35. And I described how fractal relationships would let us build up a big picture from just a few clues—how knowing something about a part means you know something about the whole as well, since parts and whole all look alike.

"But don't the turbulence mess all that up?" my tormenter persisted. "I mean, you talk about atmospheric physics, but we already got those kinds of models. Even a bunch of yokels like us are experimenting with a multilayer baroclinic something or other. And we get some pretty good results, too. But the turbulence kills us, we get one storm racing up the seaboard and our forecasts go to hell all over creation. Why won't it kill you too, especially with that notion of yours to use teeny bits of sparse data as stand-ins for big continuous pieces of sky?"

Where'd they get this guy, dammit? He was smart all right, and had scored another direct hit. I didn't even have a flagman yet to separate atmospheric flow into mean and turbulent components. My heart raced and I tried to relax, I thought of my childhood doctor's aquarium and the yin/yang symbol on my screen and then, somehow, another idea began to form. The two dots in that diagram represent the notion that when one of the yin or yang forces reaches its extreme, it contains already, within itself, the germ of its opposite. At least that's what the sign in the new-age bookstore window said before they tore the place down.

"Actually, the most turbulent regions are also the most fractal," I said and as the words came out I faintly heard myself thinking, *That's my own voice! The words are flowing by themselves and they seem to be making sense on their own!* "It's rather intriguing, really," I told him even as I only myself began to appreciate just how intriguing, the notion crystallizing in my mind as I spoke. "By resolving the turbulent components, one can make reliable calculations based on the fractal dimension even with limited data." *What a concept!* Hidden order within chaos! The most inscrutably complex atmospheric features possessing, in their fractal identities, the seeds of their own simplicity! Could it possibly be so? "If you see what I'm saying."

"Maybe I do and maybe I don't. Let me think about it."

"Oh, I'm so glad we're into the theory now," said the chunky guy in the back, "and I have a question. Is it true that when squirrels gather a lot of nuts it means we're going to have a rough winter?"

I was still floating in the elegance of my insight, but welcomed the opportunity to debunk a silly weather myth. I said, "No. If N stands for nuts and t is time, than the nut-gathering rate dN over dt is proportional to N, see, so the number of gathered nuts is really nothing but the exponential function *A* times *e* to the negative *kt*..."

"Ah, *signor BOO-sta-montay*," interjected Rita, "you are so, how shall I put it, *drôle*, since all you say is that squirrels gather a lot of nuts when there are a lot of nuts around. It is much the same in Tuscany, you see. But perhaps you will now tell us more about the finances..."

"I still don't see any real near-term potential," said the well-packed woman.

"And perhaps you might speak more slo-owly," Rita said, exaggerating the word to make some kind of point. "In deference to my limited English."

Actually it seemed to me that everyone in the room spoke slowly, I was the only one talking at an ordinary clip. Were they learning disabled? Or was I galloping through my speech like Wiseman? Could it possibly be that Don Boyer was the only one at MIT who spoke normally and the rest of us were stuck on fast forward because spoken language is so inefficient it drives us crazy?

I stared at Rita. Her face was serene, and bits of my speech slowly seeped back. It had been data compression overkill. The situation was so terrifying and the financial considerations so dreary I'd crushed them all into an inaccessibly dense pellet, and now, somehow, I would have to allow it to dissolve and redisperse in my speechmaking thought centers.

I looked over at the woman in black, then ruffled slowly—or maybe it only seemed so—through the transparencies. I remembered now. I found the one with projected revenue growth. "Well, certainly one can't expect returns in years one or two," I told her, "but if you discount the future revenue to present value, I think you'll agree that the, how shall I put it, the *adjusted* near-term potential is quite favorable."

Rita flashed me a discreet smile. We had connected. I uttered the words I could feel her thinking—*how shall I put it?*—and I had to fight the urge to speak with Italian inflections. Rita was in my head now.

Then the pace of questions picked up. The nondescript bald fellow asked about note three to the financials, which I'd never even seen before, so I looked over at Ronald. Someone asked about performance incentives. Someone else wanted to know about progress reports. They were coming at me from all sides now, it was like a press conference. But all the information was accessible once again thanks to Rita. Ronald and I worked together like twin time-division multiplexers, sorting out the overlapping messages and parsing out discrete, orderly responses. There was a transparency for just about every question.

Rita helped things along even further with a couple of skillfully placed rhetorical questions and cleverly contrived misunderstandings: "Am I misreading the dilution terms? They seem so overly generous to first-round investors."

"We done yet?" the old guy asked finally.

"If there are no further questions," said Ronald, "I'd like to thank everyone for coming. We'll be in touch with each and every one of you. Thank you again."

Rita stood motionless against the bay window. When the last of the audience filed out the door I walked up to her.

"I thought you weren't any good at contrived situations," I whispered.

Rita studied me sternly with one eye, her head askew. Then she extended her arm, revealing a mongo patch of sweat that had soaked her jacket maroon underneath, and pressed her finger into my chest. "You're very lucky, *signore*," Rita said in a slow hiss, "that your proboscis hangs low." She removed her finger and walked off.

Ronald came up to me. He was satisfied. "Terrific job," he said, provoking Rita to clench her shoulders and draw her hands into fists as she walked through the door. "We'll get a syndicate together for sure."

"What about a term sheet?" I asked, trying to sound knowledgeable.

"We'll fax one to you tomorrow. Listen, start thinking about milestones, and come up with a more detailed use-of-proceeds analysis. Budget ten thou for the attorneys."

"What happens next?" I asked.

"*Domus placens*, my friend. That's Horace," said Ronald as he left.

Before I left I took one more look out the bay window. A black cloud hovered just over the clear horizon, its irregular bottom drifting above the airport like the toothed edge of a wood saw that would rip the hangars and planes to shreds were it to descend. I thought of the sudden thunderstorm that doused me on my way to Central Square last spring. This was pretty important stuff I was working on, notwithstanding the obvious hype I had to pursue to keep the project moving ahead. Just a shade more forecast accuracy would provide measurable improvements in people's everyday and economic lives. It was all becoming real now. I would propose challenging milestones, not just fluff, to keep my work true to itself. If I couldn't achieve genuine benefits, why bother trying?

The room was empty now. I'd faced a group of skeptics and emerged triumphant.

They were ready to support me. I couldn't wait to log onto EDGAR and get started again.

The room was empty, and Andre Dupree was nowhere in sight.

"Enough already," said Rita after I'd gotten back to our dorm. "No big deal, all right? Stop lavishing the praise, you're just elevating me to submerge your own self-doubts. You did fine, you really did."

"What a show you put on in front of all those people!"

Now Rita looked at me suspiciously. "A show? You think I did it to show off? Is that what you're saying?"

"Of course not. I'm just saying I owe you big time," I told her.

"Now you're insulting me. Are you trying to insult me?"

Dex was due to return at six. I was afraid to meet him. I didn't know what to say, he'd gotten beaten up pretty badly on the *Today Show*. Things had gone so much better for me. Already I had e-mail from Jeff. He'd scheduled a teleconference with Mo Herman for the next day. Word sure propagates fast, I thought.

"What should we do for D-cube?" I asked Rita, happy to change the subject.

"What should we do *for* him? I want to know what's going to be done *to* him, bamboozling that ignorant woman out of her money like that."

"Rita, he's been through enough. Maybe I'll just wait for him myself."

"I'll control myself," said Rita.

"I really think it might be better if I just waited here myself."

"Are you telling me I can't control myself? I just save your ass with the performance of my life and you're kicking me out of the house because you think I can't control myself?"

"I didn't say that."

"Not in so many words, but that's what you meant."

"No, it really wasn't," I told her.

"Well fine, then."

"All right, fine."

So now I was really worried.

Dex showed up right on time, trailing Don Boyer, calcium transport, behind him. He lumbered into our room with great effort and dropped into his desk chair.

"You look like shit," Rita observed. She eyed him from my bed like a cross-examining lawyer.

"I've been up since 4:30," Dex replied. He took a deep breath and looked out the window at the occluded front that promised stagnant, precipitating weather for at least a few days. Then he smiled and made fists and shook his head from side to side and said, "Were we great or what? Huh? Uh-huh!"

Rita almost hit the ceiling. "How can you live with yourself? Didn't you hear that woman's voice? She doesn't know the first thing about investments or bioactive materials or clinical trials or anything else!"

Dex's smile vanished. "What?" he asked. He was incredulous.

"Rita..." I tried.

"Your five minutes of televised fame exposed you for the predators you are. You sleazebags finance your escapades by selling pipe dreams to ignorant techno-groupies. There," she said, turning to me, "I've controlled myself. I've stuck to the facts." Rita folded her arms.

"Wait just a minute," Dex protested. "This was a Reg D offering. Blue skied in three states. Every investor was carefully screened. Every investor is fully accredited. Mrs. Mendoza is a multimillionaire."

"Right," sneered Rita. "An heiress from Spanish Harlem, perhaps?"

"Colombia, actually."

"Oh." There was some hesitation in Rita's voice. Very rare.

Now Don chimed in. "The friend she referred to is the head of one of the biggest investment-consulting firms on Wall Street."

"But God, I just don't know how we're going to handle the fallout from that show..." Dex said.

"Don't take it so hard, D-cube," I told him. "Look, you did your best. Just get on with the science, right?"

"Who's got the time?" Dex lamented. "We're getting inquiries from all over the country. It seems like every dentist and oral surgeon on the planet wants to be in on the ground floor. These guys are smart now. They know products still in clinicals have investment potential, that as soon as the FDA grants preliminary approval the pharmaceutical companies dive in—then there's blood in the water, as I've told you, and the stock price skyrockets out of sight."

"They're converting our second-stage financing to a mezzanine round," said Don. "They're talking about a public offering in late spring."

"*Our* financing?" I asked.

Don immediately blushed. "So how did *your* little spectacle go today?" he asked.

"The VC rep was very positive," I said. "Looks like we're moving right along."

"How many people showed up?" Don wanted to know.

"At least twenty."

He laughed. "Twenty potential investors for a lousy twenty-five K investment? I guess they're taking no chances."

"What does that mean?" I asked.

"Just that Star is obviously reluctant even to put up pocket change in your little project. They're passing all the risk through to other investors, and they'll probably garner some hefty brokerage fees to boot."

"That's enough, Don," said Dex.

"And these twenty investors, they seem interested?" he persisted.

"Quite interested," said Rita. "I saw it myself. What are you getting at now?"

"They quiz you about milestones?"

"We don't have milestones yet, I'm working on them," I said.

"Oh really!" said Don. Somehow he seemed to know everything about my research, about Star, about the deal. "And these smart young MBAs in suits and briefcases didn't object to your setting your own milestones? Didn't that seem strange?"

"They were all very mature and sober," I said, "and they bought it. Bottom line: they bought it."

"Ah, mature and sober," said Don. "No suits and briefcases, then?"

"Don, really, enough," said Dex.

"If Star were serious about anything but making a quick buck on you, they wouldn't have invited a ragtag group of dilettante investor losers to throw nickels and dimes at someone's unproven guesswork."

"*I said enough, dammit!*" screamed Dex. He rose from his chair and collared Don. "We obviously need to talk," he said as he pushed Don out the door. Turning to me he said, "Sorry. I'll see you in a bit."

One day later—one day!—the unthinkable happened.

I'd been at it with EDGAR most of the night, trying to puzzle out a way to test out my fractal idea on turbulent conditions. It wasn't going to be easy. First you'd have to peg a fractal dimension based on how fast the air is churning. Then you'd have to use that dimension to hop scales—but how? At this point I didn't even have a fully working model for the easy, calm stuff.

I marched over to Jeff's office for our conference call with Mo Herman. Again that woody straw smell as his door opened.

"*Ma-cha,*" said Jeff, apparently noticing the involuntary scrunch on my face. "Japanese ceremonial green tea. A prelude to meditation. A laxative, too. Like some?"

"I'm kind of meditated out right now," I told him, suppressing my nausea. It seemed there was always something putrid in the air around here. "But thanks anyway."

"Tell me of your encounter yesterday."

I gave him the complete run-time version. Jeff began to lean forward over his desk as I explained my fractal conjecture. He grinned broadly when I mentioned yin and yang.

He said, "You have done well then."

"So you think I'm on the right track?"

He smiled again. Then he said, "Who the hell knows."

The phone rang. Jeff pressed a button and said, "Top of the world."

A breathy voice that seemed to emanate from Jeff's terminal replied, "Uh, yes, good morning, this is Opal Wintermeyer, Dr. Herman's secretary. Dr. Herman is waiting to speak with a Dr. Watt and a Mr. Bustamante." The voice was smooth and professional.

Doctor Herman? Jeff and I looked at each other. "And we're waiting for him," said Jeff.

"Hold please," whispered the voice. Then we heard a muffled

bellow: "Hey! Mo! They're ready!"

No intercoms. Jeff and I sat and waited, staring intently at the phone.

"PICK UP FOR GOD'S SAKE!" The secretary's piercing words crackled through the speaker.

"Yes. Yes?"

"Mo?" I said.

"Ah, gentlemen. A pleasure, to be sure."

"Maybe we should call you Doc," said Jeff. "I didn't know you have a Ph.D."

"I am a juris doctor. An attorney."

"I see," said Jeff. "Is Sue there?"

"Well, I ... actually, I'll be handling this case personally. It's that important, you see."

"Super," said Jeff. "But could we have Sue on the line anyway?"

The connection kicked in and out, as if some muttering and rustling of papers on the other end of the line were clogging transmission.

"Actually," said Mo Herman, clearing his throat sharply, "Sue is, ah, no longer with our firm, you see. But I can assure you we have every capability..."

"These guys make me sick," Jeff said, looking up at me.

"What? Excuse me? What was that?" squawked Mo Herman's voice. Good thing even Jeff's speaker phone couldn't receive and transmit simultaneously.

"Actually, the more I think about this, the more I like it," said Jeff. He stroked his beard. "Yes, this works out quite well indeed."

"Well, I'm certainly appreciative of your confidence," said Mo Herman. I could picture the scowl. Jeff looked seriously at the phone. "I am generating a first draft of the application," Mo Herman continued, "and it will require significant thought and comment on your part. I would ask you to provide me with the same at your earliest convenience."

"Absolutely," said Jeff.

"Then I will have a package delivered to you no later than tomorrow."

"Can't you just e-mail the thing?" Jeff asked.

"Yes, as I said, we'll express-mail it," Mo Herman said impatiently. Jeff smiled, looping his index finger into his thumb in a gesture of satisfaction. I wondered what he was up to.

"Okey-dokey," said Jeff. "And thank you."

"Thank you both," said Mo Herman's voice as it disappeared.

"What I think you'll need to test your theory," said Jeff as he looked at me across his desk, "is a special type of computer program. You know what an engine is?"

I'd heard of engines before, but Jeff could see I hadn't heard much. "An engine," he continued, "is the generic heart, the karma, the essence of a program that can be used in many ways. The engine is what makes the software work. It performs the fundamental tasks. Once you've got the engine running you can make it do whatever you want. Put it under the body of a VW bug or a van, just keep truckin' on and on." Now Jeff was tapping his desk.

"Yeah…" I began. What was he getting at?

"So construct your basic model first but keep it as open as you can. Leave lots of ways to get at your variables. Make it work smoothly. Then write a module to implement your fractal scheme. If your engine is sufficiently extensible, the fractal module hooks right in and the engine makes it run. Then, if you're right in your conjecture and get your programming straight, your module will optimize engine performance like a turbocharge." Jeff looked at me closely. "A lot of if's."

Indeed.

When I returned to our room, events leading to the unthinkable had begun to unfold. We were only two weeks into classes and already I'd run out of the Pentel Hi Polymer Super 0.5 millimeter No. 2B lead sticks that I used to feed my stable of mechanical pencils. It turned out that Dex had exhausted his supply, too, and a frantic trip to the MIT Coop found them fresh out of stock; these are very popular items and they sell fast at the beginning of the semester. So we raced to the Red Line and boarded a train for Harvard Square, hoping to get there before hoards of desperate empty-penciled MIT techies had fully depleted the shelves, and just as we emerged from the subway a girl walking with two of her friends stopped dead and looked at Dex with a sudden shock of recognition: "Hey. I saw you! Yesterday! On the *Today Show*, that was you, right? Oh, I can't believe it!"

She was absolutely gorgeous. She had long ginger hair, partly gathered in a white lace ribbon, that cascaded generously over her shoulders like the most perfect laminar flow. She wore that same sleepy, WASPy look that Dex always had on, only hers disappeared instantly into a sparkling, high-wattage smile. Her error-free complexion was milky, her white turtleneck confirmed an ample volume-to-circumference ratio, and as she turned to talk with her friends I noticed that her blue cotton pants, loose over the legs, were drawn at the hips to define tight, shapely, undeformable gluteal regions.

Dex said: "Ummmm…"

She told him how much she hated Bryant Gumbel and how upset she was at the obvious sneak attack. She didn't let her friends get a single word in as she gushed how important his work sounded, how it must have been so exciting to share it with so many people.

So she was nice.

"And how shrewd of you to schedule all that publicity before you've even obtained official approval, good heavens, the investors must be pounding on your doors!"

And smart.

The nerve of him! It was as if one day he accidentally tripped over the search logic and somehow called up a dream, a fantasy, his to simply download into reality!

Her name was Penny, as in Penelope; Hammond, as in Brahmin. As in big bucks, Boston high society. She was studying at Harvard, if that's what they really do there. And Dex didn't have to take her number, no, *she* took *his—our!*—number before strolling off with her friends whom she hadn't bothered to introduce, just as Dex had completely ignored *his* roommate during the entire episode.

Dex looked at me, frozen. He said: "Ummmm…"

The Harvard Coop had a full supply of pencil leads, probably more than they could ever hope to sell, the cashier seemed positively thrilled to get rid of some. We rode back to MIT on the Red Line, the tunnel lights flew across dark windows like a television's raster scanning pulses, and I said nothing.

12

A LITTLE LESS THAN TWO WEEKS LATER DEX FLOPPED DOWN IN A HEAP onto his bed, bobbing up and down on the bedsprings like a beached whale struggling for air. He was smiling. He'd gone out on his third date with Penny and had just returned. EDGAR's clock window indicated 11:03 AM.

"You missed breakfast," I told him. "Your favorite: overcooked oatmeal, Cap'n Crunch and particularly revolting coffee."

Dex moaned, "Mmmm hmmm."

So what did he expect me to do now, beg him to share the details? He'd never shown the least interest in my amorous adventures; why should I permit my low curiosity threshold to give him any satisfaction? I resolved to ask nothing, say nothing.

He continued to grin conspicuously as I typed, trying to ignore him. It was perfectly obvious that he was taunting me with his smug smiley smarmy silence. It was pure meanness, a deliberate distancing. Almost a betrayal. I remembered what my mother said shortly after meeting Dex my first day at MIT: "He's no different from any of us. He's just someone you don't want to get too close to." (Of course she was referring to matters olfactory.)

"So what's she like?" I asked at last.

"You've met her. She's terrific."

"I mean, what's she ... like? What happened?"

"Oh, cripes, Paul. Give me a break."

"Fine. Be that way," I said.

"All right, if you must know, she took me to this dumpy little Chinese restaurant in Harvard Square, and then, well ... one thing led to another, and of course I did all I could to accelerate the process, and she did nothing to oppose it..." He turned to me. "What else do you want to know?"

A dumpy Chinese restaurant! How quintessentially and Ivy

Leaguishly romantic! I would have moved mountains for the chance to draw Penny's giggle by glowering over some tasteless Peking Ravioli with a food critic's pretentiousness and fumble my chopsticks so one of the dense boiled dumplings splashes in the soy sauce and we laugh and laugh at the grease stains on our shirts and then I catch her merry electric blue eyes ...

As I listened I was certain I could detect in Dex's voice a certain satisfaction—a gloat over the abject failure of my circulation model to predict actual events. Sure the numbers had been wrong. But who could have foreseen such monumental tunneling, a resonant amplification of his every mediocre variable by unexpected fame and anticipated fortune?

I realized I still hadn't responded to Dex's question. "Nothing. You've fully satisfied my curiosity," I told him.

Now I returned to my screen. I was working on the use-of-proceeds analysis Ronald had asked for, and it was starting to make me uncomfortable. First of all, I was sadly aware of exactly where the money would go. After days on the telephone peeling back the bureaucratic lamellae I had discovered just what it would take to put together even a simple pseudo-field test.

The idea itself was simple. The atmosphere is three-dimensional like a thick orange peel around the fruit. I'd need measurements at the surface and measurements up above, enough to get the statistics rolling, enough to model a chunk of that peel. The surface part was no problem. The National Severe Storms Project maintains a dense patch of weather stations in Texas, Oklahoma and Kansas. I'd ask nicely for some historical data and hope they wouldn't be too stingy.

For the upper-air readings, I'd turn to GARP. Combine the stormwatchers' surface observations with the GARPers' loftier measurements, run the numbers, do up a forecast. Then check the accuracy of the forecast against the historical records.

The comparison part would also be easy. It would be like an electronic horserace, my model against the Weather Service's model, running side by side on a big computer. MIT's Department of Earth, Atmospheric, and Planetary Sciences (Course 12) already had the huge Weather Service system up and humming on their machines; we'd add my model, feed in the numbers, post the results, and declare a winner. It would be a cinch all right.

It was getting to that point which seemed impossible.

Here was the problem. GARP had finished well over a decade

ago. What was left of it sat gathering dust somewhere in the bowels of some administrative agency—thousands of computer hard disks, columns of old-style tapes, which was bad enough; and truckloads of moldering printouts, strip charts and handwritten entries, which was even worse. First we'd have to get our hands on all that stuff. Then someone, somewhere would have to type all the manual records into a computer.

That mind-numbing, wallet-draining task would consume fifteen K in a jiffy. So I typed: USE OF PROCEEDS—DATA ACQUISITION. No spreadsheets, no budget line items; just data drudgery.

As I stared at the screen and tried to ignore Dex, loudly sipping the air as he drifted off into what was either a maddeningly well-deserved slumber or an exquisitely vicious fabrication to draw my attention, I realized that more than oppressive hordes of data had lain siege to my equanimity. What was bothering me was Don, or more specifically, his taunts before Dex had silenced him. It was indeed odd for a venture capitalist to treat use of proceeds and milestones as mere afterthoughts. It was strange that they would give a college kid free reign to design his own self-serving goals and budget *after* the investors had been charmed or turned off. And yet clearly they were serious, since Star had already formed Atmospheric Research Group, Inc. as a corporation and the handsomely compensated Mo Herman had by now filed the patent application. Star's term sheet seemed generous enough—they and the investors were putting in all the money, taking all the risk, yet they left Jeff and me with 75% of the equity. No vesting schedule. No right to buy back our stock and kick us out. The whole thing just left me wondering.

Rita did not wonder. She pronounced the whole enterprise the most prodigiously tedious, unfathomably boring way to spend probably the rest of my MIT career. Rita was in a bad mood these days. Her adviser had without warning departed for sunnier climes at Cal Tech and she was having trouble with his replacement.

Late one night she returned to her room from the speech lab and screamed, "That idiot thinks the variance of a sum equals the sum of the variances!" as she slammed the door behind her. Apparently she had forgotten the presence of Wiseman, who had been standing just outside; he frequently walked her back from Tech Square, all the way on the other side of campus, late at night. I pictured his newly flattened nose and peered around Rita toward the door.

"Oh, shit!" she said and turned back and opened the door. She looked to one side, then the other: no Wiseman. She yelled, "Sorry!" into the hall and slammed the door again.

I thought about her gripe for a moment as she stared at me to respond. "Variances, sums … that's a harmless enough statistical relationship, isn't it?" I asked her innocently.

She shook her fists and rocked back and forth and seethed, *"Only for independent random variables! Otherwise you've got to add a multiple of the covariance, goddamn it!"*

"Oh, well, sure—I mean, I'm sure you're right. I'm no authority."

"Damn! You admit you know nothing yet right away you're ready to take his side! *My* project has covariance splattered all over the place. And this little pinhead, this visiting birdbrain who will never, ever receive tenure at any self-respecting academic institution tells me, no, Rita, think a little more carefully about your work, avoid the blind alleys. That's his favorite aphorism—avoid the blind alleys! I hear it in multiple iterations every day. Avoid the blind alleys!"

"Maybe you should just tell him about the covariances…"

"I. Will. Not. Work. With someone who thinks the variance of a sum equals the the sum of the variances!"

Rather than ask me to vacate her desk chair Rita wrapped her arms around my head and began typing on EDGAR. She saved my screen and pressed the <CTRL><ALT><PAUSE> key combination, which brought up her project. "Watch this," she said, and as she stepped back the screen cleared and turned a quiet shade of light blue.

"French," she said. The word **FRENCH** appeared in red letters at the top left corner of the screen.

"*Je m'appelle Philippe*," she said in a casual tone of voice. The entry
>JE M'APPELLE PHILIPPE
appeared two lines under **FRENCH**. "*Je m'appelle Philippe*," she repeated, this time barking the words quickly with no pauses in between. Again the computer transliterated the words correctly, adding an exclamation point.

Then Rita said, "English," prompting the appearance of that word two lines under the last entry, and once again she said "*Je m'appelle Philippe*." This time the computer responded
>GEM APPLE FEE LEAP

Rita folded her arms and, with the command of a drill sergeant, ordered, "Rationalize." After a moment the computer responded:

FRENCH

>JE M'APPELLE PHILIPPE

"You think I could do that without covariances?" she asked me.

I had no idea whatever but the display certainly was impressive.

"If you think the variance of a sum equals the the sum of the variances I would like you to leave. I will not share the same bed with such a man," she told me.

"I stand corrected," I replied.

"Will you criticize my work in complete ignorance?"

"I think your work is marvelous," I said and then, realizing I hadn't answered her question, hastily added, "No."

"Will you advise me to avoid the blind alleys?"

"Never."

That had taken care of things, but only for the night.

Dex, meanwhile, was still sleeping. And I was still typing, still brooding over use of proceeds. Outside my window I could see ace dorm tutor Eric strolling across the small courtyard with his clipboard; he'd signed up for another year at good old W70, bless him, undoubtedly out of eagerness to continue right up to his graduation the great rapport he'd cultivated with us. George and Seth from down the hall had also retained their room for another year, and were busily engaged in a game of techie catch with a ball-popping toy. Each of them held a plastic game piece with a funnel-shaped basket for receiving a small orange ball and a spring-loaded ejection mechanism for launching it out of the basket. George had the stopwatch; Seth was measuring distance. They were calculating the spring constants.

The population of our dorm was remarkably stable. Sure, a few social climbers left each year for the prestige high rises, a few joined frats, a few graduated; but otherwise most remained not only in the same building but in the same rooms and with the same roommates they'd arrived with as sophomores after drawing W70 in the residence lottery. Even the decor was stable; in our room the only embellishments that ever changed were the titles in the row of books Dex and I each kept atop our bureaus. This semester I'd finally outgrown Thomas & Finney, the bible of calculus and analytic geometry that sustains even the most hardened math nerds through their sophomore years, and replaced it with a nonlinear dynamics textbook. Turbulence and Random Process in Fluid Mechanics, Past and Present Climate, Statistical Physics—it looked like quite an exciting semester, all right.

And our lives had acquired certain predictable tendencies, found their steady states. During the day Dex and I were usually in class, and when we weren't in class I was usually at a terminal and he was usually off at BioVitrics, and after dinner we would usually buzz through our problem sets in short order, and after that Dex would usually head back to BioVitrics and I back to EDGAR, and finally I would head over to Rita's room. Wiseman, a competent mechanical engineer but a computer moron, was usually in her room receiving counsel at her terminal. Despite the spelling of his last name Wiseman pronounced it *shoo*, and that's just how I characterized his nightly enforced exit: The Wiseman Shoo.

All of this was about to change.

"How would you feel about a double date?" Dex asked me when he finally deigned to awaken a short time later. Now he was fully recovered and refreshed and, apparently, eager to flaunt his statistical miracle. "There's a new production at Hasty Pudding. Penny can get all four of us tickets for the Saturday after this one."

"Boyer won't be coming along, will he?" I asked.

"Of course not. This would be a true double date, not some five-membered ring with a stray heteroatom. Besides, Don's having some ... well, problems."

"What kind of problems?"

"Let's just say he's unavailable."

Come to think of it, I hadn't seen the great Don Boyer around since Dex hustled him out of our room. That had been weeks ago.

"Is he angry with you?"

Dex sighed. He knew I'd persist. "He's in a bit of academic hot water. Fritz Sauer, you know, his adviser? He's gone. Never should have let him teach here. He'll stop at nothing."

"What's that got to do with Don?"

"Everything."

"What are you saying? That Don's involved in some ... what? Theft? A scandal?

Dex looked down at the floor, as if deciding whether he should respond. At last he said, "Someone falsified some lab data. Someone else found out."

"Why would they do that?"

"Well ... it seems that Sauer's company needs research money, and Sauer himself was running low on credibility."

"Really! But Don—he wouldn't sink that low; would he?"

"It's not clear. Sauer signed his name to the paper and faxed it all over the place. One of his grad students blew the whistle. MIT quietly booted Sauer, who never implicated Don. Now the Ad Board is questioning Don, who so far has refused to accuse Sauer. Quite honestly, I don't know what happened. Except that it's a good thing they never started human clinicals."

"Who's the grad student?"

"What does that matter? Look, I've said too much already. This whole incident may become a tremendous embarrassment to the Institute and its faculty."

Dex always referred to MIT as the "Institute." That usually prompted me to quip, "You mean, *the Institution*," but this time I held off. "MIT has nothing to be embarrassed about if it got rid of Sauer. The more public they make it the better, it seems to me."

"Well, my young American friend, it's not that simple," Dex explained. "Sauer is a one-man public-relations campaign for the virtues of corporate sponsorship. A lot of people—influential people—think consulting for industry compromises a professor's objectivity. Those people are making more and more noise, pushing for this restriction or that guideline. The faculty wants the money for obvious reasons. The Institute needs the money to keep top-flight faculty. And Sauer's made a name for himself fighting with the critics. He's constantly being quoted in the *Times*, in the *Journal*, telling everyone that scientists can be trusted to speak the truth even when it hurts them financially."

"So everyone wants to keep this hush-hush."

"Right. The Institute has no desire to become a high-profile target for critics of corporate sponsorship. Sauer is officially leaving on a voluntary basis to pursue other research, and his company—this is his *fourth* company—is quietly severing its ties with the Institute. It's in no one's interest to get into the gory details."

"Don being one of the details?"

"Exactly."

"So what you're telling me is, even if Boyer is innocent, MIT might want to make an example of him—sort of, like, to prove the capacity of the system to keep itself clean by discharging the rotten elements."

"I didn't say that," Dex responded, carefully measuring his words. "The Institute would never stoop to such levels. But innocence is in the eye of the beholder."

"This is ridiculous. If MIT jettisons Don unfairly, he'd broadcast his story to the world, wouldn't he?"

"Not if he ever wants to work in molecular biology."

"So Sauer and his company can just step over Boyer's body and walk away. Maybe even refine and resell the technology somewhere else."

Silence.

Only in Course 7 could this ever happen, I told myself. Only in Course 7.

"Anyway," said Dex, "please get back to me on these Hasty Pudding tickets as soon as you can, okay?"

A performance in Harvard Square; it sounded fun, actually. I hadn't seen Penny since the day Dex first met her. I'd probably overrated her. I wondered what she'd wear.

Of course Rita would be a complication. Clearly, the only way to get her out on the same date with Dex would be to raise the issue at an inopportune moment.

At exactly 6:15 I entered Building W32. And as expected, Rita was fully absorbed in the details of some textbook or other, building up a profuse sweat. Her legs glistened as they flexed and extended, and perspiration droplets fell from her eyelashes. She was on the Stairmaster. She'd been climbing for at least twenty minutes now, mind and body thoroughly exhausted; she looked, actually, pretty damn good.

"How would you feel about a Hasty Pudding performance?" I asked her, shattering the concentration.

She looked at me as if I'd just arrived from a different arm of the galaxy. "You want to go out? Like on a date?" she asked. Her voice followed the rhythm of her leg movements.

I mentioned the particulars and she said, "Great!" and returned to her twin toils.

"Oh, someone I recently met will be coming along," I said casually as I walked away. The room was noisy, and at least two dozen other people were working out on treadmills and exercise bikes. "Someone from Harvard."

"Fine," said Rita.

I was almost at the door now, and at least four bobbing, shaking heads intervened in my line of sight. I prepared to deliver the *coup de grâce*. "And her boyfriend," I said, practically yelling over the ambient noise level.

"Fine!" Rita shot back, clearly anxious to be rid of me.

"Terrific. I'll tell Dex, then."

I marched out the door as Rita's yells of "Hey, get the hell back here you bastard, goddamn it this is bullshit!" faded. I'd hoped for greater decorum, quite frankly.

It was a production about some people planning a stage parody of some mainstream television shows. A performance about a performance about other performances. Penny pronounced Hasty Pudding's efforts "very meta." I, for one, didn't enjoy it. The play was tedious. The acting was pretentious. And there was a picture fixed in my head that I couldn't shake.

On the way over Rita and I had collected Dex at BioVitrics headquarters since it was so close to the Red Line. After making us sign our name in the guest register, the suspicious after-hours receptionist reluctantly led us down a well-lit corridor to Dex's lab. The space was small, only a few equipment-filled rooms, and completely silent; it appeared that we were all alone. As the three of us exchanged pleasantries on the way out of Dex's lab, my eye caught the quiet glow of twilight emerging through the vertical blinds in the window of the next door. Through the blinds, before the deepening azure sky that spread across the much larger window on the opposite wall, the backlit silhouette of Don Boyer stood out like a black cutout portrait—his head bowed, hands folded together on his knees. Don's strained, fleshless shadow stayed with me like a persistent retinal afterimage.

Of all the absurdities! I was feeling a germ of sympathy for the repugnant Don Boyer.

After the show we headed to the Starbucks for a snack. Rita was stiff as a board, totally uncommunicative. Penny looked magnificent in a colorful skirt and frilly white blouse.

"Why so quiet?" Dex asked Rita as we walked down Mass. Ave.

Rita said nothing. She was punishing me for cajoling her along, making me feel awkward. It was working.

"Her new faculty adviser is driving her crazy," I responded, returning the punishment by making an excuse for her. "He sounds like quite the airhead."

"How so?" Dex asked with the concern of an old friend.

Finally Rita spoke. "He doesn't understand the first thing about statistics, and he's making me pay the price for his ignorance every single day."

"How do you mean?" Dex pushed.

"I mean he's always on my case. You know how it is, when someone gets on your case and just won't get off?"

Dex got the message and promptly shut up.

"Are you sure it's his statistics you're bothered about?" Penny asked, maneuvering next to Rita.

"And exactly what do you mean by that?" Rita demanded.

"Well, it's just that ... you reminded me of something that happened when I first got to Harvard. Freshman year I had a European Lit TA who absolutely infuriated me. He would needle me in class. Scoff at my ideas. He laughed at my every word, and when I said nothing he challenged my silence. I assumed I'd somehow offended him with some inadvertent slight and now he would exact retribution every day of class. But one day I realized, well, perhaps it's not pure meanness. Maybe he's soliciting attention. Maybe this little twerp has eyes for me!"

We stopped walking. Rita looked at Penny with rapt attention. It seemed as though she was beginning to unclench.

"It made me extremely uncomfortable, of course" Penny continued. "I was afraid to go to class. But I talked to my roommate, and she totally wised me up. She said, hey, consider yourself lucky. *This* you can *do* something about. And I did. I smiled at him when he wasn't expecting it. I looked at him languorously when he lectured. And as soon as he sensed I might be interested he retreated like a startled vole; he avoided me as if I were rancid meat and gave me an A minus. Rita, you're a very attractive woman. You've got to recognize the effect you can have on men, and the discomfort their attentions can cause you without your even realizing it."

Rita just stood there, stunned, the way Dex had been stunned after his first encounter with Penny. Finally Rita looked deeply into Penny's eyes and said, "I *love* your scarf. Where did you get it?"

"This? Oh, I've got a million of them," Penny replied. "You know where the best place to buy scarves is? There's a little shop just across from Faneuil Hall downtown..."

They walked off. They were bonding.

Dex and I tagged along behind them. He had his hands in his

pockets, relaxed, with the indulgent smile of a content family man. I hadn't noticed before, but his taste in clothes was certainly improving. The stained jeans had been exchanged for pleated wool slacks and the tee shirts for striped button-downs. He was blow-drying his hair. He wore contact lenses more often. I couldn't believe it: my roommate almost looked handsome in a ruddy, warthog way. This would take some getting used to.

13

At the end of September we closed the venture financing. I had twenty-five thousand dollars to play with, although only Jeff and Star had authority to sign any checks. And if things went well another twenty-five K would be waiting just beyond the first milestone.

By early October Rita and Penny had become close friends. The four of us went out together nearly every weekend, usually just for a couple of hours, after which we would pair off by gender. Dex and I would return to MIT. Rita and Penny would go shopping.

Shopping! Go figure.

Penny led us along brick-sidewalked roads with names like Acacia and Ash and Appian Way, where iron filigree decorates carved stone walls and clapboard houses hide behind flowing ivy beards. This was the nice part of Cambridge—the part that generates all those silvered visions. Around us colorful leaves fell silently, like puffs of luminous confetti, and soaked the air with their sweet organic scent. Penny remarked, "The New England fall is such a masterpiece of nature, don't you think? You know, I've lived here my whole life and the miracle impresses me every single year!"

"Well, it's not a miracle, really," I pointed out. "Chlorophyll ordinarily colors leaves green. As it decomposes the natural russets and yellows begin to emerge. Scarlet hues come from sugars, which accumulate in the cool weather, and through a complex chain of reactions turn into the red dye anthocyanin."

Penny glanced back at me as if bemused by a sideshow freak. Rita said nothing.

"Just beautiful," Dex agreed.

Now that politic surrender really was too much. Since when had Dex shrunk from his responsibility to unravel the mysteries of science and disabuse the gushings of the uninitiated? It had been *he* who had taught *me* about anthocyanin!

Penny's thumb hung on Dex's belt. As we walked she drew her hand up the back of his shirt, rubbed his shoulders, and cupped his neck. Unconsciously I reached for Rita's hand. It was limp and a little cold. It didn't want to be held.

"I don't do affection," she whispered.

Dex and Penny ducked behind an arched stone entry to Harvard Yard, pausing for a discreet, presumably passionate kiss before Dex and I would descend the stairs to the Red Line. Rita gripped my hand as we stood outside.

"I just don't do affection," she repeated. "I *do* do sex, however, and you're getting it more often per unit time than anyone else at MIT. Consider yourself lucky. Most guys would."

As she spoke I could practically taste the stabbing, throbbing pain growing behind my eyes. I knew the pleasure Dex was experiencing, the rushing thrill of the love he felt, the unquantifiable joy of greeting the entire world each morning feeling as if its every detail had been constructed to divine specification, just for him. I saw how he engaged Penny's every peripheral and accessory—the way she lifted her fork, the angle her head made when she cocked it in jest, how her clothes always seemed to match her eyes, the stares she provoked from others. I saw the same perfection he saw, and through recollection I felt all the warmth and fullness he felt. I'd been there too, once.

My only consolation was the knowledge that Rita didn't harbor any unrealistic, sentimental notions about our relationship. At least her departure from MIT come graduation wouldn't be complicated by the painful shards of emotional commitment. Rita held little sympathy for others and sought none for herself; that simplified things considerably.

As Dex and I walked down the stairs to the train I wondered if he could feel the bitter streaking cold the handrail transmitted up my spine. I wondered if he noticed how I would slip into silent standby mode whenever Penny was around. I wondered if he could detect the extra snap I gave the keys on our computer terminal when he spent time on the phone with her. I wondered if to him I was as transparent as a slab of his bioactive glass, and whether he could have cared less.

In November, after the crush of midterms had passed, we began to spend entire weekend days together. And not only together. Occasionally we would be exposed to clutches of Penny's friends, her *Harvard* friends, who chattered everything they learned or touched or felt into inane triviality. One Saturday she dragged us down to Newport in a van stuffed full of these chosen few, these brawny intellects who clogged our ears with punctuationless commentary on the proceduralistic patriarchal prison of dead, white Eurocentric culture and the emerging enlightened emancipation of multicultural sensibility, about the sheer fascist enormity of Fritz Lang's *Metropolis* and the cool formal grace of Robert Mapplethorpe's leather fantasies and on and on. It was enough to make you sick. Everything was 'PC' this and 'PC' that. Since when did Harvard prisses get so worked up over personal computers?

We finally lost them on the cliff walk. Fog and rain had been predicted, sending the cackling Harvard invertebrates scurrying through Newport's tangle of boutiques and bodegas, but instead the sky was fully blanketed by striated bands of sleek autumn clouds. There would be no rain. And as we meandered along the edge of the Rhode Island Sound, the water on our left and the huge, ostentatious Newport mansions on our right, I decided I didn't like Penny all that much after all. Her logic was peculiar, her thoughts lacked precision, and to her everything was just *soooo* miraculous.

So it was no surprise when, near the end of the walk, she suddenly stopped dead and pointed with excitement as we turned a corner. A hulking gray battleship, festooned with a gaud of radar dishes, antennas, gangplanks and guns of various sizes, was slowly wending its way east. It had caught Penny's attention and she said, "Who would believe such a metal gargantuan could possibly sit atop the water like that instead of sinking to the bottom like a stone. It's amazing, don't you think?"

A miracle! I thought. *Please don't say it!*

I wanted to tell her that it's one thing to be impressed by a large body finding its level of neutral buoyancy but quite another to bubble over with such mindless wonderment. I hoped wanly that Dex would be merciful enough to explain how any immersed body displaces its own weight in fluid, and perhaps even mention Archimedes' recognition that this accounts for the body's apparent loss in weight.

But no. Instead Dex put his arm around Penny's shoulder and said: "Will you look at that."

In what she obviously thought was a private instant Penny

slipped her mouth suggestively over Dex's outstretched thumb, and pretended not to catch my eye as she returned her attention to the ship and the endless sea—standing tall next to Dex, the stiff off-shore wind scattering her hair like wild streamers, obviously not giving a damn what I observed or thought or wished or felt.

"You still haven't noticed what I'm wearing," said Rita, startling me slightly. She smiled playfully.

It was true, I hadn't noticed, but what was so momentous? Her latest fashion exoskeleton was just more bounty from her shopping safaris with Penny—a stylish denim jacket, a maroon turtleneck, a dark Pendleton skirt. Somehow on her it looked wrong. What gave Penny a certain *je ne sais quois* on Rita looked like I don't know what.

"I told you you were having an effect on me," she said. I wished I had just the slightest inkling of how her mind worked. "Don't you like it?"

"I can't say I don't like it," I told her. "Maybe I just need to get used to your new look."

Now Rita studied me carefully. "You think I've sold out, don't you? You think I've betrayed my principles. Well, you're wrong. Staying true to your values doesn't mean you have to spend every waking minute projecting them like a billboard. It's not hypocritical to ... hey, Penny," Rita called, "do you think I've sold out?"

In what was either a fortuity of the rushing wind or Penny's deft tactfulness she replied, "Sailed out? No, I think it's heading in, probably bound for Boston Harbor. They have dry docks there."

"Wiseman, do you think I've sold out?" Rita asked him as he made his way to the door that evening. I had just told him he was being relieved of his nightly duties as Rita's student and caretaker. It was my latest attempt at humorous execution of the Wiseman Shoo.

"I advise you to be careful, Rita," he said.

"So what do you think of California?" Rita asked me. "Specifically, Pasadena?"

"You mean where Cal Tech is?"

"And my old adviser. I'm thinking about their master's program."

"That sounds really exciting," I told her.

"What if I said I was pregnant? How would you feel then?"

My heart pounded. "Are you ... you can't possibly be—"

"No, I'm not. I said 'what if.' What would you think of Pasadena then?"

"Well, I ... I guess I haven't heard anything particularly awful about the place. Cal Tech students aren't getting robbed and murdered every day of the week, right? I'm sure it's an okay place to raise kids."

"Even if they were your kids?"

"Well, I, uh ... why are you asking me these questions?"

"I mean, you wouldn't impose one set of standards on your kids and another on mine, would you?"

"No. Of course not."

"And what about for yourself? Are you saying you'd enjoy living in Pasadena? You wouldn't impose one set of standards on me and another on yourself, would you?"

She had me utterly baffled at this point, and seemed to sense my hesitation.

"Ummm ... no."

"Then why do you keep me shielded from your family as if I were a gamma emitter?"

Now the confusion level was reaching absurd proportions. "Rita, what are you saying?"

"No, what are *you* saying?"

"Are you ... asking me to move out to California with you?" All of a sudden this was starting to get complicated. Just what I was hoping to avoid.

Rita rolled her eyes. "Of course not! That is most definitely *not* something I asked you. Is it, Wiseman?"

Wiseman fidgeted nervously by the door. "Evidently you choose to ignore my advice to be careful. Very well," he said, lacing his burst of words with a growl of irritation. He flitted out of the room.

"Is it so much to ask to meet your family? To know that you're not ashamed of ... us?" she asked.

"Absolutely not," I said. What a relief! "Want to have Christmas dinner with the Bustamante clan?"

"Took you long enough to ask," said Rita.

It was right around this time that Jeff summoned me to his office to discuss progress. He expressed dissatisfaction.

"I know you're dating Rita," he said. "I can tell from your EDGAR log-ons, originating in her room late at night."

"You mean you're monitoring my log-on habits? Jeff—isn't that illegal or something?"

"My point is this. If you spent more time at the keyboard and less time in Rita's pants, maybe you'd be farther along by now."

"Rita doesn't wear pants anymore," I told him ruefully.

"Must I be crude, then?"

"But I'm ... it's just ... Jeff, weren't you ever young?"

"Nonsensical question. Everyone no longer young was obviously once young. But if your intent is nonliteral and you're asking me whether I've ever experienced romance..." Jeff rubbed his hands together; they made a dry sound like sand paper. "Look, I know how it is. I went to college also. Tried intercourse once. Twice, almost. Didn't like it."

I looked around his office, desperate for any excuse to change the subject. Behind his desk, under the table that supported his computer, was an odd piece of equipment—a translucent red tube attached vertically to a base support, with a short metal-tipped conduit extending diagonally outward near the bottom. I pointed and said, "Say, Jeff, is that some kind of laser fitting? The housing of an optical storage device you're building?"

"Leave El Kabong out of this," he replied. "Listen. I'm not trying to turn you into me. I've made my choices. This"—he gestured toward the spherical computer behind him—"is my dancing partner. It's a horridly complex piece of iron but it behaves logically. I created it, I understand it, and it does exactly what I tell it to do. I'm no longer surprised by idiosyncrasies. Now if you want to merge yourself into a world of random human errors and relationship instabilities, be my guest. But at least get your priorities straight! Remember how much time you've already invested in this work! You've only got six months to reach the first milestone, and if you fail, this project will never see another dollar."

"I'm really concerned about data acquisition," I said. "I still haven't gotten any response from Noah on my request for all those surface and upper-air measurements."

"I have," Jeff replied. "They communicated with me directly. They want about a million dollars. More or less."

I sank back into the plastic seat back. "A million dollars," I repeated. "Why didn't you tell me? We're screwed!"

"Obviously my attitude differs from yours. I will not let myself get screwed," said Jeff and, immediately regretting the pun even as it slipped out, he hastily continued, "I believe I have convinced the bureaucrats to part with their data for the sum of $15,000."

"How'd you manage that?"

"Well, quite honestly, I abased myself. I emulated greatness. I told them I was Edward Lorenz—it was a marvelous simulation, I wish you could have seen it. Of course it was rather humiliating—telling them how critical the data are to my Nobel-laureate work, thanking them profusely for their magnanimous concession to my budget, requesting that they send all their piles of material to my faithful assistant and flunky, Jeffrey S. Watt—that's W-A-T-T, care of the Hayward Garage; yes, that's right, G-A-R-A-G-E, as in fumes and horns, yessiree, Jeff's the Quasimodo of Building E42 and gives us all quite the chuckle with that hunched back and carbon-monoxide cough of his..." He trailed off, staring directly into my eyes, but then suddenly smiled. "See? It was easy."

"Jeff. You're incredible. You're absolutely incredible."

"No one uses that word correctly anymore," Jeff said with a frown. "So what's your first milestone?"

"A wide-area forecast improvement of ten percent over the Weather Service's best efforts. Sound impressive enough?"

"Not if you never get us there." His voice seemed a little sad, as if burdened. "Just get something done, all right?"

And I did. It was no problem, really. Rita's confusing demands and Penny's mindless gushings and her perfect face and the ceaseless affectionate gestures she heaped on the man she called "Dexter"—*Dexter!*—were beginning to get on my nerves anyway, and I was just as happy to spend more of my time with EDGAR. A lot more time.

By the end of November I completed the basic mathematical framework of my weather model. EDGAR and I, really. We did it together. We'd learned to communicate on equal footing. It was purely a matter of thinking together, of matching neural thought patterns to computer processing patterns—knowing how the machine will execute its instructions, what any one instruction will accomplish, and what effect that will have on all the remaining instructions. It takes enormous concentration to replace relaxed, unreliable cortical thinking with digital logic and efficiency. I began to slip into the routine of a true hacker—days without nights in the sealed environment of one of the windowless, acoustically isolated, fluorescent-lit computer labs; cans of Coke for breakfast, lunch and dinner; increasing disregard for hygiene and appearance; and phenomenal progress.

I was never alone in the lab. There was always someone at another terminal who had been at it longer than I, who would stay at it longer than I, and who could probably blow the doors off my computer code with minimal effort. Soon enough I realized the true reason for these marathon sessions. It had nothing to do with mystical attachment to computers. It did not reflect disdain for the company of humans.

The reason was fear.

Fear that sleeping or taking a shower would decimate the concentration. Fear that eating a sandwich would somehow alter the body's chemistry and destroy the peculiar synaptic circuitry necessary to maintain awareness of how all the processing loops nest into one another and where the recursions leave off. Fear that success is but an instruction or two over the run-time horizon and the slightest interruption will postpone the triumph indefinitely or—worse—crash the system and sweep away hours of work in a furious torrent of error messages and meaningless characters. So much fear that the friendliest voice is greeted with misfit antisocial snarls that raise the intensity level of an already overcharged atmosphere, and no one minds, since only in just such an atmosphere can the marathon sessions continue. The natural consequences of exhaustion would prevail anywhere else.

EDGAR and I were speaking the same language. We understood one another. So I explained patiently that, first, we needed a discriminator function—a flagman to separate turbulent regions from still regions. That would certainly be doable, we realized. Funny but characteristic things begin to happen as chaos approaches. Measurements taken at different times begin to correlate with one another. What looks like random noise actually harbors strange constant patterns, and from these, with a little math, we can not only recognize turbulence but derive its fractal dimension! It would be easy!

Remember, EDGAR, I remonstrated, we're conceiving a world together. We've got to populate a whole grid of spatial coordinates with living, breathing numbers before we can flip back to the time domain and make our predictions. At first our world is mostly empty; we'll have actual measurements only at a few points. That's enough for non-turbulent regions, where we can lace them together with our statistics. Too bad those statistics go nuts in the turbulent regions. That's where things get tricky, EDGAR. Very tricky.

The fractal dimension is our zoom lens. With it we can jump

between spatial scales, they all resemble one another, so we can use measurements from a wide area to imagine ourselves into a much smaller region. Pretty slick, eh? As if you could sharpen a grainy photograph by blowing it up and shrinking it back down. Oh, we'll leave them speechless when our fractal pogo stick lets us forecast weeks—months!—into the future. When we revolutionize meteorology! When we start cashing the royalty checks!

EDGAR understood all this.

And then there was the computer code. It had to be perfect. They say a good hacker can peer into another programmer's heart, know how his mind works, just by reading his code. EDGAR was the ultimate hacker as well as the ultimate hack. Course 6 people claimed EDGAR could write its own instructions. That it sometimes fixed the bugs in people's programs without their even knowing it. That it formed an opinion of you early on, and if you were a loser, you'd get no help from EDGAR. I couldn't afford to embarrass myself. I couldn't jeopardize any possible source of advantage. That would be even worse than taking a shower before I was done.

And by the end of November, there it was. The framework was complete—ready to chew on some weather data. Soon I'd expand it into an E-M engine that could swallow anything. The whole weather model would be just one special case, like a plug-in module, and the engine's generality would provide the power needed to fine tune the model.

Before long I'd be in a position to determine whether I was forging genius or chasing snipes.

"Well, how do I look?" Rita asked as she swiveled her hips in front of the mirror behind her door.

I was getting used to the new Rita, and she didn't look half bad, really. Her dark skirt and the muted greens and salmons of her blouse combined to satisfy every tenet of color theory; hue, value and chroma were fully compatible. She told me that Santa Fe colors were like, really big in California.

"You look great," I told her.

She sniffed the air. "And I notice you're bathing again. I take it you've rejoined the human race?" Without waiting for an answer she fired another self-conscious question as she affixed a seashell earring. "What do you think of these? Penny lent them to me."

"Great, really. Look Rita, I haven't told you this yet," I began, "but there are a few things you should know about my family before you meet them."

"Tell me in the car," she said as she clasped the other seashell earring. "We're running late."

As we drove along the Mass. Pike I told Rita what she'd be in for. I told her about Larry, about Larry and Tracy, about Tony and Tracy, about Artie.

"What about your parents?" Rita asked. "Let me hear more about them."

"Not much to tell, really," I said. "Father's a computer engineer. Mother's in fund-raising."

"Isn't that more of a man's world?" Rita asked.

"Well, I suppose so. That never stopped Mom."

"And your father. Didn't you say he was civvie before he went electrical?"

"That was ages ago. Although, actually, he still does a bit of civil engineering as a side line. He redesigned the access roads at one of IBM's buildings in Armonk, for example."

"You sure about this thing going on between your uncle and Tracy? I mean, you've got solid evidence?"

"Beyond question. You'll see for yourself."

Larry and Tracy hadn't yet arrived when we pulled into the driveway. My parents were waiting at the door, full of smiles, hearty greeting and, I'm sure, a certain amount of relief that their elder son hadn't turned into an asexual curiosity.

After the amenities Rita fumbled through her purse and said to my father, "I came across this in the AI lab, and thought you might get a kick out of it." She produced a 3-1/2 inch floppy diskette labelled SIM CITY.

My father inspected the disk like a glass of aged Bordeaux. "Wow," he said and immediately repeated, "I mean *wow!*" He turned to my mother. "You know what this is? This program lets you build cities on your computer! Oh, not real cities of course, but you pretend you're the mayor and city planner of a hypothetical metropolis trying to stave off natural disasters or overcome the effects of poor early planning."

He raced up the stairs just as Larry and Tracy pulled into the driveway.

"Why don't you kids follow us in the Dodge," said my mother. "Six is a crowd in either of our cars."

Soon my father bounced back down to the living room, waving a laptop over his head, still holding the diskette in his other hand. "This is the perfect machine to run Sim City—IBM's latest full-color portable," he told Rita as Larry and Tracy came in the front door.

"With the 64-bit Pentium chip?" asked Rita.

"Yes ... yes!" said my father with growing enthusiasm. "You certainly know your x86 architectures." He turned to me. "Good taste, son. Good taste." Then he looked over his shoulder. "Oh, hi Larry. Hi Tracy."

My mother said, "You're not bringing that thing to—oh, never mind. Let's get going."

By the time I got the keys from my parents and climbed into the front seat of the Dodge, Larry was already going on nonstop about Tracy. About how they met at camp. About how she took pity on a desperate, rotting soul and lifted him from misery with her tender glance. About how she loved Larry and animals and the homeless and Elvis.

"How special," said Rita.

"Hi," Tracy said to Rita as she climbed into the back seat next to Larry. "No one introduced us. I'm Tracy."

"And I'm gonna hurl," said Rita with a congenial smile.

At this point I sensed trouble.

"So you're Paul's girlfriend?" said Tracy.

"Are you asking me or telling me?" Rita asked.

"Well..." said Tracy after a pause. Larry changed the subject. "You two have been together now, what, almost a year?"

"I suppose it depends on how you define 'together,'" I said. "Let's keep the conversation delicate."

Rita smirked at me sarcastically. "Where do you go to school?" she asked Tracy.

"Binghamton? SUNY Binghamton?" Tracy replied.

"Are you asking me or telling me?" Rita demanded.

"What does she mean, Larry?" Tracy asked.

"It's the way you talk," Rita explained. "What are you majoring in?"

"Well, it's like I haven't made up my mind? But I'm thinking of psychology?"

Rita rolled her eyes. "You must be joking."

Tracy was not joking. "What does she mean, Larry?" Tracy repeated.

"I'm talking about your intonation," said Rita. "Your voice

rises at the end of your sentences like you're asking a question." I hadn't noticed this mannerism before, but it was firmly embedded in Tracy's speech patterns.

"I've always found that so charming," said Larry.

Rita was unimpressed. "It's a sign of diffidence. Don't be ashamed of what you have to say. You're an intelligent woman, right? Don't apologize in advance for your views."

"Wow," said Tracy.

"I still find it charming," said Larry, smiling at Tracy. It was so sickening.

"It's a charming way of subordinating her individuality," Rita said. "That's what you're doing. That's why she keeps asking you what other people mean. You're encouraging submissive behavior. Maybe you weren't aware."

"I know about submissive behavior!" Tracy exclaimed like an eager pupil. She turned to Larry. "Encouraging it is patriarchal. It's like male dominance? I mean, IT'S LIKE MALE DOMINANCE!"

Larry said nothing. That was pretty much it for the rest of the ride.

We arrived at the Sebastianis' right on time but Tony was annoyed anyway. As each of us queued past his artificial smile and deposited a coat into his arms he said, "And how are *you* this evening?"

"Fine," said my mother.

"Fine," I said.

"Terrific," said my father, straightening Tony's tie. Tony's eyes widened into white-hot flares but his smile stuck.

"Actually, I've got cramps that could stop a truck. Thanks for asking," said Rita, dumping her coat. Tony's smile vanished.

"Why Tracy," said Tony, pushing past Rita into the doorway. "It's so nice to see you." And then he added, "Oh, hi Larry."

When we reached the living room Gina was setting up the usual complement of hors d'oeuvres and drinks on the new pink, polished-granite server. Shaped like a massive staple, it had curved edges and nothing but empty space between its heavy sides. Gina wore a billowy flowered skirt; she'd put on a couple of pounds. The kids were absent but their residue—a sweatshirt, popsicle sticks, a mangled shoe—was scattered around Uncle Artie, who was talking to himself on a small matching polished-granite bench that occupied the space once claimed by Artie's plush wood-trimmed cushiony chair. Form had fully triumphed over function and comfort in the Sebastiani home.

And the Christmas tree had gone fully electric. The colored lights danced spasmodically, as usual, but now large rotating ornaments revealed decoupage nativity scenes as they turned. Servo-operated electromechanical bear ornaments banged out Christmas carols on little bells attached to their bodies.

Gina took Rita's hand and said, "So you're Paul's girlfriend!"

"I guess you could say that," said Rita.

"Have a clam, they just came out of the oven," said Gina. "I won't take no for an answer."

"She won't take no for an answer," echoed Tony, entering the room and dropping onto the long polished-granite bench that had replaced the couch.

"What does that mean?" Rita asked Tony.

"Yeah, what does that mean?" repeated Gina. It was instant solidarity. "You're always criticizing me."

"And you're always eating," he retorted.

"Hey, that's different. That's a psychological condition, a phobia. Fear of starvation," said Gina.

"So what?" Tony retorted.

"So you should respect it."

"I do respect it, my income buys the food. But it's getting out of control."

"It's a phobia," said Rita. "Maybe she needs help."

"I can't afford food *and* help," said Tony.

"But you can afford to criticize everything I say because that costs you nothing, right?" Suddenly Gina was on a roll. "Why should my phobias bother you? They do you no harm."

"Hey, you're my wife, right? I look at you every day of my life just about. I want to like what I see."

"Bulldozer," said my father from the other end of the granite bench. He'd booted up the laptop and was fully absorbed in the game.

"Bulldoze her? You mean Gina?" asked Tony. "Oh come on, it's not that bad."

Gina had her hands on her hips. "Are you comparing your very own sister to earth-moving equipment?" she demanded.

Finding himself the unexpected center of attention, my father looked around and said, "It's an icon on this game. See, you can only build on clear land. I'm using the bulldozer to get rid of some trees. Did someone ask me something?"

"I begged you to let me go to Albuquerque with Rosa!" Gina raged, returning her attention to Tony.

"That place is for sick people," said Tony. "You just need to eat less."

"How do you know I'm not sick?" Gina retorted. "That's what they told Marty Larusso." Gina turned to the rest of us. "Dropped dead on the stairs to the subway one week after the company physical that gave him a clean bill of health, thank you very much. God bless his poor soul. I can't even talk about it."

She exited into the kitchen. Larry, descending the stairs on his return from the bathroom, called out, "Hey, who's Star Ventures?"

"Star," I responded proudly, "is the venture-capital outfit that just financed my project to the tune of twenty-five thousand bucks, with more on the way."

"No kidding," said Larry. "They the same ones who bankrolled your roommate?"

"Yeah. But how did you..."

"Hey Gina!" whined Tony. "When're we gonna eat already?"

Gina came out of the kitchen and announced, "I guess it's time for dinner, if my husband will allow dining to take place in his palace. Can I invite our guests to seat themselves?" she asked Tony. "Are you sure it's all right for them to eat?"

"As long as we're not feeding anyone's phobias," Tony retorted as he led the way to the dining room. He looked back us. "Phobias, anyone? Is anyone in need of pre-*mangia* counseling?"

Gina began passing out bowls of *manast*, a clear Italian soup with leafy greens and little meat dollops. She also set out a dish of steaming baked codfish.

"So," said Tony, flapping open his napkin, "you're Paul's girlfriend?" He was sitting directly across from Rita.

"I guess you could say that."

"You must be from New York."

"No. What makes you think so?"

"Oh no, nothing. Really. It's just that we were beginning to worry about Paul."

"Worry?" Rita asked.

"Sure. You know, like whether he'd ever, like, lose his, how shall I say..."

"Inexperience?"

"Right, exactly!"

"And you were worried about this?"

"Sure we were. I was, anyway. This is a totally normal family." Tony sliced the air over his bowl with his hand. "Totally."

"And you were relieved to find Paul had met a New Yorker who might exhibit, *how shall I say*, a certain moral lassitude?"

"Well…" Tony cocked his head: the sentiment speaks for itself.

"Rita, I don't think that's what Tony meant," said my father. Soup dribbled onto his tie. It wasn't the first time.

"Sure he did," said my mother. "Didn't you, Tony?"

"Bada-boom, bada-bing," said Rita, push-pulling her fists like a smug boxer, mocking Tony's strut, "end of innocence. Is that it?"

"Jesus H. Kee-rist! Am I being cross-examined? Is that what's happening?" Tony whipped his head from side to side.

"Tony, I really don't think that's the intent here. Loosen up." said my father.

"Too loose, Lautrec," said Artie.

"And what if it is the intent?" my mother snapped. The women were united.

"Maybe we can find a New York lawyer to make an assessment," said Rita.

"Hey Tracy," said Tony, veering sharply, "Tell us how your sophomore year is going?"

"Are you asking me or telling me?" asked Tracy.

Tony thought she was joking. He pointed at her and bent back in laughter.

Artie said: "Ho ho ho Henry Higgins." He sipped his soup noisily. Gina studied Tony as his laughter subsided, then glanced at Tracy.

"The difference is important," Tracy persisted. She turned to Rita. "Isn't it?"

Larry jumped in. "You shouldn't ask questions to hide your feelings or opinions," he told Tony.

"I was only asking her because she knows what she's talking about!" quipped Tracy. She thought Larry had been speaking to her, mistaking his expression of support for criticism.

"Okay, okay," said Larry. "What are *you* saying?"

"I was just saying *something*!" Tracy retorted. She looked confused; her eyes were blank. "Fine. I just won't say anything anymore."

"Can I have the codfish?" said Tony, looking down the table.

"You never understand anything I say anyway," Tracy said to Larry.

"How can you talk like that, baby? I always..."

"And don't call me 'baby.' It's like male dominance?" She glanced over at Rita and said, "I mean..."

"Did you teach him that?" my mother snapped at my father.

"Baby, baby," whined Antonia, taunting Johnny. They started shoving one another.

"Pass the codfish!" said Tony.

"Why's everyone mad at me now? What did I do?" Larry asked.

Artie suddenly rose, sending his chair tumbling backward. "I have an announcement," he told the startled company in a loud, gravelly voice. "I am retiring from what I do for a living. Now I know most of you think I've already retired, that I spend my days gaping at television or putting up with the abuse I get around here like some meatball. Like some looney tunes! But you're wrong, all of you! I'm an artist, see? Have been for years. With these hands I have made a fortune! I have influenced the lives of everyone at this table with my art, and none of you even realizes it. That's why I am great. But now I'm done with all that, okay? I have left my mark. In a couple of months I'll be moving to Kiawah Island in South Carolina. I'll lounge in the sun and all of you can sit around here, regretting the years of ridicule and, uh ... torment! I hope you'll be happy."

"But why?" I asked, incredulous.

"Ah, it's the CDs," said Artie. "They're so small. Everything's pint-sized these days. There's no room left for the art, real art. Now it's just packaging. Besides, I'm sicka the marble and all this rock furniture around here. It hurts my butt."

"What will you do with yourself all day long?" I asked.

"Bocci, for starters. Beyond that, well, who can say?" Artie responded, his palms outstretched as he shrugged his shoulders. Then he picked up his chair and sat back down. The stunned silence was almost overpowering.

Finally Tony exclaimed, "So is anyone going to pass the goddamn codfish?"

Gina slapped his forehead and pointed at the kids.

"Stop with the friggin' head!" said Tony.

Gina slapped his forehead again. Tony pushed his chair back and yelled, "Enough with the head!"

"Good one, Dad!" said Joey.

"Can't you have some respect?" Gina said as she smacked the table.

"Way to go, Mom!" said Antonia. "Baby, baby," she whispered at Joey.

My father leaned back and smiled. "Listen, you two…"

"Oh, shut up!" Tony and Gina yelled in unison. Gina retreated to the kitchen.

"But tell me how you really feel, why don't you," joked my father. He wouldn't give up. My mother was shaking her head, rubbing her temples with her fingers.

Tony looked at Tracy and said, "I'm sorry you had to be here for this. Sometimes the Sebastiani men get, well … *appassionato*!"

My mother said, "They certainly know how to charm the ladies."

"Well, maybe not if they're from New York," said Tony, directing his anger at Rita out of fear of my mother. That was a mistake.

"Why so much concern about Tracy, anyway?" Rita came back. "Is she your fantasy object or is there more to it? Well? Is there? Is there more to it than simple unfulfilled lust?"

Gina heard this. All at once so much made sense. She leaped from the kitchen wielding a wooden spoon dripping tomato sauce, holding it aloft in a gesture of assault. "SNAKE!" she yelled at Tony, who slumped back in his chair, exasperated.

"Shoot me, please!" said Tony. "Somebody shoot me!"

But then, realizing the tomato sauce on the spoon would be replaced with his blood if he didn't act quickly, Tony darted out of his chair and ran for the stairs.

"SNAKE!" yelled Gina, racing after him.

We all sat quietly and watched the unfolding drama taking place on the balcony at the head of the stairs, where Tracy had fallen exactly one year ago. Gina bolting after Tony into the bedroom. Tony racing out of the bedroom, then gracefully sailing down the iron banister with his arms outstretched for balance, catching a last look at Tracy before flinging himself through the front door.

"SNAKE!" yelled Gina, hoping to head Tony off by bounding down the steps to the basement and into the garage. Feet scuffed on rubber stair treads. Doors slammed. Tony's BMW roared into action outside. We could hear the tires screeching backward, out of the driveway, onto the street and into the distance. Then silence.

"What now?" asked Larry.

"It might be a while," sighed Artie. "Where'd my toothpick go, anyway?"

My father returned to the bench and rebooted the laptop; all three children immediately gathered around him, completely unconcerned about their own father's desertion. My mother had begun to clear dishes when Gina emerged from the basement, her apron still around her waist. "Now who wants clam sauce and who'd like plain tomato?" she asked brightly, scooping up a heap of dried-down appetizer plates. "Pasta in just a minute."

The bell-beating bear ornaments began playing *Joy to the World*.

"Maybe we should just drive home now," I suggested to Rita and my mother, who took Rita's hand in both of hers.

"It's not your fault," she said. "We don't blame you." In a hushed voice she added, "Tony had it coming."

"That's my boy," said Artie as he worked on his teeth. He'd recovered the toothpick. "His mother's favorite, all his life. Too bad she didn't have more of what this kid has," he said, pointing the toothpick at Rita. "Would have saved all this trouble if she'd had just a little more—"

"Bad manners? Indiscretion?" Rita interrupted. "No. I overreacted, I—"

"Shaddap a minute!" Artie shot back. "I'm trying to make a point here. I was getting a little worried about my baby nephew here."

"Well, I certainly seem to provoke an undue amount of Sebastiani concern," I huffed in discomfort.

Artie directed the toothpick at me as he addressed Rita. "See what I mean? The way the guy was beginning to talk. The attitudes he was starting in with. His brains were going to his head. A big shot. Like a certain son of mine. And I figured that's what they teach you at, what's-it, MIT. Only now I'm not worried so much anymore."

"Now that you mention it," said my mother, "I'm feeling rather better myself."

Rita added, "'Feeling Alright.' Joe Cocker 1969. I love that song."

"Not bad," said Artie. "Not terrific, either, but yeah, not half bad for a start. Let's hope it's a talent you never have to develop."

Heaps of savory macaroni found their way into Tupperware containers and then into our hands as we exchanged parting pleasantries, leaving before coffee only over Gina's strenuous objection. Tracy seemed to harbor no bitterness, only admiration, for Rita. No one mentioned Tony. My father never left the bench and his laptop.

"See you back home, Dad," I said to him as we walked out.

"Glad you like the game, Mr. Bustamante," said Rita.

As I closed the door behind us I heard my father say "What?"

"Tracy's not bumping fuzz with your uncle," said Rita as we drove back to Armonk.

"You weren't here last Easter, when it was fully apparent," I replied. "He's visited her at school, during some dental convention. She eats his attention up. And I know the way she falls for macho guys. I worked with her in summer camp and saw it first-hand."

"How do you know he visited her?"

"You weren't here last Easter," I emphasized. "Gina mentioned the Binghamton convention, and Tracy practically bit my head off when I asked—just asked—whether they might have run into each other."

"So what? I probably would have bitten your head off also. Maybe she was embarrassed. Maybe Tony really did make a pass at her and for some reason she blames herself. Maybe she was trying to avoid damaging Gina's marriage. Who knows?"

"Wait a minute. If that were true, then why would she let you get away with the same thing? You flat out accused her! Why wouldn't she bite your head off?"

"I don't know, maybe she figured Tony deserved it at this point. Look, I can't tell you what the truth is. All I'm saying is, one, I don't think she's the type, and two, your hypothesis isn't the only one that fits the facts."

Now I was really confused. "So if you think nothing is going on, and you're concerned about the marriage, why on earth would you confront Tony like that and cause such a scene?"

"Who says *I'm* concerned about that ridiculous excuse for a marriage? Your uncle is an asshole, he deserves to experience Gina's long-suppressed rage, and besides, I knew no one would suspect what you suspect. Gina doesn't really think Tony's sleeping with Tracy; if she did, she would have been wielding something pointier than a lousy spoon. You seem to be the only one sure of Tracy's transgression." Rita turned to face me as I drove. "Now why do you suppose that is?"

"My penetrating mental acuity, perhaps?" I suggested.

"Or your latent jealousy. Are you jealous of your brother?"

I felt heat spreading over my cheeks. "I don't think so."

"You know, there's no such thing as a neutral observer. Everyone's got his or her own biases filtering their observations. When you draw conclusions about people, you should keep that in mind."

"I think I hear Heisenberg calling."

"The Uncertainty Principle? Well ... maybe. I hadn't thought about it that way. You sure you're not jealous of your brother?"

"Well, I'm not aware of my every pre-conscious thought, so I can't be positive. But I'm pretty sure."

"What about Dex? You jealous of him?"

Now that was a shocker. "Definitely not," I said firmly.

"Good," said Rita. "Of course, if you were, that would explain the melancholia you invariably exhibit around Penny as well as your recent departure into full-time communion with EDGAR. But as I say, there's always more than one hypothesis to fit a set of facts. Don't you agree now?"

I surely did.

When we got back to my dorm the next day there was a transmission waiting for me in Dex's fax machine. Ronald had sent it. Just half a page long, it looked like a report spit out by a database service. The information concerned a company called E/Mtex, which, apparently, was a Massachusetts corporation, had no financial assets, and whose corporate purpose was to "research, develop, procure and market consumer, industrial and scientific applications of the E-M Algorithm." The report listed a single director and a single shareholder: Jeffrey S. Watt.

I flipped back to the cover sheet, feeling as if I'd just received a body blow. The only handwritten comment under the Star Ventures logo said: *We felt you should know about this—A. Ronald Sweetwater.*

No wonder Jeff wanted an engine.

14

"THIS IS A FINE DAY, A TRULY FINE DAY. CONGRATULATIONS TO YOU and to ARGI." Ronald looked positively flushed with excitement. He had begun referring to our little company, Atmospheric Research Group, Inc., by the acronym ARGI as soon as the early results started to look promising.

The people seated around the set of tables arranged in a U-shape applauded politely as I powered up the overhead and tamped the ragged-edged pile of transparencies. There was nothing to be nervous about this time; I held in my hands exactly what they wanted to see. The ambience in the small banquet room overlooking Boston Harbor was thoroughly relaxed, so unlike the last investor meeting, and somehow the posh decor seemed entirely appropriate. We were saluting success.

"Thank you, Ronald, and thank you all for coming today. Now that we've reached our first milestone, and you're all on the hook for more money"—(hushed laughter)—"I'd like to give you some idea of what we've done, where we are and where we see ourselves going from here. Our mission in corporate life is to enhance the predictability of weather forecasts. I'm pleased to report timely and worthwhile progress."

First transparency. "You probably think you're looking at an amoeba colony, but actually it represents weather patterns over Oklahoma and northern Texas in June of 1978. The red blobs are peak-intensity fields of severe thunderstorms that occurred during the course of the month. There are plenty of them. When I overlay this second transparency on top of the first … you see that now some of the blobs have little blue dots in them. These are the storms that our current forecasting systems would have correctly localized 24 hours ahead of time—about 85-percent of them. Using the same data, the ARGI system successfully predicted all of these"—

next overlay—"and also the ones that now have green dots. So we were over 90 percent.

"Now I'll remove the overlays and start again with the same red amoebas. Here's how many of the storms the current technology would have predicted a full week in advance. This time not very many of the amoebas get blue dots, maybe a third of them at most. And again, when I introduce this second overlay, we see that the ARGI system has enhanced the accuracy significantly. We would have pegged twice as many of the storms." *(Some impressed 'hmmphs' and nods.)*

"Finally, let's look at the results for a month in advance. Here we took data from the entire hemisphere for our predictions, since the atmosphere does a lot of moving in a month. The results?" (First overlay.) "A measly 20 percent. That's not prediction; that's random guessing. A monkey or even a venture capitalist would have done as well throwing darts." *(More hushed laughter.)* "ARGI, as you can see from all the green dots, has boosted that figure fully to one-third. Any questions so far?"

"Yeah, I got one," said the older fellow who liked to stare at the ceiling with his hands in his pockets. "All this tells a nice story. But you got anything systematic to back it up?"

I wished I could remember his name, the guy who persecuted me into recognizing the connection between turbulence and fractals at our first investor meeting. But that was so many months ago. This time, of course, I welcomed his skepticism. It served as a buildup to my climax.

"Certainly do, and that's exactly where I was headed. While I hope what I've shown you is impressive enough, scientists turn up their noses at this sort of storytelling. They call it anecdotal. What a scientist wants to see is how well you can forecast the progress of a specific weather element over time. A scientist wants to know *exactly* how your predictive accuracy varies with your time horizon, and how much it's improved by adding more sources of data. That's objective.

"So what we're going to do is follow one single weather variable—the height of the 500 millibar pressure level. As you all know, atmospheric pressure decreases with altitude. Here in Boston it's a comfortable, lung-filling 1000 millibars. But at the top of Mount McKinley it's a blue-faced 500 millibars or so. The key is 'or so.' The more accurately you can predict the exact height of that 500-millibar pressure level, the more accurately you can forecast the weather. That's how scientists rate their meteorology models."

Next transparency. "And so here it is. This graph plots the error in our ten-day prediction against the density of weather-observation sources. As you can see, if our sources are spaced really far apart, the ARGI approach offers no improvement over the National Weather Service: the ten-day prediction is at least 75 meters off either way. But look what happens as the sources get closer together—the ARGI model begins to overtake the Weather Service, particularly when we add upper-air measurements to the sample matrix. When we have a real crowd of sources, when they're no more than 100 kilometers apart on average, we're better by over ten percent. Under ten days, we're still well ahead of them, and look what happens when we go out to a month—we really beat their brains out."

"In other words," said Ronald, eager to move things along, "we've reached our first milestone. At this point we can look for government funds. We're applying for a Small Business Innovation Research grant even as we pursue a development and license agreement with the National Weather Service."

"Then why do you need any more money from us?" asked one of the audience. "It sounds like the product is finished, or at least saleable."

"Ah, well," laughed Ronald, "we're still engaged in development, you see. We're still testing the limits of the system, arranging for actual field tests..."

"Wouldn't the government pay for that if they're interested in the project?" asked someone else. I couldn't believe it. Success was making these people skeptical and tightfisted!

"Maybe, maybe not," Ronald replied politely. "And don't think for a moment we're finished with our research. What we have now is a first-generation product. Nothing more. We've got to explore optimization strategies, extensions, additional features ... rest assured the money you're contractually obligated to contribute will be well-spent."

"You really figure you can get improvements?" asked the old guy. "My comp'ny's ready to exercise our license option with you boys, but we ain't gonna plunk down all that dough until you got something that's, well, finished."

"I'm certain that exciting advances will be forthcoming. You'll learn of them in our quarterly reports to investors. As for the license, I'm sure we can negotiate a right to any and all improvements."

"Well, I guess we're done then," said the old guy as he rose from his chair. He always knew how to end a meeting.

"Aren't we ever going to meet the genius behind the technology, that elusive Professor Watt?" asked the woman who really should reconsider those stretch pants.

"It will be difficult, given his many academic and industry commitments," said Ronald, "but I will make every effort to have him available at our next meeting."

Yeah, right, I thought as I followed Ronald out of the room. He stopped me in front of the door as the last investors left.

"This isn't for general consumption, but Uncle Sam—that is, Uncle Noah—is ready to buy in on a trial basis. We're about to fulfill our second milestone. Now about that third one..."

"Applying our technique to different forecast models? Gee, we haven't really explored the full capabilities of our current implementation..." Ronald was getting me nervous now.

"Hey, Paul, seriously, don't sweat that! You've already succeeded! We met the first milestone, we've got the Noah deal practically wrapped up—got to give Blair credit, she knew a ten percent improvement would set the federal meteorology mouths to watering—so we're in great shape. Just have to do some further testing..."

"I don't know if I've got the time for that kind of undertaking right now," I protested.

"Nooo problem," I was told. "We've got experts, consultants. We'll look at what you have ourselves. If any unfavorable issues arise we'll tell you; otherwise, say hello to another twenty-five thousand bucks."

"Can't argue with that, I guess. I'll send you a disk with the engine."

"No, no, don't bother. Just give me your password. We'll get what we need through MITnet."

"Sure, it's ... wait a minute. You're positive Jeff is fully out of this loop?"

"You mean Watt? History. He's history. We were as shocked as you must have been when we made that discovery."

"Well, I hope you don't mind, but I want to put everything in a protected file first. Can't be too careful."

"And then you'll call me?"

"I'm not even sure my phone line is secure; I think Jeff's got a blue box in that computer of his. I'll fax the password and access information to you."

"Positively Elysian, my friend."

I hopped the train back to Cambridge. Now I'd have to begin the arduous task of adapting my system to different forecast models, hoping for marginal performance boosts. As if I really had time for any of this. As if I didn't already know what I'd find. As if it possibly mattered anyway.

When I returned to the dorm I found that Jeff had left me an e-mail message. It requested my presence in his office.

"Where the hell have you been all this time?" asked Jeff, picking himself up from his chair as I entered his dark, stuffy enclosure. "You never call, you never e-mail anymore..."

"Busy busy," I told him. "Seems like there's always more to do."

"You presented today, right? How'd it go?"

"Perfect. We're getting the second round of funding."

"And what about your paper? I'll need to review and sign it before you send it off to *Tellus*."

"Oh, well, actually, I thought I'd spare you the trouble. One of the new Course 12 professors was interested, and of course he's a meteorology specialist anyway, and since I'm taking a class with him I just figured..."

"Fine," said Jeff flatly. "I'm sure that's preferable. Now how about your model? I know you've gotten some good results, but what about the structure? Did you create an engine as I suggested?"

"Jeff, you always seem to know what I'm up to. Surely you're familiar with every detail of the system."

"Some months ago you raised the issue of privacy, and since that time I have refrained from invading your personal network space. Therefore I ask you again..."

"Then how do you know about my results?" I asked.

"What is this, *koan* time? Do you propose to pelt me with an endless series of mystical Zen riddles? I am in contact with people at Star Ventures, of course; in fact, more so lately than I am with you, in case you hadn't realized."

"I see," I told him.

"Please prepare for me an update in the form of a progress report. I will review it, and then we can decide together how best to apply the money you have been awarded."

"I'll have it for you in a few days."

"Very well then."

"How on earth can someone be so glum after achieving his first scientific milestone and getting a bunch more money?" Dex asked me soon after I returned.

"It's actually the only scientific milestone," I told him. "The others have to do with licensing and business terms."

"Then why, tell me, are you hunched over the desk with your face buried in your hands like some morose grouch? Did you get the money?"

"Yes."

"Weren't people impressed with your numbers?"

"Yes."

"So spill it. What's the difficulty?"

"Dex, we..." I took a deep breath. "I'm afraid we've hit some sort of predictability limit. Up to a point, everything's log-linear—add more data points, increase predictive accuracy. It almost makes you giddy, like you've pierced through all the knowledge barriers, like the solution to every unknown is at hand. But when I do calculations for the few regions where I have closely spaced clusters of measurements, bang, nothing. The magic ends. No further improvement."

"Have you told Jeff?"

"Of course not."

"Well, that's good. But look. You weren't expecting to eliminate forecasting error altogether, were you? I mean, that's ... fantasy land."

"No, of course not," I assured him. "But I didn't expect to hit a concrete ceiling at ten percent, either."

Now Dex was getting animated. "Soooo ... WHAT?" he bellowed. "You were given a single scientific milestone. You have satisfied it. Now you've got more money, real credibility, and you'll probably garner some publicity, too, when your paper gets published. The science is done. The engineering begins."

Somehow that sounded profoundly depressing. "What do you mean?"

"Engineering. Where the rubber meets the road. Don't be afraid of it. You've got to take the principles you've established and work out the kinks. Be thankful you have the resources to do it."

"God, it took months to digitize all that data, months! And now it's back to the drawing board? They won't accept that. They're looking for improvements, D-cube, they're waiting for more breakthroughs."

"Who's 'they'? The investors? They've already gotten all they've paid for, and more. They bought in knowing you might accomplish nothing. And besides, you'll give them improvements. You'll optimize, vary parameters ... we do it all the time at BioVitrics. That's what *real* science is all about."

"Real science?"

"Real, honest, useful science. The kind of work that doesn't end with a discovery. You don't think it was all over for us when Pap formulated his earliest glass compositions, do you? We've spent years tinkering with different reagents, purity levels, reaction times, temperature variations, cooling protocols ... we've taken a concept and made it practical. So will you. You're at the threshold."

"How can you call it honest? The investors have no idea where this technology is headed, and they're about to double their stake."

"There is no pursuit more honest than engineering," Dex insisted, entering lecture mode as he pinched thumb and index finger together and began bouncing his hand. "If you're a scientist, you can offer one hypothesis and spend the rest of your life debating whether it's true or not. Engineers produce things that *work*. If something doesn't *work* it's an engineering failure, period, and you move on. Whatever improvements, if any, you make on your system, everyone—you, me, your investors, the public—will know whether they're real or not, and your rewards will match your success."

"Don seems to think he's an engineer, and right now he's still facing expulsion, isn't he?"

Now Dex stopped lecturing. He spoke slowly, weighing each word. "Don's situation just proves my point. Data was falsified. The fraud was detected promptly. Little research money was wasted, and no one suffered injury. If the work hadn't had such practical application and financial potential, no one would have noticed for years. And as for Don himself, well, the Ad Board's investigation is over, and he's been reinstated. But he won't graduate this year. He still refuses to point any fingers, and they've revoked his course credit for lab work with Sauer."

"Too bad," I said with genuine regret, since this meant an unfortunate extension of his presence at MIT. "How much more time will he have to spend around here?"

"If he can get another research project he'll be out by the end of the summer. Otherwise he won't finish until after first semester next year, and without lab credit he'll face significantly greater difficulty finding a job."

"Too bad," I said and, realizing I'd just repeated myself idly, added, "really."

"Oh, I almost forgot," said Dex. "The money from Star finally came through. My so-called facilitator's compensation. Here's your half." Dex slid a check for a thousand dollars across my desk; the corner of the check bit into my finger, and the tiny wince of pain only emphasized my discomfort at Dex's gesture.

"This really, *really* isn't necessary," I said. "You deserve every cent along with my undiluted gratitude."

"Right now I've got more money than I know what to do with, and I'm happy to share this with you. Please. Take it."

One thousand dollars. Just like that. I could chip away at my student loans. I could get a new radio for my car. I could ditch my summer TAship.

I stuffed the check in my shirt pocket.

"So? Well? Huh?" asked Rita, marching into our room. "You score big? You knock 'em dead?"

"Welcome back," I told her. "Sure, things went fine here, the money's in the bank. But you—what happened out in Scottsdale? How was the conference?"

She'd planned to give her paper at that speech-recognition conference and return immediately, but then she called to say she'd be there for the full three days, and then she left a message that she'd be interviewing for a few more days after the conference ended. No one had any idea when she'd return, and her appearance now was entirely unexpected.

In answer to my question she leaned her chest forward so we could read her tee shirt. White with green lettering, it was set up like a little word puzzle. On the left side the characters **ICSR-3** were arranged vertically, each laying on its side. In the middle there was a low-resolution computer drawing of an ear, rendered in clunky little blocks to emphasize its digital origins. And to the right of the ear stood a stack of binary numbers:

10010010
10000110
10100110
10100100
01011010
01100110

As we read this oh-so-clever epigram, which advertised the Third International Conference on Speech Recognition by illustrating a successful reduction of the conference's abbreviation into binary computer code, Rita withdrew a leather-bound certificate from her backpack. It said

BEST OF ICSR-3

"YAPPER"

RITA DORFMAN, MASSACHUSETTS INSTITUTE OF TECHNOLOGY

Dex and I expressed the appropriate congratulatory sentiments.

"I wouldn't have flippantly titled it YAPPER if I thought my speech program would be such a hit," Rita said.

"Is that an acronym?" Dex asked.

"Yet Another Phoneme Processing and Expansion Routine," Rita explained. "It's accurate enough, and yapping is what speech recognition is all about, but I don't know, it just seems overly self-effacing." Now Rita was starting to crank up. "You wouldn't have believed it to see me. There I was, making technoid chit-chat with these guys from Xerox PARC, Stanford, Berkeley, Apple, Cal Tech—and actually *liking* it big time! And the interviews were no problem, I mean *no* problem at all. They were asking for *me* on the strength of my presentation, and every interview felt almost like natural social interaction! Who would have believed?"

"That's just great, Rita," said Dex.

"You know," she continued, "Penny gets such a kick out of all this. She says speech recognition is like a window between electronic and human worlds, the only hope for bridging the divide between people and the machines that run our lives."

She would, I thought. But I restrained myself.

"Let me show you some of the new features I added..." She took command of the keyboard and activated EDGAR, then summoned her project. Nothing happened. "Where the hell is my goddamn program, anyway?"

After deciding she had waited long enough Rita said, "Screw it. That's what I hate about timeshare, it's taking forever to load. I'll show you later. Anyway, I've got to get dressed—and so do you." She was looking directly at me. "You haven't forgotten what day this is, have you?"

"Not for a moment," I lied shamelessly. What was she talking about?

"We're going to celebrate our one-year anniversary in style," Rita announced.

Oh, yes. One year. It seemed like a long time.

"Where are you going?" Dex asked.

"Maison Robert," Rita replied enthusiastically and with impeccable pronunciation. "We've got 7:30 reservations for *haute cuisine*, as Penny is fond of saying..."

"For crying out loud, Rita," I couldn't believe myself saying *but there were the words just pouring out*, "who cares what Penny says? For seven months now she's been the locus of your entire existence. Penny says this, Penny says that ... sometimes I think you're covalently bonded to her."

Instantly I regretted my outburst but it was too late. Rita went white, she backed up to the door without taking her eyes off me, feeling for obstacles with her arm extended behind her. One such obstacle was the large figure of Don Boyer, presently blocking the doorway. "Well, well," she said as she turned to face him, "if it isn't the dapper DonBoy. So well-dressed. Death in the family?"

"I really don't need this, Rita," he told her.

"Neither do I," she said and walked briskly down the hall.

"You about ready?" Don asked, looking toward Dex.

"Almost," Dex replied, withdrawing a tie from his closet.

"What's the occasion?" I asked.

Don was eager to respond. "BioVitrics' public offering is the occasion. I find it hard to believe no one's told you."

"Believe it," said Dex. Turning to me he added, "It's far from official. We've reached agreement in principle with an investment bank, and Pap's invited the whole company—all four of us, that is—to his house for steaks."

All at once I felt a wave of disgust.

"Where'd he get the meat?" I asked, barely containing my revulsion.

"What? What do you mean?" asked Dex, annoyed at what seemed a lunatic question.

"Oh, man," said Don, shaking his head. "Don't worry. It's not Oscar. That cow is too valuable to dress with A-1. It'll be monitored throughout its lifespan to track the safety of the glass." Don Boyer still spoke slowly, but something was missing from his voice. Something whose absence represented a clear improvement.

"Don, would you excuse us for a minute? I need to talk to Paul."

Don gestured obediently, with exaggerated humility, and left. "I have no intention of prying into your relationship with Rita," said Dex. "But your rather unprovoked tirade before raises a separate issue. You are familiar, of course, with the three-body problem?"

"I am," I said, wondering what he was getting at with this strange reference to the classic physics conundrum. Objects everywhere attract one another according to Newton's law of gravitation. It's easy to plot forces and trajectories for two mutually attracting bodies, but chaos reigns as soon as a third body enters the picture.

"Do we have a three-body problem with Penny?" Dex asked. Now I got it.

"We do not," I told him.

Dex sighed with relief. "Good," he said. "Please forgive me for asking. I hope you understand my concern."

"You have every right to express concern."

"Yes, well ... I'll go fetch Don now," Dex said, plainly eager to be through with the matter.

Don re-entered the room with the self-pitying manner of a chastened child. "You were talking about girls, weren't you?" he asked glumly.

"Oh, come on, Don..." said Dex.

"I know, I know," he continued. "Don Boyer obviously has nothing to contribute to such a discussion. I know how woeful I must seem to you. But think about it. They say that for every person there are no more than 50,000 suitable matches out there. In a world of billions! Dex, you've hit the end point—you've fallen in love. And you, Paul, you're at least satisfied on a temporary basis, and who knows—maybe your statistics program is dead on, maybe its prediction that you'll find a perfect romantic match by the time you graduate will turn out to be true. But what happens to the rest of us?"

"Don, that circulation model is just guesswork," I told him. "It was totally wrong about Dex, and I'm probably no closer to eternal bliss than you are."

"Give yourself a chance," said Dex as he fidgeted with his bowtie. "MIT isn't the real world."

"The real world!" Don replied theatrically. "As if I'll ever see it. As if I'll be appreciated there any more than I am here. As if there's any meaning to—"

"Earth to Don!" Dex snapped. "Hello? Anyone home? You are twenty-one years old now. It's decades too soon for a midlife crisis. Stop wallowing, for God's sake, there's just no reason for it."

"Sorry, sorry," said Don, raising his palms. "Didn't mean to contaminate your good fortune. Didn't mean to precipitate on your parade. Who knows, maybe someday I'll get to join you out there. We can trade disillusionment memoirs."

"Are you done yet?" asked Dex.

"Yes," said Don. "And I'm hungry. Can we go now?"

"Thank heaven." And turning to me as he left Dex said, "Enjoy yourselves tonight. You and Rita both deserve it."

We really did, and I despaired of my earlier attack. It was entirely gratuitous. Rita and I had been together a long time, watching our individual lives begin to take shape, and now there were all sorts of reasons to celebrate. She was on the brink of a rewarding graduate or corporate research opportunity far from the frustrations of undergraduate research and the harsh Cambridge winters. I was on the brink of more funding and further successes, right here at MIT. So what if I would face an endless life of engineering to turn my discovery into practice and the constant threat of treachery by Professor Jeffery S. Watt? With all that was at stake, it didn't seem all that terrible. And it certainly portended a clean breakup.

Fully moussed, cologned and generally spiffed for an evening out, I had the apology fully loaded into the output cache as I opened Rita's door. "Look, about before, I'm really sorry..."

But the words trailed off at the sight of Rita, standing erect and stiff as a statue in front of the terminal on her desk. From the waist up she was dressed for the town in a light wool sweater and her pearl necklace, but from the waist down she was naked except for panties. It was as if someone had cryogenically frozen her in the act of getting dressed. Clearly the process had left her metabolism intact, however, because her complexion was undergoing a pronounced red shift even as she stared at me, and her whole body seemed to be accumulating vast quantities of energy for some fearsome detonation. A tear spilled down her right cheek. My heart began to race.

"What's the matter?" I asked cautiously. "I said I'm sorry, it wasn't right what I said before."

"I just want to know this," said Rita. Her voice was husky, her words restrained. "What am I to you? What have I meant to you all this time?"

I tried to answer. Nothing would come out.

"I thought we had something. I thought there might be some

kind of future for us. What's it been for you? Were you just waiting for program execution to terminate at graduation?"

"I don't understand what you mean. What did you see happening?" I managed.

"I guess I didn't have any specific plans!" she yelled. "I didn't have the nodes and arcs of this relationship mapped out in some kind of solution space. I thought it would be something we would develop. Together."

"So then let's—"

"I signed on to the Master's program here, you know, in spite of the idiot they have me working with. I was going to tell you tonight. It was going to be a surprise. Good thing I said nothing, it was a stupid, stupid thing to do—totally incompatible with your life architecture's run sequence."

It was only when my eyes wandered to her terminal's live screen that I realized what had happened. The red lettering, bold against the light-blue screen background, said:

YOU PAUL YOU'RE AT LEAST SATISFIED ON A TEMPORARY BASIS AND WHO KNOWS<.> MAYBE YOUR STATISTICS PROGRAM IS DEAD ON<.> MAYBE ITS PREDICTION THAT YOU'LL ADSORB A PERFECT ROMANTIC MATCH BY THE TIME YOU GRADUATE WILL TURN OUT TO BE TRUE<.> BUT WHAT HAPPENS TO THE REST OF US<.>
SPKR1> DON THAT CIRCULATION MODEL IS JUST GUESS-WORK<.> IT WAS TOTALLY WRONG ABOUT DEX AND I'M PROBABLY NO CLOSER TO ETERNAL BLISS THAN YOU ARE<.>
SPKR2> GIVE YOURSELF A CHANCE<.> MIT ISN'T THE REAL WORLD<.>
SPKR3> THE REAL WORLD<.> AS IF I'LL EVER SEE IT<.>

Her YAPPER program had finally loaded, booted itself on and captured the entire conversation. Rita accessed the transcription. It was becoming dangerous to live around technology.

"Look, Rita, I was just trying to comfort the pathetic bastard," I offered.

"You're the one who's pathetic!" she replied, tears rolling freely. "You've been encapsulated in your room for almost three years and operate your life at EDGAR's instruction."

"Rita..."

"Tell me when to get up in the morning! Tell me how to solve nonlinear differential equations! Open the pod bay doors, Hal!

Tell me when I'm supposed to meet my dream mate so I can scrub myself off and make sure I pack a condom!"

"Rita, didn't you take pains to tell me you don't do affection? I thought we had the same view of things. I'm not saying I want to break up."

She laughed and threw her head back. "I guess that's right, she's not due to arrive until you graduate, so lucky me, I've got another whole year. You just don't get it, do you? I'm not asking if we can stay together. *I am breaking up with you.* Understand?"

"Just wait a minute, will you? Don't get so extreme. We've had such wonderful times, let's not—"

"This isn't calculus, goddamn it! You can't integrate isolated worthwhile moments into a history we never shared. We've obviously been inhabiting different realities all along." Pause. "Haven't you noticed? I've changed. Dex's changed. We've turned into real people, Paul, we're ready to enter the non-MIT universe where humans touch other humans without machine mediation."

"What are you saying?"

"I'm saying I'm done! I'm saying the speed of light in a vacuum will still be the same after you leave. *I'm saying get the fuck out!*"

She planted herself on her bed, facing away from me, sitting upright and staring at the opposite wall. But as I walked through her door I saw that she was actually smiling at me, tentatively, out of the corner of one of her soaked eyes. Crazy. It made no sense.

The next day she was gone, her room completely empty of her belongings.

"Hi, Paul. Where's Rita?" Penny asked. She always looked so cheery in the morning.

"Well, actually, I don't know, I guess."

"You guess that you don't know?"

"I'm sure I don't know. She's gone. Didn't announce her departure or destination."

Now it was Penny's smile that departed. "Gone, like, outta here?"

"I'm telling you, I don't know."

"I see." Penny eyed me carefully. "Did you two have some sort of blowout?"

"You know," I said, avoiding her question, "you really did her a world of good. It's almost as if you transformed her into a different person."

"How nice of you to say. I hope that doesn't mean you blame me for your falling out."

"Oh no, that's not at all—"

"Good, good. Because that would be quite unfair. Whether you realize it or not, you were far more responsible than I for any transformation."

We looked at each other momentarily. I couldn't read her expression or the thinking behind her words.

"And I hope Rita's absence doesn't end your run of success," Penny continued. "That would be most unfortunate—to discover your life is intertwined with that of another to a much greater extent than you'd thought or hoped. A most unwelcome surprise."

As I watched her walk out, as I studied the way her perfect waist descended into her perfect hips and legs, it struck me how casually unconcerned Penny always seemed about her appearance. And how despite such unconcern, she carried a naturally sensual elegance that all the exercise and careful eating habits and fashion consciousness could never give Rita. Rita was structurally angular; Penny was smooth and rounded (like June). Rita looked counterfeit dressed in anything but sweats; Penny exuded sprightly sophistication in anything she wore (so did June). Rita was forever damping her natural combative and defensive tendencies; Penny was unfailingly, pleasantly confident (as was June).

Somehow that made Rita all the more admirable.

15

"HELLO?"

"It's Jeff. I suppose you've got some reason for ignoring your e-mail. No matter. We need to talk. Right away."

"Gee, Jeff, I've got a Quantum problem set due tomorrow and it's a real bitch. Can we do this some other time?"

"I consider it imperative that we exchange thoughts now," Jeff persisted. "Please."

Back out the door, back past Rita's empty room, back across campus, back to Jeff's world. It was noisy in the air-conditioned corridors of E42. A dissonant orchestra of banging and clanking from above suggested growth of a new office floor above the one Jeff called home.

"Thank you for coming," said Jeff, looking at me with unusually serious and businesslike decorum, his hands folded on his desk. He wasn't typing. His keyboard lay off to the side of his desk, and the computer didn't even seem active. Jeff would have appeared entirely dignified were it not for the occasional wisps of plaster that escaped from the ceiling and settled quietly on his hair, within his beard, on the poncho he'd draped over his terminal. The focus of the construction noise seemed concentrated directly above his office.

Jeff said, "I feel as if we have lost our bond of trust. Perhaps I am to blame for keeping certain things from you in deference to various inescapable realities. But I sense more. I sense you have somehow lost your way. What is it, at this moment, that you are trying to accomplish with this project?"

"I want to reinvent weather forecasting," I told him firmly, stressing the first-person singular. "I want to enhance predictive accuracy, extend time horizons—"

"Just as I thought," Jeff interrupted. He shook his head sadly.

"You sound like a Star Ventures prospectus. Now, I know it may seem like a lost age but can you recall our early conversations? You weren't some meteorology minion back then. You were tormented by the mysteries of everyday existence! You sought to understand the world around you! You wished to solve the most fundamental *koan* of all—deterministic chaos and its maddening, terrifying secrecies that cloud your vision and draw the future through your fingers like dust!" Jeff inhaled deeply. "Remember that?"

"Sure I do. What's that got to do with anything?"

"Don't you see how we've grown apart from one another? Of course our trust has lessened—our research goals, our *life* goals have divided. Your purpose has individuated and once again you labor under the ignorance of *avidya*! You've become a … a…"

"An engineer?" I offered.

"Yes! Yes! Don't you see? Why do you think I let myself get involved in this project in the first place?" *So you could rip me off*, I thought, but I let Jeff continue. "Paul. I … I, too, have been hurt. All right? I am also fearful of chance, of the unknown. I must understand more before I venture from these precincts into an endlessly changing nonlinear world. Your work, your insight—you seemed to have found that forbidden key! And don't you see that once you unlock one nonlinear secret you have conquered them all? Brahman. Dharma. Tao. Gestalt. Don't you remember? You stand on the threshold, your breakthrough points the way to a grand mandala of all things nonlinear!"

"I'm not following you. All what things? Are you saying that forecasting the weather is the same as forecasting behavior? Simulating thought?"

"Don't look so surprised. It's not such a new idea. More than a decade ago John Hopfield at Cal Tech suggested that cognitive functioning may be nonlinear—that thought itself is, ultimately, a chaotic process at the neural level. He showed that if they're set up correctly on a computer, neural networks undergo a sequence of nonlinear state changes that result in absorption and application of knowledge. Know what I said when I read his paper? *No shit!* I'd known all that for years! already. Know why you've never heard of Hopfield? Because he couldn't get his electronic model to work like a brain. He didn't have the right equations, and even if he had them, he wouldn't have been able to solve them! I have identified scores of cognitive equations these many years. I have built a parallel processor with shared memory that will enable each node in a neural network to think for itself while remaining connected with the thinking of every other processor. I have the computer. You have the statistical tools and a fully adaptable engine. Together we'll produce the most powerful simulation ever! A fundamentally new approach to artificial intelligence!"

"So you can claim it for E/Mtex?" I accused him. The need to shout over the construction noise exaggerated the drama of our exchange.

Jeff drew back warily, clasped his hands behind his head. "Ah, E/Mtex, yes indeed. What do you know about E/Mtex?"

"I know its corporate mission, I know its goals, and I know who owns it. What else do I need to know?"

He stared at me for the longest time, as if waiting for something. Finally his hands slipped to the arms of his chair and he said, "E/Mtex is for both of us. It was my little concession from Star."

"You mean in exchange for their piece of the weather application, Star gave you everything else?"

"Star could care less about meteorology. What they're interested in is finance, a category off-limits to E/Mtex. Star wants to predict stock-market trends and to price options and futures. They believe your approach will enable them to acquire great wealth."

"I can't imagine how it could."

"You can't imagine because it *won't!* I've already sim'd the E-M approach in a finance context and it fails miserably. I suspect it's because people don't behave like dynamic systems, they won't change their actions in direct proportion to stresses like price shifts or tax incentives; instead they react in steps and jerks, rendering your approach irrelevant."

"Then how did Star come up with this crazy idea?"

"Well, perhaps I am the source of their particular confusion. Remember the letter I had you deliver?" The precursor to a smile crept across the bottom of Jeff's face.

"And on the strength of your letter they put fifty thousand bucks into a technology they could care less about?" I asked.

"Actually, more on the strength of the MIT letterhead than the words of my letter. But they were not entirely uninterested in weather. Fifty thousand is peanuts. They assumed, rightly, that they could toss a group of fat-cat amateur investors together, offload most of their risk and profit by a quick sale of the technology to a gullible federal agency. But none of this matters. I called you here now because they are pressing me. I have given them nothing since we closed the first financing, and they have grown impatient. They are threatening to bring in consultants to set up the stock-market system. There is much we must do."

The impact of these sudden revelations was nearly overwhelming. My face burned with shame and yet, despite how neatly Jeff's explanation connected all of the facts, I still didn't fully trust or believe him. There was too much confusion, too much data, too many alternative scenarios that satisfied the data.

"I would like you to read these," said Jeff as he slid a set of thick stapled documents across his desk. They landed in my lap. One was a $2.5 million grant proposal to ARPA, the next was a detailed outline for a scientific paper, and the last was a patent application.

"Please read the final item first. If it is acceptable, sign the forms at the end and return them to our patent attorney. I want to have this on file before Star realizes it's been groping down a blind alley."

"You want me to send this back to Herman?" I asked. "Won't he just talk to Blair and—"

"E/Mtex's patent attorney is a young, energetic solo practitioner in Kendall Square," Jeff interrupted. "Her name is Suzanne Harris. In addition to drafting the document you now hold, she was instrumental in making sure the weather application wouldn't overlap with anything E/Mtex might wish to pursue. Doctor Maurice Herman certainly failed to diagnose the significance of her editorial changes."

I still didn't trust Jeff. He said E/Mtex was for both of us but I didn't see him handing me any stock certificates. Instead he was asking me to sign away my rights to the company he and he alone owned.

The construction noises suddenly stopped.

"We'll need many resources to make this work, of course," Jeff continued quietly. "We'll need to hire programmers, acquire substantial hardware support for my little computer masterpiece here ... by the way, don't worry if the grant doesn't come through. I've learned quite a bit about VCs from this experience, and Sue assures me most of them are honest. She thinks they'll eat this deal up like ginger rice porridge after a smoky night of intense meditation."

So maybe he'd had a falling out with Star and was craftily

playing me for a dupe as he chased other sources of money. Maybe this was his ticket out of MIT. Who knew what he really had on his mind.

All at once the thought occurred to me: "Wait a minute. I gave Star my password. They said they wanted to test the program's extensibility."

"*Extensibility?*" Jeff repeated with mock seriousness. "How polite a way of saying they want to steal your code. Well, be sure you make at least two floppy backups before you delete the file from the system. It's not in an XCOM path, is it?"

"Uh, well ... yes. I just wanted to make sure it was secure."

"Secure from me?" Now Jeff was accusing me.

"Oh, well, Jeff, I mean..."

"Well, isn't that just great! Just terrific! Have you any clue as to the vast depth of the deep shit you've cast us into? XCOM files are secure because the network worms distribute them all over the place! Big pieces of your program have been deposited every node cluster—hell, maybe every active node in the entire MITnet system!"

"Network worms?"

"Don't tell me you know nothing of the system you interact with every day! Network worms are mobile programs that keep MITnet operating efficiently. They travel around the network looking for unoccupied machines to perform unfinished tasks, and while they're at it, they distribute XCOM files among unused memory slots in many terminals. That way no one can get your whole program by breaking into a single machine. But if someone knows the password and the access protocol—"

"They can gather the pieces from multiple terminals."

"And put them together with the XCOM utility even after you've deleted the primary file. That's just what XCOM was constructed to do—put the distributed pieces back together when you want to run an XCOM-protected program."

"Does any of this really matter? I thought you said our patent lawyer has everything sewn up for us."

Jeff glared at me. "You just don't get it, do you? If Star lifts your engine they'll be able to duplicate whatever we create, we'll never be rid of them. Do you want to spend the rest of your life in court?"

"All right, all right," I conceded. "But can't I just change my password?"

"Sure. You fill out a form, present ID to the provost and wait three to four weeks. Or maybe you'd like to try changing the access protocols. They're system-wide, they're fully embedded ... should be a real challenge! But enough of this cycle-wasting interchange—when did you give Star your password?"

"Just a couple of hours ago."

"Fine. Make your backups. Then I want you to start deleting the engine file from every accessible computer terminal with a resident memory. There are hundreds of them. So what are you waiting for? Go! Get out! Get started!"

When I left Jeff's office he was reclining in his chair, hands tensed over his face.

Still I didn't trust him. But following Jeff's instructions seemed the safest course, since it preserved all options. By nightfall I'd sanitized only twenty-seven terminals. The procedure was time-consuming, and I couldn't very well interrupt someone's marathon hacking session to access his terminal's memory partition. It was a good thing Rita wasn't around. I hated feeling stupid and powerless in front of her, especially when her advice could have spared me the misery. She never would have let me save into an XCOM file had I discussed the issue with her.

Dex rose from his chair as I trudged into our room. "You've been a very popular absentee today. Your brother called, his girlfriend called, Wiseman's having a fit ... and some of us were getting a bit worried, what with this Rita situation and all."

It occurred to me that Dex just might be part of some conspiracy with Blair, Ronald, Jeff or some subset of them. It was strange how violently he had silenced Don's attempt to make me aware of Star's motivations after the initial presentation to investors. And of course BioVitrics and Star were like larvae tightly wrapped in the same cash chrysalis. So I just told him I'd been with Jeff, that he wanted me to try a out couple of new user-response features.

Then I wondered about Tracy. What could she possibly want? More blackmail tribute?

Dex was looking at me with concern. "You still haven't mentioned anything about that prediction ceiling you seem to have hit, did you?"

"Not a thing." I cringed as I said it. Once again I was gratified Rita wasn't around, listening to the way I was pushing blithely ahead without so much as hinting at the possibility of limitation. I remembered her reaction to Mrs. Mendoza. I could anticipate her incredulous retort as she assumed the voice of my conscience: *You extolled your progress and kept the problems secret? You want to spend your time cheating people and fine-tuning a kluge?*

"Good," Dex told me. "That really would have been silly. You've got plenty of time to explore the origins." He kept looking at me. "What's the matter?"

"Oh, nothing," I said. "I was just thinking of how Rita would react, that's all."

"Look, I'm sorry about what happened and all that. But it's easy for her to set lofty standards. She doesn't need to worry about research funding since ARPA's so keen on speech recognition. Did she ever tell you why? Did she mention that the government uses S/R software to snoop on telephone conversations worldwide? I'll bet they just drooled over her program's interlinguistic capability."

"There you are!" huffed Wiseman, pushing his way into our room. "So there you are!" he repeated. "I must talk with you. Right away."

"I guess I'm off again," I groaned to Dex. I'd barely gotten my jacket off.

Wiseman's room was completely unembellished; he'd added nothing to his complement of MIT standard-issue furniture. No reading lamp, no clock, no radio, no floppy disk organizer. He scooted me in with impatient gestures and began barking at me as he closed the door.

"Have you not been worried? I certainly have been. Have you not wondered where she went? I certainly have been worried. I advised her to be careful. I advised her to avoid emotional engagement, it is inappropriate at this time…"

"Take it easy Wiseman," I said, trying to halt this incoherent stream of nonsense data, "she's probably just moved her stuff back to her folks'. Finals start in a few weeks, she's got to get back for those."

"Oh, you fool! You understand nothing! And you, who have known her as long as I! You, who have been intimate with her!" Wiseman's wire-rimmed glasses bucked wildly on the end of his nose, and his thick black hair shook like a grass skirt; he was rubbing his fingers together. "Do you not know her class schedule? She has no examinations this semester. And she does not have what you call folks, either; were you not aware even of this?"

"A lot of people come from broken homes and do just fine," I said, but there was no calming him down.

"Broken indeed! How mindlessly apt! How improbably correct of you! Rita's home has been broken because her mother is no longer extant, in the sense of being dead. A suicide. It is two years now."

I was stunned, completely floored. Rita had lived on our hall for six semesters and never said a thing—not when it must have happened, not ever. I sat down at the edge of Wiseman's bed and listened.

"A suicide," he repeated, driving the word inside me so hard it smarted. "Like my sister. She also took her own life, many years ago now. Such an event hurts not only for itself but for its effect on others as well."

"But she said her parents were divorced," I responded. I could hear the sudden numbness in my own voice.

"That was the truth. Her father appears to have blamed himself for what followed, and prefers to avoid his guilt by distancing himself from Rita. Perhaps he cannot help his behavior. I do not know. But Rita would not be with him now."

Instantly so much made sense. The unrelenting toughness, her hesitance to express affection or any other feeling, even by her style of dress. And all the time she spent with Wiseman—the two of them were a miniature support group; Wiseman's doting reflected his concern. Perhaps Rita's grueling daily workouts served her as an emotional outlet.

"How could you not know these things?" Wiseman demanded. "Did you not wonder why she did not invite you to meet her parents?"

Of course I hadn't wondered because I had been too busy feeling gratified for a relationship free of unwanted commitment. I had been so eager to shut her out that I'd never even gotten to know her.

"So that's why she became so close to Penny," I speculated aloud. "She was a new female role model, almost a replacement."

"Your thoughts are so perverse that I must soon ask you to leave. But listen now. When my sister ended her life our family grew closer to one another. Excessively close. We were told it was unhealthy, that we must seek in each other support but not solace. This can only come from within. It is most dangerous to entrust to another emotions that have not yet healed. And so I was afraid

Rita might seek too much from you, more than you could give. Of course I was correct. She went so far as to adopt the manner of Penny because she thought this is what you wanted—that it would make you feel for her what she felt for you. I told her she was mistaken. I assured her that you could not love her if you sought the heart of another. She did not listen."

Now Wiseman was pacing in a small circle in the middle of his room, tapping his fingertips against his lips. "She changed so much for you, I saw this," he continued. "I noted that she had altered the setting on her radio from easy listening to rock. I saw the box her lingerie came in. I advised her to be careful and she did not listen." Wiseman stopped abruptly and looked at me. "Please leave now."

"Where is she?" I asked him.

"She is safe now," he replied.

"I asked you where is she and I'll be damned if I'm leaving before I get an answer!" I hollered, drawing close to him.

Wiseman was unfazed. He didn't move. "She does not wish to hear from you. Now leave." Wiseman's voice was firm; there was nothing more to say, nothing to do but comply. As I opened his door Wiseman added, "You are a very foolish and selfish young man."

That hurt. That *really* hurt.

"Hello?"

"Where the hell have you been?"

"Larry?"

"Tracy and I have both been trying to get hold of you. It's about Tony. We think he's trying to steal whatever it is you're working on."

As he said this I was typing on EDGAR, flipping through menu screens and trying to hack my way into the registrar's electronic files. Some kind of forwarding address for Rita would surely be there.

"What?" I asked as my multitasking mind finally attached meaning to Larry's words. I continued typing.

"It's good that you decided to sit this Easter out. Your absence gave us a chance to follow up on something I spotted last Christmas. I couldn't imagine why Tony would have a Star Ventures brochure lying around on the reading table in the bathroom. Then I started to think, well, maybe your roommate had left it with him last Easter, and maybe it was just hanging around, but then again…"

I wished simultaneously that he'd get to the point and that the registrar's files hadn't been XCOM formatted; they were completely inaccessible. The next place to look would be the electronic bulletin boards.

"...and so finally I figured maybe his interest was more than casual. And I figured that if he was involved, but you didn't even know, he might be up to no good. So Tracy hung around with him all day Easter. She turned on the flattery. She told him she hadn't had a real dentist in her mouth since he sewed up her lip. She told him how much she's turned on by investment acumen, which, of course, is untrue. At least I think it's untrue. Anyway..."

Entries in the main EDGAR bulletin board were arranged like a library's card catalog—a staggered stack of graphical index cards, one behind the other, only the front one visible in full; the others receded until they disappeared above the screen border. The cards were in no particular order and there were thousands of them. What a stupid system! And what a treacherous uncle!

"...so he figures he can make millions. Is it true? Can your system really predict the stock market?"

"Of course not," I told Larry. "They'll find out for themselves soon enough." *But not too soon!* I thought, suddenly remembering my still-unfinished mission to sanitize the terminals. There were so many of them, and right now I was desperately occupied. If Rita had left her address on the bulletin board, it meant she wanted me to find it, and if not, there was probably nothing I could say to put things right. How could Tony be so craven? How could he have learned about Star? His introduction must have come from Dex. That certainly seemed to implicate my roommate in the scheme, although not necessarily; it could have been unwitting. Maybe. Or maybe he was personally uninvolved but saw no reason to get Star in trouble. Life as nonlinearity. Each new layer of complexity multiplied the possibilities without yielding a clue to which was truth. Chaos abounding, chaos ascendant. There was no one I could trust. Except Rita. Except Rita. I continued to flip through the infuriatingly stupidly designed bulletin board.

"Aren't you worried?" Larry asked me. "Aren't you afraid that they'll come after you or something?"

"Here it is!" I shouted. "She's at Cal Tech!"

"What the hell are you talking about?" Larry demanded. "Have you been listening to a word I've been saying?"

"All of them," I assured him as I selected the index-card entry, only to find no specific address listed. "Don't worry, I'm not going to let them steal anything." I was lying; even now Star's faceless computer-consultant moles might be draining the lifeblood code of my engine from any of the terminals where XCOM had scattered it. "I'm just preoccupied. Rita took off. We had a ... well, I guess you could say a falling out. It's a good thing she's not around to see me chasing after her new address like some ridiculously tormented, obsessed artist."

"Well now that's not very nice, Paul. Tracy and I went way out on a limb to rescue your ass and now listen to you. You're deliberately insulting my field of study. Do you hear me denigrating scientists?"

I'd forgotten about Larry's infatuation with art history. But could he be in on the conspiracy too? Maybe Larry had been helping Tony, who had now decided to cut him out of his end, and Larry was telling me all this in revenge.

"And another thing," Larry continued. "What makes you think you're not an artist? I still think your comparison of art to engineering is a load of horseshit, but you're chasing after something, the unknown, it's like—"

"It's like something that won't work," I interrupted, inexplicably eager to confess, conspiracy be damned. "It's like a prediction system with its own mysterious built-in limit. Progress has come to a complete halt at ten percent. I've hit a brick wall, Larry, and I can't figure out why."

"God, you are so lucky!" he cried. "A brick wall! Brilliant ecstasy followed by crashing agony! It's just like all the artists I study, like Michaelangelo struggling high above the Sistine Chapel, like Leonardo—"

"Larry, cut the crap already! I'm your brother, not a character out of one of your textbooks. I've just blown my social life, I've invested my heart and soul in a dead-end project and everything's going nowhere, don't you get it?"

"You know, it's easy to avoid moving ahead by obsessing over the details of what's wrong now. But what good does that do? How can you know where you're going if you're so sure of where you are?"

His words snapped into my head like a shaft into its boss but the mental coupling was disrupted by the instant obliteration of everything on my screen. All at once there was nothing but silence and stillness.

"Hello? Paul? You still there?"

Now gold words began to weave across the screen, filling the empty space like lace embroidery. The words were JACK IS GONE BUT THE BEAT GOES ON, repeated over and over again.

"What's that noise? Did you just turn on the radio?"

"Bebop jazz," I told him. "It's the computer, it's…"

"FUUUUUUUUUUUUUCK!!" wailed someone down the hall.

"And right now I'm watching my adviser commit career suicide before my very eyes." As I said this I realized how little I really knew Jeff, or anyone else at MIT, or for that matter, about Jack Kerouac—other than that he traversed the country along both directional axes most of his life, searching for something. Maybe it was something he lost, something he never had, I couldn't begin to imagine.

"What are you talking about? Is everything all right?" Larry asked urgently.

"Everything will be fine. I have to go now. I'll call you later, okay?"

"Sure. Just take it easy. All right?"

The fastest way out of MIT is along the twisting Charles River on Memorial Drive. You climb out of an underpass and now the Charles is on your left, over the grassy island that separates seven lanes of traffic and parked cars. Soon the island disappears and then the last of the MIT buildings are behind you; nothing but hotels and gas stations and office buildings to your right, the broad stretch of greasy dark water and Back Bay skyline to your left.

Rain pecked at the car as I drove. The old clutch ground noisily into gear like the serrated gnawing of my hopeless confusion. I wondered if Larry could possibly fathom the significance of his words—*how can you know where you're going if you're so sure of where you are?* Did he know that this represented a perfect statement of the other, better-known strand of the Uncertainty Principle, the one my father never found occasion to explain? It was a good thing Rita wasn't around to witness this senseless, disoriented reverie, this sadly misguided tribute to Heisenberg.

What had she intended with her final glance as I retreated from her room that last time? Why had she left me with that crazy nonsensical pointless smile even as I left her?

The entrance to the Mass. Pike came up on my right. I fingered Dex's check, still uncashed, in my shirt pocket. The toll collector took my change without expression. Traffic was light. I was on the road with a thousand dollars in my pocket and, evidently, heading west.

○   ○   ○

"Hello?"

"Ya know who this is?"

"Is it … Artie?"

"You bet your sweet caboose it's Artie. I missed you last Easter. I wanted to see how you're doing."

"Artie, where are you? Are you in South Carolina?"

"Naw, I'm still stuck here in Jersey. And I'm back to doing covers, can you believe it? I got a hot one for some what-do-you call, wrap group or something? Buncha 16-year-old hooligans. I don't know. I'm doing it for the kids. My genius son lost his shirt on some investment scheme that turned to crap. All their money, everything, gone. You know how many root canals we're talking about here?"

"Are you still inventing?"

"Nope. Gave all that up. Look, let's face it, I was no good at it. You can't be an artist and a mechanic at the same time, you know what I'm saying?"

"Do I ever."

"So how's that girlfriend of yours, anyway? You know, some of us don't think it's right—"

"What do you mean, 'right'? If it's because she's Jewish…"

"What are you, a wiseguy? What kinda meatball question is that? I don't even care if she's Sicilian, for chrissakes! When I was your age I used to knock 'em over like ducks in a shooting gallery! Like wooden ducks!" A pause. "Now what was I saying?"

"You were reassuring me that—"

"Oh, right. What I was telling you is that it's a new day now, a different generation. When I was your age we didn't take up with a girl unless we were ready to marry her. You two gonna get married?"

"Maybe someday. Not right away."

"Well, I guess that makes sense. It's a new day. Hey. When are you coming back, anyway? I'd like to see you, you know."

"Sooner than you think. I promise."

"Well, then we'll see you soon, right?"

"You bet your … what was that? Caboose?"

"You're a good kid. See you around."

There was nothing else to say, no particular need to point out that the sun was just beginning to peek over the San Gabriel Mountains in fiery spectral hues and it was, indeed, a new day.

GROSSLY AMPLIFIED UNCERTAINTIES

*The pioneers of divergence theory
describe the inevitability of chance, the limits
of understanding, and why we should not be afraid*

by Jeffrey S. Watt, Ph.D., and Paul C. Bustamante, Ph.D.

In 1931 a twenty-five year old mathematician named Kurt Gödel published a relatively short paper entitled "On Formally Undecidable Propositions in *Principia Mathematica* and Related Systems." Like its author, the paper remained largely unknown for years, its startling conclusions buried beneath more intellectual heft than most of Gödel's contemporaries could fathom. The section benignly titled Proposition VI advanced the heretical notion that mathematics—that most ruthlessly formalized of

JEFFREY S. WATT is director of the Synthetic Intelligence Laboratory and professor of electrical engineering at Brown University. He received his Ph.D. from the University of Michigan, after which he travelled to western Australia "for no particular reason" and accepted his first faculty appointment at MIT. PAUL C. BUSTAMANTE studied under Professor Watt at MIT and at Brown, where he received his Ph.D. He is currently associate professor of physics at MIT. Professors Watt and Bustamante are co-founders of E/Mtex Corporation.

worlds where logic reigns supreme—had for too long enjoyed an undeserved reputation for completeness and internal consistency. Gödel demonstrated, as a matter of pure logic, that this world necessarily contains propositions that simply can't be decided one way or the other. What's more, such doubts arise not as untidy exceptions to otherwise unblemished mathematical principles, but instead follow directly from—are *required by*—those very principles. In other words, mathematicians would just have to live with limits on what they could be sure of. Kurt Gödel had driven fissures into foundations unquestioned for centuries, foundations that supported a near-religious faith in the certainties of mathematics.

If his fellow math scholars were less than overwhelmed by Gödel's Proposition VI—today sanctified as Gödel's Proof—physical scientists were particularly unimpressed. They had fundamental limits of their own to worry about. Four years before publication of Gödel's paper came word from Copenhagen that uncertainties permeate all physical systems at microscopic dimensions. Werner Heisenberg's Uncertainty Principle showed that the more you know about the momentum of a moving object, the less you can know about its position, and vice versa. In addition, while you can specify an object's energy over a period of time, restricting the time frame means accepting greater uncertainty as to precise energy level. (See Figures 1 and 2.) Once again, a boundary had been drawn around our powers to observe and to know.

But physicists could take heart. By its own terms the Uncertainty Principle makes a difference only for extraordinarily tiny, fast-moving particles like electrons. At larger scales the uncertainties pale in comparison to the measurements themselves.

At least that's what we all thought.

The third shock came decades later. Edward Lorenz, plotting values for certain kinds of nonlinear differential equations that crop up frequently in many areas of physics, thought his computer had gone haywire; in 1961 that wouldn't have been so unusual. Lorenz, a theoretical meteorologist, was running one of his early digital weather models. He wanted to replicate the results from part of an earlier run. Instead of reexecuting the entire procedure, Lorenz had painstakingly entered intermediate values from that run as initial conditions for the new run. Needless to say, the graphical output patterns should have been identical. And for a short while they were; but then the patterns started to diverge. The farther he extended the time horizon, the less the outputs looked like one another. Eventually

they shared no resemblance whatsoever. How could the same initial conditions lead to different outcomes? Where was the "bug"?

Before long Lorenz recognized his own hand as the source of the error. The computer stored numbers out to six decimal places; Lorenz had copied only the first three as grist for the new run. So sensitive were his model's nonlinear equations that they amplified tiny fourth-order round-off discrepancies into significant, observable differences in result. Lorenz understood that if real systems like the atmosphere exhibited such amazingly fragile dependence on initial conditions, trying to forecast the long-term behavior of such systems would be impossible. There was no way you could fix the starting values with infinite precision.

Once again discovery of a fundamental limit went largely unnoticed. But the world eventually caught up with Lorenz, and by the late 1970s the science of "deterministic chaos"—studying systems whose unpredictable futures develop from microscopic roots in the present—had begun to occupy the attentions of world-class researchers. Such systems abound: in the orbits of comets, in fibrillating hearts, in the growth of snowflakes, in swirls of smoke. Chaos is everywhere around us.

S everal years ago the junior author became interested in weather forecasting. There is something endlessly seductive about the weather—constantly changing, violently unpredictable, yet possessed of immutable cycles like seasonal variation

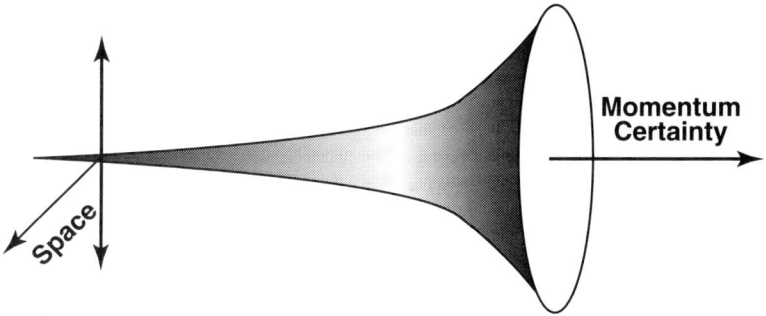

Figure 1. WHERE'S THE PARTICLE?
As knowledge of a moving particle's momentum becomes more and more accurate, its position in space becomes less certain. Here space is represented in two dimensions, with momentum certainty plotted along the third axis. The expanding cone represents an increasingly broad region in space where the particle cannot be localized.

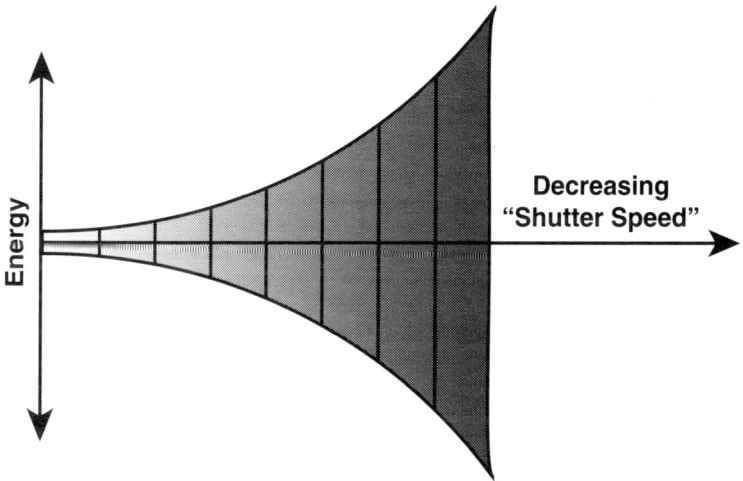

Figure 2. HOW HOT IS THE PARTICLE?
Suppose you had a camera that could record a particle's average energy. As you increased the camera's shutter speed to pin down the energy level over a shorter and shorter time period, you would find your picture growing fuzzier. Aveage energy becomes less and less certain as the measurement time shrinks.

that give our lives structure and reassurance. Somehow a hidden order seemed to cry out for discovery among the raucus strains of thermal clashes, freak storms and chance rainbows. The junior author thought he might have found a route to that order—a way to cast light onto chaotic darkness.

The idea was straightforward. Up to a point, unpredictability can be viewed as the result of insufficient starting data. The more we know about the initial conditions, the longer before what we don't know becomes chaotically amplified and spoils our forecasts. Now suppose money were no object. We could simply launch new weather satellites and build new land stations until today's sparse weather network became a teeming crowd of data-happy broadcasters telling us all we wished to know about any point on or above the Earth.

Money being a considerably prominent object in the real world, however, the junior author proposed an approach that accepted large gaps between observation points. His answer came from a branch of statistics that traffics in missing data. Instead of trying to obtain real measurements at all points, let's use a few real measurements and knowledge of the atmosphere's behavior patterns to guess the values at unobserved locations. Then we can combine statistically educated guesses with actual data as our initial conditions.

Using a crude iterative version of the E-M algorithm, a tried-and-true statistics technique for coping with missing data, the junior author immediately obtained a ten-percent increase in forecast accuracy over the National Weather Service's best efforts. He figured he had beguiled nonlinearity into submission, that soon chaos would be tamed. The senior author did nothing to discourage his enthusiasm.

The senior author was, in fact, busy pursuing his own nonlinear adventures at MIT. While the junior author cavorted the summer away in Pasadena, the senior author and his able research assistant, Donald Boyer, succeeded in implementing a computational model of human neural processing and response. Working with a slightly more refined E-M construct and various nonlinear equations that characterize calcium-mediated nerve action potentials, they were able to generate the coarse equivalent of stimulus reflexes, pattern recognition and stepwise logical reasoning. At one point the senior author, having surreptitiously attached electrode contacts to his slumbering research assistant, observed a 250 ms response time to his sudden cry of "DonBoy! Come here! I want you!" and the simultaneous delivery of a mild electric shock. Mr. Boyer's reaction delay very nearly matched that of the computer model when exposed to a programmed stimulus of equivalent amplitude. This experiment, which resulted in only minor injury to Mr. Boyer, confirmed the fidelity of the model. It seemed too good to be true. And indeed it was.

Upon his return, the junior author confided that he had encountered unexplained limitations in prediction accuracy using the E-M

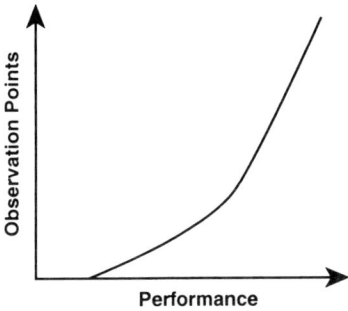

Figure 3.
THEORETICAL PERFORMANCE of the authors' E-M statistics technique for improving weather forecasts. After reaching an initial threshold, performance—how far in advance one can accurately predict the weather—first increases logarithmically with the number of additional observation points, then rapidly approaches infinity after surpassing a second threshold.

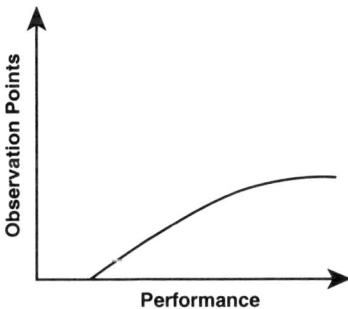

Figure 4.
ACTUAL PERFORMANCE falls far below theoretical expectations. Regardless of the number of observation points, the technique failed to yield improved predictions beyond a certain maximum performance level.

approach. We agreed to postpone investigation of this disquieting observation and instead focus on spending our ARPA grant money. This we did with relish. By the end of the next year, when both of us departed Cambridge for more hospitable surroundings in Providence, R.I., we had a dense-array neural network implemented on the senior author's high-speed parallel processor. The efforts of seven full-time and three part-time programmers had given us a fully integrated platform ready for any cognitive application.

The senior author viewed the hardware architecture of this neural network as his crowning achievement. Its heart was an array of 4,096 microprocessors, or "nodes," in dynamically changing communication with one another via optical transmission channels. Each node had an instruction set slightly different from that of the others; each accessed a shared memory with all other processors. This arrangement permitted the nodes to process independently or cooperatively, depending on the demands of a problem. It was ideally suited both to neural simulation and to complex statistical processing. When programmed, the system's nonlinear features enabled it to work with input that failed to match known patterns exactly; our computer could guess and learn and come close enough.

Early applications proved astounding. When provided with basic concepts of finite set theory and requested to hypothesize conjectures relating them, the system "discovered" natural numbers, prime numbers and elementary arithmetic operations within minutes. It proved able to discriminate among known facial templates based on miniscule recognition data. Ported to a graphical interface, our computer learned to play poker with reasonable competence and even to demand its due tribute with surly appropos.

And yet the senior author felt a creeping sense of dissatisfaction. He wanted to know why the computer could rapidly accumulate a considerable number of mathematical notions but then stop dead, as if suddenly witless. He wondered why the system never bluffed at poker. He became depressed and didn't tell anyone why.

At this point, investors in ARGI—the company set up to commercialize our weather application—were getting restless for greater research attention. Having recently renegotiated its capital position and divested itself of certain troublesome business ties, ARGI had too much money sitting in the bank to neglect an aggressive development agenda.

We hired programmers, we retained research meteorologists as consultants, we leased a state-of-the-art multiprocessor from Thinking Machines Inc., and for approximately fourteen months we burned up our keyboards as we spent down our bank account searching for ways to improve performance. In our simulations we obtained virtually limitless accuracy. After priming the system with a threshold number of observation points, we found that the reliability of our simulated forecasts grew in log-linear relation to the number of additional observation points; finally, at a second threshold, the statistics would suddenly take over and drive reliability toward theoretical perfection. (See Figure 3.)

The key is "theoretical." Because that's not what actually happened. Despite all our efforts, we were simply unable to embarrass the already-available models—the very ones we used in developing our statistics ensembles. In fact, the best we could do was a fourteen-percent improvement, and then only in a single case. (See Figure 4.)

Certainly we were ready to accept that our statistical flashlight could provide only limited wattage in the real world. But why a fourteen percent maximum? What was it about the weather that provided an iron resistance against more intimate probings?

The junior author flippantly suggested Heisenberg's Uncertainty Principle as the cause of our frustrations. To his amazement, the senior author concurred. The reason for the amazement can be discerned from Figures 1 and 2. With particular reference to Figure 2, note how increasingly precise knowledge of a particle's momentum reduces one's ability to pinpoint its position in space. (Actually, it's not a matter of our inability to find the particle; it simply *possesses* no fixed position.)

While the horn eventually flares outward, at which point the particle becomes hopelessly lost in space, this only occurs at absurdly high levels of momentum certainty. For example, if we can bear just a millimeter's worth of doubt over a particle's position, nothing prevents us from knowing its precise momentum to thirty decimal places!

What this means is that measurement errors stemming from Heisenberg's uncertainty relation are pathetically puny. It means that the amplification needed to elevate such uncertainties into deviations we can observe with our senses is not merely huge—it is inconceivably enormous. And it means that, given what we know about the rate at which errors evolve in nonlinear systems, it is simply impossible to blame the Uncertainty Principle for taking our models off course; they just don't amplify that fast.

Unless, that is, we don't know all the equations. In a famous 1982 article, Lorenz observed that the apparent rate of error amplification seems to grow with the sophistication of the model under study; the more equations you have, the faster mistakes seem to evolve. Soon the senior author revealed this reasoning as the source of his depression. He had begun to suspect that our system's cognitive shortcomings and prediction limitations reflected flip sides of the same nonlinear enchilada. If the equations that *really* govern weather patterns contain an endless progression of smaller and smaller nonlinear terms, perhaps errors as small as Heisenberg's really can grow to observable levels in short time spans. And if cognitive processing depends on a similar pattern of equations—drawing intuition and creativity from grossly amplified uncertainties—modeling thought would be as hopeless as a perfect weather forecast. There would be too many mathematical terms even to catalog, much less process.

Two years and another ARPA grant later, the authors were still searching for hints that the true equations governing real physical systems contain cascades of nonlinear terms. We were able to identify but a few such terms. And while the tiny contributions they made seemed to explain their escape from the attentions of previous researchers, it also suggested their individual unimportance. We now believe that the nonlinear cascade, while real, is largely situation-specific—in other words, infinitely mutable as conditions change. Even if we could somehow process the math, the terms themselves would thwart our efforts by constantly reinventing themselves. A complete description of ourselves and our surroundings is impossible. The physical universe is as unknowable, as fundamentally resistant to fixed rules as the mathematical one Gödel explored so many years ago. We have lifted one barrier only to find another.

What implications does this theory—which we call the divergence hypothesis—have for our everyday lives? One must exercise caution in extending scientific discoveries into non-scientific realms. Even universal laws of nature apply only to particular phenomena and under specific assumptions; turning them into sloppy metaphors merely dissipates their scientific validity by taking them where they don't belong.

Yet in this one case, perhaps, the metaphor really is the message after all. There are irreducible limits to what we can know about the world, about each other, about our futures. We now realize how much closer to such limits science had brought us than we'd dared to suspect. But these are frontiers whose persistence we can live with if we remain unafraid, if we can accept chance as opportunity rather than lurking disaster, if we can take joy in the mysteries of love and laughter rather than trying to pinpoint their origins.

Besides, while we may not be able to simulate the human mind in all of its kaleidoscopic visions and behaviors, we can still do a pretty good job duplicating its purely analytical capabilities; that's why every sizable research institution has one of E/Mtex's DENSE-NET computers and why the authors are now rich as all hell. And while we may remain unable to chart the weather with scientific precision, we can still gaze at the frigid snow drifts piling up outside the front door and look forward, with entirely justified certainty, to the first mellow hints of spring. Θ

Steven J. Frank writes patents by day and fiction by night. He studied chemistry at Brown University, learned to hate the lab, and traded the lure of discovery for healthier lungs at Harvard Law School. He's authored numerous short stories tinged with humor and empathy, articles filled with incomprehensible jargon, and the legal primer *Learning the Law*. He lives outside Boston with his wife and word processor, and can be reached at sjf@c-m.com.